Mike Jefferies was born in K... ... ... early
years in Australia. He attended the Goldsmiths
School of Arts and then taught art in schools and in
prisons. A keen rider, he was selected in 1980 to ride
for Britian in the Belgian Three Day Event. He now
lives in Norfolk where he works, among other
things, as an illustrator, with his wife and family.

*The Road to Underfall* is the first volume of the trilogy Loremasters of Elundium of which the second
and third books are *Palace of Kings* and *Shadowlight*.

Voyager

MIKE JEFFERIES

# The Road to Underfall

*Loremasters of Elundium: Volume 1*

HarperCollins*Publishers*

Voyager
An Imprint of HarperCollins*Publishers*
77–85 Fulham Palace Road,
Hammersmith, London W6 8JB

This paperback edition 1996
1 3 5 7 9 8 6 4 2

Previously published in paperback by Fontana 1986
Reprinted five times

ISBN 0 00 617346 2

Set in Ehrhardt

Printed in Great Britain by
HarperCollinsManufacturing Glasgow

# The Bondbreaking

'I will teach you,' whispered a voice in the darkness. 'I will tell you what it is forbidden to know; of how the Granite Kings arose out of the great darkness.'

'Lord, there is a curse on stories about time before the darkness came,' answered a shy nervous voice. 'It is forbidden to meddle in magic.'

Laughter crackled, almost seeming to split the blackness in two.

'Listen, child, and I shall tell you of a time before night was ever thought of and how it came to a world of perpetual light, in a time when the sun endlessly circled Elundium.'

The voice paused, and in its place a tiny speck of light began to glow.

'It was the age of the Mason Kings, the architects of all that is beautiful across the length and breadth of Elundium. City after city, each one more intricate and delicate; each one mirroring the beauty of a perfect world, rose up, glittering in the soft changeless light, until . . .'

'Until?' pressed the younger voice, eager to hear the story, yet terrified that the Nightbeasts might be listening in the darkness.

'Until King Mantern took up his mason's chisel. He was driven by strange dreams to fear the sunlight, and all he built shadowed what the other kings had built. On the outside in hard bleak lines he used only dark stone, rough hewn and quarry raw, while within there was black marble, traced in silver; it lined every room. He built the Granite City, sheer and windowless, a dark place of inner courtyards and secrets, and in its midst, rising in brittle points, stood the Towers of Granite.

'He sought tirelessly for the purest black marble, and his quest

7

led him deeper and deeper into the marble valleys until, amongst the blackest shadows, he found a pure seam of the richest marble ever known. It was etched in veins of silver.'

The point of light had grown stronger as the story unfolded and it reflected fine feathery veins around it.

'Mantern raised his hammer and swung a mighty blow at his chisel and that hammer blow broke through the surface of Elundium, and from that tiny hole night burst out.'

The young voice gasped in the darkness.

'Night roared and screamed around King Mantern, tearing the hole into a great split. Earthquakes shook the marble valleys and black storms tore at its surface. Mantern tried to stop the earth splitting but the more he held on to each side the more violent the earthquakes became until a great mountain had formed beneath the struggling King and he stood in total darkness beside a black entrance. Wise men say it was the first moment that the world turned, but among the Masters of Magic it is known that this was the moment of Krulshards' birth.'

The voice paused and the point of light grew smaller and smaller until it became lost in the blackness.

'Without the sun, King Mantern was blind. He reached out shaking hands against the raging storms but all around him the winds began to laugh, cruel shrieking sounds of torment, and his hand touched the Master of Night.'

'Krulshards!' gasped the young listener, huddling against the floor.

'The one whose eyes are the black holes of despair and whose breath will overshadow the moon or blot out the stars. He had arisen to destroy Elundium.'

'Did he make all the darkness?' asked the younger voice.

Again the laughter rekindled the point of light.

'There were, before that hammer blow, two worlds in perfect parallel. One above the ground, at peace with nature, in harmony with the sunlight. While in the darkness beneath the surface in the other world unnatural things had grown, nightmare images that hated the light. The Mason Kings had stripped the surface of Elundium in their search for the purest stone, weakening and drawing the two worlds together, and in their ignorance they had awoken Krulshards, the Master of the Darkness.'

'Which world have I come from?' asked the listener in confusion.

'Patience!' hissed the other voice. 'Listen. The storms of night gradually receded, leaving King Mantern face to face with the one he had touched and he cried out, clutching at his withering hand. Before him stood a mirror image of himself, the black inner self of his nightmares that had driven him to make that hammer blow. Krulshards. Before him stood a figure more powerful than any being that had ever walked in Elundium. Shadowy and terrible to look upon. Wrapped in a black malice which covered corrupted rotten flesh that hated the sunlight.

'He sneered at the King, gripping him with bone black fingers, laughing in his face. "I have summoned you, Sun King, to set me free and now I shall take everything and cover Elundium with darkness."

'King Mantern struggled helplessly as Krulshards lifted him high above his head and cast him down the mountainside. Night winds screamed and tormented him and savage storms lashed at his body as he fell, but eventually battered and bruised he reached the lower slopes and came to rest on the edge of a steep slope of living granite. It sparkled and glowed in the dark and as the King slid across its surface, searching for a way down, he saw within the rock face a sleeping form.'

'What form?' urged the young voice.

'Shush!' hissed the voice of wisdom, feeling a slight change in the flow of air, 'Nightbeasts are near.

'It was the sleeping form of the first Granite King. The terrible storms had eaten away at the granite cliff and as King Mantern reached out to touch the surface of the rock it crumbled away and the first Granite King arose. Mantern offered up the handle of his hammer fearing a greater magic than the nightmare of Krulshards and the winds of night that screamed about his ears, but the Granite King refused the hammer and, drawing his sword, split night in half, and a little light shone in that dreadful place. Just enough light for Mantern to see the ruin he had caused to the gardens of Elundium, for the storms had broken the branches of the trees and smashed down the beautiful stone buildings, and night had robbed all the colours from the flowers and they had shut their petal cases against the darkness. Mantern threw himself down at the feet of the Granite King but strong hands lifted him up and a gentle voice soothed him in the twilight.

'"I am Holgranos, the first Granite King. I shall win back what you have lost. I shall win back the light."

'With that he swept his sword against the granite cliff and it shattered into a thousand crystals of light, each one brighter than the sun. Krulshards fled back into his black hole beneath the mountain.'

'But the darkness? Who brought back the darkness?' asked the young voice.

'Crystals are not suns. Nor is their magic powerful enough to keep out the night. Mantern saw the ruin he had caused and fled back to the Granite City, where he spent the last remaining days of sunlight fortifying the granite towers against the night he knew must come and always his eyes were drawn towards the horizon that hid the raw black mountain that had grown up out of the marble valleys.

'Holgranos, the first Granite King, climbed to the top of Mantern's Mountain, the darkest and most feared place in all Elundium, and, lifting huge slabs of black marble, he blocked up the mouth of night, trapping Krulshards in the darkness. But each time the seal was almost complete the Master of Nightbeasts broke out, hurling rocks and stones at the Granite King. It was a time of giants, when the two mightiest forces in

10

Elundium stood face to face before the gates of night. Each time they fought upon the boulder strewn ledge before that dark hole, Krulshards shadowed the sun, hiding his one weakness from the Granite King; bringing with the darkness bitter winters that changed the marble valleys into a bleak desolate place that the ordinary people of Elundium dared not go near, and in time the marble valleys lost their true name and became known as World's End and a place to dread.'

'Weakness?' asked the younger voice, 'There is nothing but fear and terror here in the darkness.'

Pure laughter blazed in the darkness showing a glimpse of the older voice, splashes of colour dazzled the listener.

'Strong magic! Beware! Krulshards will destroy anything that knows of his weakness, for he has the strength of ten Granite Kings, yet children could render him helpless and ready for the killing stroke.'

'How so?' gasped the other voice, searching the darkness for the beautiful colours.

'Know me now, and I shall tell you, for I am Nevian, the Master of Magic, the Lord of the Daylight and the Keeper of the Sun.'

The light blazed again, and there in the darkness stood a figure wrapped in a rainbow cloak of many colours.

'Tread on his shadow, if you can get close enough, for that is his weakness. Here in the darkness he is shadowless and terrible, but in the daylight if you can step upon that nightmare shape he is yours to destroy, for he cannot turn to fight or escape into the City of Night. It took my greatest magic to make that part of him real, and jump as high as he likes or run faster than the wind he cannot get away from it. Holgranos saw the secret of the shadow but it was too late, he had fought for many winters on Mantern's Mountain and his bones had grown brittle from the cold. He had grown old and too weak to chase the Master of Nightbeasts and by then Krulshards was not alone or so vulnerable, for he had spawned the Nightbeasts

11

deep inside the City of Night and formed them into a shadow circle that protected him, and who could tell which was the master's shadow amongst so many hideous shapes?'

'Are the Nightbeasts afraid of the daylight?' asked the young voice.

Nevian laughed, casting back the rainbow cloak. 'Nightbeasts are afraid of the daylight, they are weak and blinded by the light yet their fear of Krulshards will drive them out to form a shadow circle wherever he commands it. They wear the skins of those they kill, fashioned into hideous armour and that protects them a little in the light. Holgranos could no longer find the strength to climb the mountain and in despair he sent for King Mantern and asked as payment for the light that the last Mason King should build him a shelter at the foot of the mountain, somewhere strong and fortified where he could rest from the battles with Krulshards. Somewhere the Master of Night could not enter.'

'Did he build such a place?' asked the young voice.

'Yes,' whispered Nevian, drawing closer, 'It is but one daylight from here, clinging on to the mountain's lower slopes.'

The young voice interrupted, 'What is a daylight?'

Nevian laughed, 'You have so much to learn. A daylight is the measure of time between the moment the sun appears in the morning at World's Edge until it sinks from sight behind World's End in the evening, four hundred daylights add up to one sun.'

'But how long is a daylight?' pressed the young voice, full of curiosity.

The magician sighed, 'A daylight has many lengths, for those who toil unwillingly at a task it can seem to take forever, while in what seems no time at all a fast horse can travel a great distance in one daylight.'

'Horse?' queried the young voice.

Nevian laughed again. 'The horse is a living being. People ride on them; they are strong yet gentle; quiet, yet brave. But I

12

was telling you of the fortress King Mantern built at the foot of this mountain. Holgranos named it Underfall, the palace of Kings. Sheer and terrible it rises, granite grey against the mountain slopes. It is set with many galleries each one shadowing the one below and they are cleverly edged with iron spikes that no Nightbeast could ever pass or force an entry through. It is a bare place of many Granite Kings.'

'Were there more than one?' asked the voice, finding his mind muddled and crowded with all this wisdom.

'There were many,' replied the magician, 'stepping proudly out of that granite cliff to win back the daylight and they all grew old, like weathered stone, before the task was even half finished, and came to the final resting place at Underfall. It is in truth the palace of the Kings.'

'Are there no more Granite Kings?' asked the young voice. 'Has darkness finally covered everything?'

'King Holbian is a Granite King,' whispered Nevian, 'and he is on the road, marching towards this nightmare place and he may carry your freedom in his sword arm.'

'If he comes, who shall I say I am, and where shall I tell him I come from?'

'You are no-one, my child. Born without a name in the darkness, a tragedy of Krulshards' greed. Your forefathers were stolen by the black monsters from a place long forgotten by the world that lives within the light. You have been condemned by the accident of birth to live in the darkness, a slave to the Master of Nightbeasts, to labour wherever he wields the lash, hollowing out the City of Night, spreading his darkness under the world of the sunlight.'

Nevian sadly sighed, and reached out comforting hands in the darkness, saying, 'But I have not forgotten you. I have travelled through great danger searching in all the dark holes beneath the grim mountain to give you back the memories and the knowledge Krulshards stole when he first walked in the light. Watch with me, watch the point of light and it will show you all the wonders of the world above the ground.'

Together they stood, hand in hand, and watched the speck of light grow and change from a million stars in the dark above their heads into soft flowers swaying in a summer wind. And then it changed into a tall forest that marched beyond the edge of sight until each and every wonder, no matter how large or how small, had passed before their eyes.

'Choose a name,' whispered the magician. 'Choose one part of all the wonders you have seen and keep it as your own.'

After a moment's hesitation the voice cried out, 'Leaf! I choose a leaf. They are so beautiful, so delicate, as they dance in the wind.'

'Then you shall be called Leaf, the first Elder, and those you find in this black place shall be your family, and you will teach them of all you have seen and you shall name them, each one, after the leaves on the trees; oak, elder, apple. Name them well and forget nothing I have shown you.'

'Lord, Master of Magic,' Leaf cried out, feeling the hand he held begin to melt away. 'Do not leave me here in the darkness. Do not take away the light!'

Nevian smiled and the rainbow coat glowed with warm colours. 'I must return. I can hear the tramp of marching feet and the shouts of the great army. King Holbian grows impatient and runs hard on Krulshards' heels. I hear the scream of the Battle Owls and the neighing of the Warhorses, bridled and ready for war. The light is yours now to keep, and share amongst your people. Tell them of its beauty, for it will burn ever bright in your heart. Look inward and see the green fields, remember the colours and follow them as quick as butterflies from hedge to hedgerow. You have a great power in the darkness now for you have a name and a purpose, Leaf the Elder.'

'Wait, wait,' cried Leaf, turning in every direction.

'Look for the sign,' called out the vanishing voice of Nevian. 'If this King fails, look out for the sign of the great black Warhorse and the boy who risks all for love.'

14

As Nevian hurried back towards the light he stumbled on a snag of black marble and fell heavily, driving the point of his sword into the dusty floor. It snapped, leaving a splinter of bright metal on the floor of the City of Night. Nevian cursed, and searched blindly but he dare not wait too long, for he could hear the Nightbeasts in the lower levels, roaring and screaming as they rushed up towards the black gate, driving a foul wind before them that buffetted and jostled the Master of Magic. Rising from his knees he fled on to the high plateau, and the steep descent on to the Causeway Fields, for the great battle of Underfall was about to begin.

'Lord, Underfall is yours! World's End lies beneath your feet!'

Nevian's voice penetrated the dying sounds of battle. He paused for a moment, surveying the slaughter, weighing the balance of night in the one hand and day in the other before he whispered, 'Do not look back lest the payment for this final victory breaks your heart.'

Slowly King Holbian turned away from the bleak fortress that rose before him, searching for the rainbow cloak. 'What place is this?' he cried, striking his sword impatiently against the rough granite walls, casting sparks into the shadows.

'This, my Lord,' answered Nevian, arriving breathlessly at the King's side, 'is the palace of Kings. It is yours by right, just as it was your father's and his father's before him, as far back into legends as the people of Elundium can remember.'

'To Mantern, the last Mason King,' whispered Holbian, the colour draining out of his face. 'Is this a part of Mantern's curse that you have taught me of? Is this the place where he set night free?'

'Yes, my Lord, it is the place all Granite Kings must seek, for it is here that night is made.'

King Holbian shivered, drawing his cloak tightly about his shoulders and touched the spark he kept well hidden in the inner folds before he asked the magician, 'Have we reached Battle's End, is this enough slaughter to keep back the night?'

15

'It is not enough,' whispered Nevian fiercely, 'It is not the darkness you have fought to destroy but Krulshards, the Master of the Nightbeasts that he spawns in the City of Night. Look, look, there on the lower mountain slopes where the shadow circle follows the sun, that is what you have crossed Elundium to destroy, for Krulshards is at its centre. Would you leave him free to spread more terror throughout this land and leave him free to creep back under the cover of darkness across the causeway fields and feed upon the dead flesh of your great army, feasting on the ones you love?'

'No, Lord,' hissed King Holbian, raising his sword to catch the last dying rays of sunlight, 'I shall follow the Maker of Night beyond World's End and seal this victory before the sun sets.'

Nevian stretched his hands towards the setting sun and the rainbow cloak he wore cast a thousand threads of light across the Causeway as he called to the Lord of Horses, Equestrius, and to the Lord of Owls, Orundus. 'These shall be our witnesses,' he whispered as Equestrius answered his call and galloped into the shadows of Underfall. Grannog the great Border Runner ran at his heels, fearing nothing that moved in the shadows.

'Now let us ride upon the edge of the wind,' cried Nevian, 'before the night gives more power to the shadows' circle.'

King Holbian felt the rush of cold evening air against his face and the smell of pine resin filled his nose as they galloped up through the forest that grew on the steep mountain slopes.

'Mantern's Gate!' cried Nevian, as they halted on the edge of a wide heather plateau. Before them stood a black gate filled with darkness and in the centre, surrounded by the shadow circle, walked Krulshards.

'What is this place?' cried Holbian, clinging on to Nevian's sleeve. Orundus spread his wings and shrieked at the dark shapes in the shadow circle. Equestrius struck his hoof against the heather plateau and crouched ready to spring

16

forwards. Grannog growled, baring sharp white fangs as the hackles rose along his back.

'This is a place of dark legends, my Lord,' whispered Nevian, 'a place where giants stand, their heads touching the sky while they battle over the fate of things to come. You, great King, stand at the entrance to Night, on the threshold of all men's fears.'

King Holbian dismounted and crept forwards, nearer to the gates of night, lifting the heavy double hilted sword with both hands. Orundus stooped on to his right shoulder, wings outstretched ready to strike, Grannog the Lord of Dogs stalked one pace ahead of the King, his yellow eyes fixed on the black shape of Krulshards where he stood in the centre of the shadow circle.

'Granite Kings!' mocked Krulshards, spitting the words with black hatred across the centre of the circle. 'There are no Kings here in the blackness of the night,' he hissed, pushing the circle forwards, 'Only I hold power here!'

Krulshards snarled exposing rage-ragged teeth. The shadow circle began to move as the Nightbeasts interlocked their spears and swayed backwards and forwards until the circle had become a glittering wheel of black spear points protecting the Maker of Night.

'Kill this King,' screamed Krulshards, 'and bring everlasting night to Elundium.'

'Kill the King!' chanted the Nightbeasts in the circle as it swept forwards to engulf King Holbian.

'Now!' urged Nevian. 'Before the sun sets. Now is the moment!'

Holbian swung the great sword above his head and with all his strength brought it down into the circle, crying aloud his forefathers' names as he shattered the Nightbeasts' spear shafts with the force of his stroke. Orundus lifted from the King's shoulder into a bright evening sky and for a second hovered high above the shadow circle waiting for the moment

17

to stoop, waiting for the moment when Krulshards would look out towards the setting sun.

'Now great bird of war!' cried the Master of Magic, lifting his arms, and spreading the rainbow cloak to catch the dying sunlight.

Orundus plunged to earth, the shadow of his talons crossing Krulshards' face as he struck at his eyes. The force of the owl's strike sent Krulshards staggering backwards, – the circle was broken. Grannog leapt upwards at the Nightbeasts' unprotected throats. Equestrius charged into the circle killing with each hoof-fall all the Nightbeasts that stood in his path.

'Curse the daylight!' screamed Krulshards, raising his arms against the evening light that had entered the broken shadow circle. 'I will destroy your daylight, Granite King,' he cried, 'and lay a curse of ruin on all Elundium. You shall rule in shadows and sit in fear of the darkness each night. None shall be free of this fear and you, Granite King, shall fear it the most!'

'Nevian, help me!' shouted King Holbian, as he stood at the circle's edge, 'Guide my hand against these evil shadows. Help me make the killing stroke.'

Krulshards laughed harshly as he wove more shadows into a tighter circle, this time keeping the King with him beyond the evening light. Only Orundus, the Lord of Owls, could rise high above the shadows and see King Holbian's peril, for Krulshards was drawing the circle towards the Gates of Night and with each step he took more Nightbeasts to strengthen the circle.

Face to face within the circle they fought spear against sword in the growing darkness. Grannog flattened himself into the heather and slipped unnoticed between the Nightbeasts' armoured legs until he had found a place to fight beside the King. Orundus stopped tearing at the Nightbeasts, trying to break the circle. Krulshards raised his spear and with all his force lunged at the King's heart, Grannog saw the danger and leapt at Krulshard's throat, breaking the spear shaft with one snap of his jaws, turning the blade harmlessly against the sword. The force of the thrust knocked the sword out of the King's hands, taking it beyond the circle. Orundus stooped into the heather collecting the fallen sword and delivered it back into King Holbian's hands.

'I shall break your curse,' cried Holbian, lifting the sword above his head for the killing stroke, but as he brought it down fear made him hesitate. The centre of the circle was empty, the Nightbeasts had gone. Before him, as close as the hilt of his sword, stood the Gates of Night.

'Follow me, Great King of the Daylight,' mocked a voice from the darkness, 'Follow me, if you dare, and lift my curse of night.'

A sharp hot wind blew against King Holbian's face and from far below laughing, shrieking cries rose up.

'My Lord,' whispered Nevian coming to the King's side, 'you must follow Krulshards into the City of Night and finish this day's work.'

'I cannot do it!' hissed Holbian, turning to face the Master of Magic. 'Even if I wished otherwise, I cannot enter that place.'

Nevian took the King's arm, gently turning him back to face the entrance to night. 'My Lord, you must follow Krulshards. You are a Granite King, pledged to protect the daylight. You cannot stand here and let him escape. All Elundium will fall under his curse and all you have won will fall into ruin.'

'I cannot enter that place!' cried the King, falling on to his knees and clenching his hands in despair. 'Nothing,' he whispered, 'nothing in all Elundium could make me walk into that dark hole beneath the earth.'

'Lord,' cried Nevian, resting his hands on Holbian's shoulders, looking deeply into his eyes, 'your line was born for this moment. Remember how your forefathers sprang from the living rock to battle with the powers of the night. Remember how through the ages, league by league, they brought the

19

daylight to all Elundium. Now you, my Lord, the mightiest Granite King, stand here at journey's end at the mouth of night, with Krulshards' sword a thrust away yet you hesitate? Step forward, Great King Holbian,' urged Nevian, 'and snatch the richest victory that could ever rest across a sword's blade. Strike the balance between night and day.'

'I cannot,' cried Holbian, catching hold of the rainbow cloak in both hands and burying his head in its folds. 'I fear the dark and I fear the very blackness of night. I cannot follow Krulshards for one step into that darkness no matter what it cost me in defeat.'

'Lord,' answered Nevian harshly, drawing himself away and wrapping the rainbow cloak tightly about his shoulders, 'Kings are more than mere men. They carry the future in their swords. There is no room for doubt or fear. Fail now to kill Krulshards and you squander every hour of precious daylight you have won!'

'Do you think I want to fail?' cried Holbian in despair.

'Everything you have won will be lost,' whispered the Master of Magic turning his back on the King and walking towards the plateau's edge.

'Do not leave me,' implored Holbian, stretching his hands towards Nevian.

Nevian halted and turned, casting a long sunshadow across the King. 'You are still a great King, my Lord, but you shall be the last Granite King to rule Elundium and you shall stand alone in a world of growing darkness.'

'Nevian, Master of Magic,' Holbian cried, an edge of anger creeping into his voice. 'This is a cruel payment for all I have striven to win. Elundium would still be in the twilight if I had not built the great Greenways and chased Krulshards to this forsaken place at the end of the world.'

'You are a great King,' Nevian repeated quietly 'and you have won all your heart sought after. If only I had known of your secret fear of the dark we could have trod a different path and trapped the Maker of Night in the daylight.'

'Were you blind to the candles I lit?' asked Holbian bitterly, 'did you think Candlebane Hall a hollow mockery of the daylight?'

'I thought that Candlebane Hall was for those that followed you,' answered Nevian, seeing for the first time past the King's weakness into a flaw in his own judgement and the councils he had cast to win a balance between night and day.

'Lord,' he whispered, returning to the King's side, 'Without Krulshards the Nightbeasts cannot rise again, and only you have the power to destroy him. But since you cannot enter the gates of night, new Nightbeasts will rise in the shadow of your victory on the Causeway below and they will turn it into defeat, bringing a new terror to all Elundium.'

'Is there any way that I can defeat him?' cried Holbian in despair.

Nevian turned his face towards the dying sun and thought hard, searching for an answer. 'Too long have the Granite Kings tried to win the light and failed within sight of victory. Elundium must now wait for a new King who can step into the darkness.'

'No!' shrieked Holbian, snatching up his sword. 'Nobody shall rob me of the crown. Nobody shall take my place. I am the rightful King of Elundium.'

'Then enter the darkness, Lord, claim what is yours,' answered Nevian.

Holbian strode forwards, slashing at the blackness between the gates, but he could not enter. He turned, red-faced with rage, and raised his sword to strike the magician. Orundus stooped and snatched the sword from his hands, Grannog leapt between them, fangs bared, Equestrius reared up, thrashing the air above the King's head with razor sharp hooves.

'Do not harm him,' shouted Nevian, 'his weakness is my doing, his faults are my haste. I have driven this King too hard. If he raises his sword against me in anger I am to blame.'

21

Equestrius stood undecided, Orundus hovered, talons spread, while Grannog stood his ground, saliva glistening on exposed white fangs.

'You shall stand alone, the bonds between us are broken,' neighed Equestrius, the Lord of Horses.

'Alone!' shrieked Orundus, stooping to Nevian's shoulder. 'You shall be alone and blind in the dark without my sharp eyes to guide you.'

'Alone,' growled Grannog, lying down in front of Nevian, his head across the magician's feet.

'What treachery is this to ruin an empty victory?' shouted Holbian, crouching, empty-handed. 'What magic twists have you ensnared me with now?'

'None, my Lord, that were not of your own doing,' replied the magician. 'You have broken the bonds that bound the Warhorses, the Battle Owls and the dogs beneath your standard. It was you who raised your sword against me.'

King Holbian glared darkly across the plateau and whispered. 'And now you will abandon me here alone on the edge of night for the Nightbeasts to destroy, and give my throne to a new King. Is this the final reward for the last Granite King, battle-pressed at the end of a desperate road?'

Nevian stepped forwards, taking the King's hand and led him to stand on the edge of the blackness. 'Lord,' he said, pointing out the black Nightshapes that hurried past across the twilight, 'there are the carriers of darkness, mere shadows that hold no menace. Far and wide they carry night across all Elundium, bringing sleep to the weary and rest to the just. Why, even to Candlebane Hall they will come, to weave amongst the flickering flames, casting soft shadows of beauty in the light.' Nevian paused seeking for words of comfort that could help the King.

'Lord, I did not foresee this sad end to the road; nor can I change or mend what has taken place. Return now to the Causeway below and gather together all those that survived

today's slaughter, for we shall meet before the doors of Underfall as the new sun rises.'

'To name a new king,' hissed Holbian, remembering the
magician's words. 'Lead me back and I shall slaughter every
man . . .'

'*No*! None shall sit in your place without your leave.'

'Never! Show him to me now and I will finish this day's work
with his death.'

Nevian laughed, casting the rainbow cloak back across his
shoulders. 'Would you cut down the oak tree before it has split
the acorn seed, or spread its first infant root? He is not here,
brave lord, but this place where we stand will be his making and
you shall know him long before he wears your shoes. Enough of
this squabbling, we talk of days so far away that even you will
have forgotten my words. But remember, Lord, he will grow to
manhood despite all the treachery that surrounds him and he
will love you more dearly than his own life.'

'How shall I know him, this King?' asked Holbian, 'if his
coming is so far away that I shall have forgotten your counsels?'

'He will bring to life old memories, my Lord, and you will see
in him an image of things long lost. Remember, his coming will
drive the Nightbeasts out of Elundium.'

'How can I keep this land worthy of Kingship if I stand alone
against Krulshards' nightmares?' Holbian asked bitterly.

Nevian sighed, watching for a moment as the Nightshapes
filled the heather plateau, bringing the soft evening with them.
'Strong men will help you keep this kingdom safe and be at
your side in the dark years ahead.'

'Dark years! Empty thrones! Where can I find these men
that will help me to keep back the darkness?' cried Holbian, full
of despair.

'Lord, I can only tell you what I see, not where you should
look for the answers to your fate. Go now and search amongst
the wreckage of this day's battle. Look below upon the
Causeway. Go quickly before night draws its mantle of darkness

23

over those you must find. Ride back to the Causeway Fields, for with the rising of the new sun the bonds will be broken and Equestrius, the Lord of Horses, will be free.'

Holbian sank on to his knees, weeping, 'I am lost and truly alone.'

Equestrius moved to Holbian's side and brushed his soft muzzle against the King's arm. 'Rise, Lord,' he whinnied softly, 'and spend the last moments of magic in the saddle. Ride once more upon the edge of the wind before we part.'

It was twilight now upon the causeway field and grief seemed woven amongst the Nightshapes that crowded there. Ghostly echoes and cries of pain filled King Holbian's ears as he walked, uncandled, through the shadows of his great army. Everywhere he looked blind, lifeless eyes stared back and everything he touched had the feel of cold dead flesh, but somewhere close at hand little more than a whispered sob broke through the cries of death, and the King remembered Nevian's words, 'Gather all the men that still live.'

King Holbian took the spark from his pocket and in its feeble light searched amongst the twisted bodies of the dead warhorses that blocked the Causeway road. At last he saw where the voice came from. 'Here, boy, give me your hand,' he cried, settling his armoured boot against the flanks of the Warhorse that had fallen across the boy. 'Who are you, child?' he questioned, casting his eyes over the lad's battle clothes.

'Thunderstone, Sire,' answered the youth, kneeling beside the dead Warhorse, stroking his cold muzzle.

Holbian lifted the spark above his head and looked quietly from left to right before asking harshly, 'Who sent you here, child, to fight amongst the Nightbeasts?'

'The Captains, Sire, they sent all of us, apprentice Gallopers and Marchers, to face the Gates of Underfall. We were to draw the Nightbeasts out, Sire.'

'And the Warhorses?' asked the King looking down at the lifeless bodies.

24

'The leader found me,' whispered Thunderstone, his lip trembling as tears filled his eyes. 'I was all alone, surrounded by Nightbeasts, blackness had covered the causeway, Lord. Then he came, when all hope had fled, and using his great strength he drove the shadows back, rising up in the clear morning light to take the spears they thrust at me. He was so beautiful.'

Holbian looked down at the broken, bloodstained spear shafts driven deep into the horse's side and gently lifted Thunderstone to stand beside him. 'He was a Lord amongst the Warhorses, child, it should fill your heart with pride that he spent his strength to save your life. Here, lad, take my sword and gently cut some strands from his tail, keep them all your days to remember his sacrifice and his beauty.'

As Thunderstone bent, blinking back his tears and cutting at the Warhorse's tail, Holbian heard other voices crying out in the darkness across the battlefield.

'Come, lad,' he commanded the boy. 'Help me gather those that still live beneath our ragged standard.'

King Holbian lifted the spark high above his head and walked amongst the dead, pretending that he was not afraid of the coming of the dark.

Nevian walked quietly amongst the slain, searching for those not called by Death, laying his healing hands on any with a beating heart, calling to them in a soft voice, freeing them of their pledges to the Granite Kings, but mixed with his words of freedom he took new promises, that if any man should win their trust through love or care, they must rise again and offer help, even with their lives.

Up flew the remnants of the Battle Birds, to scatter in the winds that tugged at Mantern's slopes, but Silverwing and his brother, Eagle Owl, settled for a moment on Nevian's shoulders. He laughed, reaching up to stroke their chest feathers.

'You two, great birds of war, will have much to do with the keeping of Elundium, yet many nestlings will grow old before

25

you fly to war again. You shall have a great gift, the power to see in the dark, and you will fear nothing that moves by night but . . .' lowering his voice, he whispered, ' . . . already I fear for King Holbian; but he must rule alone even if fear drives him to light a thousand candles to hold back the night.'

Moving amongst the Warhorses Nevian brought his gentle touch, but for many life had fled forever. All night he walked the causeway road searching for a thread of life, a whisper, twitch or movement that would heal beneath his hands. Long before dawn broke, he had gathered all those that he could mend, but they were few, for his magic could not bring any back from the dead. He bade them to return in peace into the wild forest, beyond the call of man, 'No more shall you feel the saddle on your backs, or the touch of spur upon your silken skins unless in time, through love, you wish it otherwise.'

There was one though who stayed when all others turned to go. She loved the youth who had ridden on her back to war and wished to stay with him. Nevian stood before her, troubled in his wisdom. 'Why should you labour in harness when you have been given your freedom?'

'Thoronhand, the child Galloper, found me after wolves had killed my mother. Even as they turned to kill me, a helpless foal, he jumped into their closing circle, slashing at their blood red eyes with his knife. Afterwards with gentle hands he built a mound of stones over my mother's body, setting many sharp pointed sticks around it to keep Night-beasts away. I cannot leave him; love binds us.'

Nevian called Equestrius to his side saying, 'You must stand in judgement with me. I have broken the bonds but I cannot break what love has built.'

'Your name?' commanded Equestrius, turning his gaze on to the Warhorse.

'Thoron named me Amarch, near the place where my mother's body lies.'

26

'Which would you choose?' snorted Equestrius. 'To be free to live or bound, as Amarch, to this Hand child, the Galloper?'

'A life-time of toil, pain and hardship,' added Nevian seriously, glancing through the high window on many tomorrows.

'I am Amarch,' the grey mare snorted; Nevian smiled, wondering at the power of love.

'We must find this child Galloper called Thoronhand if he lives. One pledge, it seems, will not be broken. Show me where he fell.'

Thoron sat in grief. He thought Amarch had been killed and lay somewhere amongst the heaps of dead. He had searched and searched but he could not find her. Soft was the hand upon his shoulder, softer still the velvet muzzle that brushed against his cheek.

'Amarch, you are alive!' he cried. Nevian stepped back as Thoron threw his arms about Amarch's neck, and he spoke these words as a seer for he saw much that they would achieve. 'Great is the power of love, for it will be with you all your days. Both joy and tragedy are woven into your lives; men will know you by your deeds upon the roads of Elundium. Much of your real greatness will pass them by, Thoronhand, and now join the King beneath his standard, for I have much yet to do before the new sun rises.'

'What of Silverwing the owl who came with me to war?' shouted Thoron after the receding figure of Nevian.

'You will have many meetings on the roads to Underfall.' called Nevian as he drew the rainbow cloak tightly about his shoulders, vanishing into the mist. At last he stood before Grannog and as he ran his fingers through the War Dog's hairy coat he whispered, 'Lord of Dogs, I can give you nothing, for you already have loyalty beyond the bondbreaking, and courage beyond the understanding of Man. You are already free and shall always be so.' Grannog barked, wagging his tail and licked

27

the old magician's hand before turning and bounding into the darkness.

Dawn had broken, pushing the grey hours before it. King Holbian stood before the doors of Underfall, waiting for Nevian, the Master of Magic. About him were the remnants of his great army. None of his captains had survived the battle for World's End. He was surrounded by a shadow of the greatness of yesterday, by mere lads, apprentice Gallopers and Marchers.

His heart was heavy, he doubted the Wizard's words. How could these children keep Elundium safe from his enemies and hold a kingdom where better men had perished, and who amongst them held the seed of greatness that would spawn a king? His eyes studied them in the half light and his heart darkened.

'Great King!' echoed Nevian's voice from the highest gallery. Sunlight caught the patterns of his rainbow cloak.

'I bring you gifts to bind your victory and wise counsels for tomorrow. If Underfall should fall or come to nothing, the powers of night will rise again at World's End. Nightbeasts and the shades of shadows will overrun Elundium and all that you have won. Guard it well.'

'How, Lord?' shouted Holbian. 'With nothing but underlings and boys? I cannot call this an army.'

'Look not on what you see, look rather on what they will become. Mighty trees grow from small seeds.'

Nevian descended to stand before Holbian.

'Underfall, and each Wayhouse upon the Greenways' edge must have a keeper chosen from amongst these gathered here. Let the deeds of yesterday set the measure of each house.'

'But they are children!'

'Think not of them as children. The skill of their arms kept them alive to stand with you at this place; the courage in their hearts defeated the shadows they fought against. Your captains, in their wisdom, put them first into battle, yet they survived. Now choose.'

Holbian looked from face to face and saw nothing but half-starved awkward youth and knew that he dare not choose. He would not be a Kingmaker, nor throw his throne at a child's feet.

'I cannot,' he replied bitterly, turning away. 'Pick whom you will, for you see deeper than the last Granite King.'

Nevian laughed, taking Marcher Tombel's hand, he said, 'Child, you shall be the Keeper of Woodsedge. Guard it well, but I will pledge to you yet another important task.'

'Lord, I am your servant. Ask and it shall be done,' cried Tombel, falling on to his knees.

Nevian cast back the rainbow cloak and gently lifted Duclos, the Swordsman, from within its folds and put him into Tombel's arms. Dried blood had filled his ears and as his head slumped forwards it stained Tombel's collar.

'This is the greatest Swordsman Elundium has ever known. He shall have the mark of the Kingsman on his arm and yet he will not serve you, Lord. Such was the skill of his arms that alone he broke the shadow circle and stood before the Master of Nightbeasts, daring to lift a blade against him. Krulshards has shouted him into deafness and destroyed his balance. Tombel shall take him and watch over him within the boundaries of Woodsedge, and there in time a little of the greatness may return.'

With the middle finger of his right hand he traced a tattoo on both boys' arms, an owl in blue and gold, holding a sword in its talons.

'This mark binds you to the King. If it should ever fade Elundium will fall into darkness.'

Strange magic passed before Holbian's eyes as the morning wore away, for as Nevian traced each tattoo he saw the bearers of the mark as they would be in the fullness of time, proud men with steady eyes and hearts that feared nothing in the dark. Yet not one hint or clue did Nevian give as to who would take the throne of the King.

'Trueflight Orm!' called Nevian in a clear voice, 'step forward, child. Many that stand here today owe their lives to your steady eye. Give me your hand, child, and kneel before your King.'

Trueflight knelt shyly, blushing at being called forward. Nevian continued in a loud voice, full of majesty, 'Yesterday, when these doors burst open and blackest shadows filled the road, when brave men fled in terror, casting their bows and quivers on to the ground, you put fear behind the light that shone in your eyes; you held a whisper of victory and made every arrow you shot find its mark until your quiver was empty and the Bow of Orm lay still in your hand. As the measure of your courage I name you Archerorm and place into your care the tower Wayhouse on Stumble Hill. Guard it well, for it rises above the black lands of Notley Marsh and holds the road to World's End and this fastness of Underfall.'

Holbian looked past the bowed head of the young Archer, and saw only two the Master of Magic had not called forward. Nevian followed his eye, smiling before beckoning Thunderstone to his side.

'Great deeds have set the measure yet the greatest deed has so far gone unrewarded, for this child, beyond hope, held the Causeway when all those around him fell. With only a broken blade, and a shattered helm, he fought against a wall of shadows. Thus it was Equion, Lord amongst the Warhorses, found him and gave his life that you, my child, should rise up in the morning and keep the light forever bright at World's End.'

'Lord,' stammered Thunderstone, falling on to his knees, tears of shame coursing down his cheeks, 'I let that beautiful horse die. I am not worthy.'

Nevian reached out his arms and cast the rainbow cloak about the lad's shoulders calling softly, 'Be calm, be calm; listen to the music of his hooves; see the sunlight on his silken skin; be calm and wise, for you are the Keeper of Underfall, the last Lampmaster in a troubled land.'

'It must be him,' muttered King Holbian, under his breath, 'the Keeper of Underfall.'

Such was the power of the cloak that all those gathered about the doors saw nothing of Thunderstone's grief but saw a mighty warrior, grown to cast a giant shadow, who feared nothing. He had in his hand a sword, with a silver horse tail woven into its hilt, that glistened in the sunlight. Beneath the magic mantle, Thunderstone heard again the thunder of hooves heralding the morning, and he saw the black wall of shadows crumble to nothing as Equion rose up to break their power, taking the bitter shafts of death aimed at his heart, and he saw the purpose of the sacrifice.

'Lord,' he whispered, 'although I am not worthy of the task, I will keep back the darkness at World's End all my days and live near the place where Equion fell, so I may see such beauty once again.'

'Keeper, take your sword!' cried Nevian. 'It has great power, for I have bound within the hilt those strands of hair you cut from Equion's tail. Keep it all your days as some small comfort in the dark.' His voice became a whisper as he guided Thunderstone to stand with the company. 'As much will fall to ruin, so amongst the chaos you must stand alone and keep a light burning in the troubled times to come. Let courage keep the tattoo bright upon your arm, my children.'

'Thoron. Thoronhand! Come forward, lad, last but by no means least. You are called before your King.' There was laughter in Nevian's voice and his eyes twinkled with delight. 'King Holbian,' Nevian continued, 'there stands before you one that will have no house to call his own. I could not break the pledges between this boy and the great Warhorse, Amarch. Love still binds them together. It is no small matter to be passed off lightly, my King, for through their love you have the last errant rider to serve the Granite Kings. Thoron shall now be his name, though no Wayhouse shall bear this title above its door. Every place from this great fortress at World's End to the

31

most lowly woodman's hut will welcome his presence, for he will bring hope in the morning and chase fears away at night.'

Holbian moved forward to take Amarch's bridle but she reared, striking at the air above the King's head. 'No, Lord,' shouted Nevian, pulling the King clear of the glittering, razor-sharp hooves.

'The bonds are broken, you cannot touch the Warhorses or ever again ask an owl to perch on your shoulder. Amarch chose to remain with the lad, Thoron, and take the name that he gave her. Remember my Lord that it is only Thoron who serves you, the bond of love between these two is theirs alone to share.'

'Thoron,' Nevian spoke sharply as he led the lad and Amarch beyond the great doors, 'beware, child, that your bond of love does not spread a web of jealousy across Elundium, for you are blessed with love and you will make much happen in a long life. Others will hate you for it. Tread carefully and do not step beyond World's End; that much I will tell you. Now go, and Kingspeed on whatever road should press beneath your great steed's hooves. Kingspeed!'

With the speed of a silver arrow Amarch leapt down upon the Causeway road, sparks scattering from the rings of steel upon her feet, and raced for Mantern's Forest.

'Great King,' Nevian said quietly, taking the King into the shadows of the inner courtyard, 'I have laboured hard to keep Elundium safe beyond today.'

'Is it the boy, Thunderstone? Will he take my place and steal my throne?' interrupted the King.

'Enough!' snapped the Master of Magic, his patience at an end. 'Yesterday you raised your sword against me and today your greed for power tramples on the safety of Elundium. You try my patience too far!'

Moving closer to the King, his eyes glittering with anger, Nevian continued, 'Yesterday Orundus would have torn out your eyes, but I stayed his talons. Grannog was ready crouched to spring at your throat, but I bade him sit and wait. Even

32

Equestrius pulled hard at the bridle to defend me. I did not spare your life on the heather plateau before the Gates of Night to haggle over thrones. I spared your life and all its weaknesses to serve the people of this land, to keep Krulshards and the terror of the shadow circle out of Elundium.'

Nevian paused, holding the King with his eyes.

'You have seen all those who survived yesterday's battle pledged to serve you with a binding mark upon their arms; study it well, my Lord, for as the owl protected me before the gates of night so shall they help you to protect this kingdom and keep safe the throne you sit upon.'

Nevian paused, glancing from the King's face to the steep mountain slopes that shadowed the fortress of Underfall.

'Remember,' he whispered, drawing closer to the King, 'I know your secret fear of the darkness. It is not my place to betray your weakness to lesser men. You alone must carry that knowledge. For only we know that Krulshards hides in the City of Night. You must labour to hold back his black terror until a greater King can face the darkness!'

'All your talk of Kings and tomorrows,' replied Holbian bitterly, 'but what of today, what of the empty world you have fashioned through the bondbreaking? How shall I cope with that, knowing that the Warhorses and the Battle Owls have returned into the wilderness? Will they return? Will they come with the new King and help him to step into my shoes?'

Nevian wrung his hands in despair. 'Lord, Lord, nobody shall steal it. The one who will be King is as yet unborn, and fate must travel many twists before he stands before you and even then you may not see him for the looking.'

King Holbian looked away sadly, seeing in the cold afternoon light all that his fear of the darkness had cost. 'Tell me,' he cried, 'who will spawn the King? Tell me and I shall guard him faithfully, as a son, as the most precious jewel in all Elundium. You have my word as the last Granite King!'

Nevian sighed, seeing beyond the words into the pain of the

33

King's sorrow and regret that yesterday had loaded on to his shoulders. Reaching beneath his rainbow cloak he lifted up a heavy bundle of cloth that sparkled and flashed in the shadowy courtyard.

'I cannot tell you, Lord, no matter how you ask me, who this new King will be. He must be allowed to grow to manhood alone, for that will be his making.'

'Then he will be as alone as I am,' whispered the King, shivering as the thought of the coming night came to him.

'No, Lord,' replied the Master of Magic, shaking out the bundle of cloth into the shape of a cloak sewn with a thousand jewels. Each gem had been cleverly cut to catch and hold the light.

'You need never face the darkness alone, my King. This cloak will catch the candlelight and give you comfort in the dark.'

'This is treasure indeed!' cried Holbian.

'It is all you could desire; and probably more,' answered Nevian. 'But hidden in the threads are snags that only wise men need not fear. Your saddle days are over. Government will send you back to keep Elundium safe. This gift will lie heavily on your shoulders if not used with caution. Keep it well, for it was woven with a speeding shuttle on a secret loom before the grey hours fled in the face of a new sun.'

'How shall I use it?' asked Holbian, forgetting about new Kings as he caressed the jewels, screwing up his eyes against the blinding light.

Nevian shaded his eyes against their light and began instructing the King. 'Each day, as the sunlight fades, put on the cloak. It will give you strength in the darkness no matter how long the night may last. Use the comfort it brings to grow wise; rebuild and garden the wilderness that war has left throughout Elundium.'

'Riches beyond desire,' laughed the King, lifting his arms and spiralling until he became giddy with the wealth that flashed before his eyes.

Nevian frowned at the dancing King. He stretched out a hand

and stilled him. 'Riches, my Lord,' he said sternly, 'are a snare if you hoard them for their own value. Each jewel in the cloak is worth a kingdom, that is plain to see, but its real value is to guard you in the dark. Compare the cloak against a new sunrise and it is nothing but glittering stones, hold it up against a black night of howling winds and it is a treasure beyond measure. The cloak is but a part of the new world you will rule. Before the sun climbed above the horizon's rim I reset the secret door locks of this Wayhouse and every Wayhouse on the roads of Elundium. They will open at the first hint of sunlight and slam shut before night falls. Let no man step beyond the doors if he fears the dark. Now you must rule alone, for you are a great King who stands on the threshold of wisdom.'

'I can enter the City of Night,' laughed the King, lifting his spark high above his head, 'and destroy the creatures of darkness wearing this cloak.'

'No, Lord,' answered Nevian, forcefully, 'there is no light to reflect in that dark place and your spark would be swallowed up one pace beyond the gates. Do not enter the City of Night unless you overcome your fear of the dark. Be warned. Tread carefully, my King, and trust only those who hold the tattoo mark.'

Distracted by the wealth about his shoulders King Holbian was deaf to reason, and he missed Nevian's final words of counsel for the dark years ahead. Looking up he saw the rainbow cloak fading into nothing, and for a moment felt the emptiness of despair as he reached out a hand and touched the cold granite walls of the grim fastness of Underfall that clung to the black mountain at World's End. He shivered, drawing the cloak of jewels tightly about him.

'Now we shall see,' he muttered, through tight lips. 'What secrets are there in this fortress? Secrets that the Master of Magic has hidden from the last of the Granite Kings! Nothing?' he cried, drawing his sword.

'No, Lord,' whispered Thunderstone, retreating out of the

sword's reach. 'We have searched every chamber, every gallery, there is nothing but shadows.'

'Shadows!' screamed the King. 'We fought to win shadows?'

'Lord,' a young voice called out, interrupting the King's anger, 'legend says that this place is the tomb of Kings. Perhaps that is why there are only shadows.'

'Tombs?' shouted the King, his face black with anger. 'I see no value in tombs.'

'There are steps that lead down beneath the earth. Perhaps they will show us.' The voice tapered off nervously.

'Take me to this place,' commanded the King, beckoning the lad and asking his name.

'Tombel, Sire,' he replied, 'the Keeper of Woodsedge.'

'Well, Keeper of Woodsedge, lead the way. And be quick, night is but an hour away.'

Tombel led the King through a maze of empty courtyards and passages, each one narrower than the last, darker and more foreboding, until they reached the cold walls of Mantern's Mountain and there in deepest shadows they found the granite steps that led down into the darkness. Tombel shrank back away from the steps; his fear of the dark would not let him go forwards. King Holbian lit the spark, and laughed harshly as the jewelled cloak burst into brilliant blinding light, driving the shadows out of the tiny courtyard.

'Stay here, Keeper,' the King hissed. 'You fear the dark and I can tread where others dare not go.'

Holding the spark carefully King Holbian descended the stairs. He wore a cloak that would drive the shadows out, he need not fear the dark, yet his hands trembled and his footsteps slowed. He remembered Nevian's words of caution and hesitated. What if the spark failed? What if night should overtake him here alone, beneath the ground? A cold draught of air touched his cheek, the fingers of death seemed to be caressing his face. He screamed, stumbling backwards against the steps. The spark blazed pure white as it flew from his hand

36

and in the moment before it fell, extinguished, he saw them in the cloak's reflecting light. Blind-eyed they stood amongst the fleeing shadows, petrified and ageless, beckoning to him to come forwards and take his place. Stumbling and scrambling in the darkness King Holbian fled up the ancient stone stairway, his heart pounding as he raced for the small square of light above. With each step he took upwards the cloak grew brighter until on the last few steps he slowed, gathered his faltering courage and stepped back into the courtyard, a brave and powerful Granite King.

'Guard it well,' he commanded Thunderstone as he hurried to leave Underfall, shivering under his cloak at the thought of what waited beneath the cold grey fortress at World's End.

'Build a great lamp, a beacon on the highest galleries to drive back the darkness. Do it quickly, before the night comes.'

'Lord, I will,' cried Thunderstone, but his words were lost in the bitter winds that blew down from Mantern's Mountain.

Seasons came, blossomed into fullness, mellowed and decayed. Leafmould thickened the forest floor, muffling the hoofbeats of the great Warhorses as they roamed in secret freedom. The owls kept their own counsel, blending into the wildness that grew about them, but little escaped their unblinking eyes of how badly things stood for King Holbian, for he soon forgot Nevian's words amongst the shouts of those who sought the treasure that he wore.

Thoron saw ruin spreading close on the heels of neglect but he was powerless to stop the shadows gathering and as the years passed, even the King refused him an audience, for those that stalked the cloak of jewels let no man with the tattoo mark into the bowers of granite. Small comfort came to him in the dark and gave him courage to keep his pledges to the last Granite King. Owls flew to his shoulders and the Border Runners ran at his heels for they knew much of his deeds that never reached the King's ear and loved him, for as Nevian had foretold, he brought hope with the morning and feared nothing in the dark.

As swiftly as Amarch ran, Thoron became a part of legends while he lived, keeping the great Greenways open that led towards World's End, but time and wildness overtangled all his efforts and gradually Underfall fell once more into dark whispers, besieged by the growing shadows of Mantern's Mountain.

Thunderstone kept his pledge, growing through need to cast a giant's shadow between the doors of Underfall. Nightbeasts hammered on the doors and tore at the sheer granite walls, but none could enter without the Keeper's leave. He stood alone amongst a world of nightmares, abandoned through the treachery of those close to the King. Even the wretches sent to help him guard the fastness of Underfall arrived in chains, bound and branded, to end their days in the darkness of World's End. It became a place of fear and exile where Thunderstone drove the condemned at the point of his sword to overcome the terrors of the night, and though they hated him and cursed his name, he made them into new men who, in time, walked with pride in the half light, and little by little Underfall rose above the shadows and the lamp set above its highest galleries burned with a blinding light through the darkest years of King Holbian's reign.

Without Nevian's presence King Holbian soon forgot the wisdom of his final counsel and quickly turned his back on all the Master of Magic had ever said. He cursed the bondbreaking and all dabblers in magic but most of all he cursed his own fear of the dark, knowing that it would one day lose him the throne. Sending for his stonemasons and architects he ordered them to rebuild Candlebane Hall, and fortify it against the night.

'Polish the walls,' he commanded the masons. 'Rub them so smooth that even the tiniest flicker of light will endlessly reflect. Carve new candle stems and set them in concentric circles, some raised, some lower, but each must have a fluted channel for the melted wax,' here the King paused, gathering his architects into a tight circle. 'Build me a throne, a centrepiece raised above the tallest candle stem that I might see the truth in men's eyes.'

'And the channel for the molten wax, my Lord,' asked an anxious voice, 'Where do we direct it? What is it for?'

The King laughed, a cruel empty sound that froze the blood. 'To test the truth in men's hearts.'

Turning, the King overturned two huge candles, pouring the molten wax that had collected around their wicks into a stone vessel. Into this he plunged his hand and kept it there until the wax had cooled and solidified. Raising the wax encrusted fist he brought it down against an edge of white marble, smashing the wax into a thousand pieces. 'Kings do not melt in the wax. Kings do not melt in the fire,' he snarled. 'Build the channel for the molten wax in a curve before my throne. There I shall find him, there in the heart of the fire I shall find the one who will steal my throne!'

The cloak of jewels became a terrible beacon in those dark nights of judgement as the King sought to find the one he feared. 'Bring him to me!' he raged, and any poor wretch found beyond the safety of his house after dark was dragged into Candlebane Hall, to face the rising tide of flickering candle-light and the last Granite King, high-throned and terrible.

'Can you see in the dark?' he would hiss, bending forwards across the channels of molten wax. 'Only Kings can see in the dark and only Kings are brave enough to risk the fire and feel no pain.'

'No, Lord, no,' cried the accused, throwing themselves on to the King's mercy, but the Chancellors pushed and pulled them towards the channels of wax, deaf to their pleading and blind to their pain, for there was no mercy in Candlebane Hall, only the screams of the innocent as their limbs melted in the wax, rising up to be lost amongst the high, smoking rafters. There the

Nightshapes wept tears of pity to see such cruelty in the candle flames.

Only in the evening of his days did the King for a moment hesitate and see the horror of what he had done, and come to know the true meaning of despair. For he saw from the high windows in the granite towers a river of wax woven with the webs of his treachery and lies that he had spun to find the throne stealer, and they choked Elundium's beauty. He called his Chancellors to Candlebane Hall, standing them amongst the inner circle of candles and he cursed them, daring any man amongst them to step forwards and tell him why. Why had they let him cause such misery and pain to the people of Elundium?

'Were you blind?' he screamed, smashing frail candle stems with his clenched fists. 'Were you deaf to the suffering? Who would want this throne now that I have kept it so jealously?'

'You commanded us, Lord,' whispered Chancellor Proudpurse, 'It is your laws we obey to keep this rich kingdom safe from throne stealers.'

'Rich?' shouted the King. 'Rich?'

'Lord,' answered Proudpurse, kneeling before Holbian, 'the cloak of jewels is the richest prize in all Elundium. We only sought to protect it from the throne stealer.'

Holbian laughed, bitterly, looking from face to face. 'This piece of cloth and coloured stones you value so much is worthless. Its only purpose is to reflect the light. Is this what we have plundered the people of Elundium for? A cloak of worthless jewels?'

'Worthless?' gasped Proudpurse. 'Worthless?' echoed the Chancellors, stepping backwards, shaking their heads in dismay.

'Lord, greatest of Kings,' Proudpurse called out, growing bold and snatching at the moment, 'you cannot say that the cloak of jewels is worthless. Why, each stone is worth a kingdom, and men would kill each other just to touch it. Lord, you must not abandon the search for the throne stealer, that would render all our work amongst the people pointless. Lord, we know the secrets within the secrets and we have almost found the one who will take your throne.'

Holbian stood for long moments, surveying his Chancellors while wax dripped from the burning wicks and Nightshapes moved silently in the high dark corners beyond the candles' light. He shivered, wondering just how powerful these Chancellors had become. Clearly he could see the greed and envy reflecting in their eyes as they watched the cloak of jewels but beneath the greed he could sense a terrible lust for power.

'Fools!' he shouted, tearing off a handful of the precious stones and casting them at the Chancellors' feet. 'These will not save you when the Nightbeasts come, nor will they buy you a kingdom in the darkness. If everlasting night should fall again who amongst you will take up my sword and face the terrors of the dark? Who?'

'Nightbeasts?' whispered the Chancellors, hesitating in their scramble for the jewels.

'Yes,' replied Holbian, stepping up on to the throne's dais and wrapping the cloak about his shoulders. 'I have heard them, echoes of the terror that I fought and defeated at World's End. They have spawned again and are loose once more in Elundium. They are the ones who will snatch this throne and spread the blackness throughout the land. We have been blind in our purpose. You!' Holbian paused, pointing a shaking finger at the Chancellors, 'You have turned your backs on the safety and the welfare of Elundium in your quest for power and I . . .' again the King paused, looking inwards at his weaknesses and for the first time spoke of his dread, 'and I have failed the people of this beautiful land through my fear of the dark, leaving only ruin and chaos as the inheritance of the one who will take my throne.'

Proudpurse could wait no longer, his fingers ached to touch the jewels that lay at his feet. 'Nightbeasts,' he laughed, 'are a phantom for those with tattoos on their arms. I fear nothing. I am a Chancellor.'

'Then you are a fool,' replied Holbian, 'for every bearer of the tattoo mark knows something of the truth of what could one day return to plague this land, and they would willingly have shared that knowledge with you if you had not driven them away in your thirst for power. You laughed in ignorance and you jest in the shadow of real terror. You do not understand. Now take the jewels and in their light see a little sense.'

The Chancellors rushed forwards, pushing and barging to snatch up the precious stones, but the more they fought the less they took and stone after stone slipped through their fingers and fell into the channels of hot molten wax.

'Fools,' whispered Holbian, seeing clearly how they would destroy Elundium by squabbling and fighting among themselves while the Nightbeasts would rise to power. Only one figure did not chase the glittering stones. He stood quite still, hot wax from a spluttering taper splashing unnoticed on to his hand.

'Candleman!' the King called, softly motioning the figure to come forward. 'When the Chancellors have gone, set the candles straight and give me light that I might see a way into the darkness.'

The Chancellors stopped fighting and each one, it seemed now, had something he wished to hide, and they all begged King Holbian to let them leave Candlebane Hall as soon as possible. He dismissed them in disgust, turning his mind back to the battle for World's End and Nevian's last words of wisdom.

'Where are they, Ironhand?' he asked, turning his gaze towards the candlelighter, 'Where are the bearers of the tattoo mark?'

Ironhand looked towards the King with vacant, childlike eyes, his left hand immersed in the channel of molten wax. 'Who, Lord,' he sang, 'calls on the Candleman to send him to bed. Who, Lord, calls on the Candleman to pour hot wax on his head?'

'Ironhand!' the King hissed, leaping from the high throne, 'Your hand, can you not feel the hot wax?'

Ironhand laughed, withdrawing his hand and opening it, palm upwards towards the King, 'Lord, I am only here to please, and to keep for you what you have won. Here, my Lord, are the stones from your cloak.'

'Throw them back into the wax,' Holbian replied, 'and come and sit at the foot of my throne, for there is much I must learn before the sun rises.'

Ironhand smiled as he knelt at the King's feet, 'Lord, Lord, I am nothing but the Candleman. In the tallow hall where the candles are made the Master cursed me as an idle child and plunged my hands into the hot wax as a punishment. The molten wax burned the skin from my hands leaving them raw and bleeding. I was cast out into the darkness to die.'

'And? Tell me how you grew new hands that have no feeling. For that is a strange and powerful magic.'

'Lord, you will kill me if I tell you the truth, for you have cursed meddlers in magic.'

The King laughed, searching with his eyes amongst the candle flames for eavesdroppers before he pressed the rest of Ironhand's story from him. 'The Nightbeasts are growing strong, Candleman, I have heard them roaring in the night. Now is the time for magic, tell me!'

Ironhand swallowed and searched back into his muddled memory to find the pieces. 'My father, Thoron, had come to see you, my Lord, with grave news, I think, but the Chancellors drove him out of the city and he found me in the shadows of the Great Gate, bleeding and raw from the molten wax. He took me by strange and dangerous paths into a place of tall trees and there I saw a tall man wearing a rainbow cloak. It was put across my hands and I wept as the pain left me.'

'And Thoron brought you here to Candlebane Hall,' inter-

43

rupted the King, 'and he begged me to take you in as a fool and a witless simpleton, into service as a candlelighter.'

'Lord, the price for my hands was my wits. I am a simple man who knows nothing.'

'Yet the Master of Magic touched you with the rainbow cloak,' muttered the King, darkly, 'and I took you in out of love for your father for he served me well until the Chancellors drove him out. There is more to this than simple magic. Have you a son, Candleman? Have you?'

The candlelighter shook with fear, 'Do not kill him, my Lord, he is dull-witted like his father and a baby amongst the wicks and snuffers of this great hall.'

King Holbian laughed and drew the Candleman up until their faces were almost touching. 'It is the Chancellors you must fear for they will kill you both if you so much as dip a finger into the hot wax. Be warned, Ironhand, the Chancellors have grown into a terrible power in this city. We must hide your son somewhere, somewhere the Chancellors will never think of looking for him, just as Nevian hid you here in Candlebane Hall.'

'Lord, I am nothing,' protested Ironhand.

'Quiet! Play the fool for the Chancellors, not for me! Now listen. Nevian once predicted that the one who would take this throne must grow to manhood alone, and yet if I leave your son unhelped he will grow to be ignorant and ill-prepared to face the Chancellors and they will find him easy meat to kill.'

King Holbian left the throne and descended to the inner circle of candles and there trod a shadow on the smooth polished floor as he paced the night away, going over and over in his head those words of Nevian's that he could remember. 'I have it!' he cried at last just as the grey hours were filling the sky. 'Tomorrow I shall pass a law that all the children of Candlebane Hall must attend the Loremaster in the Learning Halls. He will not grow up in ignorance but he will become well-prepared to face the Chancellors and they will never think to look amongst their own for the throne stealer.'

44

'Lord, shall I bring him to you before the new sun rises?'

'No! no!' cried Holbian, remembering clearly now the wizard's words. 'I must remain ignorant of him. Even his name you must not utter and if he comes into this hall to serve you I must not see him. So go now in peace, Candleman, and guard our secret well, for we shall have to be clever and cunning to outwit the Chancellors.'

'Who, Lord, calls the Candleman . . .' sang Ironhand, as he moved amongst the candles extinguishing the bright flames with his snuffer. 'Who calls on the Candleman to pour wax on his head . . .'

'Who indeed?' muttered the King, retreating into the Granite Towers. Wearily he climbed the circling steps until he reached the highest window that would face the new sunrise, and there he paused to look across the Granite City and think of all the changes he must make. Below, the city had awakened to the hint of the new daylight. Cooking fires hazed the air with thin spirals of blue smoke and criers moved amongst the crowded houses shouting the people out. King Holbian swept his gaze across a forest of weather-bleached slate roofs, followed the ribbon-winding lanes and dark alleyways until they were lost in the shadows of the outer walls, and there, built in rough grey granite, stood the stables and the breaking yards. Once the first line of defence against the world outside, now the King trembled to see them fallen into such neglect, weed-choked and desolate in the early dawn light.

'My Chancellors are fools to think that stone walls and strong doors will keep the Nightbeasts out. Where are the Gallopers and their proud mounts? Who can help me?' he wept, resting his head in his hand. 'There is so much I cannot change alone.'

As if in answer to the King, the clear singing voice of the Candleman rose up out of the narrow streets that lay in the shadows of the Granite Towers. 'Who calls on the Candleman to put him to bed? Who calls on the Candleman to light him to bed?'

# Within the Mouth of Night

Hidden from the sun beneath a million tons of rock the City of Night brooded in silence.

'Leaves,' a voice whispered, gathering the tunnellers into a tight circle.

'Yesterday was full of rain and today will be as bleak when the Nightbeasts drive us to work, but while they sleep we will share the light.'

Leaf bowed his head and brought his hands together as if holding a delicate cup. Then he began, as the Master of Magic had taught him, to build the point of light. He used the tree picture, the one with all the leaves in golden colours, bending in the wind. The point of light grew, warming his hands. He passed it on to the next tunneller who took up the story and so it went the rounds of the circle.

'Tell us the story of the great black Warhorse,' whispered Willow Leaf, interrupting the Elder who had taken up the story of the bending tree. 'The one who haunts the tunnels. Is he real?'

'He is real, Willow,' replied Leaf the Elder, smiling in the darkness at the young boy, 'and he is a great blessing to us, for he hunts the Nightbeasts and they walk in fear of him.'

'Have you seen him?' questioned Willow, his heart beating faster.

'Hush, child, the Nightbeasts are near!'

'Why does he come here?' persisted the child. 'If I were free I would . . .'

'Hush, hush, Willow,' snapped Leaf the Elder, taking back the point of light and holding it against his chest in his cupped hands. 'I will tell you when he first appeared if that will silence your questions.'

49

Willow grinned, knowing how much the Elder loved to talk about the Warhorse.

'It was after the noise of the Great Battle had died away. Krulshards returned, surrounded by the Nightbeasts in the shadow circle. It seemed from their talk that the Granite King had won the battle but he was afraid to follow the Master of Nightmares into the darkness. It was a time of great despair for us, as new Nightbeasts were spawned in the lower levels of the darkness and we wept, waiting patiently for the signs the magician had spoken of.'

'But what about the Warhorse? What of him?' asked Willow, impatiently. The Elder had never spent this long telling how he had arrived.

'He comes to protect the horses that the Nightbeasts steal from the land of Elundium and to put to work pulling the rubble sledges here in the City of Night. But you must be careful not to get in his way.'

'Has he ever harmed a tunneller?' asked Willow.

'Never! Not a single hair has he ever touched amongst us. Why, long ago, just after he first appeared, I saw him and felt the wind he stirred up as he galloped past.' Lowering his voice, almost as if speaking to himself, the elder added, 'he could have crushed me to death, but he left me crouching against the tunnel wall, unharmed.'

A slight noise distracted Willow from the Elder's tale and broke the pictures in his mind. There was a scuffle beyond the arch where the sledging horses stood. Willow started to rise, pushing a hand into the deep heavy dust; he froze, half standing, as a great black shape moved silently through the arch. It paused, and soft eyes surveyed him, searching his soul and held him still. Willow's heart was pounding and the sound of his own blood thundered in his ears. To see such beauty, to see the Warhorse, it was beyond any words the Elder could whisper. The great arched neck and rippling sheets of muscle, the power and the majesty – all this was standing so close to

50

him. Drips of water splashed into the pools and the group huddled around the Elder, listened to his whispering, oblivious that the horse stood almost close enough to touch them. A voice within Willow's head commanded him to be still and silent. It was not a threat, just a command. Willow felt his fear melt away and a great excitement bubbled up inside him. Nothing like this had ever happened in any of the Elders' stories. He blinked his large round eyes and the Warhorse disappeared. He searched the shadows, wondering if it had been a dream. Quietly he struggled to his feet and crept to where he had seen the horse; gingerly he felt the ground, spreading his fingers and there, pressed into the dust, were hoofprints, far larger than any left by the shackled horses. It had not been a dream after all. Quietly Willow took his place amongst the circle of tunnellers, but he felt somehow different, changed from the scrawny youth who had started the Elder whispering the story of the Warhorse. To those about him he still looked the same person, Willow Leaf, the rubble sledge boy, but he had seen the Warhorse and had heard him whisper his name. The edges of a great adventure were at his finger tips.

With cracking whips and roaring voices the Nightbeasts appeared to drive the tunnellers to work, and as the group split up to scurry to the rock face Leaf the Elder clung on to Willow's sleeve, for he had seen the change in the boy's eyes.

'One day our people will be free again. You have a part to play. I see your fate spun in choices, and the right choice will set us free. Remember, boy, if you ever come face to face with the Master of Nightbeasts, tread on his shadow.'

'What choices? What shadow?' cried Willow, grabbing the Elder's frail arm. 'I know nothing but the black tunnel and the grating sledge.'

A lash cracked across the Elder's back and sent him reeling in the dust, a clawed foot crushed his rib cage hard against the ground and, as life fluttered out of his broken chest he

51

whispered to the boy, 'Follow your heart, child; let it make any choice you have. And tread on the Nightbeast's shadow, it renders him helpless.'

Gritty tears blurred the sledge as Willow grieved the Elder's death but the old mare he looked after pulled hard against the traces and often rubbed her face against his in the dark winding tunnels, and through his loss a great bond grew between them. Her velvet-soft muzzle brushed away his tears and both of them sensed Equestrius near at hand.

Willow worked the sledge during the months that followed the Elder's death. His back grew raw from the lash and he took many beatings meant for the old mare to ease her plight. He had named her Evening Star, for she had a splash of white on her forehead and he imagined that was what a star looked like. During the short rest periods he would lie beside her and touch the star and dream of a thousand white points of light across the tunnel roof, just like the night sky in the Elder's stories, dark and yet full of light. And then he wept.

Willow sank into himself and spent all his time with the old horse. He kept his distance from the other members of the group and a bitter resolve grew in him to avenge the Elder's death, but how? The Nightbeasts were giants against him. Their armour made of strips of other beings' skins was tough and it rattled when they moved, and could not be cut by any metal he knew of. Their scythes or whips or spears were always in their hands and they were rough and very quick for all their size. But he would avenge somehow.

Willow, in his anger, developed the habit of clenching and unclenching his hands deep in the dust and sifting it through his fingers. Sitting by the mare one freezing night, sifting in the dust, a sharp pain made him cry aloud, and gingerly withdrawing his hand he found, sticking in his middle finger, a treasure beyond belief. Hanging from a bleeding puncture wound, gleaming dully in the dark, he saw a long broken splinter of steel from an ancient blade. A hand's span long, still razor sharp along its cutting edge, jagged on the fractured side, it ran down to a needle point. No King or wizard could have granted a better gift to little Willow. The tunnellers had only the rags they stood in, even the meagre scraps of food they ate were thrown down to them to eat off the floor. No tools to eat with, or bowls to eat from. But chance, or fate, or magic moves, had armed young Willow with a deadly blade which he quickly hid inside his ragged shirt and the touch of cold metal against his dirty skin made him feel strong, and his hands itched to use it. He snuggled in tight to his horse's side and closed his eyes to sleep. Dreams tumbled through his mind. Dreams of swords flashing high in the sun that he had never seen, of galloping horsemen on rolling hills with a forest of gleaming spears above their heads. He stumbled in his dream and came awake, the jolting that had woken him was a small convulsion in the old mare's side. He put his hand gently on her and felt a kick against his hand. Puzzled, he felt her ears and her neck. She did not seem distressed. So much had happened since the Warhorse had first appeared; he shrugged and drifted back to sleep, eager once again to ride with the spearmen.

Near him a horse nickered softly as Equestrius, the great black Warhorse, moved closer to Star, blowing her a gentle greeting and smelling her side just above Willow's head. His lips and nostrils brushed over Willow's sleeping face and he saw in a vision the boy ride to war with him. Nightbeasts fell beneath his galloping hooves and the sun streamed through his flying mane. Willow tightly held the jagged blade which glittered and flashed in the sunlight.

# The Passing of Thoronhand

'Late again, Candlebrat Hand!' snarled the Loremaster, advancing on the ill dressed youth hovering in the doorway. 'Get to your place before I thrash the daylight out of you. Move boy, move!'

Pinchface, the Loremaster, struck out with the lash, cutting across the back of Thane's knees, felling him with one stinging stroke. 'Boy, it was a black day that our King smiled upon the rabble who serve at Candlebane Hall letting them loose to steal a little learning, for it is a dangerous thing among the ignorant. Is that the truth my boy!'

'Yes, Sire,' Thane replied, feeling the blood heating his cheeks.

'Yes, Sire,' mimicked the Loremaster, winking at the other boys seated in the Learning Hall, 'What else, boy?'

'Sire, I am a Candlebrat from . . .' Thane hesitated, looking down at the rough string shoes and ragged leggings he wore. He could see without looking and hear without listening, the cruelty in the Chancellors' sons who filled the hall. They were waiting until the Loremaster had dealt with him then they, without mercy, would torment him. It was the Lore of the Learning Hall just as it was the Lore of the Granite City. 'Chancellors are the power of Elundium and their wishes are the will of the people.'

'What else, boy?' prompted the Loremaster, an edge of impatience in his voice. Thane lifted his head and brushing back untidy straw coloured hair from his pale blue eyes faced the assembled class. 'Lord, I am a Candlebrat from Candlebane Hall. I am ignorant, ill-mannered, unlearned and untaught.'

'Unclean,' sniggered Silverpurse, Chancellor Proudpurse's son.

'Uncouth!' laughed another.

'Boys! Boys!' called out the Loremaster, finding it difficult to suppress his delight at mocking the children of Candlebane Hall, for he hated them and their low beginnings. 'That is enough, my children,' he chided gently.

Turning cold eyes back to Thane he instructed him to go to his place below the other learners and sit on the broken stool that had only two legs. 'And pay attention, Candlebrat,' he roared, 'for today I shall teach you of the Galloper who won the battle for World's End.'

Thane forgot the pain behind his knees and carefully balancing on the stool waited on every word the Loremaster uttered, eagerly longing to hear how his grandfather, Thoronhand, had fought his way through the black mass of Nightbeasts, urging Amarch, the beautiful grey Warhorse, towards the fortress of Underfall.

'Morning was breaking into a glorious new daylight and the ranks of Nightbeasts covered their eyes against the light before the gates of Underfall.' The Loremaster paused and looked into each upturned face and saw the picture he had begun to paint. 'Bravepurse, the Mighty,' he continued, letting his voice fall to little more than a whisper, 'drove Amarch forwards, slashing at her sweating flanks with the flat of his sword. Fear was in her eyes but he forced her on at spur point, for he was the strongest and most feared Galloper in all Elundium, always first into battle and always lifting men's hearts with the skill of his sword.'

'It is a lie!' Thane cried, jumping to his feet and interrupting the Loremaster. Anger boiled in his heart and his fingers clenched and unclenched at his sides as he fought to control his voice. For fifteen whole suns he had done his father's bidding and kept a bridle on his tongue while the Loremaster told lie after lie and the Chancellors' children bullied and beat him,

58

but they would not call Amarch a coward or say that a Chancellor had sat on her back. 'There were none! None in all Elundium, be he Chancellor or King, who dared to put a hand on Amarch. Only my grandfather, Thoronhand, was allowed to ride upon her, for there was a bond of love between them.'

The white-lipped rage in the Loremaster's face and the grim stares of hatred from the Chancellors' sons should have halted Thane, but he ran on, defending the great Warhorse without pausing for breath. 'When my grandfather died somewhere in the wilderness beyond this city Amarch came to us, wounded, and asked for help but your fathers were deaf to her cries and locked the city against her. For three whole daylights she screamed and neighed, pawing at the Great Gates before she turned away and vanished into the wild lands. How can you say that a Chancellor ever rode upon her back!'

Thane's voice fell away to nothing. He stood defiantly in the silence knowing that he had said more than enough to be thrown into a vat of molten candle wax in Candlebane Hall. All that remained now was for the Loremaster to call for the Learning Hall guard, but he did not move. The silence continued; bees hummed beneath the window sill and sunlight streamed through the vaulted windows. Dust eddied in gentle draughts and caught by the sunlight formed patterns that shifted, broke and reformed, almost imperceptibly, as the Loremaster rose and turned towards the door. The patterns changed again and re-arranged themselves into the shape of a man, old beyond time, heavy with wisdom, who had about his shoulders a rainbow cloak.

'Stop!' commanded the ancient figure, pointing his finger at the Loremaster. 'For too long you have twisted the truth and whispered lies in the pictures you paint. Come forward now and tell us the truth of this great kingdom.'

'Lord,' cried Pinchface, falling on to his knees, 'I only do as the Chancellors command. It is the law to obey.'

Nevian laughed and shook the rainbow cloak, filling the

59

Learning Hall with blinding colours. 'Am I not stronger than a thousand Chancellors?'

The Loremaster cried, burying his head in the folds of his cloak. 'Lord, Lord, I am but a servant.'

'Then serve me and all of this great city by telling the truth, for without it you are lost, stumbling on the edge of everlasting darkness. Come to me, Loremaster, and teach these children the truth.'

With that the voice faded and the rainbow cloak changed into many pictures that matched the droning Loremaster's voice as he told the learners the truth of the great battle for World's End and the fortress of Underfall. 'Nightbeasts issued out of Mantern's Mountain in black waves of terror, hideously spreading the shadows of death across the Causeway Fields. The men of Elundium could not look upon them and turned to flee but Duclos, the Swordsman, gathered all those that could hear his voice above the Nightbeasts' screams and on to each one he tied a blindfold of white silk. "Look into the cloth," he whispered to each man, "and listen only to my singing. Follow my voice."'

'And the Gallopers,' prompted Nevian.

'Thoronhand, my Lord, he galloped on to the causeway upon the Warhorse, Amarch, and found all the Gallopers milling about in disorder. Terror had made the common horses shy and their riders were seized with panic. He marshalled them into quiet ranks and led them towards Underfall and always Amarch was a length ahead, rearing and plunging, where the Nightbeasts were thickest.'

'And the Archers? How did they fare in this battle?' questioned Nevian.

'Lord, Tombel, the Marcher, had rallied the Marchers time and again but the black waves of Nightbeasts drove him backwards until they fought in the shadows of the great dyke beside the causeway road. Trueflightorm, the Archer, saw Tombel's plight and formed those Archers he could find into a strike, and he led them deep into the Nightbeasts' black shadows and the song of the Great Bow of Orm lifted the Marchers' hearts and they swept up out of the dyke across the causeway fields, bright swords flashing in the sunlight.'

Nevian laughed, 'Truth has such beauty. But what of our King and his Chancellors?'

Pinchface looked nervously at the Master of Magic and saw beyond the coloured cloak and the twinkling eyes a terrible power, far greater than anything he had ever seen before. 'King Holbian feared nothing, my Lord, tirelessly he fought upon the raised Causeway sending crescent after crescent of the riderless Warhorses galloping against the Nightbeasts' spears. He called upon the owls and they honoured their pledge, plunging in countless stoops from a clear sky to tear at the Nightbeasts' eyes.'

'But the Chancellors, what of the Chancellors?' insisted Nevian.

'They, my Lord, could not face the black terror of the Nightbeasts and stayed here in the Granite City, governing the people and keeping everything in order for the King's return.'

Nevian turned towards Thane and his ancient face softened into a smile that the other learners did not see, and he spoke in gentle tones that only Thane could hear. 'You cried out for justice, Thane, a dangerous thing to do amongst the Chancellors' sons, for now they know the truth and will hate you all the more for it. Prudence should have stopped your tongue.'

'Lord,' whispered Thane, stepping backwards and tripping over the broken stool, 'I did not mean to incur your rage, only my grandfather brought Amarch into the Granite City before he died. He let me sit on her back and he called owls down out of the sky to perch on the pommel and the cantle of the saddle while he told me all about the world beyond the city walls. And – and, the Loremaster always seems to lie about what really happened.'

'Be at peace, child, the Loremaster must tell the truth while I am here. Listen and watch for the tale he is about to tell you. It is of the Lord of the Warhorses, Equestrius, but as the pictures fade run for your life, for I cannot undo your foolishness here in the Learning Hall. Take the secret alleyways and dark lanes that lead down to your father's house that shelters in the shadows of the great wall. Tell him what has happened here today. Remember! Go by the dark alleyways, the Chancellors' sons will not follow you into the shadows.'

'Legends tell us that Equestrius is the Lord of Horses. He is as black as night's shadows and as fast as the East wind. He first appeared in Elundium at the beginning of King Holbian's struggle against the Nightbeasts and he helped him to drive the nightmares towards World's End. Great herds of Warhorses galloped besides the men of Elundium and they feared nothing in the shadows. Equestrius gave all the Warhorses their freedom after the battle for World's End and they now roam wherever they please. It is a foolish man who goes anywhere near the Warhorses for Nature armed them with rings of steel upon their feet and they mistrust us.'

The voice of the Loremaster receded as Thane watched the picture change into a desolate place of sheer cliffs, broken paths, thorns and tangled undergrowth. Amidst this wreck of Nature, hard against a black mountain, stood a grim fortress. On its uppermost iron edged galleries one light burned. It looked to Thane as he had imagined Underfall would look, it matched the place in his grandfather's stories of World's End, but there was movement in the picture. Horses came and went, hard-pressed with fear on their heels. Sparks scattered from their hooves in the dark and gloomy cobbled yards. There was a flash of mail shirts and swords beneath the Gallopers' cloaks. The rainbow cloak swirled, scattering the picture, and as it faded into nothing a grey Warhorse reared up, pierced with many Nightbeasts' spears.

'Amarch!' Thane cried, recognizing the Warhorse. The sun

had moved behind a mighty buttress and the Learning Hall was full of shadows. Nevian had vanished. Thane was alone amongst the Chancellors' sons.

'Stone him!' voices cried out.

'Melt him in the wax, the filthy Candlebrat!' joined in others.

'Tear out his tongue,' hissed Silverpurse, rising to his feet.

Thane moved quickly, dodging and ducking amongst the hands that reached out to stop him and reached the doorway ahead of the mob. For a moment he turned and stood his ground, 'Truth! Know the truth!' he shouted. Then, laughing, he turned and fled for his life, running as hard as he could through the maze of corridors towards a little used entrance at the back of the Learning Hall. Behind him he could hear the clamour of pursuit as others joined in the chase but always above their angry shouts he could hear the Loremaster's curse – 'Kill the Candlebrat and curse the name of Hand!'

Thane leapt through the doorway out into the afternoon sunlight and ran down the stone steps, four at a time, left and right he turned, jostling and pushing his way through the crowded streets. Quickly he dived into the first dark alleyway that would lead him home and stopped for breath, listening for the sounds of pursuit.

'Kill the Candlebrat!' echoed through the busy streets, but nobody turned aside into the dark alleyways that led down to the Great Wall. Thane smiled in the half-light, and carefully worked his way home, thankful that the high city dwellers feared the alleyways or what they thought dwelt in their shadows.

Ironhand could hear the Loremaster's curse as the mob combed the well-lit upper streets of the city and he feared for his son's life. Just after darkness fell he heard the outer door softly open and waited for the closing click of the latch before he lit his Candleman's spark and looked into his son's face.

'Fool!' he whispered harshly, unstrapping his leather belt and raising it to beat the boy. 'All these years I have kept you safe and well hidden in the Learning Hall, all for this!'

He pointed with a dirty tallow-stained finger towards the upper circles of the city where the chant of the Chancellors' sons could still be heard, 'Kill the Candlebrat, Kill the Candlebrat!'

'They will sack the city, boy, mark my words! Whatever you have done today many poor souls will have to pay for it.'

'Father!' Thane cried, falling to his knees, 'I called the Loremaster a liar and Nevian, the Master of Magic, the one whose name we are forbidden to say, came and made the Loremaster tell the truth. Father, the rainbow cloak was so beautiful!'

Ironhand smiled in the soft light of the spark, remembering when he had seen the cloak so many suns ago. 'Tell me about it, child,' and Thane told him all that had happened in the Learning Hall.

After Thane had finished Ironhand whispered to him as he extinguished the spark, 'I must go to Candlebane Hall for I am the Candlelighter.'

'No!' The Chancellors will kill you for what I have done. Let me go in your place. I am not afraid.'

Ironhand smiled and then laughed in the darkness, a dry sound without any joy in it. 'Thane, you could not take my place any more than I could take yours. A million candles will not melt away what happened today in the Learning Hall just as all that light will not stop the Nightshapes entering Candlebane Hall. The Chancellors will not melt you nor would the Bondsman be waiting to take you away in chains. If you step into that place the Chancellors will kill you two paces from the door. You have made them see the truth, or even worse, you have made their sons see the truth!'

'But if what happened goes unpunished, the night will grow angry. That is the Lore, isn't it?' Thane asked.

'I am the simpleton! You are the one who has had the learning. Listen to me, boy, for even I know a little of the truth. Night pays no heed to Candlebane Hall but comes no matter how many candles I light.'

'But what of the Nightshapes? I have seen them in Candlebane Hall. They will take me if . . .'

'No!' shouted Ironhand, his patience at an end. 'They are the harmless carriers of the darkness. It is not against them I light the candles. Forget what the Loremaster told you. The real fear in Candlebane Hall is the King's fear of the dark, and the greatest danger there is the Chancellors' power. Now go to your room and wait on my return.'

Thane climbed the narrow stairway and crept into his grandfather's empty room. It was musty and damp from the lack of use yet here he did not feel alone or afraid. He whispered to Thoron in the darkness, touching the bit rings Amarch used to wear and setting them jingling with the music of the Greenway turf. 'I bet there are plenty of people out there in the wild world who can remember you without seeing a rainbow cloak or can speak your name without a pack of blood-hungry Chancellors on their heels.' Thane put his head against the cantle of Amarch's saddle and wept, remembering the last part of the vision in the Learning Hall.

'What shall I do?' muttered Ironhand over and over as he walked towards Candlebane Hall.

'Go not into Candlebane Hall tonight without a body to cast into the molten wax.'

'Who is that?' asked Ironhand, searching the shadows, 'Who calls on the Candleman like a thief, afraid to show his face?'

'Who indeed? Who else would waste his time on Candlemen and their brats but I, Nevian, the mover of small things. I have come to warn you and to direct you down into the Breaking Yards outside the city wall. There you will find the body of a young lad who died today in the sand school beneath the hooves of the wild horse nobody can tame. The body is yours to take if you are brave enough to go beyond the safety of the city and claim it.'

'How can I enter the breaking yards? The city is closed against the night,' asked the Candleman.

'Follow the death bell and it will show you a little used tunnel that buriers travel to collect the dead from the breaking yards. But hurry, the Chancellors are growing impatient with every flicker of the candle's flame.'

Ironhand hurried down into the shadows of the outer wall and waited for the buriers' cart. He shivered with dread and listened for the toll of the single bronze bell that would herald its arrival. He thought of his father, Thoron, and the trouble he had caused the family with his talk of Warhorses and Kings. Close by he heard the rumble of iron-hooped wheels across the cobbles and saw the Buryman's cart piled high with the day's deaths.

'Buryman,' he called softly, reaching out and muffling the bronze bell with his hand, 'my son was killed in the breaking yards today. Let me buy the honour of bringing his body home to rest for a daylight with us. Here in payment are two pure tallow candles.'

The Buryman snatched the candles and peered closely into Ironhand's face. 'Fetch him, carry him, do as you please. There, through that hole, that's the way to carry the dead.'

'Where? I cannot see an entrance?'

'There!' laughed the Buryman, pointing down to a low archway close to the ground.

Ironhand thanked the Buryman and crawled into the darkness. Black echoes ran past him, unseen nightmares touched his hands and face. 'I am the Candleman!' he shouted at the darkness, 'I do not fear the dark!' and his tormentors faded into silence. Starlight suddenly blazed above his head and a deep voice called out his name.

'Ironhand! What are you doing in the Buryman's tunnel?'

Ironhand straightened his back and breathed a sigh of relief, 'Breakmaster! I have come for the boy who died beneath the wild horse's hooves. I have great need of a body to throw into the molten wax.'

'I have heard ugly rumours that the Chancellors hunt a Candlebrat. What is he to you?'

'They hunt my son,' answered Ironhand, spilling out his heart before the Breakmaster, 'and I must save him if I can.'

Breakmaster laughed, putting his arm around Ironhand's shoulder, 'I will save him for you, old friend. We will hide him here in the breaking yards. It will be a hard life, full of danger, but at least he will be beyond the Chancellors' reach. He can take the place of the boy who died today, few saw the death and less will care who pushes the broom or carries the bucket tomorrow. Send him by the Buryman's tunnel before the new sun rises. He will be safe with me.'

Humbly thanking the Breakmaster, Ironhand dragged the young corpse through the tunnel into the Granite City. The Buryman's cart had moved on, and far away on the opposite side of the city he could hear the mournful toll of the bronze death bell. The street was silent and empty. Ironhand shouldered the cold lifeless body and hurried up through the darkened city towards Candlebane Hall and the Chancellors' wrath.

Ironhand paused to catch his breath beside the outer wall of the Candle Hall and, putting his body into the shadows of a rising buttress, he could hear the muffled shouts of the Chancellors inside and, moving closer, pressed his ear against the smooth stone wall to listen. Unknowingly he had chosen a place where the channel for the molten wax left Candlebane Hall and passed into the tallow house. Clearly he could hear each word and secret whisper from inside the hall.

'How many more will you kill?' he heard the King shout, defensively, from the high throne.

'Every Candleman, and all their children. The Candleman's boy, he must be cast into the channel of wax. He brought the magician into the Learning Hall to tell a pack of lies to our children. He must be punished.'

'Chancellors! He is dead!' Ironhand burst through the inner circle of candlestems and flung the body he had carried through the city across the polished marble floor towards the

67

channel of molten wax. It turned once, bruised arms and legs splaying out in the shape of a star. The head twisted, staring blindly into the Chancellors' faces showing broken teeth and torn cheeks as it slid past and fell with a splash into the channel of wax.

Proudpurse sprung forwards and grabbed one of the dead boy's feet and pulled the body out of the wax. Turning it over he examined the face, 'Is this your son, Candleman? Come forward and answer me!'

Ironhand reluctantly came forwards, wringing his hands. 'He shamed me today in the Learning Hall with all his talk of his grandfather and Battle Horses. I beat him for his lies, my Lords, and I beat and beat and beat the truth into him until he lay dead at my feet. Forgive him, my Lords.'

Ironhand caught his breath as he looked into the face of the dead boy. The hot wax had burned and smoothed the features beyond recognition. The nose had been melted away, fine threads of cold petrified tallow hung from the open mouth and one eye stared out through a film of dried wax straight into the Candleman's heart.

'Thane! Forgive me,' called out Ironhand, falling on to his knees. King Holbian leaned forwards in his high throne.

'Are you satisfied now? You have the boy, let that be the end of the matter. Cast his body into the channels.'

'But tomorrow, my Lord, in the Learning Hall, how shall the Loremaster treat the other children from Candlebane Hall?' asked Proudpurse.

Despair weighed heavily on the King's heart. He could not bring himself to look at the body beside the channel of wax, he felt alone and defeated amongst his enemies. 'Send them to the tallow house,' he answered in a broken voice, 'let them learn the craft of the Candlehall as their fathers did. Now go and leave me in peace and you, Candleman, push the body of your son into the channel and be gone forever from this hall.'

'Lord, let me serve you in penance for my son's crimes. Let me clean the guttered wicks or polish the candle stems.'

King Holbian sat unmoved, staring blindly at the flickering flames below the throne. The Chancellors had departed, only the Candleman remained, kneeling beside the body of his son. 'Everything I touch has the feel of death about it. Are you next, Candleman? Your son died because I thought he might be King. Look at his face, half burned and hideous, and I am powerless to stop them. Even the Lore they change to suit their purpose. This is no longer my Hall of Judgement, it has become their hollow whispering house. Here the Chancellors plot and scheme. Soon I will be like your son, of little use to them and ready for the hot wax.'

Ironhand rose to his feet and pushed the body into the channel of wax, where in moments it had dissolved away. The King and the Candleman stood side by side. Eventually the King broke the silence, 'I have hurt you, Candleman, and I know that there is not a jewel in this cloak that could pay for your loss. I am sorry for your sorrow.'

Ironhand turned to the King and, pressing a single finger on to his lips, led him out into the dark and stood him near the hot wax channel. 'Wait,' he whispered and ran back into the Candle Hall.

A voice suddenly filled the darkness where the King stood, making him jump. 'Lord, the greatest of Kings,' the voice boomed, 'there was a purpose in my son's death. Through the danger and chances I took bringing his body here tonight I found the secret listening hole. It is near where you stand, and will unmask all the Chancellors' schemes.'

Ironhand laughed as he returned to the King's side. 'Lord, forgive me my haste and give me leave to return home. The night is going too fast for all I have to do before the new sun rises.'

With a puzzled expression on his face the King re-entered Candlebane Hall and paced away the dark hours. There was something about the Candleman that had the smell of wizards about it, but the King could not place it.

Before dawn chased the grey hours away Ironhand called Thane down into the cubbyhole beneath the stairs and there whispered out his fate. 'Thanehand is dead. The dreamer of Warhorses and Battlebirds is gone forever. With the breaking of a new daylight you will be apprenticed to the Breakmaster beyond the city walls in the stableyards.'

'Dead?' asked Thane in bewilderment.

'Yes, my boy. You can never again enter the Granite City, even your mother will think you dead when she returns home tomorrow from her father's deathbed. You will take the place of the boy I threw into the channel of molten wax, wear his clothes and think his thoughts. You will be him forever.'

'Did you kill him?' asked Thane. Ironhand was silent for a moment, going over the events of the night in his simple mind.

'I would have, child, if need had been that hard a master, but no, I stole him and now you must take his place. Quickly, follow me.'

Through mean, narrow and dirty alleys Ironhand led his son to stand in the black shadows of the city wall. The great doors were closed and heavily guarded but where they stood a low arch, barely high enough to crawl into, echoed with drips of water and the night movements of the rodents that lived within the buriers' tunnel.

'Follow that tunnel,' whispered his father, 'It leads into the breaking yards, beyond this arch only fate can keep you safe.'

He gripped his son's hand, and darkness robbed Thane of the tears his father shed at their parting.

'Keep safe, my child, tell no one of your name, only the Breakmaster knows who you are, and he has pledged to keep your name a secret. He knew and loved old Thoron and has agreed to take you in. Remember, tell no one your name. The grey hours are upon us; hurry boy!' Ironhand hissed in the darkness, pushing his only son and firstborn into the blackness of the tunnel.

70

'Father,' whispered Thane, 'I love you.'

'I know, child, but sometimes we are not the masters of our own fate. Remember how much we risk that you still live.'

Thane crawled into the tunnel, his elbows scraped the sides, his knees soaked up the slimy wetness of the floor, fear made his teeth rattle and rats ran across his hands as he felt his way forward. The tunnel seemed endless and full of Nightshapes, he cried out for courage, screwing his eyes tightly shut. He could not go back, there was no room to turn around, he knew he must go on.

A rough leathery hand grabbed him by the scruff of his neck, broken nails dug into his skin and pulled him clear of the tunnel, Thane hung dangling from a strong arm.

'Welcome, Thane, to a new beginning,' whispered a rich, deep voice, showing a hint of disappointment as its owner inspected him. 'You hardly seem worth all the fuss, but if you are the one they hound to death, follow me; be quick, child, dawn breaks.'

Thane followed in the Master's shadow, shivering as much with the fear of what lay before him as from the foul-smelling dampness that clung to him from the tunnel.

'Walk beside me, boy, hold your head up and pretend to be a part of this place. I shall call you Boy; that is now your name. If anyone asks about your past, tell them you came with the last batch of wild horses gathered beyond sight. You are an orphan.'

'Master,' called Thane, 'will I ever see my mother again?' The rich voice laughed in the darkness, the Master stopped and turned to Thane. 'Child, I am Master here because I have lived the longest amongst the wild horses we break to serve the King. Who knows how long you will live amidst their crashing hooves, or how many men I will bury before another sun sets, but,' continued the Master, lowering his voice to a whisper, 'You are Thoron's grandson, and I shall protect you, if I can.'

71

Thane was shown where he was to sleep and given brooms and buckets to sweep and scrub the stable floors. As the Master turned to leave, he held up his left hand. 'Sleep with your hands inside your clothes for the rats will eat you alive if they get the chance, and stay clear of the main sand school at noon, for we have a rogue to break who has killed many bigger and braver than you.'

'What is his name?' Thane asked in innocence.

'Name? Name? He has no name yet, but many have cursed him and died for their trouble. Keep away, boy, if you value your life.'

As the days passed by Thane lost all sense of time and he soon found the rough and tumble of the breaking yards a place to escape his shame and forget the learning hall. It was a brutal place, full of cursing, shouting and the crack of rawhide lashes as the breakers fought to overcome the wild horses. Thane saw, to his horror, many proud beasts brought to their knees, bloody and injured before defeat stole their pride and they were ready to serve the King. Whole trees were piled shoulder high around the yards to take the crash on breaking days and only brave men stood amidst the dust and lived. Often, during the busiest times, Thane would catch the Master looking up towards the window far above their heads, set into the tower wall, but it was beyond his courage to ask whom he looked for.

With the noon bell tolling out the hour a single barred door was opened on to the main arena. Silence lay as heavy as the settling dust; inside the darkened stable a horse snorted, kicking violently at the walls. Curiosity drew Thane daily to step closer and closer so that he could see the horse that nobody could break. It was rumoured that even the King left his chair to watch from a high window, for this horse was, the breakers whispered, a mirror image of the great Warhorses of long ago.

Thane held his breath, peering over the wooden wall. Before him, pawing the sand, a full seventeen hands high, was the most beautiful horse he had ever seen, just like the horses his grandfather wove into his tales of long ago, before the battle to win World's End had broken the pledges. Yet there was something about him that made him different, a hardness in his eye, the way he flattened his ears and bared his teeth at the slightest movement beyond the wall. Sheets of muscle rippled as he moved across the sand; his mane shone like threads of silk as he shook his head.

He knelt to roll in the hot sand. This was the moment the horse breakers had waited for, crouching in the shadows. Now they would master him with hobbles, ropes and chain halters. Perhaps as many as twenty strong men swarmed noiselessly over the high barricade and disappeared into the cloud of dust the horse had churned up. Fear stalked amongst them – the horse had killed before and was highly dangerous. Neighing fiercely the wild horse fought them, rearing and plunging, scattering the breakers. Kicking and biting he drove them back against the barricades.

'Clear the sand school. Get out before he kills you!' shouted the assistant Breakmaster, urging the scattering horsemen back to safety. One by one they scrambled out, cursing their luck, knowing that they must try again in the next daylight to tame this wild horse.

'Look,' cried Thane, pointing at the last horseman trying to leave the sand school, 'he is injured and cannot climb the barricade. Aren't you going to help him?'

Cruel laughter shut Thane's mouth as two coarse-faced horsemen grabbed him by the arms and lifted him on to the top of the barricade. '*You* can help him, boy, and die for your trouble,' sneered a voice, and a strong hand pushed him forwards until he was toppling on the edge of the wall.

The horse was cantering in circles around the injured man, sending up small puffs of sand with each footfall. Tighter and tighter closed the circle, ears flattened and eyes glittering with hatred, ready for the kill.

73

'Breakmaster!' the fallen man screamed, the horse's hot breath on his face. 'Save me!' he cried without hope.

'Go on! Save him,' sneered the cruel voice behind Thane, and the hand pushed him stumbling on to his knees in the sandschool.

From where Thane landed in the sand he saw it all too clearly. The muscles bunched and tightened along the horse's back, a moment's pause and then the hindleg lashed out, cutting short the horseman's screams. With that one blow he snapped his neck and crushed his skull into the sand.

'That will teach you, boy, to hold your tongue,' laughed a voice behind the barricades.

Far above the breaking yards King Holbian watched from a window in the Towers of Granite. At his side, trembling lest what went on below displeased his Lord, stood the Breakmaster.

'Lord, he is wild to the point of being dangerous. Shall we kill him?'

'And put an end to such pride?' replied the King, raising his eyebrows at the Breakmaster. 'Is that what you would do? Kill what you cannot tame? Should I put to death every man that displeases me? Have I done that during my long reign? Have I edged the metal spikes along the city wall with those that would not bend to my demands?'

'No, Lord,' answered the Breakmaster, weakly, knowing that he dare not speak his mind. 'I have failed to tame the best, the most beautiful horse to ever stand in the Granite City. Daily my most skilled breakers and horsemen fall beneath his hooves. Lord, none can touch him.'

King Holbian interrupted the Breakmaster, holding up a hand for silence and beckoned him to come closer to the casement. 'Who is that boy kneeling in the sand?'

'Who, Sire?' asked the Breakmaster, craning his neck and seeing Thane's imminent death below. The horse had finished crushing the breaker's skull and was advancing across the sand towards the boy. Deceiving the King was treason and led to a slow death and the Breakmaster hesitated, searching for the right words to perhaps blunt his punishment for hiding the Candleman's son. King Holbian felt a stir of movement behind him and turning quickly found the Chancellors on tiptoe, trying to look over his shoulder.

'Leave me in peace to watch my sport. Another horseman has died beneath the wild horse's hooves. It is nothing more than that. Leave me!'

Reluctantly the Chancellors retired, leaving the King alone with the Breakmaster. 'Who is that boy in the sandschool?' the King asked again.

The Breakmaster felt his hands growing damp with sweat. 'He is Thanehand, the Candlelighter's son. The boy the Chancellors' sons chased through the city after the Master of Magic appeared in the Learning Hall.'

A smile touched King Holbian's lips. 'And you would risk your life hiding this boy from the Chancellors?'

'The Chancellors never venture beyond the great gates of the city. Even the bondsmen fear to step into the breaking yards for they fear the horses, Sire.'

'Enough!' interrupted the King, speaking as he watched the sandschool below, 'If that boy lives beyond the first chime of the afternoon bell then you shall also live. Now watch with me, since your life hangs on such a slender thread.'

Thane knelt in the sand, pushing his hands against the ground to rise but the shadow of the horse was almost upon him, the dull thudding of his hooves drowning out all other sounds. He opened his mouth to cry out but nothing came. From a dark corner, high in the stable wall, an owl hooted and was silent. The great horse stopped, his hooves almost touching Thane's fingers; another step and he would have crushed them beyond any healer's art to mend. Stretching his neck he sniffed the terror-stricken boy, snorting in his face.

The horse was so close that Thane could feel his breath.

75

Flattening his ears, he struck Thane hard in the face, the blow sent him crashing backwards into the wooden barrier where he lay, trapped in dark dreams, unable to move.

'He will kill him now,' whispered one of the breakers behind the barrier, watching through a space between the boards. 'He will smash his skull with one kick. I've seen him do it to others.'

A hoof pawed the sand beside Thane's head, almost touching his forehead, grains of sand fell into his hair. The hoof was raised, muscles in the horse's shoulder flexed and tensed to strike, his ears were now completely flattened and his lips curled back exposing fearsome teeth. He had charged to kill, only the owl had bade him stop.

With gentle ease he placed the hoof upon Thane's head pressing just hard enough to leave a sand-filled print across the boy's cheek. The breakers waited, breath held, for the skull to crack. The Master saw clearly his own death, the moment the horse put his whole weight on that foot. King Holbian smiled, glancing at the Master. 'What say you now, Master?'

'I hid him out of love for Thoron, Lord,' whispered the Master, his fingernails cutting into the palms of his hands.

The owl hooted again. The horse removed his hoof, and lifting his head roared out a challenge that made the blood course hotly through King Holbian's veins. He grasped the Master's arm, shouting with excitement. 'Not since the battle for World's End have I heard that call. If you cannot tame him, then set him free for he must be a Lord amongst the horses. Although I know not why he has no rings of steel upon his feet; was he not foaled in the lower pastures within sight of this window?'

'Yes, Lord, he cannot be a true Warhorse,' replied the Master.

The horse moved, placing a foot across Thane's body, pulling and rolling him until he stood once more in the centre of the arena, the unconscious boy lying in front of his forelegs. A single bell tolled, Thane groaned, regaining his senses and, looking up, saw how close death stood. He could see clearly the skin of the coronet where it met the hooves and tiny grains of sand clinging to the silky hairs on the fetlocks.

'Grandfather,' he whispered, 'give me courage to stand and not be afraid.' But his hands shook and his legs felt as if they were filled with liquid as he struggled to rise. The horse stood perfectly still watching him. The afternoon sun burned the back of Thane's neck, dizziness made him stagger as he moved forward, a hand outstretched, calling out the name of the greatest Warhorse in all his grandfather's stories.

'Equestrius, Equestrius, Lord of Horses. Protect me.' But the horse crouched on his hocks, rearing up and his shadow blotted out the sunlight. His hooves hovered just above Thane's head, striking the empty air. Grains of sand fell into his eyes as he sank on to his knees in despair calling out his grandfather's name. 'Thoron!' Again the owl shrieked, flying low across the sand, and the horse neighed with rage, lowering his forelegs, striking Thane hard on the shoulder, sending him sprawling on to his back. Snorting in anger the horse turned and trotted into the dark stable.

King Holbian stood deep in thought, looking down into the sandschool. Breakmaster hardly dared to breathe as he awaited judgement on his fate. Nobody climbed over the barrier to help Thane to his feet, whispers of dark magic went the rounds amongst the breakers. 'Did you hear the name he cried as the horse reared? Send word to the Chancellors, this boy is not what he seems,' they muttered, gripping the hilts of their daggers.

'Breakmaster!' commanded the King. 'Stand by my chair and put the jewelled cloak about my shoulders while we talk on this matter. Be careful with it for it has grown a little each time I have plucked a jewel.'

'Lord, it is so beautiful,' gasped the Breakmaster, afraid to touch it with his calloused hands.

King Holbian laughed, 'It is only coloured stones,

Breakmaster! Fear not to touch it, it is the wolves of the government it keeps at bay. The Chancellors have schemed and plotted to take it from me, but now it is too heavy for one ordinary man to carry and they cannot find the trust among themselves to steal it together!'

'But, Lord, how do you carry it?' asked the Breakmaster, struggling to arrange the cloak to the King's satisfaction.

'Nevian, the magician, fashioned the cloak for me to wear. He said there were secrets woven into the cloth. Once, in anger, I tore off a handful of the jewels and threw them at the Chancellors' feet and the cloak grew a little. At that moment I saw the power Nevian warned me of, the power of greed. So I use the jewels to divide them by throwing them one by one at the Chancellors' feet. They fight over them, some growing richer while others think themselves poorer. But with each squabble their power fades. I have brought many daylights for the one who will eventually take my place. Breakmaster, I thought I had lost everything to the Chancellors but little by little, through the cloak, I have kept the throne and now I have ways of finding out the Chancellors' secrets and thwarting each move they make. Why, two handfuls of jewels saved the breaking yards from ruin. But we must talk about the boy. Thane? Is that the name you called him?'

'Yes, Lord,' answered the Breakmaster, hanging his head. 'The Candlelighter's father taught me to ride and break horses and it was in memory of him that I took the boy in.'

'Whom did the Candleman throw into the channel of wax?'

'Lord, it was the body of a young boy the wild horse had killed earlier that day. Why, sire, you watched his death from the window over there. The Candleman came to me after dark by the Buryman's tunnel asking for help.'

'Did he light his way through the tunnel?'

'No, Lord, I heard him cry out as he crawled towards me that he did not fear the dark.'

King Holbian laughed quietly, repeating to himself, 'He did

not fear the dark.' Turning to Breakmaster, Holbian motioned him closer. 'The Chancellors will kill Thane, even if they do not do it themselves they will find those who can. But I will not have him hurt. Today we saw some of his magic and we must keep him safe until he grows in power.'

'What power, Lord?' asked Breakmaster, puzzled by the whole affair. By rights he should have been tortured and put to death for deceiving the Chancellors but here he was listening to the King's secrets.

'Breakmaster, if you had been a Chancellors' man Thane would be dead. Your love for the boy's grandfather and the act of hiding the boy is proof enough that I can trust you. Do not ask why you must guard him, it is my command. Each day he shall face the wild horse.'

'Lord, he will die. I cannot guarantee his safety in the sandschool.'

'Perhaps,' mused the King, remembering the horse's neighing challenge and the owl's shrieking hoot.

The King called after the Breakmaster as he reached the chamber door. 'The boy shall name the horse as custom demands. It must be a simple name that hides the truth for there is much about them both that we do not understand.'

'Name him?' mumbled Thane, rubbing gingerly at the bruises on his head, 'Me? Name him?'

'Yes, boy, you are to name him tomorrow when you enter the sand arena and stand before him, now think on a suitable name and keep it simple.'

Without another word the Master turned and disappeared into the night before Thane could tell him how the breakers had turned their backs on him, spitting on the ground, as he left the sand school. Thane sat long into the night listening to the rats gnawing at the wooden boards of his cot. Yesterday he would have feared them, and driven them out with a broken broom handle he kept hidden for that purpose, but now they were nothing compared with facing the wild horse in the morning. He wondered what he should call him, trying to remember all the names his grandfather had used when he spoke of the great Warhorses at the battle for World's End. 'Well, one thing is for sure,' he whispered to himself in the darkness, 'Grandfather wouldn't have done tomorrow what he could do today.' He arose, quietly left his bed and crept across the sand school to meet his fate head on. Fate has many twists, for as Thane left his bed and ventured across the darkened sand school, grim figures moved in the shadows, making towards the bed he had slept upon.

The stable door creaked on its hinges as Thane pulled it open; the startled horse snorted, striking the ground with his hoof. 'Quiet, great Lord,' whispered Thane, as he gathered his courage and stepped into the dark stable.

He pulled the door behind him until it stood just off the latch. 'I come in peace,' he began to say; the door snapped shut behind him and cruel voices laughed in the darkness outside. 'Die, boy, and rid us of your magic.' Something was jammed across the latch. Thane was trapped alone with the most dangerous horse ever to stand in the breakers' yard.

An owl hooted high up in the rafters, the horse moved towards him. He felt the horse's presence rather than saw him, and almost jumped out of his skin as a velvet-soft muzzle touched his cheek. At that moment a quiet voice called out in the darkness above his head, 'I am Mulcade, Chief Loftmaster Owl, the son of Silverwing, the Lord of Battle Owls. You came to name the horse; your King commands it but you cannot think of a name for him. Perhaps that is because he already has a name handed down from father to son, a name carried on the wild wind from where his father roams in freedom.'

'What is that name?' whispered Thane into the darkness.

'Esteron, Esteron,' chanted the owl. Thane tried the name, reaching out a shaking hand, feeling for the horse's shoulder to caress. 'It is just the name Grandfather would have chosen for you,' he whispered, waiting for the horse to strike, but Esteron gently nudged him, pushing and pushing until Thane lost his balance and fell on to the soft warmth of the bed. Esteron stood close to Thane, listening to the night sounds beyond his stable door, alert and ready lest any should try and kill the boy who had given him his name, for above his head Mulcade, Loft-master Owl, chanted out the Lay of Thoronhand, whose grandson now lay at his feet. 'Harm him not, for he is but a child driven by fate to your door, worn out with worry, trembling with fear, his hand may touch you in love even as his grandfather's hand gently closed your great grandfather's eyes upon the battle field at World's End, at the bondbreaking.'

The owl tilted his head, searching for the slightest hint of listeners beyond the door, and continued with his story. 'You are a Lord among Horses, in the line of Equestrius, none shall tame you or sit upon your back unless you wish it.'

'What of the boy?' Esteron asked in soft whinnies. 'He has to tame me when the sun burns overhead. If I am a Lord among the Warhorses, how can I let him use me, even to save his life?'

Mulcade, wisest of owls, sat in silence for a long time before answering, 'Thoron, his grandfather, was considered a Lord amongst the free; thus in love for him all free beings will in time come to the aid of his grandson, bringing hope in the morning to chase fears away. Fate has called you to be first, Esteron, son of Equestrius, to treat him as you will. But remember, he came alone tonight, putting fear behind him, with nothing but the love of his grandfather to give him courage.'

Esteron snorted, peering closely at Thane; Mulcade swooped to perch on the manger.

'I cannot stop you killing the boy even now as he lies there if that is your wish. Yesterday you held his life beneath your hoof but you spared him.' Esteron looked up at the owl, 'You bid me spare his life; he carried no whip, nor any anger in his heart, and he cried aloud Equestrius's name.'

81

'The grey hours are upon us,' hooted the owl. 'Before a new sun drives the shadows back, you must decide if he will live or die. Think hard Esteron, Lord of Horses.'

Pandemonium and rage erupted in the breaking yards overshadowing the birth of a new day.

'Where is the boy?' shouted the Master Breaker, wielding a rawhide whip at his men. 'If that boy dies I'll nail all your hides to that wall. Where is he?'

Somewhere at the back of the throng of men beneath the sand school barricade a voice answered, 'Perhaps he ran away, Master, we're best rid of him and his magic.'

'Magic?' screamed the Master. 'Who said anything of magic? The King has commanded me to put the boy in the sand school at noon. Who among you will take his place?'

Fear held an uneasy silence as the breakers looked from one to another.

'Alone in the sand school,' was the King's command, and I shall choose who shall stand in his place. Before the noon bell tolls, I shall find the guilty. Now! Search for that boy – your lives depend upon it.'

The Master turned towards the winding stair, dread of reaching the King's chamber in every step. A shout from the sand school made him hesitate and look down.

'Master! The latch is jammed shut on the wild horse's stable.'

'Then the boy is dead,' muttered the Master to himself, 'and my death will come before this sun sets.'

# Esteron

'Send word below,' ordered King Holbian, 'to open the stable door at noon, and you, Master, shall wait with me to see how your fate has turned.'

'Lord, if I am to die, let me face the wild horse and meet a death with some small honour.'

Holbian laughed, dismissing his Chancellors and holding a finger against his lips until they were alone, and said, 'You have little faith in the boy, and yet you gambled your life on his.'

'Great King,' answered the Master quietly, 'Thoron brought hope in the morning and soothed away our troubles at night. Thane is but a boy, raw and awkward, who has much to learn.'

The morning hours dragged by slowly; uneasy eyes were turned towards the sand school and fear moved through the breakers like a shadow crossing the sun. Who would the Master choose to stand alone, when the noon bell rang?

'It is time, my Lord,' whispered the Master, watching the striker lift his hammer beside the bell. Light flooded into the open stable; Esteron snorted, flattening his ears and curling his lips back before he charged the door, bucking and kicking to stand in the centre of the school, pawing the ground. Total silence surrounded Esteron; not a man dared move lest he caught the Master's eye. Sweat trickled down their backs; tight hands held their rawhide whips.

'Esteron. I name you Esteron,' Thane called from the stable door. He was still slightly dizzy from sleeping so late, and the light made him blink.

'Lord, he lives!' shouted the Master, forgetting where he stood.

85

'There is more to this boy than most men see,' muttered the King, leaning on the casement to watch what was about to happen in the sand school.

Thane advanced across the sand, his eyes growing accustomed to the sun's glare, calling again, in a softer voice, 'I name you Esteron, a Lord amongst Horses.' Lowering his voice to a whisper, he thanked the horse for sparing his life, adding scarcely audibly, 'I have to tame you, but I don't know how.'

Esteron turned his head, whinnying, and pushed Thane hard in the chest; then he reared up, thrashing the empty air with his forelegs and thundered, cantering and plunging, across the school. Thane had watched the breakers pull smaller horses down, sit across them and hang on until they became quiet through exhaustion, he had seen them hobble and cast the bigger ones, only reaching down to cut the blood-soaked ropes after the horses' spirit had been broken. He had no whip or hobble ropes nor did he wish to have them, for he remembered Thoron's hatred of the breakers' cruelty, hearing the old man's words echoing in his head. 'How can the proud be expected to serve when their pride is broken?'

Esteron charged towards him, churning the sand into a cloud of stinging dust; Thane reached out, springing up to lock his arms around the horse's neck. Esteron stopped abruptly, pirouetting violently away from the boy's arms, sending him crashing against the barrier. 'Gently,' hooted the owl, Esteron trotted to where Thane lay, and pulled him away from the barrier with his head and gripped the boy's collar between his teeth. Thane's battered senses cleared and he stood up slowly. 'Keep him safe,' hooted Mulcade. 'Many beyond the barrier wish him dead; keep him at your side.' Esteron nudged and pushed Thane towards his stable, herding him into the safest place in the Granite City, where none dared enter for fear of the wild horse.

'Well, Master,' mused the King, 'it seems you have done me

86

a great service hiding young Thane from the mob. Perhaps, just perhaps, his fate is bound by many invisible threads to mine, just as Thoron's was. Set food and drink outside the stable, and we shall watch each day the taming of this horse.'

Thus through high summer and a glorious mellow autumn Thane strove to tame Esteron. In blissful ignorance his hand touched the silken skin of Equestrius's son. Had he known with whom he wrestled in the sand, he would have fled, for the bonds were broken at World's End and none could ride the wild Warhorses. Choking dust ground between his teeth; gritty-eyed and bruised he hung on to the lunging line as, bucking and plunging, Esteron dragged him helpless around the breaking yard. Raw, bleeding hands and broken nails made dressing and eating an agonizing feat but with each day Thane drew a little closer to understanding the horse that no one could tame. Yet, for a time, he was confused by Esteron's contradictory behaviour. His gentle, biddable softness and sensitive obedience in the stable was replaced with determined, untameable pride before the eyes of men and the boy could scarcely approach him.

First winter's snow was in the air, frost bit deeply into the sand school, breaking Esteron still seemed no more than a far-off dream. Thane blew on to his numb fingers as he adjusted the tack and tried for what seemed the thousandth time to ride the horse that he had grown to love and admire.

'Don't hurt me today,' he whispered. 'The ground is bone hard, much too hard to fall upon.'

Galloping hoof beats interrupted Thane's whisperings; along the Greenway below the city wall, through the great gate and up the steeply sloping cobbled streets, thundered the sound of hooves, bringing back to Thane's memory his grandfather's races along that same path to the King's door; bringing grave news of far away disasters upon the road to World's End. He sighed, leading Esteron out to collect the day's bruises.

87

Mulcade, too, heard the running horse and rose on silent wings to perch high in the King's chamber.

'Let me past,' a strong voice called out as the chamber door burst open. 'None but the King may hear Thunderstone's message.'

A travel-stained warrior filled the open doorway, pushing the Chancellors before him.

'Guards! Guards!' shouted the Chancellor, waving his fists at the messenger, 'seize this intruder. Seize him!'

The Warrior laughed, drawing back the sleeve of his mail shirt to show the bonding brand of Candlebane Hall. 'You sent me away in chains to die at World's End, Chancellor, but Thunderstone gave me back my pride. I do not fear you or your guards.'

'Chancellors, stand aside!' commanded the King.

'Lord!' called out the Warrior, falling on to his knees, 'I am Errant of Underfall. Thunderstone pledged me to bring you news of World's End and the black shadows that live out there.'

'Is your message a warning of the Nightbeasts?' asked the King, looking past the bowed head of Errant into the Chancellors' eyes.

'Yes, Lord,' whispered Errant, trembling as he remembered all he had seen at Underfall.

'Then let the Chancellors hear it, for they govern this land and they should know what might one day come, even to the gates of the Granite City.'

Errant reached into a sack tied across his shoulder and pulled out a dispatch pouch, engraved upon it was an emblem of an owl in blue and gold. 'This is the bondsman's pouch, my Lord, that and the chains that bound the prisoners was all that was left of the poor wretches you sent to us during the last sun. Before the winter set in we found their bones in Meremire Forest strewn along the crown of the road, still chained together. Nightbeast footprints had burned the ground all around them.'

As the King listened to Errant he watched the Chancellors and saw their fear rise, draining their faces white.

'Who now wants this cloak of jewels? Now that the Nightbeasts have come again, who will wear it and stand before the gates of the Granite City? Proudpurse, you are always the boldest, come forward and take the cloak.'

'No, Lord, it is too great an honour. I could not be so bold.'

Holbian laughed, putting his hand upon Errant's shoulder to stop him leaving and dismissed the Chancellors, telling them to find strong holes to hide in. When they were alone the King bade Errant to fetch himself a chair. He offered him meat and drink and asked him how Underfall would stand now that the Nightbeasts had arisen again.

'Lord, the Nightbeasts have plagued Underfall for suns beyond counting, but it is a mighty fortress manned by strong men who fear little if Thunderstone, the Keeper, is amongst them. Thunderstone sent me, Sire, to ride through great danger and warn you that the terrors of the night are spreading beyond Mantern's Forest. Soon, he fears, they will be strong enough to spread across all Elundium unless you can marshal an army to fight against them.'

'Strong enough to travel in the daylight?' whispered the King.

'They have travelled as far as Meremire Forest, my Lord, and that is only two daylights from Underfall.'

'The Greenways and the Wayhouses along the edge, how did they seem to you? How will they stand against the Nightbeasts?'

Errant spread his hands, 'Lord, the Greenways are overgrown and tangled with wildness. In some places the trees have seeded and grown up, rendering the wood impassable. Only near each Wayhouse was there any order, but the Wayhouses are in good repair and will fight bravely against the Nightbeasts.'

'The bearers of the tattoo mark, are they still the Keepers of the Wayhouses or have the Chancellors driven them out?'

Errant laughed, 'Lord, they are old and wrinkled but their eyes still shine and their swords are quick and sharp. The Chancellors have tried to starve them and kept them short of men but they are true men, pledged to serve you.'

'True men, but not enough to marshal into an army. What am I to do, messenger, send you back to Underfall with the news that Elundium totters on the brink of disaster, waiting for ruin?'

'Lord, forgive me, but Thunderstone said I was to offer you the hilt of my sword. He is a fearless Keeper who sees much that other men miss. Bit by bit from the stories the prisoners told us each year he has seen your peril and he warned me of the Chancellors. Lord, take my sword.'

Holbian laughed, 'Errant, Errant, I have a Captain at last, well mounted on a brave horse. I heard you galloping up through the city, footsure and strong, what is the name of your horse?'

'He is named Dawnrise, Lord. He is the first stallion amongst the Nighthorses and he is the bravest horse at Underfall.'

'Nighthorses?' questioned the King, leaning forwards in his chair.

'They are half-wild, proud beasts that Thunderstone has gathered from all the wild places near World's End, my Lord. He has tamed them and they stand ready each night, battle-dressed to face the Nightbeasts.'

'Will you ride for me, Errant? Now, without rest, and find as many true men as you can, Gallopers, Marchers and Archers, and bring them into the Breaking Yards?'

Errant looked out at the cold frosty landscape and shivered. Snow had followed him across Elundium, deep winter was setting in. Kneeling before the King he offered up the hilt of his sword saying, 'I will, my Lord.'

'Tell no one! Here in the city there are too many Chancellors' men,' insisted the King as Errant rose to leave.

'My lips are sealed,' whispered Errant, quietly closing the chamber door.

90

King Holbian shifted restlessly in his chair, the joy of the moment had ebbed away. He was alone again.

'Where are these warriors I have sent Errant to find?' he muttered, plucking absently with age-worn fingers at one of the jewels of the cloak. 'Who will be brave enough to stand at my side when one shout from a Nightbeast can extinguish every candle in Candlebane Hall. Thunderstone should be warned of how things stand here in Granite City but there is no one I could send. Errant must stay here and seek out every true-hearted man. I dare not send him back.'

'Thoronhand,' he mumbled, speaking his thoughts out loud, 'the roads are bleak and empty since your death. Who can take your place; who?'

Movement high above his head caught his eye, soft hooting broke into his thoughts as Mulcade strutted on the king post beam. Looking up at the owl he spoke aloud, 'If only the pledges had not been broken, the roads would be full of Warhorses and many sharp eyes to search out the way. Whom can I send, great bird; who in your wisdom would you choose?'

Holbian did not expect an answer from the owl – the bonds had been broken so long ago – but his presence filled the chamber with beauty.

'On whose shoulder would you perch, great bird of war, if you could help a tired King in the evening of his life?'

Mulcade spread his wings and stooped to perch on the casement, turning his head towards King Holbian. 'Follow, King, follow my wisdom,' he hooted and Holbian rose from his chair, hearing a call that took him back beyond the pledge-breaking, a clear note in the morning bidding him to look and follow sharper eyes.

Standing beside the owl, Holbian looked down into the sand school where Thane was about to try mounting Esteron. Frosty sand clung to his clothes and his knees were wet from kneeling while he gathered his wits to remount.

Holbian laughed, 'I cannot send a child. How would he arrive, on foot? Leading the horse he cannot tame?'

The owl's hoot rose to shrill, piercing notes, Esteron looked up, listening, for he had heard his father's name and word of the darkness on the roads to World's End. He snorted, pawed the ground and bent his front legs to kneel in the sand. Pride arched his neck, fire sparkled in his eyes as Thane placed his feet in the stirrups.

'Rise, great Esteron,' he whispered, waiting for Esteron to rear and plunge him back on to the sand but Esteron only straightened his front legs and stood perfectly still. Mulcade stooped and settled gently on Thane's shoulder. Looking up towards the King he spread his wings and commanded Esteron to show for the first time that he was indeed a Lord amongst the horses, who feared nothing that hid where the shadows gathered, who could, if he chose, protect the child upon his back and keep him safe through the blackest night. Esteron lifted his head, roaring out a challenge that rattled Thane's bones in the saddle, and moved lightly forwards over the frozen sand.

The King gripped the casement still, the Master dropped his whip, and frightened whispers went round among the breakers gathered beyond the barrier. None had seen the Warhorse paces since the battle at World's End, the easy power and elastic grace as each hoof touched the ground. Mulcade flew back to perch on the casement, hooting softly as he held the King's gaze.

'Wisdom asked for has been given. That is sufficient, even for a King.'

As early darkness gathered beneath heavy snowfilled clouds Thane was led by Breakmaster through secret passages into the King's chamber.

'Go now, Breakmaster, and guard the door. What passes between this young man and myself must remain a secret,' commanded Holbian quietly. 'Breakmaster,' added Holbian, closing his fingers around one of the jewels on the cloak, 'Your loyalty shall be rewarded.'

'No, Lord, do not try to buy me as you do the Chancellors. I love you as Thoron did or any of the bearers of the tattoo mark. To serve you, Lord, is enough.'

'Breakmaster, in time we shall make this kingdom strong and worthy of the one who will take my place.'

Smiling, the King released Breakmaster's hand and turned his gaze towards Thane.

Mulcade, unseen, perched beyond the torch light. Thane knelt, hardly daring to lift his eyes, the gems set in the cloak that wrapped the King almost beyond sight were more wonderful than any of the stories he had ever heard.

'Thoronhand's grandson. Just a boy,' he mused, as if speaking to himself. 'Stand, child, that I may see all of you.'

Thane rose, blushing, but still keeping his eyes downcast.

'Look at me, boy! You stand in the prints of a great man, whom I badly wronged. Let me see your eyes, for they will tell me what is in your heart.'

Thane slowly raised his eyes and almost forgot where he stood as he gasped in astonishment at the sight of the wrinkled old man encompassed by the cloak. 'Even Kings grow old, child; worry wears them away quicker than most with the rub of time. Come, sit by my side and tell me of the pictures you saw in the Learning Hall, for rumours are a bad cloak for the truth, and give me guidance in the grave decisions I must make. You were feared in the city. The Chancellors plot your death. Bad magic was mixed with your name and now the breakers fear you, for with the breaking of Esteron they realize who you are. The owl upon your shoulder frightened them so that they will kill you if you stay within the Granite City.'

'Lord,' whispered Thane, 'I meant no harm. I did as the Master bid. Why do they hate me so? I did not call the owl to my shoulder.'

93

Holbian looked at the boy with sadness in his eyes, 'We live in brittle times, child, and the people fear anything that might upset the balance of their lives. The watchmakers check each second of daylight and weigh it against the night before they light one candle. For they know that one too many will enrage the Nightshapes just as one candle too few may make night last forever. Envy follows the great, child, and fear treads in all the shadows, even on small beginnings.'

'How can I stop it, my Lord?' asked Thane, fighting back his tears. 'For all I have done is to love my grandfather who, while he lived, loved me.'

King Holbian reached across to a small table where a hundred candles burned and picked one up, tilting it until the hot wax had run on to the floor, 'Now child, can you remake this candle?'

'No, Lord, it is impossible,' said Thane, staring at the solidifying wax.

'Then neither can you stop what you have started,' said King Holbian, adding bitterly: 'Fate cares little for those who try and swim against the tide but remember this, child, Thoronhand planted a seed that men would trample on and destroy before it bears fruit.' The King's voice rose, growing stronger, as he lifted his hand and placed it on the boy's shoulder. It was so brittle and frail with age that Thane hardly felt its weight, yet his heart beat faster to be touched by the King.

'I will not have your blood stain this cloak. I thought that the Chancellors' plots and schemes were made to find the throne stealer. Now I see more clearly that all they have done is to destroy my name, and now they use me as an empty puppet. But you, child, they shall not have. You must grow strong, as strong as Thoron, your grandfather, far, far away from this place.' He paused, watching the boy's eyes, searching for a weakness before he whispered, 'Underfall, the fortress at World's End, where shadows hammer on the doors and the days are full of darkness; where quick men die for want of being quicker. Would you travel that road in your grandfather's footsteps and dwell amongst his memories? Would you gather up my standard and carry it into the shadows as he did?'

'Lord,' stammered Thane, his eyes shining with tears, but the King held up his hand for silence.

'Your eyes are but windows to your heart and I see all your answers clearly without words.'

Reaching deep inside his cloak King Holbian pulled out a letter, heavy with the royal seal.

'This is for the hand of Thunderstone, the Keeper of Underfall. Show it to no one else, child, and tell him . . .' Holbian hesitated a moment, remembering Nevian's words, 'Tell him that I doubted the hearts of the most loyal friends a man could ever wish for, and that I would give away this throne of thorns to stand once more by their sides in the light of the great lamp at World's End. I dare not write that in the letter. Beware, child, of those you meet upon the road. Beware, but you are not sent in punishment, remember that. Nor will you go alone into darkness, as a beggar, cast out, for I give you a great gift for the road, perhaps a gift as great as life itself. I give you Esteron.'

'Lord,' gasped Thane, blushing scarlet, 'I could not take him as mine. I am not worthy.'

Holbian's laughter cut into Thane's words, 'Child, I think he is not a horse to be bartered in the market place or measured by your worth, but by some freak of nature his blood lines are tied to those of the Warhorses. He will never belong to any man, even a King such as I could not claim him, but you are Thoron's grandson and he has let you sit upon his back, that is claim enough for the moment. You shall leave tonight. Beneath the cloak of darkness vanish; the Master Breaker will see to that. Few will mourn you here.'

'But where is Underfall?' queried Thane. Holbian laughed again.

'Follow the Greenway to World's End, my lad. No more

questions. The road is black enough to strike terror into brave Warriors' hearts. One road and all roads lead to World's End. Put your courage before you and do not look back, lest the shadows swallow you up.'

Thane rose to go, hesitating and fidgeting. 'What is it, boy?' asked Holbian gruffly, anxious to rest.

'May I see my mother before I go?' he asked. 'For I love her, and I would like to say goodbye.' The wrinkles around the old King's eyes softened and he saw before him the child he had just commanded to ride perhaps to his death, or worse, on the road to Underfall, and he was smitten with guilt, enough to make him, a Granite King, look away. A voice in his head mocked, 'How great is the man who sends a child to do a man's work, a child who goes in ignorance and trust where brave men fear to tread?'

The owl hooted, making the old King look up and the hard cold eyes held his and he shook with fear knowing that the owl had seen into his heart, right through his plots and schemes to send a messenger to Underfall and cheat the Chancellors out of a child's death. Small power in a faded King which made him want to look away. Mulcade turned his head, releasing the King from his stare and the old man, ashamed at his deceit, said softly, 'You shall see your mother tonight and take anyone you wish to make the road safer. A squadron of Gallopers, a strike of Archers; command it and it will be done.'

Thane looked from the King up to the owl and paused for only a second before answering, 'Lord, it is enough to follow in my grandfather's footsteps; he rode alone, thus shall I re-trace his steps.'

'Then Kingspeed, child, on a desperate road,' whispered the King. 'Kingspeed, little heart.'

# The Summer Scarf

The first step of the journey was the greatest and most severe. Thane was but a boy to be rudely thrust into an unknown world. He had been his mother's favourite and she had often had to shield him with untruths and half-told lies to save him from his father's wrath. Now, to hide her grief, she talked fast of trivial matters while she packed enough to clothe an army. She seemed so small and frail now, those twinkling eyes wet with tears, her knotted hands tight upon a crying cloth, keeping back those sunlit memories lest they break her heart.

He looked long into those gentle eyes, saw all his youth and his folly and wished it all undone, took her hands into his own and held them tight.

'I love you, mother, and now feel shame for this great hurt. Forgive me, please, and ease my pain upon the road. For in the darkness of the night I shall need your love.' With that he gently pulled a summer scarf, carelessly hanging forgotten from her apron pocket, which had upon it a picture of the sun. He held her tight,

'This shall be my banner, to light the dark and twisted paths I am about to tread.' He turned and left quickly, for he could only tell her of his exile, nothing of the letter in his inner pocket, nor how closely on his heels the shadows of death trod.

'Son!' called his father beside the outer door. 'Forgive my wrath, we cannot undo what has been done, so let us part with love. You will be lost from sight, perhaps for ever, so let us part as friends. A foolish man I have been, perhaps, to think and scheme for you, but take this gear to keep you safe upon the road.'

With that he pulled into sight some ancient riding gear that had belonged to Thoron. A battered helm and mail coat that, when Thane put it on, made him stoop. It was wrought of the finest steel, as yet overlarge – it reached below his knees – but was cunning in the forging, and would turn a blade or blunt a blow. 'And take this, his cloak, which, also large, will keep you warm upon the road. Finally take his saddle, bridle and the girths. Legend has it that your grandfather ran the Greenways in this gear and never fell or was unseated. There are many tales and songs still told, I hear, in the borderlands, of the making of this saddle and the forging of the bit, and perhaps one day in a long forgotten place you may meet someone who can translate the tale carved over the cantle and along the reins. The language is long-forgotten here; all we know is that the saddle and bridle must be used together but what power or charms it holds no one knows.'

Ironhand's voice fell silent, tears touched the corners of his eyes. Thane grasped his father's arm, lost for words. He collected up his gear and walked down the spiral steps to the breaking yards, pausing now and then to listen for the footsteps of pursuit; but he was alone amongst the empty shadows, alone and afraid of what might stand or creep beyond the last lamp's light.

'We leave tonight,' Thane whispered, setting the saddle and bridle on the floor of Esteron's stable and lighting a torch from the spark he kept hidden in his pocket. For a moment he stood admiring the horse he was to ride to World's End. 'I know all about your mother, Esteron,' Thane said, remembering his own sad parting a short while ago. 'She was an errant horse at World's End, the Master told me her story. Her name was Beacon Light and her rider was killed in an ambush, she fled in panic into the darkness of Mantern's Forest, tearing off her saddle and bridle against the trees that blocked her path. A year later she arrived here at the gates of the Granite City, alone and heavily in foal. I'll bet your father was a great Lord among Horses.'

Mulcade hooted, for he knew the rest of the story, but Thane could not understand the owl's hoots and missed the beauty of the mating between Beacon Light and Equestrius. Thane sighed, listening to the music in the owl's voice.

'We had better be on our way, before the grey hours herald another dawn. This was my grandfather's saddle, Amarch wore it on their great Greenway rides and she was the last Warhorse to serve the Granite Kings,' and he lifted it reverently on to Esteron's back.

The ancient saddle, though strangely made, sat well upon his back, and for all its age was soft and supple. Thane ran his fingers lightly over the legend carved about the cantle, felt the finesse of the work and wondered about the deeds of which it spoke. Perhaps it told of saddlers' halls where trees were shaped and patterns cut, leather tooled, and the whole put together with long, curved needles. Perhaps it told of charms or spells that kept the rider safe within the seat upon a dangerous road. He pressed his fingers on the leather skirts and laid his head upon the seat, his other hand upon Esteron's neck and slipped into dreaming of the road; saw sweeps of hills, blinding snow and frozen ponds and fords, black spiky trees pressing on the road; saw lights below the track, villages shut up tight, and shadows move across the path. Esteron moved, his hand slipped, the dream was broken. Perhaps the magic of the saddle lay in the things it told when touched. Esteron, tacked, began to fidget for the road. A last look round, a whispered quick goodbye to the empty stable. The girths were tight, keepers, buckles, straps were all in place, he led him to the door, mounted and set off on the road to Underfall.

First winter's snow was swirling through the narrow streets leading down to the city's gate and soon smoothed out the prints they left. Wrapped tight in the cloak and mail he passed the silent watcher at the stable gate who had had orders to let him pass. The Master Breaker stood beside the guard, sword drawn, lest treachery end the journey before it began, and watched Thane and Esteron disappear, mere shadowy forms in the snowy night. 'Keep safe, child,' he whispered.

Thane rode until the dawn, late to break, with heavy snow-filled clouds, cast enough light to take stock of his bearings. Reluctantly he dismounted from his warm-wrapped seat, icy moaning draughts set his mail shirt rattling and his cloak flapping at his heels. He had heard the dispatch riders talk of how they spelled their horses on long journeys, when haste did not press too hard, and how they walked or jogged at their horses' heads to ease the weight upon their backs and save their strength to run the further. He soon realized what men of steel these riders were, for after one hundred paces in the uneven snow, burdened with his shirt's weight, he remounted Esteron, a little disgraced with his lack of strength. 'Some Rider I'll make! A hopeless boy to fill a man's shoes,' he thought, but worse was to come. In youthful haste Thane had set out with little thought of what to take on such a journey, he had followed blindly the road down from the city and had made his way from lamp to lamp as each one rose out of the swirling snow until he passed the last, and in the blackness wrapped up tight within his grandfather's cloak, felt the snow bite against his face and sting his eyes and dreamt of dragons and great deeds upon the road. Riding for the King, paying little attention to where Esteron took him in the snowy dark.

Now he was lost, without a landmark, damp, soaked through his breeches where snow had settled on his saddle. White, he walked at Esteron's head, his hands were numb with cold and slipped upon the reins and icy draughts found hidden ways beneath the cloak. No sign of life moved upon the grey-white landscape. Bending clumps of trees tugged in the wind, moved slowly past Esteron's measured pace. No bird or animal moved and emptiness stretched in each direction. The only signs on the road were the way-posts set to keep a traveller safe from straying and they vanished in perspective before and behind.

Esteron seemed no better off, head down into the snowy wind, his flowing mane had become a tangle of wet hair, lying limp upon his neck, and snow had settled on his quarters.

All day they walked, and all day they grew colder and hungrier; towards dusk Thane's spirits were at their lowest. Wet through and frozenly fumbling in his inner pockets he touched his mother's scarf and through the numbness in his fingers felt the smoothness of the silk, wound the scarf about his hand and crushed it tight. Perhaps the movement of his hand made the blood begin flowing, for first it tingled, then burned and felt warm. He transferred the scarf from hand to hand, rubbed Esteron's neck with it and tried hard to keep back the darkness that was growing about them. He told Esteron tales he had heard of great adventures from the past, but much of what he said was pulled away by the wind, and his tales and stories faded into silence as he slumped forward, worn out with tiredness and despair. With one hand clutching tightly to the scarf, he slipped from consciousness into dark dreams.

Lost to feeling from the numbing cold, he did not notice the weight settle on his shoulder, or the talons press into his mail coat, see the sharp cruel beaks or large unblinking eyes, or see or feel the ones that followed – black silent shapes descending from the night to settle on his back, or hear the soft hoots that were used to guide the older ones, less sharp-eyed than the rest, until his back was covered with a feather blanket from his shoulders to the high cantle of the saddle. Still they sat, unblinking watchers through the night, turning a head this way and that for these were dangerous roads with many hunting in the dark where winter food was hard to find, and Thane, unarmed, unconscious, made an easy prey.

He had seen them often, but paid little heed, except to admire their beauty and silent dignity in the tall barns, stable lofts and sometimes in the trees about the court. Watching in silence, unblinking, all the comings and goings of the King. Royal proclamation protected them from being hunted and their presence was considered a good omen, for many stories from the past told of how they fought side by side with the horses, using beak and claw to defeat their common enemies, or acted as messengers, for little missed their blinkless eyes. Mulcade, Chief Loftmaster Owl, watched all the comings and goings about the breaking yards and marked Esteron's high breeding from the first day of his arrival. He saw through the gangling of youth and his awkwardness to the directness of his line and traced with his eye where great sheets of muscle would replace the summer grazing fat. He saw that trace of common blood that made him tough enough to outstay by far the other horses in the yards; he saw his father's temper and knew from whom he came. Mulcade, wisest of all the owls, with only the merest turning of his head, had seen and heard it all. In silent flight he had settled on the twisted beam that spanned the king post where Esteron stood, racked short to eat, and in quiet hoots and whispers had told him what fate had befallen Thane. In the time left while Thane held his mother close and took his father's hand he had told Esteron all he knew of the secret paths that led towards World's End, of little used Greenways, overgrown and broken Causeways, now fallen into neglect. He said he would follow and give what help he could and counsel for the roads ahead. He would fly in danger in the daylight, however, for owls had many enemies outside the power of the King.

The stable guards had let Mulcade pass invisible; high above the gate he flew, buffeted by the storm. All day he flew searching in a great circle about the city, flying through the falling snow over a vanishing landscape where everything blended in tones of grey and white except for the black hedges and clumps of trees, bent by the wind. Angry at the snow that weighed him down and forced frequent stops to shake his feathers dry, and fear that death might wait in a trap behind the first hedgerow Esteron passed. At length he saw them as last light faded; he saw Thane slumped forward lifeless in the saddle. Flying high he cast a wide circle, calling to his kind for help and looked for a warm safe place to guide Esteron to; but there was none that even the swiftest horse could reach before morning; the road was empty of enemies, but also empty of friends. The owls with great care covered all they could and kept him warm throughout the watches of the night. They kept Esteron to the snowy path and he took comfort from his extra burden, for without the owls he would not have known his way. By morning light their feathers' warmth had dried Thane's cloak and warmed right through his mail shirt; now conscious, he slept and dreamed of feather beds, soft quilts and sunshine in his hair.

# Woodsedge

Brave Esteron, uncomplaining, had now walked two nights and one day, his limbs were aching and tiredness pulled at his frozen eyelashes and a rim of frozen snow had set a coronet about the headpiece of the bridle, but still he forged ahead, now breasting drifts that touched his shoulder. Mulcade would whisper out the way lest he waken Thane and urged him on, for now just in sight between two hills, hard against a jet black wood, a spiral of smoke rose up to meet the winter sky.

Stretching their wings, looking round with tireless eyes, the owls lifted lightly into the icy air and, swooping over hedge and tree, roosted in the wood to keep a silent watch, except Mulcade who clung to Thane's shoulder, beak and claws tensed, ready lest the lonely house be unfriendly. Esteron took them to the door and pushed it with his head; but to no avail. The door remained fast and he merely dislodged some of the snow that covered his brow. He turned impatiently and, hunching up his quarters, punched out the door. One blow from those iron-hard hooves shattered the door, post and jamb, and sent splintered timbers flying into the air. Turning, Esteron stepped through the broken entrance to face a ring of bright sharp swords held in unsteady hands, for huge he looked, blocking out the light, steam rising from the melting snow upon his back, his ears flattened back and his teeth bared. Thane seemed no more than the shade of a long-dead hero, dressed as he was in errant riders' gear and lying lifeless on the horse's back. Mulcade with razor sharp claws flexed, beak open wide upon his shoulder, shrieked, ready to stoop to the attack.

What apparition stood before them from beyond World's

End? What hideous beast, wrapped in vaporous steam? What carrion of the darkness sat upon those lifeless shoulders? Tombel, master of the house, moved fearfully forwards, flexing his arms to swing the double-handed marching sword, but Esteron reared, thrashing at the air with his hooves, driving Tombel back towards the wide staircase.

The crashing of Esteron's hooves upon the stone floor snapped Thane awake and rising tall in the stirrups he grabbed in vain for the sword he had forgotten to take. Instead, in his haste, he dropped the crumpled scarf upon the floor. Unarmed amidst a world of foes he felt a fool. In that moment, while he saw his folly and looked at his scarf, Tombel saw Thane for what he was; a half-frozen boy, an owl, and a horse, lost and alone upon the winter's road.

'Easy, lad,' he called softly, putting the marching sword upon the ground and motioning his sons and his Wayhouse men to lay their blades next to his.

'We mean you no harm, lad, but we live in dangerous times and we were battle-ready at the first sound you made beyond our door.' Tombel's eyes softened as he recognized the cloak and helm that Thane wore, but he looked uneasy at Mulcade and Esteron.

Thane followed his gaze from Esteron to the owl upon his shoulder and recognized him as the one who had flown on to his shoulder in the sand school and he laughed, blushing scarlet and jumped to the ground.

'Forgive me, sir. I did not know we had reached a house. I must have fallen to sleep in the saddle.'

Looking behind him at the broken door he turned a deeper red and whispered, 'Oh dear, did I do that?'

Tombel stood staring at Thane, 'House? Did you call this a house?'

The Wayhouse men smiled, nudging one another and Tombel's sons laughed.

'Yes,' replied Thane, looking from face to face.

'This is more than just a house, my lad, this is the Wayhouse at Woodsedge. The last refuge, or the first, whichever way you travel. It is here that travellers rest their tired mounts. Mind you, we don't keep the horses in here, come, let me show you where the stables are. Bring your horse, and we shall feed and bed him down.'

Esteron, unsaddled and rugged with the best blankets that Tombel could find, rolled in the golden straw, snorted, shook himself from head to tail and threw himself on to his food. He had one foreleg lifted, ready to attack. Tombel paused at the stable door, lost in thought, watching Esteron eat.

'You have the makings of a great horse there, my boy. Even better than the one that rested here three, or even four, daylights ago. Mind you, he was leaner and run up as light as a Border Hound at the end of a hard road. Did you pass him?'

'Pass who, sir? The road was dark and empty when I left the Granite City, and all I saw during the last daylight was blizzards and driving snowflakes.'

'Come, we will talk some more on this matter,' Tombel said, leading Thane back into the Wayhouse to stand before his sons, Rubel and Arbel, and the Wayhouse Marchers that lived at Woodsedge.

'Now, lad, I want an explanation of why you journey alone in such dangerous times. There is clearly a lot to tell us. Come, out with it before my Marchers grow edgy with their swords.'

Thane told all he could without betraying the confidence of the King, but he soon began to stammer and stumble over every word to keep the purpose of his journey vague.

'And what of that owl perched on your shoulder? Where does he fit in the scheme of things? An ill-dressed, half-starved, half-frozen lad, who rides on a horse too good to be a casual gift, with an owl on his shoulder. With the black troubles we have now you had better give me a more solid story of why you use this road, or you will kick your heels locked up in my cellar. I will send word to the Chancellors and await a better

111

explanation. Perhaps they will tell me more or maybe they will even know who you stole the horse from.'

Mulcade could see how badly it was going for Thane and hooted, spreading his wings to stoop. Tombel reached for his bow, Arrah, the Marcher, drew his sword. Rubel and Arbel leapt behind Thane and suddenly the Wayhouse Marchers had encircled him in a ring of drawn swords.

'Enough of this nonsense,' snapped Tombel, stepping into the circle, nocking an arrow on to the string and taking aim at the owl.

'Stop! Stop! I have a letter from King Holbian. I am to deliver it to the Master of Underfall. That is the purpose of my journey. The letter is inside my shirt.' Ashamed at giving his secret up so easily, yet relieved to see the bow put down, Thane breathed a sigh of relief. He did not understand the owl's part or where it had joined him, or why, but he did recognize him as Loftmaster Mulcade, who had often perched near Esteron's manger, and had flown to his shoulder in the sand school. Perhaps the old legends were true about owls and horses having a common bond. He had always liked Mulcade's silent presence in the yard and now he hoped that he would stay with him.

'Keeper,' Ethric, the Marcher, called, tugging at Tombel's sleeve as he turned the letter over and over in his hands, 'the morning wears away, Lord, we must start searching or the daylight will fade before we reach the deeper parts of the forest.'

Tombel looked up from the letter's seal, his features softening into a smile; he took Thane's arm. 'Come, lad, and sit by the fire. Open your heart to my Marchers and tell them truthfully, did you cross Nightbeasts' tracks on the road?'

'Lord, the road was deep in untrodden snow. I was alone upon Esteron's back. But why do you ask about Nightbeasts' tracks?'

Tombel rubbed a hand across his tired eyes and for a moment looked very old.

'During the night, after Errant had left us to finish the last part of his journey to the Granite City, Nightbeasts attacked us, here at Woodsedge. They almost overran the Wayhouse, taking us

112

completely by surprise.' Tombel paused, drawing his eyebrows together. 'I think now it was Errant they were after, they must have followed him here. But he had gone, hardriding Dawnrise with whip and spur. Something, perhaps second sight, had warned him to flee. The Nightbeasts seemed to be searching for something or someone and finding only us they killed two of my Marchers and stole my greatest treasure before we drove them out of the house.'

Ethric gripped Thane's arms in his huge hands, 'They stole the Keeper's daughter, boy, they stole Elionbel, the beautiful Elionbel.'

Tombel sighed, burying his head in his hands, 'Where in all the wild woods shall we search today?'

'Gansyl died at the stair head trying to defend her,' broke in Rubel, honing the blade of his sword impatiently with a whetstone. 'Let us start now, father, and leave the talking until supper time.'

'Impatience will not find her! But you are right. We shall talk of Kings and the great fortress at World's End at evening time. Today, search towards Gildersleeves and while you are that way warn the Fencing Master, Duclos, of the Nightbeasts. He may have seen signs of them.'

Tombel watched Ethric and Arrah lead the Wayhouse Marchers out on to the Greenway, 'Keep safe and beware the shadows!' he called after them as they spread out and disappeared beneath the eaves of the black forest.

'Each daylight we have searched without reward,' Tombel said, returning to stand with his back to the fire. Elionbel had not gone easily and he knew she would pay a high price for putting up such a fight. Thane had slipped forwards in his chair, his head falling on to his chest. Tombel smiled down at him and pulled the cloak across him like a blanket.

'Sleep, child,' he whispered, motioning to Martbel his wife, who stood in the doorway, to tread quietly around the young man.

113

On silent wings Mulcade rose and left Woodsedge. He flew over the black forest calling in shrill hoots, summoning all who could hear him to a council in an ancient tree beside the Greenway.

'Nightbeasts are about. Tell me all you have seen while hunting in the dark.'

Mulcade sat upon the highest branch and listened to the quiet noises that filled the gloomy forest. Tombel had guessed right, a band of Nightbeasts had followed the messenger across Elundium but Woodsedge was the only house they had attacked, so far. Mulcade turned his ear this way and that but there was no news of the fair Elionbel. The Nightbeasts had vanished, it seemed, into the heart of the forest with her.

'Who will help me?' he hooted against the cold afternoon wind. 'Who will hunt the Nightbeasts with me and fly at my wing tip to find Elionbel?'

In the silence that followed Mulcade held them with his eye, unblinking for long moments. Some could hold his gaze and those he knew were true Battle Owls, but there were some who shifted on the branch and looked away. Mulcade, with the wisdom of a Loftmaster, softened his stance and hooting quietly bid them to fly home and raise the alarm. Fly, and spread the word throughout Elundium that the Nightbeasts were once more at large.

Gathering the owls that had proudly held his gaze into a stoop in the highest branches Mulcade told them what they must do.

'We must stoop here and fold our wings upon the tree before the night grows dark. Nightbeasts must rest by day so we must fly high above the forest and look for signs. They have little thought for tree or branch and wreck much as they march, so look in this dark and tangled wood for damage that Nature would not cause. Do not be seen or give alarm but mark the place and come swiftly back.'

The sky darkened to their wings. Heads low, eyes sharp, they flew off in all directions over a mass of black winter trees.

Thane slept all day, oblivious to the bustle of preparation going on all around him. Sparks flew round the grinding wheel as notched swords were honed to sharp new points and nicks and chips hacked off by iron collars were ground out. The doors and windows were barred with wooden beams. Fresh logs were carefully stacked up high about the hearth and dry sticks, tar-dipped and tied in bundles, had been heaped behind his chair.

Giggling amongst the serving girls woke him. The early setting sun was sinking behind the black forest, casting long shadows to the door. Thane stretched and rose stiffly to his feet, and saw the room transformed as if for war.

'Come, lad,' laughed Tombel, seeing the young man standing by the fireplace, 'Come and choose a sword before supper, just in case the Nightbeasts return.'

'Will they come back?' asked Thane with an anxious note in his voice.

'I doubt it, lad, not tonight anyway. They already have the greatest treasure in my house. But one day they will sweep across all Elundium, mark my words!'

Thane shivered, drawing his grandfather's cloak tightly about his shoulders. Tombel saw the fear in Thane's eyes and stretched out a reassuring hand to him. 'Soon my Marchers will return. This is a strong house, but I have yet to have a name from our guest. Who are you, lad?'

As Thane was about to answer he heard running footsteps on the snow-cleared path. Tombel spun round, drawing his sword.

Arbel burst through the newly repaired door. 'Father, father! We have found Nightbeasts' tracks leading into the heart of the black forest. I have left the others guarding the place. What shall we do?'

Tombel quickly gathered up his longbow, two double-edged swords and a close-work cutting knife.

'Lord,' cried Thane, 'let me come with you and repay your hospitality.'

'No, lad, you owe us nothing!'

115

Tombel turned away and took two paces towards the open doorway then abruptly stopped. Mulcade was silently hovering in the opening with a scrap of torn fabric in his talons, beside him another owl hovered with a bloody eye in his claws.

'Elionbel,' Tombel whispered, reaching up to the torn scrap of fabric, seeing again the laughing girl on the stairs, feeling her goodnight kisses on his cheek and the touch of her golden locks brush against his face.

Mulcade alighted on Tombel's arm and placed the scrap of fabric in his hand. The other owl let the hideous eye fall from its talons. It bounced upon the floor and rolled against Tombel's foot.

'Nightbeasts!' Tombel cried, pointing towards the eye. Bending his arm Tombel gently brought Mulcade so close that their heads were almost touching, 'You know of the mark upon my arm, you saw right through the cloth, even though I reached for my bow in temper. You understood my grief and you have searched in the wild wood outside and found Elionbel. You know where she is!'

Mulcade hooted softly and pressed his talons into Tombel's arm, then he flew to the doorway and hovered as if waiting. Rockspray, the other owl, flew towards Arbel, circled him once, and then also flew to the doorway.

'Run back to the others, tell them to follow the owl. He will lead you to your sister,' Tombel cried as he raced after Mulcade.

Thane ran out into the early darkness and quietly found the stables and saddled Esteron. He had remembered to bring the sword he had earlier chosen and clumsily gripping the hilt in one hand he wound the reins around the other. 'Gallop! Gallop!' he urged, pointing Esteron towards the edges of the black forest, following Tombel's footprints in the snow. As they galloped a stoop of owls descended out of the darkness and led them through the trees.

Thane gave up trying to direct Esteron and leaned forwards,

116

hugging his neck. He drew his knees up as high as he could in the saddle as they cantered through tight gaps, barely wide enough for Esteron. Black and scratched they came to wider glades and yet, galloping hard and silent on the snow, they could not match Tombel's Marcher's strides. Always just ahead his shadow or moon-reflected mail showed between the trees. Up steep slopes of tall pine trees or down into tight valleys where the trees grew in close dark tangles, on they ran, through the night, horses following the owls who flew in a straight line towards the Nightbeasts' camp.

Kerzolde had thought it secure. A hollow ringed with hawthorn trees and broken granite blocks. Kerzolde, their captain, had chosen it, a place to rest and torment the girl they had stolen.

They had lost the messenger, somehow he had vanished, but the girl's death would make up a little for that. They were well forward with their torture, now they were to draw her nails one by one. Kerzolde gripped her hands in his claws, sneering and dribbling, pressing his foul face against hers. Mulcade, high above the forest, drifting on an icy current, caught within his tufted ear a scream, torn out in pain, faint upon the wind. He might have missed them in all that dark wild forest, but now he had a beacon and far below, a mere speck amongst those gnarled and spiky trees, he saw Elionbel, hung up, stretched tight by bleeding wrists between two trees. In that split second before Kerzolde bit at her finger tips Rockspray, the gentle owl flying at Mulcade's wingtip, plunged to earth and as he stooped, wings stripping feathers with the speed, he unhooked his talons and spread them wide to rip and tear. Down he fell, dizzy with the speed. The shock of his stoop flung Kerzolde backwards and, hooking his talons around one of the monster's eyes, he ripped it out, then swooped off between the hawthorn trees, shrieking with victory. Mulcade had stooped silently into the Nightbeasts'

117

camp and plucked the torn strip of nightdress from a hawthorn spike and together the owls had carried their news to the meeting tree, and then into the Wayhouse at Woodsedge.

Mulcade tightened his talons on Tombel's arm, indicating that they were close to the Nightbeasts' secret camp. Stealthily Tombel crept to the hollow's rim and hid between the hawthorns. Dawn was in the tree tops and soon the Nightbeasts would be at their weakest. There, suspended as Mulcade had seen her, hung Elionbel, with fresh tears running down her face. Tombel forced his knuckles into his mouth and bit hard to stop himself crying out as he saw Elionbel's bleeding hands.

The Nightbeasts were milling about prodding at her with their spears, cruelly laughing and mocking her as she looked up towards the dawn.

'You cannot steal the sunrise, or stop the daylight painting winter colours in the trees,' she cried out, letting her head fall forwards in despair. Blinding light flashed across the hollow. Tombel could wait no longer, up he jumped between the trees, sweeping two broad swords aloft to catch the early morning sunlight.

Esteron in that instant sprang from beyond the hollow's rim, clearing the lowest spiky hawthorns to land beside Tombel.

'Elionbel! Elionbel!' Tombel shouted, plunging the great marching swords into the nearest Nightbeasts. Esteron lifted his head and neighed until an answer came that darkened the sky. Thane looked up, expecting the shadow of death, but instead, just like a part of one of his grandfather's stories, the sky was full of owls; stoop upon stoop falling out of a clear blue morning sky to attack the Nightbeasts.

Thane hung on tightly to the saddle as Esteron reared and plunged his way deeper and deeper into the hollow, matching Tombel stride for stride. 'Run! Run!' a voice shouted in Thane's head. The Nightbeasts' foul shadows were swallowing them up, his sword arm felt heavy and paralysed. Fear made him gasp for breath as huge claws reached out to pull him down.

118

'Lord, I cannot,' he cried, trying to turn Esteron away.

'Father! Father!' a voice called out across the hollow.

Thane heard her cry as clear as silver bells on a candle night and, lifting his head, he turned in the saddle and saw her, Elionbel of Woodsedge, surrounded by Nightbeasts ready to plunge in their spears.

Mulcade and Rockspray were defending her, both leading a stoop of owls at the Nightbeasts' eyes, but for each beast they destroyed another loomed up to shadow the sunlight. Thane let go of the saddle and, inexpertly, swung the borrowed sword in a glittering arc. 'Thoron!' he shouted to give himself courage as Esteron plunged forwards towards Elionbel. Thane slashed the blade wildly from left to right, feeling it shudder as it struck the Nightbeasts' armour. Twice it was almost torn out of his hands as it pierced through into their black hearts.

The owls were being driven backwards into a tight circle around Elionbel. Soon the Nightbeasts' spears would be able to reach her. Esteron saw her peril and fought his way on to the steep rim of the hollow, below where she hung. They were surrounded now by hideous Nightbeasts. Thane leapt to the ground and thrust his sword into the swarming mass of terror, while his arms grew numb and tired, the hilt of his sword became slippery in his hands from Nightbeast blood and he stumbled over their fallen carcasses as he strove beside Esteron to hold that piece of ground.

'Death!' screamed a black shape, rising above the other nightmare forms. 'Death!' it screamed again, advancing on Thane, blotting out the sunlight. One-eyed Kerzolde had heard the other Marchers. They were rapidly closing in on the hollow, now was the time to run but first he would kill the girl and perhaps the boy who stood defending her. He drove his spear up towards her heart, throwing all his hatred of the people of Elundium behind the thrust. Thane saw the flash of sunlight from the blade and, spinning round, he struck desperately at the spear shaft. He shattered it, catching Kerzolde's

119

claw with the flat of the blade. The force of the blow knocked the sword out of Thane's hands and he stood defenceless before Kerzolde.

'I will kill you one day!' hissed the black shape, its raw eye socket oozed pus and its damaged claw twitched helpless at his side. He stepped menacingly towards Thane and then, looking back into the hollow at the advancing Wayhouse Marchers, he turned and fled over the hollow's rim into the black forest.

The tide of battle quickly turned and silence descended across the hollow. The Nightbeasts fled, following their captain into the forest.

Tombel rested aching hands upon the hilts of his notched and splintered swords and quietly directed Ethric to take the Marchers and hunt the Nightbeasts beyond Gildersleeves. He then loosed the cutting knife from his belt and climbing the steep rim of the hollow cut the bonds above Elionbel's wrists.

Tombel gathered Elionbel into his arms and held her close. There were tears in his eyes as he turned towards home. A soft muzzle pressed against his arm. He turned his head and smiled at Esteron. 'Thank you, great warrior,' he whispered. Esteron pressed his arm a little more forcefully and bent his forelegs, offering the empty saddle. 'You are a true Lord among Horses,' he said, setting Elionbel gently in the saddle. Such was Tombel's relief at finding Elionbel alive and his concern over her mutilated hands that he forgot all about Thane as he walked beside Esteron, his hand on Elionbel's knee to steady her.

Thane stood for a moment on the hollow's rim, casting his eye over the Nightmare shapes that lay scattered before him. 'Nightbeasts!' he whispered, knowing now the full horror of the monsters his grandfather had told him of. Quickly he turned and followed in Esteron's hoofprints, light in heart to have helped Tombel a little and proud that Esteron had offered his saddle to Elionbel. He remembered their battles in the sandschool and laughed to see him now in gentle majesty, neck

120

arched, seeking out the safest way between the tangled tree roots, hidden under first winter's snow.

Thane soon fell far behind, but he was not alone or lost, Esteron's hoof prints were clear to follow and Rockspray kept pace with him flying from branch to branch. Now he had time to look about and he saw the beauty of the world beyond the Granite City. Tall trees, mightier than castle columns, with branches that seemed to touch the sky; shafts of sunlight more beautiful than a thousand candle flames, that fell upon the forest floor. Distant pigeons cooed and wild white doves flew in the misty light. All about him the forest was alive. Squirrels searched the ground for winter food, or leapt from trunk to trunk, sometimes keeping pace with him, sometimes in their haste letting fall a hard-sought autumn fruit. Startled deer moved through the shadows and rabbits dived for cover. Far ahead he caught a glimpse of Esteron's tail swishing as he walked or a flash of sunlight reflecting from Tombel's marching swords where they rested across his shoulder.

Hot and damp beneath his mail shirt, Thane sat a while resting his back against a tall, smooth chestnut tree whose trunk patterns twisted round and spiralled up to disappear amongst many forking branches. He drifted into sleep and he would have let the sun slip out of sight had not Rockspray pulled him back awake by tugging hard on his sleeve, for though they had won a great fight the forest was no place yet for Thane to wander alone after dark. There perched on his knee, Rockspray in all his feathery beauty sat with blackened, bloodstained talons spread to keep his balance and with eyes half hooded he looked long, unblinking into Thane's eyes and made soft noises deep inside his throat. Soft enough to make Thane reach out and stroke his feathery chest and run his hand over the horny skin on his talons. What joy to be so close to such wild beauty.

'Come, brave owl, or the Keeper of Woodsedge will have bolted the door!' Thane said, struggling to his feet. Rockspray

121

flew to perch on his shoulder and they walked together as the afternoon wore on, pulling their shadows long, making giants of them; mighty warriors striding through the woods that none would dare go near. So they came to Woodsedge and Tombel's home with early lights in the windows casting crystal patterns on the snow as the last light faded.

'Stables first to see Esteron set fair for the night,' Thane said to Rockspray, turning away from the house towards the stable yard. But the stable door hung open. Esteron was nowhere to be seen. He called his name, near to tears and ran back towards the darkened tree line. 'Esteron! Esteron!' he called, in desperation. A muffled answer came, soft at first but climbing through the scales to reach a roaring neigh that shook the window frames and set the candles dancing on the tables. It came from inside the Wayhouse, pouring through the open door, ending in a clear high note of joy that finished in soft whinnying and blowing through velvet smooth nostrils.

Thane ran, crunching through the snow, to stop and stare. Upon the threshold stone he paused for there before him, mighty in the firelight, stood Esteron. The scarf Thane had taken from his mother hung from the pommel of the saddle as a banner.

'I wish the King could see you now,' Thane whispered.

Tombel crossed the stone flagged floor and gripped Thane's arms in welcome.

'Come, great warrior. For what you did today this house is forever open to you. My swords and the bow of black forest yew I humbly lay at your feet.' With that Tombel laid his bloody notched swords and the bow at Thane's feet.

Thane stammered, blushing, 'It was Esteron that pulled me into that dreadful place. In faith, I would have fled to hide but . . .'

Tombel with a steady hand lifted Thane's chin and looked with softness into his eyes. 'I felt your fear and I heard you cry out, but you mastered the fear my boy. Why, I saw you defend my fair Elionbel. I know what courage it takes to face the Nightbeasts. It is true your horse brought you to my side and you could have clung there like a babe, cradle fresh, whining and dribbling until the fight was done but your blade and the scarf tied to the saddle brought hope in the morning and won us a great victory! Come, brave warrior, and no more talk of hiding, for your help was much needed and will be long remembered. Come, unsaddle your horse.'

Tombel led Thane over to Esteron and helped him remove the saddle and bridle. Running his hands across Esteron's shoulder Tombel exclaimed, 'You know, I haven't seen the like of him since my youth in the great battle for World's End. Yet he will ask nothing for today's labour save we keep our faith in friendship with him, a bowl of food, clean bed, or the freedom to go where ever he chooses. Today he helped to win back this house's greatest treasure and from this moment this Great Hall shall be his stable, and my best crystal bowl his manger.'

'Lord,' ventured Thane timidly, 'just before the owls brought news of your daughter you had asked me to give my name.'

Tombel laughed, his eyes full of mischief, 'I knew you, lad, even as I put my marching sword on the floor when you burst through that door. That cloak, that helm, even the saddle told me. You have his ways, his manner and the same straight look in the eyes. Welcome amongst friends, Thanehand, welcome.'

Thane looked up, startled, at Tombel's speech and dropped the scarf he had just removed from the saddle.

'You knew my grandfather and the Warhorse, Amarch?'

Tombel smiled, bending to pick up the scarf, but he quickly dropped it again as the colours burst into life.

'That scarf has magic in it!' he gasped, bending forwards to take a closer look.

'No, it is just my mother's scarf that I took in parting to light my lonely path. It gave me courage on the road and it seems to catch and hold the sunlight. It has her warmth, her strength and love somehow woven in amongst the threads.'

Thane's eyes brimmed with tears as he remembered her in that dark little room in the shadow of the great wall.

'Mother! Martbel, come quickly,' Tombel cried. Turning back to Thane he gripped his arm. 'Forgive me, Thane, I have been a rough host. Martbel, come, come show Thane the best room this Wayhouse can offer. Up, boy, for there will be a grand feast tonight and you must attend. Go now, follow Martbel, she will show you the way.'

Later that evening Thane tiptoed to the head of the stairs and peered down at the throng of people gathered in the Great Hall. He had been at a loss to know what to do with the jug of water and the bowl set on a stand beside his bed and the mirror had startled him, making him jump backwards. He had laughed at his reflection and brushed his fingers through his hair.

'Warrior!' he had whispered, puffing his chest and frowning. 'Nightbeast slayer!' he had cried sweeping his cloak across his shoulders and lungeing at the reflection. Then he had noticed the dirt on his face and, wetting his fingers, wiped what he could away. Now he stood there in the shadows, more terrified and alone than ever before. The murmur of battle talk rose up the stairway. The noise of laughter and the clink of pewter, the ring of the crystal cups froze Thane, his mouth felt dry and his heart pounded in his chest. Something moved in the darkness and noiselessly settled on his right shoulder, then another on his left.

'Mulcade, Rockspray!' he whispered, looking at each of the owls. Softly they hooted, flying up to perch on a beam and the talk in the Great Hall fell away to nothing.

'Thane!' Tombel called, climbing the stairway to find him hiding in the shadows, 'My Marchers, my sons, Martbel and all my house await you. Come!'

'I cannot. I was born to Candlebane Hall, Lord, I could not go amongst your high born folk. My place is with the tallow taper, lighting the candles.'

Tombel smiled, putting his arm around Thane's shoulder and was about to bring him down the stairs when he noticed the dirt still on his hands and face and his untidy hair. Turning he took Thane back into his room and bid him sit on the bed.

'Being highborn does not make you better, lad. It does not make you more worthy to stand with other people. You talk of lighting candles with a taper, yet today you lit a light far greater than all the candles in this Wayhouse when you fought beside me in that dreadful hollow. Come now, wash your face, here, let me show you.'

Tombel poured the water from the jug into the bowl and splashed it on his face, laughing, then dried it on a towel.

'You have stepped beyond Candlebane Hall, now, but never be ashamed of your humble beginnings, or ever forget them. Now do as I have done and wash your face and use a comb upon that tangle of hair, it looks worse than a cornfield after a thunderstorm.'

Tombel waited while Thane washed and combed his hair, and he smiled inwardly as Thane hesitated before the mirror, seeing himself for the first time.

'Marchers! Warriors of the Greenway! Friends and family, I welcome to this Wayhouse Thanehand, the Candlelighter's son, who lit today a torch that will shine forever bright in my heart.'

Silver goblets, pewter mugs and crystal cups were raised and shouts of welcome filled the hall.

Tombel spread his hands and the company fell silent. 'There are others we shall welcome, for without them it would be a black night of weeping. Esteron, the bravest horse in all Elundium, who will be known as Elionbel's champion. And,' Tombel smiled, looking up at the Kingpost beam, 'Mulcade, Loftmaster Owl, and Rockspray, a Lord amongst Battle Owls. I pledge you safety in this small corner of Elundium for as long as I can lift a hand to make it so, for we owe Elionbel's life to you.'

Again shouts of welcome filled the Great Hall and toasts were drunk to Esteron and the Battle Owls.

'Father,' a soft voice called from the far side of the Hall, 'let me thank the greatest warrior in all Elundium for my life!'

Thane looked across the hall and caught his breath, hot blushes touched his cheeks. Elionbel smiled up at him from where she stood in an open doorway. She was dressed in a simple long silk gown that reached her feet. Her golden hair fell on to her graceful shoulders in waves of tumbling light but her hands and wrists were covered in many bandages that hid the Nightbeasts' wounds.

'Lord,' she said, kneeling at the bottom of the stairs, 'I saw you jump the ring of trees, the bright banner on your saddle catching the morning sunlight. I saw your sword sweep through blackest nightmares as you fought your way to my side. Let me serve you at table as small payment. Great Warrior! I thank you for my life.'

Elionbel turned, keeping her eyes on Thane, and led the grand company through two open doors at the far end of the hall into a feasting room set with long tables in a three sided square surrounded by high-backed chairs. Thane looked in wonder at the feast and marvelled that the tables, for all their sturdy looks, held the weight without bending.

'This is a great feast, fit for a King,' he said, hesitating in the doorway, not knowing which way to turn or which chair was his.

'Indeed, it is set for a Kingsman,' whispered a soft voice at his side. 'Come, follow me, Kingsman, and eat your fill.'

Thane turned his head and looked into the beautiful eyes of Elionbel who stood there beckoning him to follow her. She showed him the Honour Seat, set above all the other chairs, raised on a dais at the centre of the main table. To his right sat Tombel, Martbel and the Marcher, Ethric. On his left sat Rubel and Arbel, Tombel's sons, and beyond them sat Arrah, the second Marcher. The lower tables, set at each end of the main table, were hosted by Marcher Holgym and his family on

126

the right and Arfon the Marcher and his family on the left. Servers waited on the lower tables and hovered at either end of the main table. Elionbel stood just behind Thane's chair. Everybody was looking at him as if waiting for him to do something. He had to start the feast. Thane looked at the array of eating tools laid out before him. Each one looked to be a little different from the rest and set beyond them were three empty drinking vessels, a silver goblet, a pewter mug and a crystal cup, all of them finely engraved with the emblem of an owl in blue and gold. On Thane's right was a small bowl filled with a scented drink. He breathed deeply, carefully picked up the bowl and sipped at it. In the deathly silence that followed a serving girl giggled, Elionbel spun round towards her and let slip the china plate she had been balancing on her bandaged hands. Tombel coughed to hide a laugh and Ethric turned nearly blue behind his sleeve hiding his face. Thane bent down to help Elionbel with the broken china and found her crying with laughter on the floor.

'Thane,' she whispered, pulling his head so close to hers that he could smell her fragrance, 'Do it again, please.'

'Do what?' he asked, feeling his cheeks burning with embarrassment.

'Drink from the finger bowl,' she replied, 'You are the guest of honour. Everybody must copy you, it is tradition. Please! Do it for me.'

Thane looked down at his blackened finger nails and could have died of shame seeing how his ignorance had already made him look such a fool and they had not even started eating yet. Swallowing the lump in his throat he looked from left to right along the tables, each face seemed to be laughing at him, yet each right hand had reached out towards the finger bowls. His mind raced forwards, imagining the nightmare meal to come. What if he used the wrong tools for each course, or drank from the wrong cups? Lowering his head again he whispered to Elionbel.

127

'I will trade with you. For every sip from the finger bowl you will lead me and tell what I should do, what tools to use and cups to drink from. Just as in the hollow each thrust of my sword brought your rescue closer.'

She stopped laughing and looked seriously at the young man before her. Here was someone very different from her brothers or the Marchers' sons who lived at Woodsedge. She touched his arm with her bandaged hand and pointed secretly to the silver goblet. 'Place your hand on the goblet and say, "Let us begin."'

Thane lifted the finger bowl to his lips and took a long slow sip. Tombel followed suit and all the Marchers and their families likewise. 'Let us begin,' Thane called, in an uncertain voice, touching the goblet.

Drink was then poured and trays of tiny slivers of a bright red fish were laid before him. Each sliver had been rolled and spiked on to a waxy yellow fruit that Thane had never seen before.

'Remove the spike and squeeze the forest apple over the fish,' Elionbel whispered. 'Use the two-pronged fork to eat the fish and do not eat the apple, that is for the servers.'

The feast was a seemingly endless procession of culinary delights all new and wonderful to Thane. Between each course he sipped from the scented bowl, and this became the signal, as the others drank, for entertainers to sing or recite or juggle in the centre of the Eating Hall. Under cover of these entertainers Elionbel revealed what next he should do or what tools to eat with; laughing, they looked into one another's eyes and the secret of the finger bowl spun the first threads of a bond between them. Throughout the feast Tombel and the Marchers seated either side of the Honour Chair laughed and told stories of the great marching men who had fought upon the Greenways of Elundium and never once did they leave a gap of awkward silence or let the talk turn to why Thane journeyed or of its purpose.

Gradually the talk died away and even Tombel began to hesitate, his eyes drawn towards the doors that led in from the Great Hall. Elionbel bent down close to Thane and pointed with her bandaged hand at a long thin dagger to the right of a large plate she had laid before him.

'Now is the moment,' she whispered, 'when you must leap up and plunge the carver into the beast's heart. Remember, it is the tradition for the one in the Honour Chair to make the first cut, but more than that remember as you move forwards: think of the Nightbeasts between us in the hollow and make such a leap that none will ever forget!'

Something heavy banged into the doors. Marchers reached for their swords, Thane sat tense, watching the doorway. Then the doors suddenly burst apart and all the feasters jumped in their chairs. Tombel half-rose, gripping his sword in his hand but Thane sprang nimbly across the table to land, sure-footed, the carver held firmly in his hand. He stood before the beast as it crackled and hissed, staring into his eyes, lips curled back in a snarl, exposing long, yellow fangs.

'Kill the beast! Kill the beast!' chanted the feasters. Thane, on tip-toe, raised the carver high above his head and plunged the blade into the animal a hand's span behind the shoulder. Down, down it sank until the hilt pressed against the prickly skin. Hot fat spluttered over his knuckles and the smell of delicious roast meat filled his nostrils. Elionbel led him back to the Honour Chair amidst shouts of praise, tradition had been fulfilled to the letter.

'What beast is that?' Thane asked, staring at the huge animal he had just stabbed.

Elionbel laughed softly and whispered, 'Nightboar. The most ferocious animal in the black forest. Legends say that one winter just after the battle for World's End a savage Nightboar attacked this house, charging through the Great Hall into this room.'

'And your father killed it thus founding this tradition?' interrupted Thane.

Elionbel smiled, putting her hand on his shoulder, 'No, Thane, it was your grandfather, Thoron, who had the Honour Chair that night. He killed the beast and fed the Marchers of Woodsedge for a whole winter on the carcass. He was the one who started the Nightboar tradition.'

Thane smiled back at Elionbel and thought of his grandfather sitting in the same chair all those years before and he shuddered knowing that if a real live Nightboar had broken in tonight he would not have had the courage to stand and face it.

'Eat some of the meat, Thane,' Elionbel's voice whispered across his thoughts. 'The feasters are waiting for you to start.'

Thane loosened his belt and attacked the meat. He had never eaten so well or from so many strange plates before. As a Candleman's son he had been lucky to eat one meal three daylights out of seven, and then only a tasteless gruel from a wooden bowl. He had truly eaten himself to a standstill. The servers carved at the flank of the Nightboar generously filling every plate but Thane declined the offer of a second helping and the beast was lifted on two strong staves beneath the carving table and pushed out of the Eating Hall.

'How did it appear to rush in upon us?' he asked Elionbel as she moved the last fork and spoon into place ready for him to use.

'The carving table has small wheels set into the legs, and the servers have developed a great skill at making the Nightboar look real and frightening as they push it through the doors.'

Thane laughed with her as she recounted how one honoured guest had fled the Honour Chair in screams of terror as the Nightboar rushed in.

'Were you serving him?'

Elionbel's smile faded, 'I am not a server, Thane,' she

130

replied, offended by his question. 'It is not the place of Wayhouse Keepers' daughters to serve at tables.'

Thane blushed and stumbled for words but Elionbel's face softened when she saw the ignorance in his question and laughed, brushing the error aside. Two of the servers who had removed the Nightboar now returned carrying a large golden pastry between them. They set it down on a table beside the Honour Chair. Elionbel cut and laid a piece on Thane's plate explaining that it was wild forest pie. A mixture of rare berries and fruits, found only in the heart of the forest and picked before the leaves turned to autumn colours and then pickled in honey. It had a spicy smell and tasted delicious, especially the bottom layer of pastry that had soaked up the sweet syrup from the fruit.

'Wonderful, the best food I have ever eaten,' said Thane to Elionbel, finishing up the last mouthful and wiping the plate clean of crumbs.

Elionbel frowned. 'Surely in the Granite City the King and his warriors must have feasts like this or better every day?'

'I am not a Kingsman,' Thane replied, looking down at the table. 'These clothes are my grandfather's. I am only the Candleman's son.'

He wanted to tell her more but he was too shy and ashamed of his humble beginnings.

A gentle bandaged hand lifted his chin until their eyes met, 'Candleman. You are the greatest warrior in all Elundium, and I honour you.'

Turning with tears in her eyes Elionbel lifted Thane's finger bowl in both hands, and put it to her lips and called the servers' toast.

'Thanehand! Who brought hope in the morning and chased my fears away.'

'Thanehand!' the feasters shouted, draining their fingerbowls.

'Thanehand, the Doorbreaker!' laughed Tombel, draining his crystal glass. 'May he always be welcome in this house.'

Late next morning with the frosted patterns melting on the windows Thane, refreshed from a dreamless sleep, made his way down into the Great Hall. Now with time to look about he saw the beauty of the room. The dark oak panels each set with a finely sculptured lamp and the fireplace, big enough to seat a dozen people. A huge log, glowing red, lay in the hearth between two fine dogs that were made of twisted and hammered brass. The polished stone-flagged floor showed some scuffs and scrapes that looked to match Esteron's hooves and in a corner by the hearth, broken stalks of straw from the horse's bed lay scattered in disorder. Thane blushed to think of Esteron sleeping in such a beautiful room and hurried towards the door to find a broom to clean up the mess. He stopped in the doorway and looked out at the brilliant landscape of smooth white rolling hills falling to a frozen sea against the black forest edge. There Esteron ran free, head tossing in the sunshine. Thane raised his hand to wave but behind him he heard a door unlatch. Turning he stared in foolish youthfulness at a world of beauty caught in the streaming sunlight. Elionbel's appearance left him breathless and blushing.

'My father bids you attend him in the Trophy room.' Elionbel seemed cool towards him, yet her eyes were full of laughter as she led him to the Trophy room door.

While they waited for an answer to Elionbel's knock on the door Thane thought of a thousand things he wanted to say to her but his tongue seemed tied in knots. He only managed to call her name before Tombel summoned him to enter. Thane hesitated on the threshold but Tombel's voice drew him in.

'Enter, Thane, the day wears on and we have much to talk about.'

He crossed the threshold and gazed in wonder at the secrets spread about the room. The banners hanging from the beams, pictures on the walls, mail shirts and swords propped and heaped in disorder, tiny coins, trinkets, spurs and ornaments between rows and rows of books.

'Come. Be seated,' commanded Tombel as he threw a log on the fire to set it crackling and sending sparks shooting up the chimney.

Tombel settled back in his chair, resting his long boots on the fender. He sighed, smiling gently at Thane.

'Now to these grave matters we must discuss. The letter you carry and its secrets would be a great prize for the Chancellors to seize, but you are beyond their power for the moment, at least until the snows clear. But you have a greater enemy now that the Nightbeasts have awoken, for it would give them a clear picture of how weak the King has become and how near to the brink of disaster Elundium totters.'

'You have opened the letter!' cried Thane, leaping out of his chair. 'That was for the Keeper of World's End. I pledged my life to deliver it.'

Tombel laughed and handed the letter back to Thane. He had resealed it with the emblem of the owl carrying the sword, drawing back his sleeve he showed Thane the tattoo on his arm. 'I am also pledged to serve the King. Who would you have trusted, Thane, if you were wearing my shoes? A half-starved boy on a wild errand, or the careful hand of the King? After all it might have been a Chancellors' trick.'

Thane hid the letter in his shirt and angrily sat down.

Tombel continued. 'You tread a dangerous road, my lad. Far more dangerous than the King could have dreamed of. Why even I cannot guarantee your safety further than one day's ride from here.'

'Why is it more dangerous now?' asked Thane.

Tombel thought for a moment putting the pieces together in his mind. 'When you first arrived I asked you if you had passed a rider on the road. From the letter I learned that he had arrived before you left. Clearly neither the King nor Errant knew the Nightbeasts had the power to reach this Wayhouse at

133

Woodsedge, who knows how many are hiding out there in the black forest or lie waiting in the grasslands to attack any traveller using the Greenways. All I can tell you for sure is that the Nightbeast with only one eye escaped, my Marchers chased him far beyond Gildersleeves but they lost his tracks in the blizzards.'

'Then, Lord, I am lost and I shall never reach Underfall!'

'If you don't, Thane, then all Elundium may falter as night closes in upon these twilight years covering the labours of honest men.'

'Lord?' whispered Thane, looking in bewilderment at Tombel, 'What does the fate of this beautiful land have to do with my journey to Underfall?'

'Beautiful? It was once, Thane, more beautiful than a fairy tale. The morning sunlight had the touch and sparkle of pure crystal, shadows were velvet black and held no more menace than gentle shade for a traveller. Yes, it was beautiful once, long ago, before the bondbreaking. A land of gardens, with the great Greenways neatly trimmed and stretching away as far as the eye could see. People laughed and travelled in safety, birds sang in the hedgerows . . .'

'But,' interrupted Thane, 'those trees in the woods, the birds, the squirrels? Yesterday . . .'

Tombel laughed, 'Only shadows, lad. If you had seen it many suns ago.' He paused, a frown creasing his age-worn face. 'Listen, Thane, we stand on the edge of the blackest night, with swords in our hands against a terror we cannot master. The Marchers are scattered, the Gallopers have vanished and who, who could form a strike of Archers? Have you read the letter, Thane? Did the King tell you what you carry?'

'No,' answered Thane, his eyes widening as he leaned closer to Tombel.

'Then you know nothing of King Holbian's purpose?'

'No. Only that I was to give the letter to Thunderstone, the

134

Keeper of Underfall, Lord. From what I overheard the King has been buying daylights from the Chancellors with the jewels and he seeks true men, but he sent me out of the Granite City because he didn't want my blood on the cloak of jewels. I think I am to warn the Keeper in some way.'

'Nothing more?'

'Well, he did ask me if I would raise his standard in the darkness at World's End following in my grandfather's footsteps.'

Tombel smiled, stretched out his hand and gripped Thane's arm, 'And so you must, my boy, for Nevian foretold your journey long ago beneath the walls of Underfall.'

Thane shuddered, whispering, 'Why me? What have I done to be hounded and cursed by the Chancellors and cast out to start a journey I cannot finish?'

'Because you shine, lad. You carry the light.'

'Light? What light?'

Tombel laughed, 'You followed me into the black forest; did you for one moment hesitate or gather a bundle of candles to light your way? Can you see in the dark?' asked Tombel quietly.

Thane thought for a moment before answering. 'Darkness holds no fear, my Lord: but I grew up in Candlebane Hall, where my father kept back the darkness, he told me at our parting that night didn't care how many candles we lit.'

Tombel laughed again, striking the table with his hand, 'Then your father is a fool, my boy, to tell you such things. He knows nothing of real night where the Nightbeasts crawl.'

Tombel paused to look closely at Thane before drawing the boy to him. 'Didn't you learn anything in the Learning Hall? Anything about the light or the balance between light and darkness? Anything about the beautiful light before the bondbreaking?'

'No, Lord, King Holbian threw a curse on stories about the time before the bondbreaking.'

Tombel sighed, resting his head on his hands for a moment

before asking, 'Then you know nothing of time before King Holbian won the battle for World's End?'

'Only what my grandfather told me in his stories,' answered Thane.

Tombel smiled, wistfully, looking past Thane's head to where storm clouds were gathering over the winter trees, 'I will teach you, Thane, how the world began long ago before the Granite Kings arose. Long, long ago before night was ever begun.'

Tombel built the fire and lit every candle in his Trophy Room and drew Thane's chair as close as he possibly could to his own before he told him all he knew of time before the Granite Kings.

After Tombel had finished the story Thane sat for a long time in silence, watching the flames rise and fall between the logs. Eventually he turned to Tombel and asked in a puzzled voice, 'Where did you learn all this knowledge? It is more than all the Loremasters together know.'

Tombel smiled at Thane, spreading his hands, 'When I was young Nevian came to me and taught me all I have just told you. He charged me to collect the history of Elundium and piece by piece keep it here in the Wayhouse of Woodsedge. Look around you, Thane, look.'

The old man paused, watching the confusion cross Thane's face as he struggled to try and understand and to find his place in the story.

'But why me?' he cried, 'I am only the Candlelighter's son!'

Tombel took Thane's hand and soothed him into silence, 'You are more than that, lad. Nevian came to you in the Learning Hall. He passed by the last Granite King and all the Chancellors to stand before you. Not since the bondbreaking has his presence been seen in the Granite City and because . . .' Tombel lowered his voice and went on, 'the owl flew to your shoulder and you tamed the wild horse that none could touch.'

136

'But I did not ask the owl,' cried Thane, his eyes filling with tears.

'Nor did you ask to be born,' whispered Tombel, leaning even closer. 'The bonds were broken, child, and we have stood alone all these years growing old amongst our fears, regretting what we lost at the Battle of World's End.'

'But I was forced to tame Esteron. The breakers spat at me and locked me in his stable.'

'Easy, child, we do not choose our fate, nor are we born with the shoulders to carry it. Now, listen carefully. Long ago, Nevian broke the bond and loosed the great Warhorses to roam in freedom; he released the owls and the dogs from servitude to the Granite Kings, because a balance had been won. Night would follow day, each having its place and alloted time. That is what King Holbian won at the Battle for World's End. Magic was no longer needed to make the sun come up or stars to come out at night. We stood alone, Thane, in a beautiful land and laughed at the Master of Magic. But we were fools for we only knew half of the truth. Even now I stumble in the darkness of ignorance to know what really happened between the King and Krulshards, the Master of Nightmares, before the Gates of Night.'

'History in the Learning Halls said that the King destroyed Krulshards, and we are forbidden to even mention his name.'

Tombel laughed at Thane's reply.

'Your grandfather found a little of the truth, Thane, high up above the shoulders of Mantern's Mountain on a bleak plateau of rocks and heather. He had been chasing Nightbeasts, hard riding them into a cloudless dawn, when Amarch caught her hoof on a black ridge of rock. Her stumble threw your grandfather and the Nightbeasts escaped into a dark gully. Thoron decided to wait for the sun to rise before descending back to Underfall.'

'What did he find?' interrupted Thane.

'He found a shadow circle, burned into the ground. How it

137

got there is a mystery, but at its centre was one shadow more hideous than the rest and outside the circle was the shadow of King Holbian. Thoron followed the shadows for they were clear to see in the dawn sunlight, weatherworn and slightly raised above the plateau they led him towards a black gate full of wailing and torment. There the circle disappeared. Only the King's shadow remained.'

'What did the shadows mean?' asked Thane.

'What indeed? My fear is that the King did not kill the Master of Darkness, Thane. My fear is that somewhere beneath this land new Nightbeasts are being spawned; but even to say that is to speak treason, let alone to believe it.'

'Do you believe it?' asked Thane, shrinking back into his chair.

'Many things have pointed to it, Thane. Nevian's gift to the King at the end of the battle, the bondbreaking, the rise of the Chancellors and their thirst for power, Errant's news of Underfall. Perhaps the truth shouts at me, yet I must believe the King, for I am pledged to it.'

'And you think that my journey to Underfall is in some way a part of it?'

Tombel shrugged his shoulders, 'Sometimes, Thane, it is difficult to know what is happening to us, or why it happens at all. Mixed up in all the things I have gathered are rumours and prophecies; which ones we are supposed to follow is a mystery to me. The King saw you mount and tame the wild horse, the owl flew to your shoulder, yet where are the Border Runners that are supposed to run at your heels? I suppose we must follow fate and chase circumstance and do the best we can.'

'Border Runners? Who are they?' asked Thane.

'Wild dogs!' laughed Tombel. 'Savage hounds. Some are as tall as a pony but beware of them, Thane, if they are your enemies. Treat them with great respect if they be your friends, for they were at the bondbreaking and roam in freedom, belonging to no man, not even the King. Nevian foretold that

138

the new King would ride a wild Warhorse with the Lord of Owls upon his shoulder and at his feet would run a savage hound. He would carry a standard that blazed with light and he would fear nothing in the darkness of night.'

Thane thought for a moment then burst out laughing, 'Esteron is not a Warhorse and I am not a King.'

Mulcade, who had been sitting quietly on the chimney beam, shrieked, hooted and stooped to perch on Thane's shoulder.

'Well, that part of the story's true,' chuckled Tombel, stretching a hand towards Mulcade, but the owl screeched, stabbing his beak into Tombel's middle finger. Thane stared in horror at the bleeding finger, expecting Tombel to strike the owl in rage, but he merely let the hand fall, forgotten, to his side, saying, 'You see, Thane, Mulcade protects you, even if the legend is not the truth, rumour is enough to get you killed. Deliver the letter as the King asked.'

Thane rose to his feet and looked out of the window at the blizzard that had started while they talked.

'Do I leave tonight?' he asked.

Tombel joined him at the window and for a moment watched the swirling snowflakes.

'No, Thane. Winter darkness is a dangerous time to travel and you do not need its cloak to hide beneath. From now on you will take the crown of the road, using every precious hour of sunlight to reach Underfall. You shall winter here at Woodsedge and learn the history of Elundium, and I shall send you to Gildersleeves as soon as it stops snowing. Duclos, the Swordsman, lives there with his wife, Morolda, in a house full of cats. He will teach you to use your sword better than any fencing master in all Elundium. Now see your horse to bed and join us in the Eating Hall for supper.'

'Do you eat every daylight?' Thane asked as he moved towards the door.

Tombel smiled, 'I will answer your question truthfully, young man, and then ask you a question in return. Marchers

139

eat when they can upon the road, using their daggers as knives and their fingers as forks, but when at home we eat every daylight, we break the fast in early daylight, noon food in the middle of the day and feast or supper before we go to bed depending on the occasion. How do you eat and toast your guests in the Granite City? Surely it is the same, or perhaps customs have changed with the passing suns?'

Thane blushed, seeing clearly the reference to the fingerbowl.

'Lord,' he replied, gathering his courage and looking Tombel squarely in the eye, 'At home in my father's house there is only one tool to eat with, that is a spoon carved from a broken saddle tree that grandfather had thrown away. There is only one wooden bowl, we shared it, passing it from mouth to mouth, drinking the watery gruel and toasting our luck to have even that. I have never seen such things to eat, or felt so many different tastes as those put before me last night. Yet in all the joy and honour of the feast I was ashamed of my lack of manners. But Elionbel rescued me, and helped me, whispering what tools to use and which plate to eat from.'

'And the fingerbowl?' asked Tombel, 'was that her idea to make a fool of you, or maybe to make fools out of all of us?'

'Lord, I drank without prompting, out of ignorance.'

'Perhaps,' sighed Tombel, still a little suspicious, not of Thane but of Elionbel's part in it. He knew how she loved to tease his Marchers.

Later that evening, towards the end of suppertime, talk turned to Thane's grandfather and his adventures on the Greenways.

'Oh, he pledged me to secrecy,' laughed Tombel, 'but that was before he passed into the shadows, now I shall bring him back to be amongst us here tonight.'

'How will you do that?' asked Thane leaning forwards in surprise.

'A person only dies when there is nobody left to remember them. That is the moment of true death. All the while we talk of Thoron he is here in the pictures we make in our hearts, here in this room or anywhere amongst a group of Marchers who are, perhaps, gathered around a camp fire, or wherever his name is called. There he still lives. We will all see him differently, but he will be amongst us, striding across the room, laughing, his iron jacket a-glitter in the candle-light.'

Thane saw him as he listened to Tombel's voice, dusty and tired at the end of a long road and his eyes filled with tears as he saw how roughly he had treated him on his rare visits to the Granite City. How, unthinking, he had begged him to take him to the top of the Granite Towers or down the countless winding steps to fish in the Great Lundium river, and all the other thousand places he had insisted on seeing. Silently he wept, hiding his head in his hands. Tombel touched his shoulder and broke the dream.

'I cannot control what you see, Thane, that power only the Soothsayers have.'

'I saw how thoughtlessly I treated him,' Thane whispered. 'I would have loved him just as much if we had sat in a quiet courtyard, while he rested.'

'No, Thane, you did not hard press him in selfishness, he wanted you to see and feel and touch everything in the innocence of childhood. He foresaw the Chancellors' rise to power and used what little time you had together, filling each moment with precious memories. Rejoice and laugh for that is how he would wish it now.'

Through short days winter deepened beneath a heavy snowy blanket and harsh winds pushed powdery snow flakes into deep, impassable drifts that blocked all the roads and would overtake any foolish traveller with a white and frozen death. This Thane, through luck, circumstance and gentle tugs on

141

the strings of fate, dodged, avoiding Nature's bitter test and weathered out the worst of the winter at Woodsedge, within the circle of Tombel's care, and learned much that would help him on the road to Underfall. He discovered his first feelings of love for Elionbel and felt confused by the way it made him feel both strong and weak and filled his head with dizzy thoughts that made Underfall seem far away and unimportant.

Tombel saw how Thane and Elionbel were drawn together, saw Thane tangle-tongued, awkward and shy whenever Elionbel turned her eyes upon him, and he saw a shining, laughing light in her that chased any doubts away that he might have. Tombel called Elionbel to his trophy room and faced her with his fears.

'He is the Candleman's son, born in the lower circles of the city. You are a Marcher's daughter, high-born to this Wayhouse. Elionbel, oh Elionbel, how could you think of him as more than just your rescuer?'

Elionbel's face flushed with anger, 'He was good enough to save my life, and you gave him the Honour Chair. And what of his grandfather? Isn't that high-born enough?'

Tombel laughed harshly, 'Thoron was not high-born, girl, fate or chance plucked him out of the lower circle of the city when he rescued Amarch as a foal from a pack of wolves. He was not born a Galloper. Why, if the bond between them had been broken he would have returned after that battle at World's End into the shadows of the Granite City to become a Server, Candleman, Buryman or perhaps, if he had been lucky, a Breaker.'

'I thought he was your friend, so close he was to you that you almost shared the same shadow. I thought you loved him,' Elionbel whispered, close to tears.

'Love!' replied Tombel, fiercely, gripping Elionbel's arm. 'I loved him, child, like a brother and matched him blade for blade against the Nightbeasts. High or low-born, it did not

142

matter, we were warriors together and fought a common enemy, but you are of my blood and I forbid you to look on Thane as an equal.'

'How shall I look upon him then?' she cried. 'As our Candleman, and snap my fingers when the sun sinks out of sight and then throw scraps to him at supper time?'

'Child, child, treat him as a warrior, with much respect, even as a friend. But I beg you, turn your heart away, turn it towards Ethric's son, or either of Arfon's boys, they are Marchers, born of this Wayhouse, and worthy of you.'

'Worthy!' she laughed bitterly, turning towards the door. 'You have always taught me to measure a person by their heart, not by the cut of their cloak or the treasure they hoard. Now I see the truth in your heart here in your treasure room!'

Tombel angrily lifted his hand to strike Elionbel, but a shrill screech from the chimney beam stopped him. Looking up he saw Mulcade's unblinking stare and uneasily looked away. Elionbel smiled up at Mulcade and he softened his stance, blinking in the firelight.

'I will do as you bid, father, and treat Thane as my rescuer and show him the honour that he deserves, but I will not change the way I value others or look upon the Servers, or anyone else in this Wayhouse, any differently. I shall still measure by the heart and the straight look in their eyes just as Thane's grandfather did, and I know that he loved us both without weighing out or measuring our worth.'

Before Tombel could answer his daughter she had crossed the threshold, slammed the door and run, sobbing, to her room. During the darkest hour of the night Elionbel gathered the courage to creep down into the Great Hall and remove the scarf from Thane's saddle. The next morning, in greatest secrecy, she began to thread her needle, but her bandaged hands made it impossible. She dropped the thread, and burying her head in the scarf she wept.

143

'Elionbel!' a soft voice whispered, 'Elionbel, greatheart, look on the bed beside you and you will find two needles already threaded, one with silver and one with gold. Use them well and needlepoint all your love upon the scarf.'

Elionbel looked up and saw for a fleeting moment a rainbow cloak dissolving in the sunlight that streamed through her window.

'Use them well!' the fading voice called out.

'Nevian!' Elionbel whispered, reaching out to pick up the golden thread. An old face smiled at her, full of gentle care, the sun disappeared behind black snow clouds, throwing her room into deepest shadow. The thread glittered and shone, seeming to catch and hold any speck of light in the darkened room. 'Magic!' she laughed, working the needle through the weave of the scarf.

Tombel was deeply troubled by Elionbel's answers and paced the trophy room for two daylights, thinking on all she had said. On the third daylight, his mind made up, he sent for Thane and sat him by the fire.

'I set great value on you, Thane,' he said, 'and I would be a selfish fool to keep you from Duclos the Swordsman a moment longer. The weather has eased a little, you shall journey to Gildersleeves today, without further delay. Go, and saddle your horse!'

Thane rose, and glanced out of the window into a darkening snowstorm.

'Lord, have I displeased you in some way?'

Tombel gave a short laugh, 'Nothing displeases me, Thane, except the fear that you will not be ready and well prepared to continue your journey when the snow melts. This snow storm will clear within the hour, follow the Greenway as it skirts the edge of the black forest, after travelling for half a daylight a small track will appear between the trees, follow it until you reach Gildersleeves.'

Thane felt the change in Tombel's manner and saw

144

beneath the smiles and the laughter a coldness he could not understand. He felt pushed and hurried as he saddled Esteron and led him out on to the Greenway.

'Remember, Thane, keep to the Greenway,' Tombel shouted against the rising wind.

# Gildersleeves

Thane shivered and drew the cloak tightly around his shoulders, bowing his head and screwing up his eyes against the storm. After travelling for many hours he felt with numb fingers for the scarf, searching in all his pockets before realizing he must have set out without it. He remembered leaving it tied on to the saddle in the Great Hall and now regretted being so careless. He almost turned back towards Woodsedge but a clear picture formed in his mind of the cold look in Tombel's eyes and he pressed on miserably for Gildersleeves. The snow storm gradually lessened, Mulcade and Rockspray shook their feathers, dislodging the settled snow flakes and lifted into the grey afternoon air to search out the way. They smelled and heard the distant danger long before they saw it. Rising on an icy wind they saw far below the shadow of a man fighting for his life, long thin blade whirling in his hand, surrounded by many foes. He danced a graceful circle in the snow as he cut and thrust, his left hand on his hip but he could not for long outfence so many ugly looking brutes. Mulcade swooped low and fast, just above the ground, the quickest way back to Esteron.

'Come, Equestrius' son, we have work to do,' he screeched. Esteron flattened back his ears and lengthened his stride.

Thane sensed trouble from the owl's call and forgot the numbing cold as Esteron forged forwards through the deep snow drifts. Clumsily he drew his borrowed sword and grabbed the mane, his reins falling in a tangled knot.

'I'm not cut out for this sort of thing,' he thought. Behind heavy snow-covered trees he heard the ring of steel and cursing shouts. Esteron roared out a challenge that shook Thane in the saddle and set his teeth rattling in his head.

Duclos was fighting for his life against so many coarser blades

149

that a few more cuts or blows and he would be theirs. The snowy ground silenced Esteron's footfalls as he galloped in towards the robber band, charging straight at their leader. Suddenly his ear-splitting neighing roar made their captain spin round as Esteron rode him down, a brief glimpse of the galloping horse and the flash of bright metal and he was dead and trampled in the snow. Esteron checked his pace, wheeled and reared to strike again. Thane swung his sword and almost sliced off Esteron's ear, but the sword found its mark upon a robber's neck.

'Kingsman!' the shout went up and panic spread amongst the evil band. Mulcade stooped and tore off a nose, Rockspray removed an eye. Esteron kicked and bit, while Thane held on tightly to the saddle. But the day was won. Some wounded villains made the safety of the woods but many lay dead upon the bloodstained snow.

'Kingsman, I thank you!' rang out an oddly musical voice. The intonation and emphasis seemed out of key but the owner of the voice looked even odder. Thin, of medium height, a wrinkled, happy face set either side with large, jug-handled ears, full of tufted hair. Heavy, horn-rimmed spectacles balanced near the tip of a dented nose behind which twinkled quick honest eyes. The Swordsman bowed his nose until it almost touched the snow to show a shiny dome, without a single hair. Straightening up he took a graceful step, turned his rapier blade faster than a wink and laid the hilt upon Thane's knee.

Again the voice began to rise and fall, 'Duclos, the Swordsman, once Fencing Master of the King, now at your service, young warrior of the roads!' Duclos laughed, sheathing his rapier. He inspected the young horseman from head to foot, casting his expert eye over him. He judged that the lad must be the one that Arbel was telling him about, there could never be two such well-mounted riders at Woodsedge.

'Come, Sir, follow and learn a little of how to swing that blade you carry.' Duclos paused a moment, looking hard at

150

Thane's sword arm before turning to disappear between the trees. He did not wait to hear or answer any of Thane's questions for deafness had cruelly shut him out of Elundium long ago. He had grown too impatient with the rudeness and the mistakes he made to waste time trying to read other people's lips. Deafness had driven him from the Granite City to seek safety within the circle of Tombel's care less than a day's march from Woodsedge.

Esteron traced the nimble swordsman's steps into the undergrowth and followed a neat and well-trimmed path. Thane sat nervous and alert in the saddle, the owls dug their talons into the metal shirt and watched the path ahead. It widened into a lawn-filled clearing, ringed with well-pruned snow covered trees; box hedges made an inner ring, each hedge sculptured to the figure of a fencing man, and in the clearing's centre stood a fairy tale house made up of turrets, balconies and windowed galleries, a jumble of the most amazing styles of architecture that Thane had ever seen. Hanging baskets filled with winter flowers, vines and creepers twisted up the walls and along winding stone-flagged paths.

A booming voice made Esteron jump, the owls flapped their wings and hung on tight, 'Ah ha! Duclos! The boy is here . . . with some birds on his shoulders. Where is that confounded man? Dancing about fencing with the cats again I shouldn't wonder, I'll have to tie his toes together. Come on, boy, you'll frighten the cats away with the horse and the birds, whatever next?'

Morolda, Duclos' sole companion, except for his collection of tail-less cats, arrived breathless in front of Esteron. It was difficult to see her shape, wrapped as she was in so many flowing silks that she billowed as she moved. A hand appeared, heavily ringed with glittering stones, and waited impatiently to be kissed. 'Cat got your manners, boy?' All this talk of cats disturbed the owls who, as Thane nervously dismounted, flew to perch in the trees that ringed the snowy lawn.

151

Thane did not manage to kiss the hand; one foot touched the ground and he tripped over his sword and fell in a heap. Soft hands pulled him to his feet, firmly jamming his helmet back to front down past his ears.

'Silly, clumsy boy. Come, let us find Duclos before another cat loses its tail!'

Thane now stood in total darkness, unable to see through the helmet's rim that covered his eyes, stuck fast, and foolishly he tugged at the metal hat.

Esteron snorted behind him. Something rubbed and wound itself between his legs, pushing at his boots. Visions of serpents coiling in a death lock made him panic. 'Blast this confounded helmet,' he shouted, kicking out in fear and anger. There was a hissing shriek, but his boot found nothing but empty air. He toppled with a crash that rattled his skull from side to side. The final thump dislodged the iron cap which rolled away across the lawn, sunlight made him blink and then stare, gaping foolishly around himself for dozens of sleek black cats stalked or sat around him on the lawn. Their purring shook the ground, curiosity drew them ever closer. Never had Thane seen so many cats, each with a silver collar, most of them without a tail. Esteron arched his neck, snorted and stamped his feet, but the cats stood their ground. As one, their heads turned, the purring reached a roar.

Duclos danced across the lawn, 'My boy! My brave knight! Don't just sit there talking to the cats, come, bring your horse, come!'

Thane rose, feeling foolish, and followed in procession a line of gleaming cats; Esteron reluctantly brought up the rear, pulling hard against the reins. Shadows fell across the lawn thrown there by a setting sun, all too soon the day had fled away.

'Well, at least we have reached Gildersleeves before night-fall!' After all Tombel's tutoring, the last thing Thane wanted was a night in the open; but who was this Duclos, retired fencing-master and keeper of so many cats? How many spells had he woven to make such an enchanting house? And who was Morolda? Was she Duclos' keeper, or was she a wicked witch? He wished the weight of the owls were on his shoulders, they would know what to do.

As if in answer to his thoughts, a long low hoot broke the early evening stillness. It seemed to say, 'Fear not a man with an owl upon his arm.' Tombel carried the mark, but Thane had not seen one on Duclos' arm – but then he hadn't looked.

If Thane thought the outside of the house enchanting, the interior took his breath away. A living garden grew up every wall and overflowed in creeping vines of many colours across the ceilings, pots of every shape and size filled every corner and overflowed across the floors. Such perfume and colour overcame Thane's senses. Duclos and the cats nimbly negotiated the flowers and plants, but Esteron and Thane overturned three heavy tubs in the entrance. Thane hesitated to take a further step, Esteron pulled back, broke free and stood well outside the door. 'No Woodsedge welcome here,' thought Thane, missing Tombel's friendly face.

'Silly clumsy boy!' Morolda's voice was softer now, all smiles and mothering charm, 'Duclos thinks I frightened you! Silly man. He thinks I frighten the cats, but who can frighten cats?' There seemed to be no end to the flow of Morolda's chatter. When Thane knew her better, he understood the relief of having an ear to listen to all she had to say. Morolda, through love for Duclos, shared his silence, spoke over-loudly, carefully forming the words with her lips, and with quick fingers drew the letters that made up the words that passed between them. She had not allowed Duclos' exile to drive him mad through idleness and isolation, she had kept him busy breeding cats, fencing with their shadows and building extravagant new follies to practise his sword play in. Morolda was the mother of invention, the power behind the rapier blade. Love had moved the forest back and chased away the bitterness that had nearly

153

overwhelmed the greatest swordsman in all Elundium when deafness had stopped both his ears, and, for a long while, destroyed his balance too. Her energy engulfed Thane and Esteron. She organized an outbuilding for Esteron which had a neat well-trimmed lawn for a bed, and hanging baskets full of the sweetest lucerne grass. 'Now mind you don't spoil the lawn with too many nasty hoof prints.'

Much to Thane's surprise, Esteron seemed to like Moralda, and let her pull his ears. Thane was propelled back into the house, this time through an open window, scattering cats in all directions. 'Quicker than the door, and fewer plants for you to kick over! I'm going to tie Duclos' leg to the table and you can tell me all about yourself, your birds and where you are going. He cannot hear you so I will tell him everything you have to say; but if he asks you anything, have patience, look directly at him and speak slowly, forming the words with your lips. Do not be shy!'

With his spectacles perched on the tip of his nose and munching a bowl of cress, Duclos did not look up until Thane was seated opposite him. 'Welcome, little knight; a name, my hero must have a name!'

'Thane.'

'Plane? That's a strange name for such a handsome lad.'

Moralda gently took control of the conversation and prompted Thane to answer slowly, and, with her fingertalk, unfolded all Thane's adventures thus far along the road to Underfall. Never once did she lose patience with Duclos' muddled understanding of the tale, and as the evening wore away, she cleverly edged Thane to answer without her help. Just like old times Duclos talked, laughed and sang, it didn't seem to matter how much he really understood, he had someone to talk to who had the patience to listen and to answer all his questions.

Thane was enthralled with Duclos' tales and hardly noticed his disability. Candles melted, overflowing on to the table in frozen streams of wax. Thane sleepily yawned. Morolda had long been asleep, her head resting on a fat black cat. Duclos, tireless in his quest for company, had forgotten how late it was and suddenly noticed his guest falling fast asleep where he sat. He leapt up, dragging the table with him. Crashing plates and spilling cups tumbled down the table top, washing in a mucky tide around Morolda's snoring head.

She rose, startled and raging, from her sleep, tangled locks of hair stuck to her face, fists clenched. 'Block the doors! Pull up the bridge! Arm the cats!' she shouted. She took much shaking before she was full awake, and what a sight they both made. There was bedraggled Morolda sticking to her silks, and Duclos still tied to the table, towing it around as he grabbed at towels to dry his loved one.

Thane laughed aloud, remembered his manners and put a hand across his face. Morolda regained her self control, gathered up her dignity amidst a tangle of half-eaten food. 'Silly man! Even if you tie him down, havoc dances with him.' But the twinkle was back in her eyes so great a love flowed between them.

None of the dignity of a great Marcher Captain existed at Gildersleeves; it was all theatre and chaotic fun. Even putting Thane to bed smacked of the pantomime. Morolda ran from gallery to gallery, gathering linen and sleeping rugs, singing and shouting as she dashed about. Cats used up many lives as she danced past. Sleep came easier than Thane expected in the Fencing Master's house. Owls hooted in the woods and lulled him safe to sleep and all night long the green-eyed cats patrolled. Fear of this silent feline army kept many foes away and gave the fairy-tale house a little peace to sleep secure in a troubled land.

Bright sunlight broke through the leaves that crowded around Thane's window. Warm and sleepy, stretching in the feather bed, he disturbed a dozen cats, who jumped to the floor hissing and spitting. He had not realized he had so many guardians through the night. Duclos, keen for company, hurried Thane through a hasty breakfast, eaten on the move. Today he had a pupil and itched to teach the mastering of the glittering blade. 'Take off that metal shirt, top boots and cloak. Here, lad, put on this padded suit and metal face guard worn by the masters of this art.'

Changed and ready to learn he found the new clothes fitted him well, and he soon forgot how foolish he looked as the sweat dripped and the muscles ached as he began to dance the Master's steps. With knuckles raw and nicked through clumsiness he trod the piste, for Duclos was quicker than a shadow and harder to catch. Before the morning ran to noon Morolda re-appeared with long kid gloves for Thane to wear that reached almost to his elbows, they took the rapier's needle point but nothing could ease the cuts he took to learn the Master's skills. The hours blurred together as repetition taught Thane the fencing moves, neat, small and accurate he became in flesche or parry to match Duclos' blade. He learned to riposte, reprise and disengage, but in the early hours and days 'touché' became the common call and many bruises and bumps showed where he had been caught off guard. But learn he did, and with new fighting skills, grace and balance became second nature. The counter moves became a game, as Gildersleeves echoed to the clash of steel and shouts of 'advance, quarte, sixte, counter, parry,' up and down the stairs, along the galleries and the quiet, flowered walkways. Laughter filled all the corners where the cats had crept to hide, but sport became hard work and kept Duclos on his toes, for Thane had a natural aptitude and already showed the makings of a great swordsman.

Early afternoons saw Thane back in the saddle, and peace and safety flourished wherever Esteron strode, but exercise was foremost in Thane's mind to ease the aching thighs and tired wrists, and feel the biting winter wind upon his face. Little by little, he became aware how much his new found skills helped his balance in the saddle. Esteron felt lighter between his knees and responded to the merest touch, and now that lightness showed how much the horseman he had become. He took the bit and ran with joy through deep snowdrifts in the woods and along the tangled tracks near the fencing master's house. But all too soon night pushed the winter sun to bed and Thane was called to supper beneath the hanging lamps of Gildersleeves.

Mealtimes were a riot of fun, Morolda saw to that. Tiredness turned aside, as dance or song, or serious talking, moved within the candle's flame, for she had once been a great soothsayer, and still held the enchantress' gift for weaving magic in the mind and building castles in the air for those who hung upon her words. Even Duclos, through her finger talk, could visit the places of their dreams. Drowsiness would catch Thane unawares amongst the purring cats that rubbed around his tired legs or dangling hands, for there was music in the voices that lulled away the early hours before the dawn came. First light had Thane on the fighting floor, rapier or sabre in his hand. Quickly he had grasped the moves and counter-moves beneath the watchful Fencing Master's eye. Now daring attacks pushed Thane into jumping the stairs and landing lightly on his feet; parry fast and clean, leap through windows, beat wide a path with flashing steel, or plunge from a chandelier, blade between his teeth, then escape to fight again. And fight he did, whenever Duclos crossed his blade.

Soon Thane would be ready for the road again, and better matched to continue his journey. In sadness Morolda knew he had to go. Fate had pulled him to Gildersleeves, now fate must set the steps he was to follow on that dreadful road to Underfall. The very name had her shivering in her silks and reaching for a woolly shawl. 'Duclos will miss him when he has gone,' she whispered to the cats, and as an afterthought added, 'So shall I.'

But neither Duclos nor Morolda showed sorrow as the last

157

fencing lesson began, and both knew that there was no more to learn when Thane's blade touched the embroidered silk heart on Duclos' padded jacket. Both blades disengaged; 'My dear boy, you are now the Master.' For the first time since Thane's arrival, he noticed again the odd musical intonation in Duclos' voice, he dropped his sword and embraced his teacher.

'No, Master, you will always be the greater,' he said slowly, forming the words carefully with his lips, 'For you taught me. If I draw the blade it will always be your hand that guides it.'

The last supper at Gildersleeves was the merriest, the noisiest and the longest. Duclos hid the grief he felt at Thane's departure in laughing, fun-filled stories from his youth, and no mention touched his lips of Underfall. Tucked into the sleeve of his flowing shirt he had a gift for Thane that in his youth had kept him safe upon the Causeway road and had helped him win the tattoo upon his arm. It was a simple dagger made of steel, forged with cunning, tempered hard, forever sharp, it never spoiled or showed a spot of rust. When thrust, it had pierced the Nightbeasts' armoured skins where other blades had snapped, and for a moment, long ago, it had held the balance of a King's battle beneath the walls of Underfall.

Morning cast shadows across the snow covered lawns of Gildersleeves as heavy-hearted goodbyes were said. Duclos took Thane's hand and placed the hilt of the dagger in it. 'When hope has fled, and Nightbeasts press on every side, push back despair, unsheath this little blade, for it knows nothing of defeat and will inspire the hand that holds it. Legend says that Duronal, the Master Armourer, hammered out its edge upon an oaken anvil, long before the Granite Kings arose. Use it well, my lad!'

Duclos turned and with him stalked the cats of Gildersleeves back into a silent world of sorrow, but Morolda stayed a moment, stirrup cup in hand, for she saw the pain of parting touch them both. 'Fret not, young Thane, spring came again for Duclos while he taught you the swordsman's strokes, and you gave him an even greater gift, for now the Fencing Master walks again with dignity. His gift to you was his greatest treasure, and the only tool of war I dared not use to trim or weed the garden. Fencing shadows may again fill Duclos' daylight hours, but during supper times the power in my words will paint you in his mind. Now ride back to Woodsedge, tread carefully on this dangerous turf, for soon the snows will melt.'

As an afterthought she added, almost to herself, 'Stay safe, my little knight.'

Thane heard Morolda's final words since her voice rang clear across the lawns of Gildersleeves and echoed back from the trees that pressed all around that beautiful garden. He knelt, gently took her bejewelled hand and, this time with easy grace, kissed it.

Esteron had stood quietly waiting while goodbyes were said; now he stepped forwards, and blew gently through his nostrils against Morolda's cheek. She pulled his ears a final time: 'Birds, boy and horse, whatever next. Begone, before I cry!'

Thane checked Esteron's stride at the lawn's edge, Mulcade and Rockspray were back on their shoulder perches, and he looked back just in time to see Morolda, silks billowing, striding back into that elfin castle. 'Well, my Battle Birds, there seems more magic on the roads than ever I dreamed of.'

Leaving Gildersleeves with a heavy heart Thane trudged through the melting snow towards Woodsedge. The trees on the forest edge looked pinched and blackened as if they had shrunk against the winter weather but at the tips of all their branches new buds were swelling in readiness for the spring. Cold and shivering, Thane hammered on the Wayhouse door and readily took the seat nearest to the fire and warmed his fingers while he told Tombel of the fencing lessons and the fairy-tale house of Gildersleeves.

'Did he really break the shadow circle?' Thane asked,

watching Tombel's eyes, searching for that coldness that had been there the day he had left for the Swordsman's house. Tombel smiled at Thane, his eyes softening, full of gentle humour.

'It was wonderful to watch, Thane, the way he jumped and leapt between the shadows, his blades flashing in the sunlight and his clear voice leading the warriors of Elundium. Yes, he broke the circle, and for a moment held Krulshards at sword's point but the Master of Darkness dodged the blade and cupping his foul hands to his black mouth he shouted in Duclos' face. We heard the shout a league away. The sky darkened and the Nightbeast army swayed like hideous stalks of corn before a storm and the noise shattered Duclos' eardrums, destroying his balance. Nevian found him as dawn was breaking and pledged me to watch after him all his days. Yes, Thane, he did break the circle.'

Servers then announced the evening meal. 'Come, young man,' smiled Tombel, 'come and eat with us for soon you must take the road and travel past Gildersleeves, through the black forest and the grasslands beyond to the tower on the summit of Stumble Hill, and then . . .'

'Father . . .' the clear voice of Elionbel called from the stair head, 'Let me take the arm of my rescuer and lead the way in to supper.'

Anger flashed clearly in Tombel's eyes and he moved to step between Thane and the stairway. Elionbel laughed, descending to face her father.

'Surely you must keep the bargain and treat Thane with all the honour of my rescuer? That is what you bid me to do!'

Turning to face Thane, but keeping her eyes fixed on her father, she took Thane's arm and secretly squeezed it. Supper was less formal than the grand affair of the Honour Chair. The Chair had been removed and the two lower tables had been drawn together. Thane had watched carefully at each mealtime and had quickly learned the customs and manners of the

160

Wayhouse Marchers and now he felt much more at ease with the array of eating tools, plates and cups put before him. Elionbel smiled, and talked freely to those about her and gave Thane all the honour he deserved, while Tombel sat quietly avoiding all conversation, intent, it seemed, upon his meat.

'Marchers!' he said at length, waiting for the table talk to die away. 'The thaw has set in, within seven daylights our guest, Thanehand, will take the road to Underfall. Use that time to check the way is safe for him. Scour the forest and teach him what woodcraft you can.'

Pewter cups were raised to toast the start of the journey and Elionbel turned and, smiling, raised her cup, 'To my rescuer's return.'

Thane was kept busy throughout the remaining days of his stay at Woodsedge, learning to build a fire ring against attack, to track or follow scent, or find a path through unbroken forest, and in the evening times Tombel kept him in the trophy room eating with him while he told him tales by the firelight of far off places, and showed him fragile flowers, blades of strange grasses or chips of wood or stone suspended in pieces of clear crystal, some so small that Tombel had to pass the eye lens for Thane to see more clearly the beauty trapped within the glass.

'How are they put into the crystal?' Thane asked, turning a crystal flower between his finger and thumb and watching the colour change in the firelight.

'Fairday is the Crystal Maker,' replied Tombel, 'but setting trinkets and trophies in glass shows nothing of his skills, Thane. Fairday is the Master of many secrets. Look at this,' he cried, unlocking a dark cupboard in the corner of the room and bringing forth a heavy chunk of crystal that required all his strength to move.

Thane stared in horror at the crystal. A gasp choked his throat and rapid heartbeats drummed in his ears. Darkness overcame the firelight as he tried to look away. A steady strong hand on his shoulder pulled him back.

161

'Look long, Thane, on this freak of nature that once again plagues the world. Do not touch the glass, none know if any power remains trapped within the crystal or what will be the consequences if the glass is cracked!'

Thane gathered up his courage to raise his eyes back to the glass.

'Easy boy, hold your courage. Steady, here, grip the hilt of the sword that slew him. The eyes that hold your gaze once held the power to freeze you paralysed or drove men mad enough to kill themselves. But now it holds only a malice to search out weakness in those that dare to look into the glass; it keeps the hatred, despite being frozen in the crystal. I buried all its spoils of human flesh that hung about its belt after I had slain the beast. Look now upon his face, and know your enemy. For many have gone before you without the privilege of knowing what they fought, and in the press of battle come face to face with a fear that they could not master. Those you fought within the hollow were brothers to this beast.'

As Tombel tutored Thane the head in the glass began to lose some of its menace and dead-eyed stared out from its prison. Hairy skin was drawn tight across its formless face, two blackened, dribbling nostrils overhung a snarling mouth whose lips stretched back to expose needle sharp yellow teeth. The eyes, red-veined and huge, glistened in the firelight and seemed to follow Thane wherever he moved.

'Nightbeasts!' Thane whispered, his voice dry, crackling in his throat.

'Know your enemy!' repeated Tombel, removing the crystal to its resting place and returning to his chair beside the fire.

'In the days and suns that followed the bondbreaking and the battle for World's End your grandfather and I and all those with the tattoo mark scoured Elundium for the Nightbeasts. We looked in every dark hole, underneath each stone. It was a time of terrible slaughter for we slew every Nightbeast we found until we had rid the world of them. But in all our care we feared we may have missed some and we sat many long watches, waiting, but each night was empty and passed peacefully. The sun rose clear and bright in the morning and we grew forgetful. Thane, beware! These creatures are once more loose in Elundium and the bearers of the tattoo mark are scattered and cannot help you. You must ride alone!'

'Lord, with your blessing I must start the journey soon, before fear makes me seek a safe hole to hide in.'

Tombel laughed, and gripped Thane's arm. 'Holes are the last place to hide, my boy, Nightbeasts love the dark. No, no, take the high ground with the sun at your back, there you will stand a chance. Off to bed with you now, at first daylight your journey begins!'

Thane descended the great stairway for the last time, sad to leave yet anxious for the road. Esteron waited, saddled, by the door, and at his head stood Elionbel.

Nearby Tombel, Martbel and their sons waited in a group, the men had dressed for battle as a mark of honour, for today Thane would ride beyond their safety and they feared for him on that dark road.

Thane crossed the hall, Martbel wiped away a tear and reminded him of his mother. Rubel and Arbel teased him lightly to stay awake and keep to the road, but Tombel held him in a last minute counsel of the road and lastly pressed into his hands the hilt of the sword he had used in the hollow saying, 'Our gift and blessing be always at your side to blaze aloft and make your courage strong, Keeper of the Hollow. Your blade!'

'What a beautiful, beautiful gift,' whispered Thane, gripping the hilt.

'Use it well, young man,' laughed Tombel, the Keeper of Woodsedge, 'for you earned the right to carry such a blade when you rescued Elionbel. It is yours now to use against the Nightbeasts on the road ahead.'

Thane drew the sword from its scabbard and found engraved along the blade his name and the legend of the sword, 'Thanehand, the Shadow Breaker, who brought sunlight in the morning and drove the Nightbeasts out.'

'Make haste, Thane,' Tombel urged, 'cover every league you can while daylight lasts, and speed back to us if you can one day. Kingspeed upon the Greenway turf.'

Thane turned and stepped through the doorway as shafts of early sunlight broke through the clouds, casting a shining halo in Elionbel's golden hair. She smiled softly and put into his hands the summer scarf she had secretly taken from his saddle.

'Read it,' she whispered, helping him to carefully spread out the scarf. Thane blushed redder than the sun and guessed the hours of love and pain the embroidery must have taken, for lovingly worked in threads of gold and silver along the borders and around the picture of the sun, ran the tale of Elionbel's rescue. It spoke of her love for the great warrior who had jumped the ring of trees and fought his way to her side and of how Esteron, a lord amongst horses, had stood between her and the Nightbeasts' spears and who had carefully carried her home when the battle was won.

'Candleman is said in silver letters. I am pledged to silence, yet my heart will shout with joy to hear your footsteps on the Greenway's edge. Come swiftly back to me when your task is done.'

Thane felt her love, and saw it in her eyes. He tied the summer scarf to his armoured arm and quickly mounted Esteron, and from his high seat looked down into those beautiful eyes, a smile crossed his face and he leaned down and whispered, 'I shall return, though all the world's darkness stands between us. I love you, Elionbel.'

Esteron pawed the ground and snorted, snatching at the bridle.

'I will return,' he shouted. The owls stooped to settle on his shoulders. A roaring neigh, a flash of sun sparkling the mail beneath his cloak, his banner, rippling with the speed, floating out behind and then Thane was gone, pacing out the leagues to Underfall.

Tombel looked darkly at the forest edge where it pressed hard upon the Greenway. 'Trouble stirs everywhere, mark my words. There are dark times ahead for all of us.'

# The Border Runners

Thus far the road had been easy to follow for Tombel's Marchers had mowed the turf and pruned the edge but as Gildersleeves diminished with each measured hoof-beat, the trees pressed harder on to the road and in places arched high above Thane's head. Dull clouds hid the sun, gloom dampened a spring afternoon and made him pull his cloak tightly about his shoulders. Mulcade and Rockspray flew ahead on silent wings, pausing often to search either side of the narrow road. Esteron turned his ears in every direction, listening for the slightest noise of danger in the tangled undergrowth. Afternoon wore on, and with it Thane's uneasiness grew stronger, they were not alone, that much he could feel, but what stalked him on either side was well hidden and he could not guess at their shapes. Esteron seemed suddenly to relax and pricked his ears, the owls returned to his shoulders and began a fussy preening. Mulcade even slept a little. Chill breezes heralded evening, and with the falling darkness, silence held its breath.

Snap! Crack! Thane's ears picked out the noises made by the pursuing beasts from just beyond the edge of his sight.

'Esteron, run! Pick us a space to stand and fight, there is no room to swing a sword in this narrow track. Run!'

Esteron did not change his pace. Thane searched his pockets for a spark, 'Light a ring of fire and stand within it' echoed Tombel's words. So far away from the safety of his friends, the woods about him seemed crowded and dark with a thousand foes. Dark shapes broke cover either side, amber and brown eyes caught the fading light. Hairy coats in sable, black and tan filled the narrow track. Sword drawn, Thane hesitated;

Esteron and the Battle Birds made no move to run or fight. The road widened into a large grass-covered clearing. Thane's fingers tingled from the tightness of his grip upon his sword's hilt but still he made no move. Something Tombel had said beside the fire in the trophy room came tumbling into his terror-stricken mind.

'The Border Runners,' Tombel had called them. 'Show no fear,' he had said. Sitting high as he did on Esteron's back some of those mighty Border Runners could brush against his boots. Thane felt more than fear, he felt total terror. There must be at least a hundred dogs crowding around his horse's legs, most of them looking directly up at Thane, tongues showing between rows of huge white teeth, their panting breath sending clouds of vapour up to mingle with the branches high above their heads.

Esteron reached the centre of a clearing and halted; before him stood three of the biggest dogs he had ever seen. They seemed Lords among the pack, and they stood as if waiting for Thane to do something or make some sort of move. He contemplated sitting the night out in the saddle, that seemed to be the only sensible choice apart from dismounting and risking being torn to pieces before his boots had touched the ground. But he need not have feared the Border Runners, for rumour of his coming had travelled fast from Woodsedge, and watchers on the roads had been set, for he would need many friends if he was to make Underfall intact.

The three great Border Runners moved aside and revealed a pile of broken sticks and twigs and with a hidden signal summoned others from the pack to carry kindling sticks in their jaws and place them upon the rapidly growing pile. The nearest dogs to Esteron lay or sat upon the ground, some with paws as large as Thane's hands, and stretched as if a long wait was over.

'I can't sit here all night,' whispered Thane. 'Grandfather would never forgive such rudeness, for he told me many tales of the courage of the Border Runners, and Tombel said that they were friends upon the road. I must dismount.'

With a lump in his throat and a thumping heart, Thane

170

dismounted and the Battle Birds stayed perched on his shoulders, for they knew the Border Runners as allies and did not fear them. The three great Border Runners waited until Thane stood before them; then they sniffed him, licked his face and hands and lifted their heads high and howled. Louder and louder grew the howling as all the dogs joined their voices and called to the clear patch of evening sky above the trees. Thane would have blushed with pride had he known the tale passing amongst the host for it spoke of Thoronhand, the greatest horseman, who nurtured and cared for all natural things who had fallen into the shadows, and of the boy now standing in their midst, who was the old warrior's grandson. 'Mark this well; we give honour to Thane, for he steps in the prints of Thoronhand and shall have comfort in the dark wherever the Border Runners gather.'

Long would have been the story, for Thoron was well known amongst the Border Runners and longer still with the added verses of Thane's journey thus far along the road to Underfall, but the howling stopped abruptly, hackles rose, the dogs' voices changed to snarls, lips curled back to expose rows of sharp, white teeth. Mulcade snatched at the spark, forgotten in Thane's hand, swooped and dropped it amongst the heap of sticks. The drier kindling twigs burst into flames, light danced within the clearing and reflected back from evil looking red eyes crowding in on every side as wicked scythes and spears shone in the firelight.

'Nightbeasts!' Thane shouted, drawing the Hollow Keeper's blade from its scabbard; in the other hand he gripped Duclos' dagger. Bright blazed the fire as the flames raced from branch to branch turning night into day, and long were the leaping shadows as the Border Runners fell on to the Nightbeasts, ripping and tearing at their hideous faces. The Warhorse challenge rang loud as Esteron reared and plunged amongst their armoured skins, crushing and killing all that fell beneath his hooves. Steely rang Thane's hammer blows upon their iron caps, sparks danced along his blades as they bit into the Nightbeasts' armour. Close beneath the jagged scythes he jumped, lunging, thrusting, using all the skills that he had learned. Mulcade and Rockspray blinded many, hooking eyes out with their bloody talons, but victory belonged to the Border Runners, for they drove the Nightbeasts back into the darkness of the woods and hunted them to death beyond the safety of the fire. Many did not return until the grey hours had lit the sky with ghostly light and they withdrew exhausted and bloody to lick their wounds.

Only the firelight danced in the clearing. Heaps of dead or dying Nightbeasts seemed to be everywhere Thane looked. Not all the dogs had pursued the fleeing Nightbeasts; many had stayed and now padded softly amongst the fallen, sniffing out the wounded. A snarl and then quick snapping or ripping teeth upon the monsters' necks dispatched them quickly. 'No prisoners' thought Thane, keeping his eyes on the fire. A giddy sickness swept over him, words from the past echoed in his mind about the Border Runners, 'The Nightwalkers cook them alive, torment them slowly over open fires.'

Still feeling a little sick, Thane busied himself collecting wood, and had a roaring bonfire of almost his own height before he remembered Esteron or the owls. Looking round he saw them a few paces away, Esteron pulling mouthfuls of grass, about to step on the reins, and Mulcade and Rockspray perched, one on the cantle and one on the pommel of the saddle. They seemed quite unperturbed by the final slaughter going on all around them.

'Well, my friends, I am glad we didn't meet those hideous beasts on our own!' Esteron snorted, Mulcade hooted and Rockspray transferred himself to Thane's shoulder, and rubbed his bloodied beak against Thane's cheek. Esteron did not seem harmed during the fight; untacked he continued to graze; the only blood spilled on the owls looked like that of the Nightbeasts, only a few feathers appeared ruffled. Tiredness

172

sat heavily on Thane's eyelids as he sat near the fire. He had intended to stay awake, watchful in case there were further attacks, but sleep crept up in gentle waves. The three great Border Runners moved close to him, one either side, and lay down to keep him warm, and the third became a pillow as Thane's head nodded back in dreamless sleep. What a story he would have had to tell if sleep had not robbed him of half the night. How as the hunters crept back into the clearing they had formed a great ring of sentinels about his sleeping body, each dog staring out into the black trees, for none would step near Thoron's grandson without their leave.

Morning sunlight cast leafy shadows across Thane's sleeping face. Mulcade pulled at a lock of hair. Waking with a start, Thane sat up quickly, rubbing his eyes, stretching stiff, numb limbs, for the road was no feather mattress.

'They have gone!' he called, not a single dog remained, even the carcasses of the Nightbeasts had been removed. Thane jumped up and searched the clearing; had he dreamed a night full of adventures? He rubbed his eyes again, felt for the hilt of his sword and found an empty space; the dagger was also missing from his belt. Looking near the fire where he had slept, he found them lying in the grass. When sleep had pulled him down they had slipped unnoticed from his hands. Dew sparkled on the steel, but sticky, drying blood spoiled both the blades. It was no dream in which the Nightbeasts overran the clearing, and he remembered clearly his first meeting with the Border Runners. Grandfather's stories had not exaggerated their power, or their dignity. Tombel had spoken of their unselfishness; in victory they had gone as magically as they had appeared. Sadness filled Thane, he wished he could have thanked his rescuers, rubbed his hands in their thick silky coats. He felt ashamed that sleep had made him seem discourteous, and most of all he knew that the Nightbeasts would have cut him down if he had been alone.

With Esteron ready for the road, Thane mounted; the Battle

173

Birds settled on his shoulders ready for the journey, but thirst rubbed at Thane's throat.

'We must find a brook or a stream, I feel dirtier than a chimney sweep after a week in the castle chimneys.'

Esteron followed the track out of the clearing. The forest looked more friendly, less oppressive, perhaps the sunlight pushed the trees back from the track, or filtering shafts of light broke up the gloom. Birds flew amongst the trees, insects hovered in the air and danced in the shafts of light. Today the jingle of the bridle bit rings blended with the forest sounds, where yesterday they had sounded out of key in the heavy silence before night closed in. Perhaps, thought Thane, terror drives the animals to hide when Nightbeasts are abroad. Sometimes far from the road between the trees Thane thought he caught a glimpse of the Border Runners, but he could not be sure. A flash of sable coat would cross the forest floor, or tangled brambles move without a breath of wind. The birds kept singing, and nowhere was there the fear of yesterday.

A different sound gradually caught Thane's ear as it rose in volume above the other forest voices. For some time Esteron had increased his stride, he had smelt what they badly needed, long before Thane recognized the sound. Cool sweet water, tumbling over stones and racing through the gravel beds of Bordern River. Down the bank they slid, knee deep; Thane laughed and splashed the clear water everywhere before drinking. Esteron sucked up the water with loud gulping sounds and the owls flew off to hunt the forest rodents. Thane's metal helm became a drinking bowl, and he drained it twice before his thirst was quenched.

Then as he stripped off his armour and washed off the journey's dirt, relaxed and happy, for an instant his concentration slipped. He was about to pull a tuft of grass to wash the Nightbeasts' blood from his sword and dagger, when something hit the bank beside his hand. A whining noise, angry like a wasp, gave just a second's warning of the deadly arrow.

174

Esteron charged across the brook, water spraying high above the saddle; he could have died, pierced by a storm of arrows already strung, for the robbers of Gildersleeves had laid a deadly trap. They had crept up to the silver brook, drawn by the midday laughter, as they had done many times before to catch unsuspecting travellers while they drank. They had waited, well hidden, while the owls flew away to hunt and Thane disarmed to wash. The first arrow had missed its mark. The big horse spoiled their plans by charging towards them across the water. Arrows were strung, strings pulled, but their aim was never taken. The Border Runners attacked. In one rush of leaping, canine might, the robbers fell beneath the snarling, ripping jaws. It was over in an instant, so quickly that Thane's hand did not reach the hilt of his sword, nor Esteron reach the other bank.

Thane waded across, shamefaced at being so careless as to need a second rescue. But it was a lesson well learned, for he would never kneel again to drink without a hand upon his sword or an eye upon the undergrowth. Mulcade and Rockspray swooped all too late and never again hunted together unless Thane and Esteron had the safety of a Wayhouse. Theirs was the gift of sight to search out safety on the roads and they sulked for days with each other over their carelessness.

The dogs were easy in victory, licking Thane's hands and face for they welcomed a chance to repay the old man of the roads. Much was still owed to Thoronhand for deeds performed along the Greenways. Curiosity drew Thane to look at his ambushers, wondering what type of man would kill an unarmed traveller on the road. The torn out windpipes sickened him, but they were hardly as gruesome or hideous as the Nightbeasts dead. He recognized two from the road near Gildersleeves; one wore an eye patch that covered Mulcade's talon mark, an empty socket still raw and wet with poison. It was doubtful that any would mourn their death.

'You have rid the world of much evil,' Thane said to the dogs as he turned to wade across the river and collect his clothes.

Thane dressed and re-armed, watched by the Border Runners; he tightened the girths and mounted Esteron. The way ahead was easy to follow, the forest soon came to an abrupt end. Open rolling country spread before them, clumps of dense trees stood sentry still, like forgotten chess pieces, knee deep in the wild grasslands. Nothing moved except the slender stalks of grass, bending before a light spring breeze. Silence stretched to the horizon's edge, broken only by skylarks singing far above them, mere specks in a limitless sky, and the swish of padded paws along the grassy track. The dogs spread out either side of the road, the owls flew ahead checking each tree-filled copse long before Esteron drew near them.

Thane broke the silence, it seemed quite natural to talk out loud to Esteron, the owls or even the dogs, if any broke cover long enough to listen, but those held by his voice tried not to be discourteous and break away too quickly for they were busy searching out the way. 'The Warhorses of yesteryear must have been great creatures to have run the gap between the Wayhouses in the space of just one day. I'll bet you could run that fast, Esteron,' Thane said, and added after a moment's reflection, 'Let us hope we are never put to the test.'

League after league passed beneath Esteron's hooves. The landscape did not seem to change, the grasslands marched to meet the setting sun which rested for a moment, angry red, upon the horizon's rim.

'Another night in the open,' thought Thane. Suddenly snarling barks had all the dogs leaping high above the stalky grass somewhere to the right in the shadows of a rambling copse. Thane wheeled Esteron round, drawing his sword which shone red, reflecting the glorious setting sun. Thane's heels drove Esteron forwards into the chest-high grass, galloping as hard as the tangled grass allowed. Giant Night-beasts reared up, hacking wildly at the Border Runners, but the dogs were badly hampered by the tangled grass. Thane counted three, one on the left, two on the right, his blade sung through the air as he swept it down upon the nearest scaly neck. He turned and galloped on to cut the next Nightbeast down but the third was more prepared and rushed at Thane. Cruel scythes swept in a bitter arch, but it was burdened by the dogs hanging with their jaws locked into its neck, Thane could not risk the sweeping stroke he had so carefully learned at Gildersleeves, the dogs were in the way. Low along Esteron's side he leaned, rein hand gripping tightly on to the pommel; his sword hand just above the pounding hooves, he drove his long sharp blade up through the monster's heart. Armour sparks burned his face as Esteron galloped past, the sword pierced right to the hilt and was wrenched from his hand with the force behind the thrust. Rockspray and Mulcade swooped down, and by the time Esteron had turned the fight was over and the day belonged to Thane.

Wagging tails and joyful barking greeted him as he retrieved the Hollow Keeper's blade and wiped it clean upon the grass. Victory eased his shame of the incident beside the brook earlier in the day.

A search for safety drove them on, cantering half the night away, but they had to rest or fall asleep as they travelled. The dogs ran, panting hard at Esteron's heels but the owls flew far ahead, for they knew rumours of a place if their sharp eyes could find it in the dark. Their tired wings beat beneath a silver moon and at last they found the place where Nightbeasts dare not tread. A rocky hill, weather worn and bare of life above the inky landscape. Esteron followed the owls' hoots, his weary head swinging from side to side; Thane, numb with ex-haustion, stayed awake just long enough to whisper his thanks to Esteron as he untacked him. He stood for just a moment, sword in hand, upon the summit rim looking out over a hostile world, so like an ancient warrior in a mighty fortress. About the rugged slopes, the Border Runners stood guard and on the highest rocks the Battle Owls sat. Dogs and owls soon nodded into sleep, for they knew the legends of the rock. It was not chance upon the wing that brought the birds to Battle Hill. No beast of the night dare put a foot upon the hallowed mound for legends whispered of a ghostly Warhorse squadron that kept Battle Hill secure for any Kingsman, horse, bird or dog to rest the watches of one night beyond all fear.

Morning light revealed the grasses trampled flat all around Battle Hill as if besieged by many in the night, but not a sound had broken the dreams of those who slept on the oldest and safest Wayhouse in the land. A pool of crystal water, fed by a secret spring, gave the host a morning drink and hunting in the grasslands provided a hasty breakfast, though Thane thought little of raw rabbit or hedgehog and closed his eyes to swallow the slippery meat.

Thane climbed, refreshed, back into the saddle, the owls alighted on his shoulders, swiftly the dogs fanned out along the Greenway's edge and started running. Time was their enemy, dawn had revealed the Nightbeasts' tramplings beneath their temporary refuge. The dogs knew that evil tidings would have gone before them faster than the bending wind in the grass, even Thane could see that the Nightbeasts' tracks were all going in the same direction.

'The Nightbeasts will be setting an ambush, Esteron. Come, we must find shelter before dark.'

Thane tightened the girths as they moved off and each bounding stride took them nearer to Stumble Hill. But they must make the doors before night fell, or perish in the dark. Esteron high-blew with each stride, sweat lathered white upon his sides, but he was Equestrius' son, and he had the heart to outrun the wind if the need arose, and from the dogs he learned that they had that need, to run and run and run, for the sun went down all too quickly and shadows fell long across the track.

All day the landscape changed, rolling grasslands became

empty downs, rising with the sun into ragged distant peaks. Dense oak forest passed on either side, rotting leaf mould squelched beneath their flying feet, resin-scented pine woods pressed hard against the road. Pine needles laid a whispering carpet, and the roar of waterfalls drowned all other noises as they passed through shadowy gorges and leapt the angry boiling streams. All about them wildness ruled. Burned out hamlets stood forlorn beside the road, but who knew what now lurked behind the doors or what crouched waiting for the dark beneath the broken window sills? 'Run! Run!' barked the dogs.

Need jostled the desperate company on a long, unforgiving road; twilight gave no hint of journey's end. The sun was it's own master, the Lord of Daylight, that none could ask to wait; not even Equestrius, Lord of Horses, nor magic in the rainbow cloak could stop one tick of the clock. But woven in the summer scarf that Thane carried was a picture of the sun, and all about the hem a legend of love and sacrifice in precious needlepoint. Mulcade tugged at the cords that bound the banner to Thane's armoured arm and as cord after cord snapped the banner spread, rippling taut behind them. For Esteron was galloping faster than the wind towards the last uphill league of Stumble Hill and a dying sun paused at the world's edge, reflecting all its glory in the banner, so that a new sun dashed the gap on Stumble Hill, and for a little while turned deepest shadows back into daylight where Nightbeasts waited in a deadly trap.

'Run! Run!' barked the dogs. 'The doors are closing. Night pulls them shut.' In a last mighty effort Esteron stretched his neck, the doors stood before them, a closing crack to safety, but still the banner blazed, catching the last rays of the sunlight. Nightbeasts filled the road's edge and swarmed between the trees. Mulcade hooted in defiance and spread his talons. This time they were far outnumbered, death within sight of safety seemed a cruel defeat after such a great race, for he knew that the dogs would stand to the last, tired and without hope. But his call was answered, no hollow echo to be pulled away upon night

179

breezes but from a thousand Battle Owls the call came back. Word had spread from Woodsedge – Thoron's grandson is on the roads, all those that loved the old man must spread a wing to help. The sky was black beneath the talons of death, sharp the beaks between those blinkless eyes that in the very nick of time stooped on Stumble Hill. But the owls and the dogs were not alone, the Archers of Orm had made ready in the Wayhouse Tower. Fear took their hearts as the banner shone brighter than the sun but Archerorm, the Keeper, held them at the casement slits. 'Magic!' hisséd a voice behind the bows of Orm, forearms bulged as fingers locked to pull the strings so tight that the oiled wooden bows began to groan and feathered flights lightly touched the archers' cheeks. In patience they would wait until the Nightbeasts blocked the road, and every arrow knew its mark, for they had great skill with the feathered shafts of death.

The owls and the dogs fought to hold the road, drawing into a tight pack around Esteron, but the Nightbeasts' trap was sprung and they swarmed in waves of black terror out of the trees and dykes on either side. Thane, twisting in the saddle, looked quickly back and saw the road behind choked with hideous Nightbeast forms. Before them towered a forest of black spears, reflecting the last rays of dying sunlight.

'When hope has fled and Nightbeasts press on every side . . .' echoed the musical voice of Duclos in Thane's head. The banner was fading, overwhelmed by the nightmare shadows all around them, and their dash to the Wayhouse Tower had slowed to little more than a walk.

Thane slipped the reins and drew both blades. 'Run, Esteron,' he shouted.

'Give us room,' he cried out to the Border Runners leaping at the Nightbeasts before them. The dogs fell back and Thane spurred Esteron, sweeping both blades in a glittering, humming arc, smashing Nightbeasts' spear shafts and slicing through their grasping hands and claws that reached out to pull

180

him down. Esteron reared and plunged, striking out with his forelegs.

'Give us room,' Thane shouted again as Esteron began to surge forwards.

'Thanehand!' a Nightbeast voice screamed out, 'I know you, Thanehand – Thoron's spawn – I shall kill you and your owls.'

One-eyed Kerzolde burst through the Nightbeasts, pointing a claw at his empty eye-socket.

'Kerzolde!' Thane gasped, swinging both blades towards the towering nightmare.

Kerzolde laughed cruelly, wading through the dogs and grabbed Esteron's bridle. Esteron reared, the whites of his eyes flashing in the darkness, turned his head and bit at the claw, pulling backwards as his teeth closed on the smooth brittle horn. The claw snapped in two, Kerzolde screamed, thrusting wildly at Thane with his spear. Neither of them heard the angry whine of the arrows or saw the careful archers draw again to shoot, but the solid wall of Nightbeasts between Esteron and safety wavered, stumbled and collapsed. Kerzolde jerked backwards, throwing his spear high into the air, looked briefly at the gleaming arrow heads aimed at him and fled into the trees beside the road. Esteron let the broken claw fall to the ground and, leaping over the heaps of dead Nightbeasts, galloped through the doors of Stumble Hill.

# Stumble Hill

With the noise of a thunderclap the doors slammed shut. Bolts and beams were shot. Thane pirouetted Esteron and made to charge back on to the road, for his friends were still beyond the safety of the doors and he would not desert them in the dark, but the barriers were shut. Esteron stood trembling with exhaustion, steam rising from his lathered sides, pools of dripping sweat forming on the cobbles. He would have run again had Thane wished it, but in his heart he knew that the fight was over. It was Thane that the Nightbeasts wanted to destroy. Evening's chill made him shiver, all was silence beyond the doors of Stumble Hill, far off an owl hooted and distant barking drifted on the wind. The Border Runners were hunting in the dark.

Thane dismounted, eased the girths and whispered many thanks, for now he knew how great a mount he rode to Underfall. A hand upon his shoulder made him jump, and raise the Hollow Keeper's blade.

'Rest, Kingsman, the race is done, victory is yours, but much is owed to those who ran with you.' The man standing before him looked too small to be a warrior, sturdy with massive arms but gentle-eyed and softly spoken. He held out a night rug with his right hand. In the other he held a wooden bow that dwarfed him. 'You have a great horse, Kingsman, keep him well and rug him warm, for I have seen few to match him in a long life.'

Thane unsaddled Esteron and spread the rug across his back while the archer's careful eye studied him, confusion pulling his eyebrows into a deep furrow. The horse seemed to have stepped out of a fairy tale. The rider was a mere boy dressed in clothes he recognized, the Border Runners ran at his heels and Battle Owls sat on his shoulders.

185

'Young man, custom bids us to give refuge to travellers on the road, but in return we take the name and a little history from those we help.'

There was an edge of hardness in the quiet voice and silence filled the courtyard of Stumble Hill. A ring of bowmen fidgeted in the shadows, Thane's life rested on his answer. Mulcade and Rockspray squeezed Thane's shoulders, needle talons kept him still to retain a place so dearly won.

'Thanehand, Thoronhand's grandson. I ride upon King Holbian's bidding, and while within your house offer you my sword for I come in peace and friendship.'

Using the skill of Gildersleeves, before an eye could blink, he turned the Hollow Keeper's blade and offered it, hilt first, to the man standing before him, the point against his own throat, and as he knelt saw for the first time the mark that Tombel had tutored him to seek, an owl in blue and gold upon the arm that reached for the hilt of his sword.

'Rise, come lad, stand again! No Kingsman, young or old, has ever bent a knee before old Archerorm. Thoron would have my life for treating you so roughly. Forgive my harshness but magic seemed in the air with legends beating on my door. Come, Thane, and see your horse to bed for he looks gaunt and tired out. And then the news of all you saw upon the road, if you had the time to look.' Archer laughed as he steered Thane towards the stable yard. All day they had watched Esteron and the Border Runners, a dust cloud passing across the grasslands, racing the road towards them. Through the Great Glass of Orm, set high in the Wayhouse Tower they had urged them on. New arrow heads had glowed white in the forge, bows had been restrung, for all who looked through the glass saw the helm and the cloak of Thoronhand racing the sun to bed, and they would be ready should he make the door before night fell.

Thane hesitated, turning to Archer; so much had happened, so quickly, he had almost forgotten. 'What of my friends, the dogs and the owls? Without them I would have been lost upon

186

the road. How will they stand in the darkness without our help?'

Archer saw in the anxious young face so much of his old friend, Thoron, always a champion of others' troubles, more often than not nursing a lame dog or a broken bird, always in haste but never without time.

'Come, Thane, and ease your heart, climb the winding tower stair, and look on what you won, disturb not the watchers at each twist of the stair for they keep us safe.'

Following in Archer's footsteps Thane ascended the great tower. The steps wound in a continuous spiral; soon they must pass through the clouds. On his right, at each twist, he passed the watchers standing in the casements, arrows ready on the strings, facing the night outside. He gave up counting the steps for fear of falling asleep as the numbers became muddled in his head, but at last he reached the top and stood beside the Glass of Stumble Hill. Windows looked in every direction, the moon rode brightly in the sky casting black shadows over a silver road far below. Archer took his arm, and gently guided him.

'There below, look and fret no more, young warrior, the road is still. Nothing moves amongst the Nightwalking dead. Not a single dog nor owl lies amongst them. Here, use the glass and take a closer look.' Archer swung the slender cylinder of polished brass, gliding on its well-oiled wooden wheels so that it pointed directly towards the heaps of dead blocking the road. Thane almost jumped backwards, falling against Archer, he rubbed his eyes and cautiously looked through the glass again.

'It brings them so close, it is almost as if they were here with us in the tower; there is magic on the roads.'

'No, lad, skill and knowledge ground the glass, now look and tell me what you see.'

'Heaps of Nightbeast dead. Broken armour full of arrow shafts, scythes and iron caps lie where they fell. But something moves amongst the dead.'

'Where? Let me look!' Archer grabbed the glass and strung

187

an arrow as he looked but let it fall forgotten on to the platform, sadness filled his face.

'Look again, Thane, with much pity in your heart upon the rewards of age and the bitterness of fate, for there, picking at the spoils of war, perches Silverwing. He was once a great captain amongst the owls, he rode to war upon your grandfather's shoulder. None feared the dark with Silverwing near at hand, now age has pulled at his feathers, cataracts have blurred his sight, and begging on the Greenway's edge has stripped all the dignity away to leave a ragged shadow that the other birds shun or chase away. They feel a great shame for one who steals what others kill.'

Mulcade hooted angrily, digging his talons deep into Thane's shoulder and seemed almost to hiss at the shape on the road below, 'The Lord of Owls, my father, a beggar!' Mulcade turned his head away then hooted softly, 'Father, father,' but the old bird was deaf to his cry, caught in the act of stealing he flew hesitantly into the trees, bumping blindly into branches he did not see, dropping a strip of Nightbeast flesh in his haste.

Archer sighed sadly, picking up the arrow, 'We leave meat for the old bird near the doors and would gladly take him in and care for him but somewhere deep in the feathered chest a spark of pride still glows. Since your grandfather disappeared, Silverwing's stealing and bad ways have increased twenty fold, he did have a brother but none have seen him since the Causeway wars long ago. Come, see your horse to bed, and then sleep, for you are tired. Tomorrow we eagerly await all your stories of the road.'

The stables were opposite the great doors, set back on the far side of the main courtyard. Whitewashed walls and polished wood beneath a gabled roof of oiled cedar, all the rings, chains and catches were wrought from solid brass and shone warmly in the torchlight. Deep bracken beds were laid in all the stalls, fresh hay in the mangers that gave out a smell of new mown grass. Three horses stood saddled and bridled as if ready for the road, swords in scabbards were fitted on to the saddles and hanging by each stall were long oiled bows and quivers full of arrows.

'We were ready to clear a way to your side if the archers failed,' Archer said rubbing the neck of the horse nearest to the entrance.

Esteron whinnied to the horses as Thane led him in, he dwarfed the three half-breds, but in no way outshone them for they were the last of the relay horses left alive on Stumble Hill and wore the scars of battle with great pride, much snorting and talking passed between the relay horses and Esteron as Thane trod wearily to bed, for Esteron was Equestrius' son and sought news of his father. The owls roosted near the horses, Thane was safe enough in Archer's care and their sharp ears were eager for any gossip of the roads to Underfall.

Morning opened the doors and a great bonfire disposed of the dead Nightbeasts. Thane took breakfast with the Archers of Orm and related his adventures on the roads, careful to keep the purpose of his journey a secret, but Archerorm was not a fool and frowned often as the stories unfolded. Later he took Thane up to the top of the great tower to seek out the truth.

'If you were not Thoronhand's grandson I would turn you upside down and shake the secrets out of your pockets,' but he laughed as he spoke. 'Come, lad, there's more to this journey. My bowmen may settle for breakfast stories but the dogs run with you, owls on your shoulders, a horse in the image of those from long ago. Will you not ease my mind to help you further on the road? The Nightbeasts want your hide and paid a heavy price in failure last night; next time it could be you who pays . . . with your life,' he added as an afterthought.

Thane looked out over a wild and hostile landscape that stretched to the world's edge, 'Which way lies Underfall?'

Archerorm's face darkened. 'You make for that dreadful place? Nay, lad, it is too heavy a burden for one so young.' He put his hands on Thane's shoulders and looked searchingly into his face, 'You have something of great value that King Holbian wishes to hide, or keep safe? He is a wise and clever King.' Almost speaking to himself Archer mused, 'Give it to a boy to creep in; secret, dangerous, but quite clever! The dogs, the owls and that great horse!' Delighted by his own powers of deduction Archerorm danced about on the platform almost upsetting the glass. But Thane brought Archer back to earth.

'No grand plan was ever made. I travel to exile at Underfall upon King Holbian's orders. The reasons are private. The horse was the King's personal gift to me, the owls were with me when I reached Woodsedge, the dogs appeared only a few days ago, unasked. In truth they have saved my life three times and still Underfall is beyond sight.' Thane felt weary of the journey. Everybody he met wanted to know his business or spoke of Underfall with such dread. And none so far had been there for a long while, if at all. He had been hoping it was not really so bad, and secretly hoped that Stumble Hill was journey's end. Well, he could not ride on today; Esteron looked run up lighter than a greyhound and still seemed asleep when he had visited him before breakfast. A quiet walk was all he would have today to ease his aching joints, Thane thought.

Archer interrupted his thoughts, and took his attention beyond his reverie, with a pointing finger.

'See that range of mountains, hazy beyond the horizon's edge? Follow that line, there! Just in sight, the tallest, that is Mantern's Mountain. Underfall clings on to its lower slopes.'

Both stood a long time looking towards the end of Thane's journey. Each was lost in private thoughts. Thane's drifted home, and he touched the summer scarf and remembered his mother's goodbyes, his grandfather's empty room and his fingers touched the threads that Elionbel had needled in and wanted the journey over and Tombel's friendly house just around the bend.

Archer was back upon the Causeway road, a strike of

bowmen at his side beneath the shadowy walls of Underfall. How he wished that they had really won that war.

A flapping of wings and hooting brought them both back to the tower on Stumble Hill. The owls stooped over the tree tops below, Archer followed them with the glass. Speaking sharply, as he saw what was hidden in the shadows. 'Nightbeasts hide in the woods. Do not leave the Wayhouse today!' With this he fled down the stairs, shouting orders as he went. Stumble Hill became a fortress preparing for a siege: during the morning the few families that lived nearby abandoned their houses for the safety of the Wayhouse, for as Archer's foot touched the first stair he had cut the rope on Orm's Bell, freeing it to clatter a warning to any wise enough to listen. The forges glowed white and sparks burnt the armourer's aprons as they hammered out new arrow heads; swords and lances kissed their grinding wheels; carpenters prepared the shafts for the arrows and oiled the wooden bows of Orm.

The three relay horses were made ready for battle, pride arched their necks as fine mail coats were spread across their backs. Special saddle cloths were fitted that flowed past their stifles, embroidered upon them was the emblem of an owl in gold threads on a blue background. Manes and tails were plaited, hooves polished until they shone; they may have been small and of common breeding but they lacked nothing in courage, standing there fretting and champing on their bits. With them stood Esteron, and they hoped he might see them hold the check and sway where once upon a time only the Warhorses were allowed to battle.

Thane was handed a longbow and quiver full of arrows, but it was soon taken from his fumbling hands. 'If it comes to fighting, use your sword, you could do a lot of damage with a bow but which side would come off better?' The Archer smiled as he said this and treated Thane with much respect.

Thane had little to do but explore the Wayhouse fortifications and watch the archers prepare against attack. Afternoon wore into early evening, the last cart full of farm children rumbled towards the doors, pulled by an old sway-backed, bony mare. Beside the cart a thin ragged man drove a flock of sheep, his shepherd dog kept a careful watch and penned them near the centre of the road. Without warning the dog's hackles rose, growling he backed against the cart. The owls screeched and stooped, arrows whined as Nightbeasts leapt on to the road. The farmer raised his staff to have it split in two, hardly breaking the sweeping arch of a jagged scythe, but a strike of well-aimed arrows drove his attacker back into the ditch beside the road. Out charged the relay horses, lances in their riders' hands, up went a shout from all the shooting butts for the little horses needed great courage to stand against the Nightbeasts and the Archers knew that, though outmatched in fighting skill, they would hold the road or die where they stood. But they were not alone: Esteron reared, broke his chain and stable door, and roared out the Warhorse challenge. Sparks flew across the cobbled yards, Archers scattered as he galloped through the giant doors. Few Nightbeasts dared to stop upon the road with such a horse abroad and those that did remain died quickly beneath his flying hooves. The air was thick with arrows, though none flew near the horses, who in a running circle round the cart, guided it through the doors to safety.

Esteron and the three relay horses snorted and stamped in the courtyard as great shouts of honour echoed all around them. The three small horses led Esteron towards the stables; he had learned much about them during the night and found many ties of blood from his mother's side in the tough little equines of Stumble Hill. The smallest, called Sprint, was a distant cousin, the fastest on the hill. Nimble, a sister far removed, who had rare glimpses of the elevated paces, and lastly, Stumble – none knew his blood lines, for he was orphaned at birth and was found wandering on the road, thus his name which fitted well for he lacked the speed or grace of the other two horses but every man who knew him loved him for he never shied or napped in tight spots and took the shock of battle in his stride. Esteron hung back and slipped quietly into an empty courtyard, for all the honours should be heaped where they were most deserved, and he was hardly missed. As warm hands slapped the relay horses' sweaty necks, Thane and the owls found him drinking long cool draughts from a water trough. Thane threw his arms around Esteron's neck, so glad to see him safe and unharmed.

'Come, Esteron, you must rest; tomorrow with the first light we race the road to Underfall and draw away the Nightbeasts that plague this house for it is us they gather to kill.'

As darkness fell, Thane climbed to the top of the tower, and through the glass studied the wild, shadowy lands that he would enter before the sun arose. It was a long and bitter night that stank of death. Arrows fell, a bitter rain upon the Night-beasts storming the hill, but nothing seemed to stop them hammering on the doors, battering with torn up tree trunks against the walls. How long could the Wayhouse stand against such a press of hatred none knew. The doors shook, the beams splintered and warped, and stone crumbled beneath the Nightbeasts' strength. All night the armourers' hammers rang upon the new-forged arrow heads. Each bolt found its mark as piles of dead built up against the walls, but still they came. Fear took the Archers' hearts, for they saw no end to the dark shapes that filled the road and choked the dykes on Stumble Hill. But Archerorm, Master of the House, had the tattoo on his arm and held his men steady.

'Make every arrow count, take careful aim; soon the dawn, soon the dawn.' Between hammer and anvil they fought, and hoped to weather out the night.

# The Great Dash

During the last hour of darkness before the grey light drove the night away, Thane went into the stables to prepare Esteron for the great dash. To his surprise he found Archerorm and a slightly built youth a little older than himself getting Sprint ready for the road.

'My son,' said Archer, a hand upon the young man's shoulder, 'Kyot.' Archer's son was dressed to match Thane, a different motif on the helm but the metal shirt, cloak and boots looked the same, 'We have a plan, to win a little time and spread confusion on the roads.'

Archerorm pulled a dirty parchment from a leather pouch hanging from his belt and spread it on the cobbled floor. 'The Roads to Underfall,' muttered Archer, pointing down at the map. 'Look closely and remember your path. There are only two Greenways still open, both of them are dangerous.' The owls alighted on the map, searching out the way. Esteron and Sprint peered over their riders' shoulders, the only sound came from the flickering torches spluttering as they burned down through the tar. 'One road is direct and kept well clear, the other is little used for it runs through Notley Marsh and none here knows how overgrown or treacherous it has become.' Archer paused, looking slowly from face to face. 'Our plan is simple, the moment the doors are sprung Esteron and Sprint will gallop out together; a league beyond the doors, the road divides,' Archer pointed carefully at the parchment, using one of the few arrows saved for the moment their flight began, 'I doubt if the Nightbeasts will be able to tell which of the two of you they seek to kill.'

Archer held Thane's eye, 'We gamble Kyot's life and little

Sprint's great heart and courage to get you safely on your way; my son begged the chance to ride with you if only for the first league, for all of us knew your grandfather and loved him dearly, he taught Kyot to ride and Sprint to run, and many times held the road and bought us time when hope had fled before the dawn. For him alone we owe it, but to you we also owe, for the tattoo binds us.'

The stable doors burst open, cutting into the flow of Archer's words, 'Archer, no man has more than two arrows left and the doors are breaking down!'

Archer looked past his bowman into the black night where a touch of grey nudged at the sky. 'The doors will hold, the grey hours are with us, clear a path just wide enough for two horses, every man will draw his sword. Now go and make ready the way.'

Thane spoke with tears of pride in his eyes. 'To find a man so loved by his friends that they will risk their lives in the memory of him, or chance all for his grandson, is too great a price. I must go alone, Grandfather would not wish it otherwise. I loved him in childish ignorance and wish I had known him better. Your love repays all debts and I thank you for it.' Thane turned away to saddle Esteron, and to hide the tears he shed in his mane, but a gentle hand turned him back.

'Do not take my chance to gallop in his memory, or rob Sprint of his dash to glory, for we all loved him and in many ways he belonged to us all, even a humble Keeper's son.'

Thane turned again, but Sprint held his eye, so proud he stood, poised for the start, neck arched, eyes bright and full of fire. The new set of road studs set into his shoes cast sparks on the cobbles as he pawed the ground. What chance had he to stay alive? But this was his choice, none would rob him of that.

With a smile touching the corners of his wet eyes Thane spoke, 'At Underfall we will meet again, though all night's creatures stand before us!'

'It is settled then, the first league you ride together. Then which road will you take, Thane?' asked Archer.

'Through Notley Marsh; I give the Greenway to Sprint.'

Sprint snorted, snatching at his bridle for he had the better road, but still it was further than he had ever run before and it would test his strength and courage to the limit. Kyot grasped Thane's arm in silent thanks, for deep within his heart he had a lot to prove: being Archerorm's son was no easy place to grow.

Both riders mounted in the outer courtyard and whispers ran the rounds amongst the Archers of Orm, for they marvelled at young Kyot's courage. Grey dawn winds tugged at his cloak and showed his secret to all gathering near the doors, he had taken off the mail shirt and wore no armour, save the helm, thin cotton breeches, parchment thin boots and the lightest rapier blade hung from the smallest saddle ever seen. Archer stepped forward, raising his bow and last remaining arrows. His face was grey and lines of grief furrowed his forehead.

'No, father, not even the Bow of Orm will I carry. Nothing but your blessing for the road lest the burden wears Sprint's great heart down.' He was indeed Archer's son, and none would ever say again that he walked in his father's shadow.

The doors creaked, a crack appeared, and dawn broke the night's power. Esteron roared a challenge, Sprint crouched, his nostrils flared. Every archer bent his bow, the crack became a gap, in that last moment Rockspray left Thane's shoulder and flew to Kyot. Such great honour Kyotorm had never dreamed of, to have a Battle Owl upon his shoulder. The doors were sprung! Arrows, noisy as a hornets' nest, felled the Nightbeasts in the gap. Esteron reared and plunged and jumped the heaps of dead and beside him, stride for stride, ran Sprint.

'May the precious drop of Warhorse blood course through your veins, little Sprint. Run, great horse, run!' shouted all the Archers on Stumble Hill as they dropped empty quivers and snatched up their long, sharp swords. Grim were their faces and tight their lips, for the son of Orm was on the roads and needed all the time their blades could buy.

Shoulder to shoulder their horses galloped, necks stretched, nostrils flared. Nightbeasts leapt at them on either side, but the sun rose and pushed them back into the shadows, for World's Edge was afire with a new sun's birth which shone upon the swords of the Archers who ran behind the fleeing horses, catching all morning's glory on the bright metal. Skylarks took to the wind, blackbirds sang along the Greenway's edge and a fresh breeze chased the night beyond man's sight for the span of another day. How the minstrels will string their lutes or weave a tale for winter by the fire none yet knew, for the ride from Stumble Hill had only just begun.

Esteron had the blood of his father and could run all day, and when need snapped at his heels could give a little more. Sprint, on the other hand, had only a trace of Warhorse in his breeding, but his size and wiry frame gave no hint of the heart full of courage he hid beneath a common coat. The first league tested more than strength in the little horse, for black shapes filled the road, reaching out to pull him down. Fear filled his eyes, terror took his heart. He pressed close to Esteron's shoulder lest he be left behind, but Esteron feared nothing that walked by night and spread his courage like a blanket around the little horse and kept him safe until daylight drove the shadows back.

So tight were the riders crouched over their horses' necks, manes streaming around their faces, that they did not see the Border Runners leaping amongst the shadows, white teeth tearing the Nightbeasts down, or the shadows of the owls that flew above their heads. Blurring speed, roaring wind, and pounding hooves were all they knew until the horses eased their pace. Birds sung all around them, dew sparkled in the grass, morning was about them, the road was theirs.

A league behind, the new sun lit up the tower on Stumble Hill, a lone figure stood on the platform, the great Bow of Orm in his hand, the last arrow on the string. Tears flowed down his cheeks, pride and sorrow mingled, for his son had taken nothing into manhood save his blessing. 'Kingspeed, great hearts, Kingspeed,' he whispered as he wept.

Cantering easily now Thane reached across and grasped Kyot's hand. 'Till Underfall, Rider Orm!' laughter was in his voice, 'You have a great horse between your knees; keep to the crown of the road, spell Sprint only in the open spaces.' The divide was upon them, Esteron and Sprint neighed their farewells, the owls hooted. Rockspray would stay with Kyot until he reached the doors of Underfall, or perish on the way.

'To many meetings at Road's End!' called Kyot as the gap widened and the road divided.

Behind them in hot pursuit ran the Border Runners, but they halted at the fork in a long noisy council of snapping and growling. None wished to leave the pack, the road through Notley Marsh was treacherous and they were pledged to guard Thane. Eventually, long after the riders had become mere distant specks in a wild landscape six of the largest Border Runners pledged their help to Sprint and Kyot for they deemed them worthy of it and this was agreed amongst the pack. Word would spread as they travelled that the Son of Orm had won his spurs on Stumble Hill.

Esteron cantered half the morning away, an easy loping gait that pushed the Greenway leagues beneath his hooves. The road was good, far better than Archer had led Thane to believe, perhaps a little overgrown, but clear to follow.

'We could make Underfall by nightfall if the road stays this clear.' Thane was full of optimism which soon eddied away.

They reached the rim of a wide valley below which lay Notley Marsh. The Greenway vanished into a total wilderness. Esteron slowed to a walk and picked his way carefully between the hangman's creepers that blocked the track. Brambles scratched his legs, quick thorn spikes dug into his flanks, everywhere dead trees leaned dangerously across the path and where sunlight forced a beam of light giant dragonflies hovered. A stink of rotting vegetation filled the air, there was no room for Mulcade to fly beneath the trees and he spent the afternoon fighting off the swarms of marsh insects trying to eat

Thane and Esteron alive. Spiders dropped off the branches on to Thane's neck, mosquitoes hovered ready to strike and the stagnant pools bubbled as Esteron trod near them releasing foul smelling fumes. The further he walked the deeper his hooves sank into the ground. They were lost! Fading light warned them that afternoon was nearing its end.

'Night must come early in this dreadful place, we must prepare a ring of fire as Tombel taught me or die when the shadows begin to move. This seems just the place for all the Nightwalking creatures to gather.' Thane shuddered as he spoke, his voice came as a whisper in the heavy atmosphere.

The dogs were still a long way behind and knew nothing of the danger Esteron had almost walked them into. He had strayed off the track and followed a Mud Wallower's path into Notley Marsh, another twenty paces and they would have disappeared, swallowed up by the mud pits in the valley floor. Even the stoop of owls had lost sight of them beneath the tangled trees and they dared not call out; Nightbeasts were in Notley Marsh.

A hot sticky evening's labour built a ring of broken branches and dead tree trunks as high as Thane's shoulders. In the centre he piled as much extra wood as he could gather before the shadows began to move. He drew his sword and read the legend on the blade with the last glimmer of twilight. He felt more alone and afraid than ever before. Esteron moved to stand beside him and rubbed his soft muzzle on his cheek and blew gently on his neck. Mulcade took the spark from Thane's pocket and it glowed in his beak casting a giant owl's shadow against the tangled trees that hemmed the tiny clearing. Thane was glad that Mulcade held the spark, he had the courage to wait, sharp eyes on the shadows, and not waste the precious fire in what could be a long and dark night. But the darker it grew the more his scalp tingled and the tighter the knot in his stomach became. He drew Duclos' little blade and held it ready, he dare not touch the scarf for that would tell the

Nightbeasts who he was. Twigs broke, creepers moved, still Mulcade waited with the spark, but he spread his wings, lightly balanced on Thane's shoulder ready for the stoop.

The last patch of sky had deepened through subtle shades of blue to black and far above a canopy of stars shone white and cold. Suddenly there was a roaring between the trees. Breaking branches, Mulcade stooped; white glowed the spark, and drops of fire fell upon the kindling wood as the owl lit their barricade. Along the dead branches danced the flames of hope and only just in time, for beyond the blazing ring night shapes had crowded in. Esteron snorted, pawed the ground and reared as scaly skin grew scorched and burned outside the homemade fortress. Seeing Thane safe within the ring of fire drove the Nightbeasts mad with rage and clawed feet trod through the flames. Again and again the Hollow Keeper's blade thrust at their armoured hides and brighter burned the ring of fire in Notley Marsh. The blaze drew the Border Runners and far above the owls had a homing mark, for none would have found Thane in the dark without the beacon's light.

Fear fled, there was no space or time to keep a tally as round and round they trod, fighting to keep the Nightbeasts out. Soot smudged their faces and smoke stung their watering eyes. Slowly the night hours passed away. Nightbeast after Nightbeast fell amidst the roaring flames and fuelled a greedy fire, sending new sheets of flame high above their heads. The collection of firewood piled in haste in the centre of the ring lay unused.

'These monsters make a merry blaze!' Thane shouted above the screams of the Nightbeasts and the roar of the fire as he drove his blade through another Nightbeast's heart. But there was a note of despair in his voice, his sword arm had grown numb and his legs felt heavy with tiredness. There seemed no end to the hideous shapes breaking through the flames. He looked beyond the swarming Nightbeasts into the dancing shadows thrown against the edge of the clearing and saw something that made him catch his breath. A black shape far larger than the other Nightbeasts that moved as he did, following his every step, driving the attackers against him.

'Kerzolde!' Thane whispered, recognizing the injured claw and empty eye socket. Then he laughed, feeling the tiredness fall from his shoulders. The assault had slackened, now he could count the monsters beyond the flames and see an end to the battle.

Suddenly the ring of fire roared, fanned by the wind of a thousand wings, stooping fast on Notley Marsh. A noise of snarling, snapping jaws drowned out the Nightbeast screams.

'The owls! The dogs!' cried Thane.

'Thanehand!' hissed Kerzolde, escaping into the shadows, 'Next time I trap you I will catch you alive and peel off your skin to make a new suit of armour!'

Thane took a step and sprang lightly over the fire ring and followed Kerzolde's voice towards the edge of the clearing.

'Thanehand!' called the voice, begging him to follow.

Esteron whinnied a warning, Mulcade stooped quickly to his shoulder and Thane hesitated, turned and jumped back into the safety of the ring of fire.

Thane blinked and rubbed his dirty face, pushed Duclos' dagger into his belt, drove his sword's point into the ground and rested heavily on the hilt. Just beyond the fire the clearing filled with friendly shapes as the Border Runners not hunting in the dark, settled for the night. Creaking branches on the clearing's edge told where the owls sat watching out the night.

Sleep did not come easily to Thane, each time he closed his eyes nightmares came crowding in. He shivered and cried aloud, and many times called his grandfather's name. Esteron stood beside him, brushing his cheeks with his soft muzzle, Mulcade whispered nestling lullabies but only in the grey hours did sleep finally come, and with it a strange dream of the other road to Underfall. His lips moved and Mulcade leaned close to listen to the mumbled words, 'Run, Sprint, run!

Daylight comes to those who chase the night.' A smile touched the corners of his soot-smudged lips for in his dream a little horse broke through the shadows and crossed the first shaft of sunlight into a new day, sparks scattered from his worn out shoes, sweat streaked his labouring sides, his rider crouched bloodied from many wounds, a broken rapier in his hand, but his eyes were full of light, for before him unfolded another day and the road stretched safe and empty before him.

The great ring of fire had burned itself to ash, distorting the fallen Nightbeasts' iron caps and jagged scythes beyond the hammer's skill ever to straighten out; half-burned armoured skin lay on the fire's edge amidst the wreck of war. Half the morning was spent dragging or pushing the refuse of the battle into the smouldering ash. A nauseating task that brought waves of sickness over Thane.

'What this place needs is strong winds to blow it clean.' None of the animals seemed to take any notice of Thane's comments. They all wanted to be gone as quickly as possible and they laboured hard to clean the clearing. At last the filthy, aching job was finished, now they would leave Notley Marsh. The dogs sniffed out a route between the treacherous bogs, so overgrown and tight that Thane walked ahead of Esteron and used his sword to clear the path. The marsh insects plagued them but nothing bigger than the giant dragonflies dared to attack so many Border Runners in the gloomy daylight. After many hours amongst the reeds and rotting vegetation the ground beneath their feet became firmer and Esteron's hooves no longer sank past his fetlocks at every stride in the sticky mud. At last they were ascending the far side of the valley. The track became wider, the tangled roof of creepers gave way to openings to the sky above, a few more steps and they reached the valley's rim and the track opened on to the ancient way to Underfall, now unused and overgrown, but it was a road bordered by mighty oaks that marched on as far as the eye could see beneath an evening sky.

'The road! We have the road!' cried Thane. He ran his hands through the nearest dog's thick hairy coat. 'Without you we would have perished, lost forever there in that awful place.'

Something made all the company turn and look back into the valley below where dense clouds of smoke billowed in a changing wind.

'The marshes are on fire!' called Thane, leaping on to Esteron's back and standing in the stirrups to get a better view. 'Our ring has fed upon the Nightbeast dead and caught the undergrowth alight. The wind is pushing the flames towards Notley Marsh! None can follow us now!'

Even as he spoke black shapes fled before the flames to a certain death in the bottomless mud pits that lay in their path and fire cleared the road that none had dared to tread for years beyond counting.

Lighter in heart Thane turned Esteron towards the avenue of oak trees.

'To Underfall, but first a stream or pool to wash away the stench of death that hangs on to us.' As an afterthought he added, 'A safe place to sleep the night away would be a great gift on a hard road,' but he sorely doubted that they would find such a place. 'I wonder how Kyot and little Sprint fared last night with only Rockspray to guard them. I dreamt that they galloped into morning but Kyot looked sorely hurt. Can dreams be true?'

Mulcade and Esteron had no answer to Thane's questions and dared not speculate or hope.

The trees thinned out and grassy clearings opened on either side of the road. The dogs spread out, moving silently, noses on the ground; barking suddenly broke out somewhere just ahead. Thane felt compelled to draw his sword, but Mulcade did not move from his shoulder perch or seem at all perturbed. The dogs had found water beside a ruined hut, tumbling from a mossy fountainhead. Carved on the creeper-covered lintel of the hut were words that Thane could just see. Reaching up he pulled the creepers clear and rubbed the time-worn stone until the legend was clear and he read, 'Though darkness holds the road, he that seeks refuge may enter and sleep in peace until a new day dawns.' Washed and refreshed Thane pondered the broken doorway. Night was closing in, dare he enter the hut? Howling far off towards Notley Marsh made the hairs on the back of his neck prickle, a shiver ran up his spine. Hackles rose on the dogs' backs, their lips curled in silent snarls.

'Wolves!' cried Thane, pushing his hand against the thorns and creepers that grew across the doorway. They should have needed hacking down but they parted easily at his touch and drew back in the shape of a curtain, revealing a dust-covered gloomy room.

'Nobody has used this place for suns!' he gasped, sticking his head inside. 'It must have been a Wayhouse once, long long ago.'

The howling was growing closer and he had to decide whether to believe the legend over the door or run before the wolves. Another quick look into the tumble-down hut showed him an empty fire-place, smoke-blackened and cold. Broken chairs and tables, once part of a hollow square now lying scattered with weeds and wild flowers growing up through the earth floor. The wolves were almost upon them.

'Quickly!' he cried, his mind made up, 'And let us hope strong magic wrote the legend over the doorway and that it still holds true!'

Esteron, Mulcade and all the Border Runners followed Thane across the threshold. The door of thorns rustled, swayed and fell back into place, an impenetrable wall.

'Strong magic!' Thane whispered, crouching by the window.

The first of the wolves reached the hut. It stopped, then trotted in circles, sniffing the ground before lifting his saliva-dripping jaws to the darkening sky and howling. Soon the road was crowded with the rest of the wolf pack, red eyes and yellow teeth shining in the early moonlight. The dogs were uneasy, lifting their lips in silent snarls but none uttered a sound. Esteron stood very still, Mulcade perched on the saddle, wings spread ready to stoop.

The leading wolf came right up to the doorway, snarling and growling. It pulled at the thorns, shaking them from side to side. Others joined in, snapping and snarling until the barrier shook and trembled, and turned its thorns towards the wolves. Yelps of pain replaced the angry snarls and the wolves retreated into a large circle around the hut, licking at their torn lips and claws. One by one they crept nearer, howling in turn at the hut. Thane loosed the dagger and drew it. The lead wolf charged at the hut, biting at the crumbling stone work, tearing at the thorns with his claws, another followed, then another until every claw and fang was attacking the masonry. Thane could smell their foul carrion breath and hear their grunts of effort as the thorn barrier began to fall apart. He leapt to his feet and drew his sword but as he advanced to the doorway he noticed a different smell filling the hut, and saw through the thorns a brightness outside the hut that was more than moonlight. The wolves were retreating, snapping at each other in their haste to escape. The legend written above the door was the truth. Nevian had built the hut and carved the words long ago and in between each layer of the stones he had planted nightflower seeds that only bloomed in darkest night when great danger threatened. Inside the hut the sweet, heavy scent of the nightflowers brought a dreamless sleep to the hunted, even Mulcade, and they closed their eyes and slept. From the outside the hut had become buried in banks of small white flowers blooming between the thorns that gave off a bitter acid scent that had driven the enemy away.

# Road's End

'Trouble stirs! Arm the horses well! Make sure that every saddle carries an extra sword throughout the watches of the night.'

Thunderstone gave his orders without turning or looking back, his voice carried authority into the furthest corner of Underfall. 'Something is going to happen, mark my words,' he muttered to himself, standing between the doors watching the black cloud of smoke drifting over Notley Marsh.

'Too many shapes are moving after dark, make fast the doors!' he shouted to the watch-keepers, stepping back into the fastness at Road's End and turning his back on the last shades of evening. 'Set the best bowmen you have on each watch.' He wanted sharp eyes in the galleries tonight and steady hands on the bowstrings. Trouble turned his heart as he checked the horse lines for the twentieth time since the smoke rose, but he could find no fault no matter how hard he looked. Every buckle, keeper and strap was adjusted to perfection. The first watch-horses stood ready, aglitter in the flickering torch-light, reflecting from the countless tiny loops of polished steel woven into their battle coats. Manes were tossing, hooves pawed and scraped the cobbles for the nighthorses fretted for the road.

'Be calm, my friends, trouble is near enough,' whispered Thunderstone, moving with a gentle hand amongst his horses, settling them quietly on their halters. 'Save your strength, be ready, be ready.'

Long after the moon had sunk from sight, Thunderstone slept fitfully in the watching chair. He awoke with a start, letting his long broadsword clatter on to the gallery floor. 'Sleep is a curse carried by the old,' he muttered angrily, rising to tread life back into numb legs, for night chills had crept beneath his cloak while he slept.

'Something moves on the road from Notley Marsh, Master,' whispered the watcher on the wall. 'Wolves are howling. Shall I fire a blazing torch to see what moves beneath night's mantle?'

'Yes, but with all your skill make the arrow curve high above the old disused road, for need drives something from Notley Marsh.'

'But none would use that path, Master, no man or horse would dare to risk the marsh, except old Thoronhand, and he has long passed into the shadows.'

Tiethorm, first Archer of Underfall, did not like wasting arrows, and mumbled to himself as he dipped the blunted bulrush shaft into the sticky tar, but Thunderstone was Master of Underfall and knew which way a leaf would fall when tossed into a changing wind. Hands froze on the bowstring as the blazing arrow lit up the ancient Greenway, the old road was full of monstrous Border Wolves, saliva hanging from open jaws, red eyes glowing in the arrow's light. 'They hound some poor devil to his death, or chase someone we have missed upon that lonely road.'

Thunderstone's voice broke the spell that held the Archers' fingers on the strings, and many arrows found a mark before the torch burned out.

During the last hours of darkness, the wolves besieged Underfall, leaping at the doors and biting at the granite walls, but the first glimmer of daylight chased them into the wilderness of Mantern's Mountain beyond the bowmen's reach, leaving Thunderstone to ponder on whom they hunted, for none had ridden or marched to Road's End since Thoronhand had passed away.

Thane awoke to a chorus of snoring dogs; the nearest must have dug a twitching elbow into his side.

'Chasing rabbits in your dreams?' he laughed, glad to be

212

alive. He stepped carefully between their sleeping bodies. The thorn barrier gave easily to his touch but scratched a little as he passed through. Esteron and Mulcade were already outside, the owl flying back from searching the way ahead. He alighted on Thane's shoulder, a forest rodent in his beak.

'Breakfast for some,' commented Thane splashing water from the fountain head on to his face. 'What a strange old hut, it looks nothing but a ruin from the outside, overgrown with thorns. It is lucky the wolves didn't stop to sniff around. I doubt if we could have held it for long.'

It was a beautiful morning; pigeons cooed in the woods, blackbirds sang in the brambles and just a breath of wind stirred the leaves along the Greenway's edge. Thane untacked Esteron, worried that the saddle was rubbing sores on his back. He looked dirty, dried sweat and mud from the marshes caked his sides, his tail was full of clinging burrs. 'What a mess you look; we can't arrive at Underfall looking like vagabonds.' Luckily he didn't carry a looking glass to show the travel stained, dirty clothes that he wore, or the smudges on his face the fountain's water had not washed away. Using his fingers he scraped as much of the mud and sweat out of Esteron's coat as he could, but he still looked to have travelled a hard road.

The dogs jumped through the thorns, stretching and yawning at the Greenway's edge, drinking quickly, they also set about a rapid grooming session, scratching at their muddy and blood-stained coats. Eventually the whole company seemed satisfied with its appearance. Esteron was saddled, the girths tightened and ready for the road, Thane gave a parting look at the ruined hut and the last part of the journey began.

Through shafts of early sunlight they strode, travelling at an easy pace that wore away the Greenway leagues. Forest and woodland fell behind, tall mountains rose, wreathed in a morning mist. 'Mantern's Peak,' said Thane, pointing a dirty fingernail; it made him shudder to look at the towering pine-covered slopes shadowing his new home.

213

'Underfall must lie somewhere below the rocky spur,' he muttered. Something caught his eye far away to the left.

'That must be the other road from Stumble Hill. Mulcade, fly high and be our eyes, there in that dark wooded valley. Fly, great owl, fly.' With a hard push against Thane's shoulder Mulcade rose on silent wings to search the countryside. Esteron pricked his ears and pawed the ground, for he had heard hoofbeats, far away, running fast, and a howling in the wind. Thane shielded his eyes from the sun, 'If that is Sprint he is long overdue.'

Now he also could hear a galloping horse. 'Run, Esteron. Run as if the wolves were on your heels. If it is not Kyot, then another Rider has great need of help.' Before Thane had finished shouting Esteron had snatched the bit and set the Greenway grasses bending with the speed of his hooves, looking for a place to jump the bordering dyke. On the first bend he found a place and leapt, plunging down towards the valley's wooded bottom, twisting between trees, jumping tangled hedges, over secret streams they ran. Throughout their breakneck descent the fleeing hoofbeats grew ever louder until down the last steep bank, trampling wild wayside flowers, Esteron and the dogs leapt on to the road, just as little Sprint galloped past, a sword's length from Esteron. Eyes glazed, and deaf to the help that had come at last, Kyot raised the broken rapier blade, slashing as though at Nightbeasts on the road.

'Go Sprint, run!' cried Kyot, his voice full of desperation, for he knew that Sprint's strength was at an end and they must perish, he dared not look back to see defeat on their heels. Tears were in his eyes as he slipped his feet out of the stirrup irons, and whispered his farewells to the best friend he had ever had, 'They shall not kill you, Sprint. Without my weight you can run the last few leagues to Underfall. Keep safe.' With a last caress of Sprint's bloody, sweat-covered back, Kyot jumped, crying out as he crashed on to the road, 'They shall not have you. Run!'

Bruised and bloody he arose, facing back the way he had come; how he wished for his father's bow and a quiver full of the sharpest new forged arrows to build a wall of Nightmare dead, but he only had the broken blade and he swore that none would pass while he lived.

Two dogs raced into view with an owl fluttering just above the road, and there was joy in his face as he recognized the two Border Runners that ran to his side, exhausted and bloody from ugly gashes in their sable coats. They were the only ones left alive on the great dash from Stumble Hill, and Rockspray, with many flight feathers hacked away, swooped just above the ground. Kyot scooped the owl up as he flapped his damaged wings helplessly on the crown of the road and tried to tuck him in the folds of his cloak but Rockspray was a bird of war and sought only his shoulder perch to fight from.

'None shall pass us,' hissed Kyot, a fierce light in his eye. The dogs moved, one either side of Kyot, crouching on their haunches, lips curled in defiant snarls. But the terror of pursuit had stopped, a roaring neighing shook the valley road; both doubt and hope touched Kyot's heart but he stood his ground. Sprint answered the call, for he had halted as the first note of the Warhorse challenge rang clear upon the morning wind.

Esteron and the dogs let Sprint run past and filled the road facing towards Stumble Hill. Their ranks silently opened for the two exhausted Border Runners and Rockspray who would take no aid even from Mulcade. Nightbeasts and all their kind heeded nothing. They believed the road was theirs, their quarry was almost run to death. They rounded the bend and their screams of pursuit turned to howls of terror and rage when they saw their way blocked. Strength and power held the road underneath the banner of the sun. Blinded by Thane's scarf, their hairy hands rent empty air, hissing, dribbling Nightbeasts trampled the wolves under razor sharp claws in their haste to flee. Esteron and the dogs leapt forward, sunlight caught the valley top and shone upon the summer scarf.

215

'The road is closed to all your Nightmare kind; begone!' cried Thane, lifting the Hollow Keeper's blade to catch a beam of sunlight and the shadows fled, wailing and grinding their empty teeth in defeat.

Kyot could not believe his eyes, he blinked and rubbed his face with a bloodstained hand. Where all hell's creatures should have choked the road, Esteron and Thane stood with the Border Runners beneath their banner of the sun. He shouted with joy and threw his broken sword high in the air.

'Though all the Greenway leagues stood between us you came when hope had fled. Sprint, Sprint, we are safe. . . .' Kyotorm turned and almost fell over his little horse who had retraced his aching steps the moment he had heard the Warhorse challenge.

'We are safe, safe,' he cried, throwing his arms round little Sprint's neck, but Sprint had run his heart out. He was beyond care, legs trembling, unable to lift his weary head more than a hand's span from the ground. He seemed to hear familiar friendly voices from afar, but even the pride of his great dash meant nothing, it was overpowered by the pounding of the blood in his ears. Each laboured breath burned his lungs. Thane snatched his dagger and slashed the girths and the bridle's plaited knot, carefully taking the bit out of Sprint's blistered mouth.

'Water! Mulcade, use your searching eyes, and hurry before Sprint dies!'

Kyot wept as Thane carefully removed the saddle, for Sprint's back was a mass of raw skin. Thane spoke with pride and wonder as he looked at Sprint, 'Great is the heart that beats beneath his ruined hide. Though worn to a shadow he is as full of courage as the best Warhorses of long ago.'

No greater praise had ever been spoken of the little relay horse, but Sprint did not hear it, he was sinking into darkness, his legs were buckling beneath him.

'Quickly Kyot, help me guide Sprint to the road's edge

216

beneath that shadowy tree.' All the company pulled and pushed the little horse into the shade, Mulcade returned, Thane's helm upturned in his talons full with cool clear water. Kyot held Sprint's head as Thane removed his mother's scarf and dipped it into the water. He gently wiped Sprint's lips and squeezed a trickle on to his blackened and burning tongue. 'Drink slowly, let it gently cool your throat,' whispered Thane, using the wet scarf to wash and cool Sprint's face and bathe the many ugly cuts upon his neck. Gradually a spark of life glowed in the little horse's eyes. Thane tipped the helm and Sprint drank it all to the last drop in the bottom. Mulcade, unsummoned, hooked his talons on to the rim and flew back to fetch more water. How many times he laboured with the heavy metal helm went beyond counting, but the last one he carried he offered to Kyot as tribute to his courage on the road to Underfall.

Throughout the struggle to keep Sprint from death Esteron stood close, calling in soft whinnies the battle honours that belonged to Sprint, and nuzzled his face. The dogs licked clean the long gashes on his sides and legs, cut deep into his flesh by the Nightbeasts' whips and scythes. All held their breath as the spark flickering in the horse's eyes grew stronger. He rose to his knees, paused a second before struggling to his feet amidst deafening barking, hooting and cheering. Kyot whispered to him while running his hand through his mane but the words could not be heard in all the noise. Sprint snorted and stamped a broken horse shoe on the ground, and then rubbed his weary head on Kyot's arm.

The Border Runners were tough and hardy and tended each other's wounds with rough clean tongues, but Rockspray's injuries were beyond any healing skills that Thane or Kyot possessed. The owl clung perilously on to Kyot's shoulder, trying to keep his balance but as they prepared to take the road again Kyot coaxed the owl into the folds of his cloak where he fell into a coma and knew nothing of the last few leagues to Road's End.

Sprint and Esteron walked together. Only after much persuasion would an exhausted Kyot mount Esteron.

'I must walk through the doors of Underfall beside Sprint,' he mumbled, as he fell asleep with his head resting in Esteron's mane. Thane checked that Rockspray was safely tucked into the folds of the cloak and would not slip or fall as they moved forward. He lifted a hand to ruffle the soft downy feathers on Mulcade's chest. He would miss the owl's weight on his shoulder as he would have missed his right hand.

'We're near journey's end now; I hope you'll stay with me in my new home.' Mulcade looked at him with large round eyes, shifted his weight and rubbed his beak against Thane's dirty cheek, pulling at the strands of hair escaping beneath his helm, and hooted softly. The dogs, in two long columns, tails waving behind them, led the way on to the causeway but would go no further. Before them towered the walls of Underfall, still wreathed in shadows, for the sun had not yet climbed above Mantern's threatening shoulders.

'Underfall!' gasped Thane, moving forward with leaden steps. 'What a dismal place it looks!'

The walls rose sheer, set with many galleries, each one overlapping the one below, but all of them were edged with iron teeth so bound and worked together that no Nightbeasts could ever enter. The lower walls were polished smooth without one single hand or claw hold for an attacker to use. Thane swept his gaze up across the galleries to the great lamp on the highest battlement, but nothing moved. Underfall looked deserted. Narrow casement slits, well beyond a giant's reach, stared empty-eyed back at him. Even the wind had fallen away to nothing but a breeze that bent the torch flames set either side of the massive iron-studded wooden doors. The doors stood open, drawn back across well-worn cobbles to reveal inner courtyards, full of dancing shadows cast from many hidden wall lamps. Narrow stone steps skirted each courtyard, running upwards out of sight and tall archways deep in shadow joined the courtyards together. The further Thane looked into the fortress of Underfall the darker it became. He shivered and turned his eyes to the newly mown lawns that swept from the raised Causeway to the granite walls giving the only splash of colour that he could see in such a bleak and dreadful place.

'Underfall. If I had really believed that it would look as grim as this I would have stayed at Woodsedge forever.'

Thane's spirits had sunk to the level of his boot straps. He shook Kyot's arm to wake him, 'Road's End, Rider of Orm. Time to put your feet back on the ground.' Kyot stirred and opened his bleary eyes but sat up quickly, reaching for his broken sword.

'I have heard winter tales to make the blood run cold about this place, but none could match the reality.' With a look of pity, he watched Thane summon up the courage to take the last few steps into exile. Dismounting, he took his friend's hand, for the great dash had made them even more than brothers; 'I'll stay for as long as you need me.'

Mulcade hooted softly, gripping Thane's shoulder tightly with his sharp talons. Thane's eyes lost that haunted look, he laughed, 'With friends like this who needs to fear the dark. Come, this was my grandfather's second home, here I can tread in his footsteps and perhaps learn to know him a little better!'

Thane drew his sword and knocked three times on the massive doors but even as the hilt touched the wood for the third time he saw that they had not come unnoticed. Beneath the lowest gallery in deep shadow sat a host of the grimmest horsemen mounted on the finest horses Thane had ever seen. Each rider held a lance and all of them were pointing towards the doors. The horses appeared to be crouching, hocks close to the ground, ready to leap forward and their battle coats flashed and sparkled in the shifting torch light.

# The Keeper of Underfall

Between the two horses opposite the doors stood the fiercest and oldest Warrior imaginable. He wore no armour save a closely woven mail shirt. His boots and leggings were made of pale calfskin, undyed and age-stained from frequent wear. Upon his shoulders hung a simple blue cloak, drawn together beneath his beard with a golden clasp, wrought in the shape of an owl. His face was angular and finely etched with care-lines and his old eyes wrinkled with concern as he looked at the two travel-weary young lads that stood before him. Thunderstone smiled and threw back his cloak to reveal a sword with a long horse tail woven into the hilt. Above the hand that held the sword was a tattoo of an owl in blue and gold that shone as freshly as the day that Nevian had traced it.

'Come! Come, fear not those who are gathered about me for they are battle-dressed and ready lest any should dare hold you up on the Causeway against your will.' Thunderstone spoke softly, yet his hawk sharp eyes had already searched each one of them and he could hazard a good guess as to who they were. But why had they come unheralded to Underfall?

Before Thunderstone had finished speaking the warriors of Underfall galloped past the weary travellers with a roar like thunder. Through the doors they charged to form a ring beyond the entrance so that none could enter without the Master's leave.

Thunderstone raised his hand and called for Merion, the Healer. 'Tend to the horse,' he commanded, pointing towards Sprint, 'for his was the hardest road to World's End.'

Merion took the halter from Kyot and was about to lead Sprint away when Thane stopped him and gently opened the

223

folds of his cloak and lifted Rockspray towards the Healer. Merion turned to Thunderstone. 'There is a great tale to tell of the road by the look of these two!'

Thunderstone frowned and pulled Kyot's cloak aside, 'I'll wager this young man was with them through the worst of it. Off with you now, go with the healer before your wounds from the Nightbeasts' blades fester and turn poisonous. Your father, Archerorm, would never forgive me if you died through lack of care in my home!'

'You know me! Before even asking my name!' exclaimed Kyot.

Thunderstone laughed, 'You, young man, have the Archers' steady hand and eye. It is the way you move even without a bow in your hand. Why, old Archerorm has grown a son few enemies would care to stand before. But Archers travel in strikes and do not roam the roads alone, I will hear why you travel after Merion has dressed your wounds.'

After Merion had led Kyot and Sprint away towards the healer's courtyard Thunderstone turned to Thane.

'When the horse that owned this tail lived and was, for a moment, the light of my life, I had two friends whose mirror images are with me now!' Thunderstone was stroking the horse tail woven into his sword's hilt, but his eyes had a distant look as he continued, 'Beneath these very walls we stood. Come, young man, and let me guess your name. You cannot be the son, you are much too young, yet the same look in the eye, the owl upon the shoulder, the dogs upon the causeway, the clothes are those of a Galloper. Thoronhand! You must be his grandson, young Thane. How quickly the years run from us!'

With more than a touch of sadness in his voice Thunderstone continued. 'How proud he would have been to see you grown this far. But my manners have grown coarse and hard like the place we stand in, let me call for meat and drink and chairs to sit upon, and then you can tell me what has driven you to take the road to World's End.'

Thunderstone clapped his hands and a table and chairs and all that was needed were set in the centre of the courtyard, even a trough of water and a bucket of hard feed was set upon the cobbles for Esteron. Thane began searching through his pockets for the letter from King Holbian.

Having found the letter, he laid it on the table before the Keeper of Underfall. It had been a very hard road, the ivory parchment was stained with sweat, crumpled and very dirty, and a fine red powdery dust fell out as Thunderstone opened the letter.

'So much for the King's seal,' laughed the Keeper, and then added, only a little more seriously, 'There is much to teach a Kingsman if he is to carry news, for the one who receives it must be able to read it!'

Thane told all that had befallen him on the road, the owls', dogs' and Esteron's parts in it all, right up to their arrival before the doors that morning. Thunderstone listened between frowns and smiles, often re-reading the letter while Thane paused for breath. The sun had become a ball of fire resting on the hill tops, shining through the massive doors, when Thane had finished his tale, the horsemen returned and the sun sank from view. The doors swung shut with the sound of rumbling thunder.

Thunderstone sat looking at Thane passing the letter from hand to hand as if settling a difficult question in his mind. Darkness had fallen and the torches glowed anew before he spoke.

'It is not often the apprentice surpasses the master before the first day's work has begun, or even before their first meeting. To have fenced within the fire in Notley Marsh, or to have held on to the Greenway road is more than any swordsman here could do alone, even aided by the dogs and the owls. To have won the road to Stumble Hill and then to have ridden out and won the road again, is more than my best horsemen and my best horses could do. Who is the Master now? What can I do

225

with you that will not feed resentment in my men's hearts or humble your feats upon the road which all men shall come to hear about soon? What can I do with you, who should have perished on the way had you been any but Thoronhand's grandson?'

'Master, I am exiled into your service and would do as you bid me and not begrudge the meanest task. Luck and all my friends saw the journey through, I am raw in learning and beg a chance to know your skills and grow a little like my grandfather.'

'What of Nevian's moving pictures in the Learning Hall that the King writes about? Is this magic? Men fear what they cannot understand.' Thunderstone waited on an answer.

'If it is magic, which I doubt, I cannot conjure it up or control it in any way. Only once has it happened, but you are right, men feared it. The Chancellors plotted my death, fearing a power I do not hold. Even the King hung much importance on my day dream in the Learning Hall.'

Thunderstone's face darkened, 'The King does not make mistakes! Never cheapen his name within these walls or mix treachery with your words. Elundium may have fallen into shadows at the hands of the Chancellors, but we are here to keep the light for a great King. We are bound to serve.'

Thane shrank back into his chair, seeing for the first time the power and the anger of the man who kept the last outpost at the end of the world secure so that other men could sleep without fear.

'You shall be apprentice undergroom, under-rider, under-dog, under-anything to make you into the man your Grandfather was. A true Kingsman. Now take your horse, bed him well, clean your tack and all your gear of war. Your place is in the straw above his stall, amongst the other curs who think they might be men!'

Thane fled from the Master of Underfall, rushing headlong into the stable yards, looking for a place to hide. But Esteron proudly stood his ground, holding the Keeper's eye. Mulcade, perching on the high pommel of the saddle, did not flinch or move. Two voices blended in Thunderstone's head, barely louder than the nightwinds that whispered through the courtyards.

'Judge him not too harshly, Keeper. He is but a boy, hard-driven to stand before you at the end of a desperate road. He loved your King enough to face the darkness alone. Look to the roof tops high above your head or watch for eyes beyond the Causeway road and see that he has gathered many friends along the way, just as his grandfather Thoron did. In many ways we are all born to serve!'

Thunderstone looked up and caught his breath to see so many blinkless eyes watching him, and a distant barking echoed on the wind.

'Keep your pledges and teach him all you can, and we, through love, will honour ours.'

As a cloud passed over the moon the owls on the roof turned away, Esteron made his way towards the stables but Mulcade moved to the saddle's cantle to watch the Keeper until Esteron had left the courtyard.

Thunderstone sat, a tired and old man, worn out with holding back the tide of fear that washed against the walls of Underfall. He rose on weary legs to find his new charge and quieten the anger in his heart.

'Lord,' whispered Thane, shrinking back from the Keeper of Underfall, 'I meant no disloyalty. I love our King more than life itself.'

Thunderstone smiled, lifting Thane to his feet. 'Child,' he said softly, 'we live in troubled times and you bring whispers of disquiet from the man I have loved and served for a whole lifetime in this shadowy place. It was not the talk of magic or how our King viewed it that made me angry with you but the tricks and treacheries that have driven him to send you here alone.'

227

'No, Master, he did not send me alone, he gave me a horse and offered me a strike of Archers or a squadron of Gallopers to see me safely here.'

Thunderstone laughed bitterly, 'Did you read the letter, boy?'

'No, Master,' cried Thane, 'I was the messenger. I dared not touch the seal.'

'Somebody has tampered with it!' accused Thunderstone. 'My anger was partly out of fear that the Chancellors or one of their spies had read the letter. Who broke the seal, Thane?'

Thane swallowed, feeling the blood rush to his cheeks, 'Tombel,' he whispered, fearing Thunderstone would strike him, 'but I didn't mean to let him know I carried the letter, only he was going to kill the owl.'

Thunderstone laughed again, only this time it came from his heart. 'Lad, I misjudged you. Tombel would not deal in treachery, or kill a bird of war, he is a true Kingsman.'

'Will the Chancellors kill him?'

'Who? Kill who?' asked the Keeper.

'Tombel,' Thane replied. 'Only I stayed at Woodsedge during the winter.'

Thunderstone thought a moment, touching the horse tail sword before he answered. 'Would you cross swords with the greatest Marcher Captain in all Elundium?'

'No, Lord, never,' whispered Thane.

'Nor would the Chancellors, Thane. It would be a different matter if Tombel entered the City of Granite but he is safe enough at Woodsedge while King Holbian lives.'

'What will happen when the King dies?' asked Thane, remembering how old he had looked.

Thunderstone frowned, drawing his forehead into deep wrinkles, 'It depends on many things, lad, fate, luck or clear-eyed judgement from the last Granite King. But if he dies leaving us without a new king the Chancellors will destroy everything, even each other, in their struggle for power. Remember, lad, only one man can rule this Elundium.'

'Who could be the new king? Wouldn't he come from amongst the Chancellors?' asked Thane in innocence.

Thunderstone laughed, looking fiercely at the boy who stood before him. 'How little you know or understand. Nevian foretold long ago that the new king would arise here in the shadows of World's End. The Chancellors fear this place and none have dared risk their lives on the chance of growing into Kingship in the shadows. Only the condemned are sent to Underfall in chains to perish.'

'But,' interrupted Thane, 'the riders at the gate were not chained.'

'No, lad, nor will you see one link of the shackles that dragged them here to die. I break their chains and make them into men of honour. Underfall would long ago have fallen into black despair if I had treated the guardians of World's End as the Chancellors wished. You see, child, if this fastness had fallen Nevian's predictions could not come true. While Under-fall stands the Chancellors cannot seize power.'

'Perhaps one of the men sent in chains will be King,' wondered Thane.

Thunderstone sighed sadly, 'No, Thane, not one single man amongst them has the makings of a King. They are proud and honest, but not the stuff of Kings. He will come one day, mark my words, child, and raise his standard on the Causeway Fields as Nevian foretold, and we shall flock to that standard in the sunshine of a new Elundium!'

'When, Master?' cried Thane, eagerly.

'One day,' replied Thunderstone, quietly. 'But I have grown old and tired waiting and you, my lad, may grow as impatient as I before that standard flutters before these doors.'

'Master,' Thane asked, anxiously, 'has my coming here really risked the King's life?'

'Yes. But it was not your doing. He could have left you to the mercies of the Chancellors, or given you to the mob, but he saw something in you, perhaps the vision, or the owl alighting on your shoulder, something that moved him to cheat the Chancellors of your death.'

'But why was it so important that I travelled here? I could have hidden anywhere along the road.'

'Could you?' laughed Thunderstone, 'With those owls on your shoulders and a king of horses between your knees. No, my boy, there was nowhere else to hide but here at Underfall. You are Thoron's grandson and had to follow your fate whether you liked it or not. Fate pushed you forward, Thane, to stand before a desperate King and you have won the road for him where greater riders have failed and delivered a ray of sunshine in the darkness, for now I know that King Holbian has seen through the Chancellors' struggles for power.'

Peace was made in the candlelight, but Thane would still serve his time as underling as any true apprentice would. Secretly he was glad; he was the youngest at Underfall and knew that he had much to learn from the men who guarded World's End.

# Sprint

Kyotorm recovered from his wounds within the space of four days, at least enough to walk about, but he grew thinner, seeming somehow older, and often his careful Archer's eyes had a distant look. Nightshapes haunted his dreams and he cried aloud in his sleep, tossing and turning, stabbing his hands at the Nightbeasts in his nightmares. Thunderstone sat with him through many watches and pressed into his hands the hilt bound with horsetail but even that talisman only eased the pain a little. Mulcade perched on his pillow but he could not drive out all the shadows from Kyot's dreams. In desperation Thunderstone summoned Thane to come down from his bed of straw and sit out the watches by his friend's bed. He brought his mother's scarf, bloody, dirty and creased and gently laid it across Kyot's forehead and sleep came; the lines of pain were smoothed away, for in Kyot's dreams he rode into morning and the sun shone on his face and the Nightshapes fled.

Many nights Thane sat beside Kyot and each time, through his troubled mumblings he pieced together the epic ride his friend had made to reach World's End. He shuddered at what he heard, and saw clearly the great courage and strength he and Sprint had spent to win the road. After they had parted at the divide Kyot had jumped to the ground and run beside little Sprint to save the horse's energy. He had spelled him often in the open spaces, rapier drawn lest any dared to attack. By late afternoon the six Border Runners caught up with them, barking softly and wagging their tails. Meremire Forest stretched before them and day was near its end, only with the last glimmer of twilight did Kyot remount, just as the shadows began to move. Gripping the rapier's hilt tightly with a shaking

233

hand, Kyot urged his horse forwards; there was no turning back, the road behind was full of shadows. Meremire Forest spread before them, its tangled hanging branches creaked and groaned and the silver star-reflecting road disappeared beneath its threatening eaves.

Rockspray flew ahead. The dogs ran on either side as Sprint gathered speed. The forest enveloped them with its blackness. A stride inside and the stars were blotted out. Nightbeasts moved between the trees, roaring and screaming; scythes glistened and whips cracked. The dogs snarled and leapt, tearing Nightbeasts down as they swarmed on to the road. Kyot swung and thrust the rapier on either side, Rockspray hooked out eyes on bloodied talons as sparks scattered from Sprint's worn studs. He kept to the crown of the road, shutting out the pain and terror as best he could, running for his life. The roaring in his ears grew louder and louder until his pounding heart mastered the Nightbeasts' screams. Kyot's arms were wet with his own blood where noisome blades had cut deep, but he heeded nothing but the road ahead. Whips cut and twisted around Sprint's legs, but such was his speed that he wrenched them out of the Nightbeasts' hands, tearing off rage-tight fingers in his haste.

Long after midnight, gasping hard, they reached the summit of a long hill and for a fleeting moment saw how much still needed to be won. Meremire stretched beyond the edge of sight, but over to their right a great beacon blazed in the direction of Notley Marsh and it fed doubt in the Nightbeasts' hearts making them waver even as they sprang to block the road. With courage and strength nearly exhausted, Sprint charged at the towering shapes, as the road narrowed to a small crack between the shadows. Kyot plunged the rapier blade so hard that it snapped, two of the dogs died on the Walkers' scythes; but even as death took them they saw Sprint win the road. In that moment they saw the little horse break free, running hard upon the Greenway's crown, sparks dancing beneath his shoes, for the grey hours had come and the road glowed like beaten silver beneath his fading hoofbeats.

Tears ran down Kyot's cheeks, and in his mumblings he vowed to raise two great mounds beside that road and set about them a ring of silver arrows, for he owed his life to those Border Runners. With morning in the sky they had galloped into sunlight and left Meremire, a dark threat behind them. Within a league Sprint had slowed to a walk, Kyot dismounted and nursed him, stopping often at pools and streams to wash his horse's bloody wounds. Rockspray, tattered and bloody, sat once more on his shoulder, while the four Border Runners licked their wounds and watched the road.

All too soon the sun began to sink, drawing long shadows in its wake. 'You must run with the setting of the sun, Sprint,' said Kyot, 'for Mantern's Forest stands across our path. It is far older than Meremire and our way looked from my father's map to be descending into dark canyons and bottomless ravines. Tomorrow we must reach Underfall or else die upon the road.'

Tightening the girths as they moved forward Kyot prepared to mount, leaving it to the very last moment. His own thin boots were scuffed and torn and blood oozed from raw blisters on his ankles. 'Run! Run!' barked the dogs, but even as they spoke other noises echoed in the wind, blood-chilling howls, still far behind, but growing louder as darkness fell.

Thus it was that Thane had found them almost run to death and nearly overtaken on the road to Underfall. Kyot had never spoken about the ride from Stumble Hill, not even to Thane, and he tried hard to shut it out of his mind, but often when standing on the upper galleries his eyes strayed beyond the Causeway road to the wooded edge of Mantern's Forest, and those near him would sometimes catch his whispers, 'The dogs, the great Border Runners, how much I owe that can never be repaid,' and then tears would fill his eyes.

Thunderstone had sat the watches with Thane and had marvelled at the boy's courage and made it known that Kyot,

235

son of Archerorm, should have the freedom of Road's End and none should stand in his path, which was a great honour for one so young.

During the weeks that followed their arrival, Thane began to understand the true meaning of the legend carved above the stable entrance. On his first evening he had passed beneath the time-worn letters without a second glance, but now each word seemed etched into his heart.

'Hardships make hard men, and hard men make nothing of hardships.'

The legend became a way of life: starting with the first touch of sunlight that opened the great doors until night drew them shut, not a moment of daylight was wasted. Stables were cleaned and scrubbed, horses groomed and kept in constant readiness against Nightbeast attacks, and whenever a moment of idleness drifted through the courtyards, the undergrooms were ordered to polish the horses' battle coats until, ring by ring, they glistened, reflecting back every precious ray of light. But the evenings were a time of uneasy rest, when fear drew the frightened together, for Nightbeasts howled in the gathering shadows on Mantern's Mountain and night, when it came, seemed to have no end. Yet the gallery boards creaked and laughter echoed in the gloomy half-light as Kyot and Thane walked together, sharing their hopes and dreams, for the great dash from Stumble Hill had bound them closer than brothers and they did not fear the dark nor anything that crept beneath its mantle.

Thunderstone watched Thane and Kyot as they walked the galleries and marvelled at what he saw, but his inner thoughts were troubled; if these two boys were the beginnings of a new age of men who could arise strong enough to rule them, this King would have to be more than a man.

Thunderstone sighed, remembering Nevian's words 'And he shall set a standard on the Causeway Fields that men . . .' Something jolted the old Keeper's memory, something about

236

that first morning a few months ago, two weary travellers surrounded by a host of dogs, the sky above Meremire Forest full of Battle Owls, a forgotten scarf tied to Thane's arm that sparkled in the early sunlight.

'No,' he laughed, 'he is but a child,' but his eyebrows drew into a frown and he whispered, 'If he is the one then I shall protect him with my life; Thoron old friend, you have my word on it!'

Summer had come to an end before Kyot was fully recovered and ready for the road back home to Stumble Hill. 'Child,' said Thunderstone, 'you must return to your father's house before winter comes and closes the road. I shall send a squadron of my best horsemen to guard you but you must leave soon or winter will cut off their return.'

'No, Lord,' replied Kyot, a smile touching the corners of his mouth, 'I need no escort home, nor would I ask for one.'

Thunderstone frowned, raising his hand to brush aside Kyot's words saying, 'Your father stood at my shoulder long ago; in friendship to him I cannot let you wander unguarded. Archer would never forgive me.'

'Lord,' laughed Kyot, 'I shall not be alone but in the company of a thousand friends.'

'Who?' cried Thunderstone. 'Who could guard you better than the men of Underfall who swept down on to the causeway as you arrived, travel weary, at the end of a desperate road and risked their lives that you should walk through these doors unharmed?'

Thunderstone began to turn away full of anger but Kyot's reply stopped him short.

'Who else, Lord, but those who kept me safe upon the road, who in the darkness came when I was all alone and stood with me in the face of defeat. Who else but the Border Runners.'

The Keeper looked mystified.

'The Border Runners, Lord, they have been gathering all summer long along the Causeway. Whenever I have ventured out on to the road they have come to me, led by the two great Border Runners that ran at my side on the dash from Stumble Hill. They will escort me home; I know it in my heart.'

'Then go with much honour,' laughed Thunderstone, his anger forgotten, 'for you have guardians more numerous than the leaves upon the trees and a greater safety than I could ever guarantee but, my child, leave before winter comes, for it will be a dark and desperate time.'

Kyot turned to go, thinking the Keeper had finished with him but Thunderstone motioned Kyot to come closer.

'The scarf,' he whispered. 'What do you know of it?' Kyot shrugged his shoulders, fearing to give away any of Thane's secrets.

'It was his mother's scarf,' Kyot replied, vaguely. 'He took it at their parting and carries it in memory of her.'

'Don't treat me as a fool, boy!' hissed the Keeper, towering over Kyot. 'I saw it catch the sunlight and soothe away your nightmares. It has great powers. Now! Tell me all you know.'

Kyot leapt backwards, away from Thunderstone, 'No, Lord, not even if my life depends upon an answer will I betray Thane's confidence and trust.'

Thunderstone sighed, holding up his empty hands. 'Neither of you will come to any harm. Let its secrets keep your tongue still, child, for a moment I thought old legends were coming true at last. I asked without hope, thinking that the scarf might be the standard that he would set up on the Causeway Fields.'

'Who?' Kyot asked, moving closer to Thunderstone.

'The new King,' answered Thunderstone.

Kyot laughed, 'Thane has no ambitions for Kingship. Finding the bones of his grandfather and raising a tower to the stars in his memory fills all of his mind.'

'But the scarf?' asked a bewildered Thunderstone. 'Perhaps he carries it in ignorance, perhaps the new King is somewhere on the road.'

Kyot sighed, seeing the Keeper of Underfall as he really was,

238

a tired old man who stood crushed beneath the worries of a lifetime's toil. 'Lord,' he said, quietly, taking Thunderstone's hand, 'the scarf, it has great power but the magic seems woven into everything Thane touches, the owls, the dogs, why even the sunshine seemed to sparkle more brilliantly as morning took the road on our dash from Stumble Hill. He is different from any other person I have ever known, except his grandfather, Thoron, who had that same touch of magic, yet if I hold the scarf it is nothing but woven silk. It holds no magic.'

'Yes, perhaps I have judged him wrongly,' replied Thunderstone, sadly. 'Perhaps I am looking for something that fills my dreams but as you say he is in many ways so like his grandfather. He could have taken Holbian's crown any day he wished, he had the power yet took nothing.'

'Oh no, Lord, he is quite different,' insisted Kyot, re-membering how Thane had stood between him and the Night-beasts on the road through Mantern's Forest, the summer scarf blazing with early sunlight. 'I think he has greater power than Thoron for the owls are on his shoulders and the Border Runners run at his heels.'

'Then I must guard him more closely than a thousand cloaks of jewels.'

'No, you cannot, unless your eyes are sharper than the owls', or you can run as tirelessly as the dogs. Nature's army has brought him here and waits upon the Greenway's edge; he will be safe amongst them until any legends there are come true.'

Late autumn had pulled the landscape into a bleak depress-ing place, mist and rain hung on Mantern's shoulders, Kyot shivered, drawing his cloak collar up around his ears, drizzling wind blew dead leaves along the Greenway's edge to fill the muddy puddles.

'Winter's in the air. Soon snow will block the road,' Thane said, huddled next to Esteron with Mulcade and Rockspray on his shoulders, hunched against the weather. Reluctantly Kyot mounted Sprint. Reaching down he gripped Thane's hand.

'Duty takes me back, Thane. I owe it to my father to return home and help him guard the tower, and Thunderstone insists I leave before winter sets in, but I would rather stay here with you and face the shadows that threaten Elundium together.' Kyot laughed, 'None could stand before us; not even the one-eyed nightmare, Kerzolde!'

'Do not speak of him, Kyot,' Thane whispered, 'I feel that he has some dark power and is watching us, growing stronger with each new daylight.'

Kyot looked back towards Underfall where a great company of horsemen had gathered to see him start the journey back to Stumble Hill.

'If the Nightbeasts hunt you in the dark, if Kerzolde or something worse comes down the mountain, send word, send Rockspray, and I will come, Archers in a strike, to help you drive them back. Remember!' shouted Kyot, turning Sprint and squeezing him into a gallop. 'Send word, and I will come!'

'I'll miss you,' Thane called after him but Kyot had gone, galloping amongst the Border Runners.

'Kingspeed! Kingspeed!' he shouted, running a few paces along the Greenway, but his voice was pulled away by the winds on Mantern's Mountain, and sadness turned his footsteps back towards the great fastness at World's End.

# A Bitter Winter of Darkness

Thane's cloak became a blanket in the dark, but it gave little warmth or comfort when the straw he slept on froze as icy draughts breached the window cracks. Only during work or while he held his steaming bowl of gruel did a little life return to his numb fingertips. Brief winter's sun could do nothing to prevent ice and blizzards sealing the great wooden doors. The tree-thick beams groaned against each other, splintering the grain. Spikes and stanchions ground their brittle metal teeth in an effort to break winter's bitter lock, but the doors stood firmly shut. Nature's springs were frozen solid. Even the owls stayed indoors, hunting for their meat between the granary bins. Winter deepened and the daylight hours became a shadow of the night. Even with all the torches burning, perpetual shadows gathered in all the corners. Only the owls could penetrate the gloom and their unruffled courage gave the men of Underfall new heart.

Never had Thunderstone known a season as bitter or one that filled his men with such disquiet, for upon the frozen drifts of snow, wolves and Nightbeasts in their thousands gathered, howling and screaming, battering on the very doors of Underfall, and he was powerless to stop them. Bow strings snapped, brittle with the ice trapped in their frozen fibres, even his spearmen found their shafts frozen to their hands as they stretched to throw. They were besieged, and Thunderstone felt his heart more troubled than ever before in his long life by the sea of hate washing against World's End.

'Walk with me, child,' Thunderstone commanded Thane, calling him to come to the highest gallery. And as he waited for the boy to climb the countless winding steps he drew his winter cloak about his shoulders, touching the frozen horse tail at his belt.

Thane stepped on to the gallery, Mulcade and Rockspray on his shoulders. Thunderstone looked into the owls' eyes, smiled and lowered his gaze.

'Already the men think much of you, lad. You win hearts even as you won the road to my door.'

As the Keeper spoke, his mind ran back over the months since Thane's arrival, thinking of his labours to hold his place at Road's End. 'Look out with me on all I have failed to win. Nevian charged me to keep a light burning at World's End, but to what purpose have I worn a life away?' Old and tired the Keeper turned towards the snowy landscape. 'There are more shadows and more fears out there now than another lifetime's toil could push back. Have I failed? What is your answer to that my lad?'

'Lord, if you had once doubted your purpose, the night would have taken over long ago and the Causeway Fields would be a black place for any new king to set his standard.' Thane dared not say more, or trip over his tongue again, but the Keeper smiled at him.

'Come, Thane, you walk with only your own shadow. King Holbian was right, the seed of Thoronhand will grow into a mighty tree. Men will follow you when the time is ripe, that much I can see. The signs were there at your arrival, but I feared it then.' Thunderstone shivered, drawing his cloak tighter, 'Will you help me, even as your grandfather did, to drive the shadows back?'

Thane felt the owl's talons press into his shoulders as they spread their wings, hooting softly.

'Look, Master, look!' shouted Thane, pointing towards the eaves of Mantern's Forest, for even as Thunderstone put his pride aside and bent beneath the wind of wisdom to ask for help from one so young, the dark shapes of a great pack of Border Runners crossed the snow, late winter sunshine glowing on their sable coats.

'The dogs, the Border Runners!' Even as Thane spoke, they fell upon the Nightbeasts and the army of terror fled. Only the wolves turned and stood their ground, lips curled back across their yellow teeth, and fought beneath the walls of Underfall. Many of the wolves died, ripped and broken in the bloody snow for the Border Runners had the advantage of numbers and greater courage and they cleared the Causeway road. As they tore apart the last wolf the sun sank into the blackness of Mantern's Forest.

In close formation, barking and leaping, the Border Runners vanished between the trees. 'Never since I stood beneath the rainbow cloak have the dogs come to our aid,' whispered Thunderstone; the warmth from his hand had melted the frozen strands of horse hair woven into the hilt of his sword and it felt soft, silky, almost alive. His speculation was interrupted by Thane's unsteady voice as he dared to answer the Master from his heart.

'Master, Lord of Underfall, not only will I help and pledge my life to drive the shadows out, but all free beings are at your side. Turn your head and look, for Mulcade and Rockspray have perched within this fortress of their own free will.'

He paused, watching the Keeper's face waiting for the frown of anger. With his courage building, he chanced to add, 'Night overcomes us all, fear draws us together, love binds us in the dark. I think the dogs came because you asked for help.'

'Thane,' mused the Keeper without any anger in his voice, 'You have the wisdom of your grandfather and the pluck to speak where fear holds others' hearts. Tell me, have I not held World's End secure through love or has this life's work been for ambition only?'

Thane considered a bumpy plunge on the end of Thunderstone's boot down the winding stair, and chanced his Master's anger to speak his mind once again.

'Men risk their lives for you, Lord. They fear you and hold you above others, for you are the Keeper. There is a grimness and a hardness like the very walls that rubs into everybody at World's End, but there is little love, little that shows.' Thane kept his eye level with Thunderstone, looking up into the Keeper's face, and dared to go on; 'At school we learned the legends of the Man of Granite who holds World's End by the point of his sword; he breathes fire and grinds bricks between his teeth. Dread fills the hearts of any who feel that fate would push them along the road to Underfall.'

'Do you fear me, lad?' There was thunder in the voice, but no real anger.

'Yes, and no, Master. I know more about you than most who tread these roads although much of what my grandfather said was beyond my understanding.'

'Thoron was my only friend. If he was in truth that close to me why do you fear me, lad?'

'Grandfather loved you and once likened you to a tall thistle that had grown amongst a bank of nettles. Proud, clothed in many thorns that waited only for the sun to open the petal case for all to see the beauty of the flower.'

Thunderstone laughed, looking away from Thane and the owls. 'Much is changing, lad, and I must change things here before spring comes, or it may be too late to drive the shadows back. What you have said of me is the truth, and it has taken a lifetime's toil to learn the wisdom in a child's words. Thoron tried to show me but my eyes were blinkered by the warrior; I never looked into the man.'

While Thunderstone strove beneath all Thane had said, to see himself as others did, Rockspray flew to perch on his shoulder, and new light shone in the old warrior's eyes. The loneliest man at World's End had friends indeed and new hope eased his heart. 'Come, Thane, tonight and every night the men of Underfall shall eat at one table. Love shall bind us together, not only pride and honour.'

Howling beyond the walls made the Keeper look out again but laughter creased his bearded face, 'We are besieged again lad, but fear moves amongst the Nightbeasts, they watch the forest eaves. Come let us set this house to rights.'

246

Thunderstone kept to his word and worked hard at changing all he could amongst the men of Underfall, but it was not an easy task to change the habits of a lifetime, hold a grip upon his temper and yet still seek standards high enough to keep World's End secure. Laughter chased the grimness out and new heart and effort had everyone from the captains down to the humble undergrooms bending their backs in preparation for the spring. In his wisdom the Keeper made every man an equal at his table and shared his hopes and doubts about the way they stood.

'Nature is gathering at World's End,' he said one night at table. 'There are owls in the tree tops, the Border Runners are beneath the eaves of Mantern's Forest and only today I caught a glimpse of wild Warhorses upon Mantern's lower slopes.'

Even against the roaring blizzards that buffeted the walls, every man who heard Thunderstone's words wanted to rush up on to the galleries and look into the blackest night to see the living legends.

'They gather for some great purpose, I am sure of that. Make sure that each one of you is ready, for we are at the centre of whatever storm should break.'

From outside Underfall stood unchanged, grey granite walls rising sheer in the snowy landscape. Carrion crows picked at the frozen wolves' carcasses lying half buried in the bloodstained snow but whenever the Border Runners or wolves came near they flew away in search of other bones to pick over. Winter slowly began its retreat back into the mountains, and each new day saw the sun grow in power, pushing against the doors of Underfall, grinding the ice to powder that clung fast within the locks and hinges.

'Soon we must saddle our best horses and clear the roads of the Nightbeasts that have plagued us through a long winter,' Thunderstone said, watching the doors straining against their icy seal. 'Walk with me, Thane, while there is still time, and watch the woods for they have filled with more than winter's snow. We have so many allies out there now; help me ponder on what is about to happen.'

Thane followed in the Keeper's footsteps, but he could not cast any light on what moved Nature to gather at Underfall, only Mulcade, Rockspray and Esteron knew that pledges must be kept, for they had heard the rumours on the winter wind and fretted to be on the roads again.

Many others along the Greenway edge were as puzzled and troubled as Thunderstone at the great migration heading towards World's End. Tombel found Warhorse hoof prints in the snow at Woodsedge and prepared his battle clothes in readiness for the spring. The gardens of Gildersleeves were trampled down and the hanging baskets of lucerne grasses eaten down to the last stalk. Morolda, in all her grumbling, bet a cat's tail that the boy with the owls had something to do with it and smiled and remembered him as she plundered the lofts searching for Duclos' war blades. Archer stood on the platform in the tower at Stumble Hill and watched shadows cross the forest floor and called his son Kyot to his side.

'Not since the Causeway wars have I seen the beauty of the Warhorses or so many Border Runners. We are witnessing the beginnings of something, son. Since your return from Underfall the animals have been gathering.'

As he spoke he looked down at the two great Border Runners lying at his son's feet. 'Silverwing has disappeared and the Nightbeasts hammer less often on our doors; you have those magnificent animals always at your side. We are on the edge of something, but what?'

'If the Warhorses and the Border Runners are making for Underfall, perhaps Thane has called them,' Kyot offered as an explanation, his eyes had a far away look as he rubbed his hands through the dogs' thick winter coats.

'I'll lay a quiver of silver-tipped arrows that he's mixed up in it somewhere, but I don't think he could call on the Warhorses; even Thoron did not have that power.' Half speaking to himself

Archer added, 'Although Esteron was as near the Warhorse as I've ever seen, I doubt that he could summon the Warhorses. They were pledged to freedom long ago when Nevian broke the bonds; only love could bind them again.' He sighed, resting a hand on Kyot's shoulder and looked deeply into his son's eyes, 'Thane may need your help before high summer comes, my heart tells me that you will go, no matter how great the danger. I see you facing an army of fear. Promise me one thing,' he paused, 'you will take the Bow of Orm, as well as my blessings; no other bow has its strength, and it would ease my heart to know that your hand was upon its string.'

Kyot knew the measure of the gift and felt a lump grow in his throat as he stumbled over words to thank his father but Archer was himself near to tears as he remembered the beginning of Kyot's ride to Underfall and turned quickly back to stare at the distant mountain tops.

'Go quickly, take as many woodsmen as will follow and cut new arrow shafts, touch not any horse that crosses your path or lay a finger on their skin for they are free and go where they wish. Nevian ordered it.'

As he spoke and Kyot turned to go the dogs licked Archer's hands and rubbed their heads against his legs for they knew the greatness of the gesture, and then they leapt, barking, down the stairs to follow Kyot.

Age does not make the Warrior, nor innocence know the measures of defeat. Thus Thane sat upon Esteron at Thunderstone's command before all the Riders of Underfall to head the flying column waiting for the doors to open. Mulcade and Rockspray sat on their shoulder perches and flexed their talons on his metal shirt. Thane wore no badge of rank, but on his arm he wore his mother's summer scarf and it sparkled, catching all the light that found its way into that gloomy courtyard.

'The legend is coming true,' whispered Thunderstone to himself, Mulcade turned his head and held the Keeper's gaze.

'Silence, Lord of Underfall!' a voice commanded in Thunderstone's head. 'Now is not the time to speculate. You are pledged to keep the light, let others follow their fate without an old man's babbling.' The owl blinked and then turned away.

Thunderstone opened his mouth but the owl turned back and stared him into silence. Horses snorted and stamped, shaking their heads and setting the bit rings jangling. Torchlight reflected from the thousands of tiny metal rings sewn into their battle clothes. Sparks danced between their hooves as they waited, fidgeting for the road. Two days they had stood ready while the doors rocked to and fro, groaning and straining against the frozen locks.

Crack! A splinter of light appeared. Crack! The horses neighed, pawing at the cobbles as the doors swung open. Crouching, hocks almost on the cobbles, the horses leapt forwards with a mighty roar and the sound of thunder. They swept on to the Causeway road, swords and spears glittering in the sunlight. The banner of the sun burned white with light, imaging the beauty of summer days.

Hard and fast they rode, in and out of the snow-filled dykes searching out the shadows that waited for the night, until, with the horses breathing hard, they reached the eaves of Mantern's tangled forest and could go no further. Sweat vapours rose in clinging clouds of steam from the horses' heaving flanks as grim-eyed Warriors sought to penetrate the banks of twisted thorns.

'The Deepling Gorge!' boomed a voice across the snow from where Thunderstone stood, sword in hand, between the doors.

'Check the way is clear. Ride to the Deepling Bridge.' Even as the Riders turned, plunging through the chest-high drifts that lay against the Greenway edge, he looked up at the sun and weighed the wisdom of his words and knew that all too soon the day would end. 'Ride like the wind,' he shouted after them, but his words fell to nothing amongst the thunder of their hooves.

All afternoon the company galloped and always just a length in front ran Esteron with the standard of the sun. But the wood was empty, the snow lay crisp, white and untouched by any foul Nightbeast claw prints. To the Deepling Bridge they rode, without a single challenge called. An eerie silence hung all around them. Thane urged Esteron across the bridge and rode on for half a league before he realized that he was alone.

'Thane!' a faint voice called out from across the bridge, 'Night will fall before we have returned, come back. Hurry!'

Thane turned, laughing at the Riders' fears and cantered easily back to the bridge.

'Warriors!' he called, anxiously re-crossing the bridge and searching the hoof-trampled snow. It was clear to see that they had gone, retracing their steps towards Underfall, leaving him all alone in the gathering darkness.

'Warriors indeed!' he muttered, drawing his cloak about his shoulders and asking Esteron to follow their hoofprints. Fear had taken the Riders' hearts.

'We must go now,' they had cried, milling about on the Greenway before the snow-covered bridge.

'Thane! Thane!' they had called, begging him to return.

'Perhaps the Nightbeasts have taken him,' one Rider muttered darkly.

'Night draws in and will claim us all,' shouted another, spurring his horse in a tight circle.

'We must ride back,' urged a third, turning his horse away from the bridge.

'Go now! Now!'

'We cannot leave Thane,' shouted Sygnis, first Captain of the Nighthorses. Spurring his horse he stood between the other Riders and the bridge.

'Wait if you wish and die in the darkness!' shouted Fagneon, forcing his way past.

Panic then seized each Rider in turn and they all fled, driving their spurs deep into their horses' flanks and beating the flat blades of their swords upon the horses' battle coats to reach the doors before night came.

In wild disorder, blood dripping from their spurs, they reached the Causeway road, jostling and barging to be first back to safety but with less than half a league to run the doors slammed shut and the riders cursed and shouted, hammering in vain, calling to Thunderstone without hope to open them. But each man knew that only the sun held that power. 'We are doomed,' they wailed, milling in disorder.

A clear voice floated down from the galleries, 'Where is Thane? Surely my best Warriors have not left him alone upon the road while you scuttled back to save your own hides?'

As Thunderstone realized the full weakness of his men, his rage reached heights he had never known and those at his side cowered, crouching on the galleries.

'Ride back! No man is to be left alone. Even as the doors shut I summoned Tiethorm with his best bowmen to man the walls and keep you safe until morning came but if that boy dies through your cowardice, not one arrow will be fired in your defence. You will stand alone in the darkness.'

In disgust the Keeper turned, wringing his hands with shame; but a musical tinkling drifting in on the wind made him turn back and peer out into the evening shadows and what he saw brought tears of joy into his ancient eyes. 'Thoron, Thoron if only you were with me now to look upon the greatness you planted long ago,' he whispered, gripping tightly on to the horse tail hilt of his sword.

'Look now, you band of whimpering curs who hammer on the doors, look and in your cowardice see who holds the Causeway road!'

The company turned, fear in their eyes, shaking hands tight upon their swords and spears, and looked into the gloom and hung their heads in shame.

'There is the only one true Kingsman beyond these walls. If you value your lives at all you will do as he commands.' Thunderstone looked beyond the men huddled below, for in truth he knew any man beyond the walls would perish before the night was done. The Keeper walked amongst his bowmen, setting by each man a flaming barrel of tar and many bulrush blunted arrows ready for a long dark night.

Esteron had followed slowly cantering easily for he had seen many friends between the trees on either side who gathered on the Greenway's edge as they passed by. Thane leaned down and rubbed his hands through the Border Runners' coarse winter coats in greeting.

'The Dogs are our true friends on the road to Underfall,' he said to Esteron and the dogs barked, wagging their tails, leaping up to lick his face. Mulcade dug his talons hard into Thane's shoulder, 'And the owls,' laughed Thane, looking into the tree tops. 'Who fears the dark with such friends by his side?'

Then he remembered the despair that took the Riders' hearts. 'Will you help me tonight to keep the men of Underfall from the terror of the Nightbeasts? They know almost nothing of your strength or courage, save through rumours. None of the Riders with me had the tattoo on their arms; will you help me? The doors will be shut and they will die paralysed with fear once the shadows move. I must stand with them and do what I can, even as my grandfather would have done had he been here.'

Thane looked in wonder at the growing host of dogs that joined him with every step Esteron took until the road was full to bursting and he laughed, 'If only Tombel could see me now!' Above his head, owls flew through the branches, Mulcade and Rockspray strutted and squawked, ducking their heads backwards and forwards. 'Without you all the world would be such a dull place.' He laughed again, looking all about him, 'but we must hurry before fear drives the Riders into the dykes.'

Night could send all its shadows to World's End, but Thane had many friends, many that he did not even see. Only Esteron heard their voices and drew great comfort from their presence. By the time Thane reached the causeway the last shades of twilight were fading, Mantern's Mountain seemed to loom threateningly, stretching shadowy arms out to engulf Underfall.

Pressed against the doors, bucking and rearing, driven to madness by their riders' fear, crowded the battle horses of Underfall, striking their hooves on the granite walls. Shrieking in terror they cast their riders on to the ground. Esteron called in a clear voice that rose and fell through neighing shouts to soft whinnies, 'Fear not! The shadows that move by night are not invincible. Be calm; I am Equestrius' son.' The majesty and pride in his eye held them still, sweating and trembling, showing the whites of their eyes; but they listened. 'No Nightbeast shall touch your skin. Look down upon the causeway, the Border Runners are gathered to keep you safe and with them stoop the Battle Owls.'

The horses drew great comfort from the multitude assembling in an enormous semi-circle from the causeway to the walls. They mastered their fear, putting aside doubt, and formed into a line behind Esteron, snatching at their bits and pawing the ground, for each one had a trace of Warhorse blood and knew the legend of their kind from long ago.

Thane had dismounted and stood before the cowering riders. He spoke in a soft voice that held no malice or anger at being left at the Deepling Bridge but lifted them and cast fear aside.

'If you fear night you are lost, overmastered with the thought of it. If you think only of the morning light it can hold no fear over you. If we stand upon this spot tomorrow and watch a new sun rise we will have won life itself and driven our greatest fear back into the shadows. Who will stand beside me, look into night's face and laugh? For there can be no light without darkness. Who will be the stronger tonight? Those who stand with me will think of nothing but the sharp edges of their swords and will see nothing beyond the great host that now gathers upon the causeway road, for you are not abandoned to die, nor do you stand alone beneath the walls of Underfall. Look to the Causeway.'

The men who had thought themselves Warriors lifted their

eyes and gazed in wonder at the Border Runners assembling. 'What magic is this?' they whispered. 'Never in all the tales and stories of this dreadful place, never have the dogs come to us, only with Thoron did they run, and then only in his stories of the road, not here at World's End.' Then they asked among themselves, 'But will they really help us when the shadows move?'

Thane replied sharply, 'Look not to what they might not do, look to your swords and see what this night's work may bring to those who put their fear behind them.'

A voice from far above their heads called out, 'Thane! You are safe? Unharmed?'

'Yes, Master,' Thane called back. 'The dogs and the owls are with me . . .'

Wild barking and deep growling broke out upon the Causeway, interrupting Thane. The men snatched up their swords, a grim light in their eyes; Tiethorm bent his bow.

'Light! We need light!' shouted Thane, and Tiethorm and all the bowmen at World's End loosed their flaming bulrush arrows high into the night sky.

Beyond the furthest dykes, Nightbeasts swarmed thicker than the tangled roots of Meremire Forest. Scythes and spears cast wicked shadows in the arrows' light. Hissing, screaming, treading the snow to ruin, they advanced. The dogs crouched, hackles spiky on their backs, waiting for the moment. As the arrows fell spluttering to the ground they leapt, fangs bared, ripping and tearing. Esteron could wait no longer, he roared a challenge and charged and with him, coats aglitter in the arrows' light, ran the battle horses, neighing out their long-forgotten fathers' names. The circle of dogs parted as the horses swept down on to the causeway and the sound of their hooves was like thunder in the wind and their speed blew the snow into new drifts that settled over those they trampled to death.

Beneath a sky of burning arrow shafts, Thane and all the besieged warriors strode on to the Causeway road singing and shouting old, half-forgotten battle rhymes as their swords rang and hammered on the nightmare iron caps. Owls stooped, dogs leapt and the horses swept to left and right driving a clear wedge throughout the army of terror, leaving a wide path of trampled bloody snow behind them. Glory lay all about them as new ballads were in the making at Underfall.

'Master,' shouted Tiethorm above the battle's roar, 'the bulrush arrows are near to finished, soon blackest night will take the field.'

Thunderstone sniffed at the wind and wet a finger, 'Even the weather blows to our advantage,' he shouted. 'Look, the clouds are breaking, moon and stars will cast a silver light upon the field.' In haste he ordered, 'Tear up the gallery boards! Split them into arrow shafts, dip them deep into the tar, use every piece of wood. Keep the night ablaze with light.' Even the stairs were plundered, ripped up and chopped into long splinters, without flights or any time to trim for balance they filled the night. High and low, some spinning as they flew, the arrows kept the sky full of fire as bowmen balanced on the newly bared joists.

Thane knew little of the strategy of war, and drew the men of Underfall into great peril, for they followed, inspired by his word and the skill of his sword beyond the safety of the Border Runners, advancing far into the centre of the swarming Night-beasts.

'Whom do we chase?' shouted Sygnis, above the roar of battle, breathlessly. He had kept at Thane's side, defending his right flank.

'A monster more powerful than most Nightbeasts,' Thane shouted back, plunging his sword double handed into a black shape that had risen up to block out the arrows' light.

'Beware of him, Sygnis, he has a broken claw and only one eye. He dogged my footsteps all the way here to Underfall. His name is Kerzolde and I know he is somewhere near. I feel his presence, I can almost smell his foul breath!'

256

Looking across the Causeway Fields towards the higher ground Thane saw him, far away, head and shoulders above the mass of Nightbeasts, driving them towards Underfall, a whip fixed into his broken claw.

'Kerzolde!' he shouted, grimly, forcing his way forwards.

Kerzolde laughed, lowering his whip and beckoning Thane to come to him. The Nightbeasts fell back, drawing Thane's small band of Warriors into a trap away from the dogs. Quickly they swept all around them, forcing them closer and closer to Kerzolde. Thane's men were pressed into a tight knot, black shadows towered on every side, only in front of Thane was the ground left open, a clear path to Kerzolde's feet. Mulcade saw Thane's danger and rose on urgent wings above the battle, searching with sharp eyes for Esteron; he called to him in shrieking hoots, begging him to come quickly.

Esteron had led the battle horses through the deep, snow-filled dykes away to Thane's right to fight amongst the Night-beasts attacking the Border Runners. Faintly came Mulcade's call above the battle noises. Esteron paused, listened and turned, calling as he ran for the other horses to follow.

'Clear the field. The Riders are in great peril. Follow. Follow.'

Beneath the very blackness of nightmare shadows Thane saw the trap he had rashly brought his Warriors into. He cried to the Spearmen to set their shafts butt end into the snow and hold the ground they stood in. Between each Spearman he set those with swords, crying, 'While we live, hope is with us!'

Kerzolde sneered, pushing his whip into his belt and lowering his spear, he gave the signal to crush the warriors to death.

'Fight!' shouted Thane above the roar and clash of arms. As the Nightbeasts closed in upon them from every side, they pushed against their ring of sharp steel. Spear shafts groaned and split, arms ached, and muscles bunched in knots of numbing effort.

257

'Hope comes!' shouted Thane, feeling a tremor through the ground, yet with each swaying movement of the battle he was being pushed closer to Kerzolde. Briefly Fagneon was jerked up above the other riders, impaled through the neck on Kerzolde's spear, only to be dropped, broken and forgotten, as the monster turned his mind again towards Thane.

From a whisper far away, the tremor Thane had felt became a roar of thunder, blotting out Kerzolde's screams of rage.

The shadows of terror trembled, hesitating, swaying this way and that, looking for weakness in man's heart, but found none to bend beneath their will, for the Warriors of Underfall looked to their blades and sang of a new morning's sun. With a great noise of neighing and a thunder of hoofbeats Esteron broke through the shadows, followed shoulder to shoulder by the horses of Underfall. Dogs leapt at the Nightbeasts' throats and owls stooped from a star-filled sky and the moon rode clear of the last cloud to cast a silver light into the Nightbeasts' eyes.

With a great shout the men strode forward, thrusting their swords and spears into the fleeing Nightbeasts and the towering walls of shadows collapsed. Leaping quickly into their horses' empty saddles, ready to sweep in victory across the snow, they stopped. The sound of hoofbeats grew louder. 'Look!' shouted Thane.

'Look!' whispered Tiethorm, a still hand upon his bowstring, 'Look, Master,' and in awesome silence beneath moon's silver shadows the men of Underfall watched and held their breath, for in a wide crescent that spread across the snowy field, manes streaming with their speed, galloped the Warhorses. Proudly they ran, and none could stand before them. Night-terrors wailed and fled back towards Mantern's Mountain. Snapping at their heels ran the Border Runners and the owls spread their wings, casting despair across their path. The Warhorses ran, pushing the grey hours before them and all the riders of Underfall marvelled at their beauty.

The field is ours!' cried Thane, 'won through hope and with

the help of the many friends who came when hope was almost gone.'

And the men of Underfall knew the truth in his words. Esteron stood watching his brothers and sisters, filled with sadness for he yearned to follow but none answered his call. He turned at Thane's touch on the rein back towards Underfall and with heavy hooves retraced his steps but from afar upon the dying wind a single horse called out, 'Equestrius, your father, bids you bide your time in the bridle, he will have great need of you soon. Be ready, by your great deeds upon the road he knows of your coming.'

Esteron bucked and plunged, the cares of battle and Thane's safety for a moment forgotten, so great was his excitement to have word from his sire.

Thunderstone trod carefully across the exposed rafters until he could look directly down on to the company gathering once more before the doors and called to them in a voice full of pride.

'Men that I thought had no honour have grown through this night's work into mighty Warriors!' And looking down at Thane he continued, 'It warms my heart that one amongst you rose up, casting aside fear, that all should see a new sun rise. Even when hope seemed at an end he held you together and never once doubted your hearts.'

The riders lifted their swords high above their heads, shouting Thane's name and his battle honours from the Causeway. Thane blushed scarlet in the darkness for in secret truth he knew how afraid he had been. Only the dogs, the owls and the great courage of Esteron had kept his heart full of hope for they did not fear the dark or anything that moved beneath its mantle.

The Keeper ordered warm rugs, food and bundles of spears to be lowered down to those beyond the doors. 'Set the spears to form a ring of bitter points that none may tread. Night may still hold a menace or catch you unawares. Guard well and wait the dawn.'

Thane could not sit easy in the saddle, something nagged at the edges of his mind, something he should do, and with a sickening feeling in his stomach he remembered when he had sat beside the fire, rescued from the shadows and watched the dogs search amongst the slain, killing any Nightbeast that still held a spark of life. He must do now what they had done then, for the dogs ran with the Warhorses and only the Riders remained. He turned to Esteron, stepping through the ring of spears, drawing his sword and screwing up his courage but the Riders followed, asking what they must do to hold the field they had fought so hard to win.

'The legend is coming true,' whispered Thunderstone, awestruck, as he watched the riders follow Thane. During the last of the grey hours the Warriors searched the field, gritting their teeth and turning their heads as they plunged their swords through the Nightbeasts' hearts, but they found many wounded Border Runners and owls amongst the wreck of battle and these were brought within the circle of spears and covered with warm rugs and treated with great honour, for without their help defeat would long have hammered on the doors.

With the first streak of dawn in the sky and the song of the blackbird already in the air the men of Underfall finished their labours. Before them stood a giant pyre ready for burning all the dead Nightbeasts in one foul heap. Thunderstone threw down a tar-dipped spear, already burning fiercely. Thane galloped and caught it in his right hand, turned and hurled it amongst the mound of death and a great fire devoured the mens' fear upon the Causeway Field.

Even as Thane threw the spear a new sun rose, red and fiery, and the great doors swung open. The riders passed through into the cobbled yards amidst shouts of welcome and victory to have lived through the dark. Thunderstone's voice cut through all other voices, 'Look to your horses, for theirs was the courage that changed despair to hope. Little will they ask of you but you will give them everything, putting their comfort and well being before your own.'

And the Riders turned and saw in the light of a new morning the great hurts they had suffered. They gazed in wonder and pride at the steel-ringed battle coats that hung in tatters and the saddles that once glowed with rich colours that were now hacked to ruin. Each horse bore the Nightbeasts' scars upon its neck but their tired eyes were full of fire that had stepped beyond defeat.

'Where is Thane?' asked the Keeper, searching among the riders. 'Where is your Captain?' Looking out beyond the doors he saw him kneeling within the ring of spears, tending to the fallen dogs and owls. 'There is the boy who with each move teaches us how love can overcome the terror of the dark.' Thunderstone and all the Warriors of Underfall went out beyond the doors, knelt and looked to the comfort of the wounded and a great bond found new beginnings within the ring of spears between the Border Runners, the Battle Birds and the men who guarded World's End.

The snows melted, winter was at an end. The sun grew stronger and the doors stood open a little longer each day. Often the woods and wild landscape that grew within the shadow of Mantern's Mountain seemed alive with Warhorses, Border Runners and many species of bird, never seen before at World's End. 'Nature gathers, lad,' became the Keeper's regular saying. He would lean on the hilt of his sword, idly stroking the woven horse tail, watching the Warhorses moving among the trees and sigh, 'Such beauty, such beauty!'

Carpenters worked at times between his feet repairing the gallery floors, but he was far away in youth and heard nothing of the hammering a hand's span from his toes.

Thane spent many happy hours in the saddle patrolling the roads towards Notley Marsh and Meremire Forest, guarding the men mowing the Greenways and trimming the edges. Both roads looked a great deal neater than they had when he had arrived. Border Runners came and sat near the road, watching the men working, coming down on to the Greenways when the men spelled their horses, wagging their tails, licking their hands and faces. Owls sat in low branches, keeping a sharp eye on the shadows well beyond the road's edge. Neither Thane nor Thunderstone nor any of the guardians of World's End knew the meaning of the owls' persistent hoots or the soft-throated growling that would suddenly start amongst the dogs, seeming to travel with the wind. Each time the chorus started, Esteron would snatch at the bit or the owls would rise into the clear sky and stoop towards Mantern's Mountain, as if searching for something or someone.

'What or whom do you seek?' whispered Thane, as he stroked the owls' chest feathers; but their reply was beyond his understanding, a mystery of troubled sounds that blended with the wind.

King Holbian scratched his brittle fingernails across the weave of the cloak, feeling in its many folds for the last jewel. The Chancellors stood before him in a whispering huddle. Proudpurse stood a few paces nearer the throne, nervously hopping from one foot to the other, his eyes greedily following the King's hand as it searched the cloak.

'When did the shadow first appear?' he asked again, looking directly into the Chancellor's eyes.

'Yesterdaylight, my lord,' whispered Proudpurse, trying to stop his hands from shaking.

'Yesterdaylight!' echoed the King, his fingers closing around the last jewel. He pulled at it gently until it lay in the palm of his hand. Stepping out of the cloak he gathered it into a huge bundle and tossed it across the channel of wax to fall at the Chancellors' feet. Crossing Candlebane Hall he climbed to his high chamber in the granite tower.

After the King had left the Chancellors fell upon the cloak, tearing it into shreds and they screamed with rage when they realized that all the jewels had disappeared. The King stood at his window, watching the shadow, it had moved closer.

Yesterdaylight it had been a faint smudge on the horizon, at this rate it would be on the gates of the city before the sun went down. His hand moved to the hilt of his sword, it felt strange after so many years, awkward and clumsy. A faint knock on the chamber door made him turn.

'Enter!' he commanded, turning back to stare at the shadows.

Breakmaster hurried to the King's side. 'Lord,' he whispered, 'Errant is long overdue. He rode out to lead the Marchers into the stable yard just before the shadow appeared. What shall we do?'

'Have you done as I commanded?' asked the King. 'Are all the horses and Warriors Errant has so far gathered within the city?'

'Yes, Lord. The yards are empty, even the unbroken horses have been herded into the lower limits of the city.'

'There, look!' shouted the King, pointing towards the shadows. 'Something runs before them. Look!'

Breakmaster stood on tiptoe, searching the edges of the black shadows. Backwards and forwards he looked until he found it, a small cloud of dust on the crown of the Greenway, less than half a league in front of the shadows.

'Pass me the glass!' cried the King; reaching out his hand towards Breakmaster he snatched the slender brass cylinder from him, putting the glass to his eye. He searched the Greenway until he found the small speck he had seen racing towards the city.

'Errant!' he gasped, adjusting the glass, bringing him clearly into focus. Moving the glass Holbian looked at Errant's pursuers.

'Nightbeasts!' he hissed, twisting the focus again. It was just as he feared, the shadow they had watched for a whole daylight was the vanguard of a great Nightbeast army advancing on the Granite City. A large swarm of Nightbeasts suddenly broke away from the main army and began gradually to gain on

263

Errant. The King swept the glass back to Errant and saw Dawnrise stumbling with exhaustion, his battle-coat torn and bloody, his flanks white lathered with sweat.

'They will overrun him before the sun sets,' muttered the King, putting down the glass and clenching his fists in frustration. 'My only Captain, cut down within sight of safety.'

Holbian turned and paced the chamber, thinking hard.

'Breakmaster!' he cried, his mind made up. 'Have you a horse for me?'

'Lord, there is none worthy of a King. There are no Warhorses within the city.'

Holbian laughed, a flash of forgotten youth shining in his eyes. 'Even the Buryman's donkey would be worthy enough now! Go quickly, find me a horse!'

Breakmaster left the chamber, running as fast as he could down the winding stairway.

King Holbian strode into the armoury and reached for his battle helm. The iron work was dusty and showed spots of rust but the three cornered crown engraved below the stooping owl shone as new, glittering in fine golden lines. The King lifted the helm on to his head, it felt heavy and made him stoop a little. A sword on the wall caught his eye.

'Thoron! Now is the hour of great need,' he cried, touching the blade. He left the armoury and descended the winding stairway to the open doorway into the highest circle of the Granite City.

King Holbian smiled at the fine chestnut horse Breakmaster held for him by the bridle. She was dressed in the finest battle coat of woven steel rings that Breakmaster could find, it flowed down past her hocks showing the emblem of the owl in blue and gold.

'She is truly worthy of a King, Breakmaster, what is her name?'

Breakmaster swelled with pride, 'Lord, she is Esteron's dam. The mother of the horse you gave to young Thane for the journey to Underfall. Her name is Beacon Light.'

Holbian fitted his armoured boot into the stirrup and mounted. He laughed as Breakmaster tightened the girths, saying, 'Then I am better mounted than I ever dreamed of to face the Night-beasts. Come, Beacon Light, and carry me into the blackest night.'

The King laughed again, pirouetting the horse and sending sparks dancing across the cobbles.

'Breakmaster! Follow me if you can with every horse you can saddle.'

King Holbian urged Beacon Light forwards, cantering her down through the winding city streets, his battle cloak flowing out behind him.

Ironhand heard the hoof beats and ran out of Candlebane Hall with the King's standard. Catching up with Beacon Light he ran at the King's stirrup, laughing and singing as the emblem of the owl fluttered above his head. Beacon Light's iron-clad shoes echoed in the narrow lanes and dark alleyways as she descended towards the great gates, but other sounds mingled with the beat of her hooves, light running Archers' footsteps, heavy crunching marching boots and the neighing shouts and clattering hooves of many horses. Their noise rose to a rumbling roar that made the King look back. He laughed, his eyes shining to see so many eager faces and he drew his sword, sweeping it above his head to catch the glory of the bright afternoon sun.

'Men of Elundium!' he shouted, looking across the sea of faces, 'Who will come with me and fight once more beneath the emblem of the owl?'

In the hush that followed the King saw the doubt and the fear of the Nightbeasts cloud their faces. Breakmaster broke the silence, mounted on a rough-coated pony he called for room as he rode through the press of warriors, behind him were twenty mounted Gallopers formed into two neat columns either side of the King.

Breakmaster laughed, pointing his neatly coiled breaking whip at the assortment of horses.

'Lord, every horse broken to the saddle is here, and every warrior Errant has sent to the city awaits your command.'

King Holbian smiled, rubbing his hand along Beacon Light's proud neck, touching the silver thread woven into her mane.

'Breakmaster,' he said, quietly, 'you have served me well, and I could ask for no better. You are indeed a true Kingsman! Marchers and Archers,' he called out in a proud voice, 'Errant is upon the Greenway, hard-pressed by Nightbeasts. I shall lead this flying column of Gallopers out to rescue him. Follow us and hold the Greenway secure for our return, block the gates with tree beams to keep them open for the sun may have long set before our work is done. Riders, to the Greenway!'

Without further delay the King rode Beacon Light out of the Granite City and the Gallopers followed him, speartips ablaze with afternoon sun.

Errant saw the King's standard before him and dug his spurs deeper into his horse's flanks and swung the flat of his sword against the torn battle coat. A roaring noise from behind told him the Nightbeasts were less than a length away. Dawnrise faltered, and seemed to shudder. Errant twisted in the saddle and saw two Nightbeasts' claws hooked into the battle coat, trying to pull the horse to a halt. He slashed the sword backwards to the left and felt it strike, and heard the Nightbeast scream with pain. He slashed again, this time to the right, but he missed the claw, shattering his blade against the Night-beast's iron cuff, the force of the blow numbed his hand and sent the broken hilt high into the air. Dawnrise surged forwards again, stumbling as he picked up speed. Something bumped against Errant's leg and, looking down, he saw the severed Nightbeast's claw and iron cuff still hooked into the horse's battle coat. Another Nightbeast was beside him, reaching out its long arm to bring them down. They were all around him now. Dawnrise was staggering, his head falling from side to side with each laboured step. Errant drew both his daggers, knowing the end had come. He turned the blades outwards against the towering shadows and lifted his eyes to

266

see the sun once more, then he laughed with joy, for less than half a length ahead of him two riders ploughed into the closing Nightbeasts at spear-shattering speed. Behind them another two fanned out, lowering their spears. Errant galloped clear of the Nightbeasts, passing through the ranks of the Gallopers of the Granite City who closed in behind him.

King Holbian rode amongst the Nightbeasts swinging his double handed sword, smashing iron caps and piercing through their foul nightmare armour, and all the time, even beneath the darkest shadows, Ironhand, the Candleman, stayed tirelessly at the King's stirrup with the standard of the owl in blue and gold fluttering in the late afternoon sunlight.

Breakmaster rode his pony up beside Dawnrise until his and Errant's stirrups were touching. 'Jump!' he shouted above the thunder of hoofbeats. 'This pony is mountain bred and strong enough to carry both of us.'

Errant loosed his stirrups and sprang across. Breakmaster held on to Dawnrise's reins and so as the sun was setting they passed through the first line of Marchers defending the Greenway and eased back into a fast trot.

'Where is the King?' asked Errant looking backwards at the line of shadows following them.

'There he is,' said Breakmaster, proudly, pointing back at the Marchers, retreating in an orderly line. 'He is a great King you know, Errant, and I'll bet a bundle of pure wax candles he is the last into the Granite City.'

Holbian secretly thanked Breakmaster a thousand times as he galloped Beacon Light amongst the Marchers for she was brave and fearless before the Nightbeasts, rearing and plunging, biting and kicking to kill, and each time he let the reins fall to take up his sword she went where he bid her, or stood rock still while he made the killing stroke.

Archer Grey Goose had divided up his bowmen into two strikes. One he placed on the high ground against the granite walls of the city. 'Save your arrows,' he commanded, 'for you are the last line of defence. Swords will be broken and spear shafts shattered in the retreat when the Marchers and the Gallopers rush for the gates. Then drive back the Nightbeasts with every arrow you have.'

'What of you, Grey Goose?' one of the Archers asked.

Grey Goose smiled. 'We shall be on the Greenway, using the skills Trueflight taught us, sweeping in wherever the Marchers are weakest, buying time with each shaft we shoot.'

Night had fallen, Breakmaster urged his pony into a canter, Dawnrise followed, his head sunk down in tiredness. The great gates loomed up out of the darkness, ablaze with every torch and lamp the city people could find. Behind them Errant could hear the roaring noise of the Nightbeast army.

'Look!' cried Breakmaster, 'Look at the walls.' Errant looked up and saw, silhouetted against the night sky, thousands of tiny lights.

'The people of the city have come to help us! Every one of them has brought a lamp or a candle. Look how it lights the Greenway.'

Breakmaster looked back across his shoulder past Errant into the darkness and saw reflected in the city lights the rippling emblem of the owl and the flash of bright steel where the King spurred Beacon Light against the shadows. The Marchers swung their swords in rhythm from left to right, retreating a step, pausing to plunge their blades, retreating, pausing, and sometimes silently opening their ranks to allow the King through as he marshalled the line. Grey Goose had followed the King, shadowing his every move, and five times before night fell his strike of Archers had saved Holbian by driving back foul beasts that threatened to overwhelm him. Now they were within half a league of the gates. Holbian drew all the Marchers, Gallopers and Archers into close order upon the Greenway. The Archers with empty quivers were sent into the city, running as quickly as they could, carrying their injured between them.

'Swordsmen between the Spearmen, Gallopers on the outside. Prepare to break order,' shouted the King as they neared the gates.

'Now!' shouted Grey Goose, and all the Archers beneath the walls loosed their arrows, halting the Nightbeasts' forward rush.

'Break the standard. Retreat!' cried the King, turning Beacon Light towards the gates.

As one the warriors quickened their pace, retreating through the gates into the city, only the King and Ironhand were still to enter.

'Lord!' Ironhand cried out, stumbling forwards, the standard of the owl toppling out of his hands. Holbian spun round, sparks flying from his horse's shoes and saw his Candleman and brave standard-bearer driven to his knees by a Nightbeast spear. Holbian spurred Beacon Light forwards and plunged his sword through the Nightbeast towering over Ironhand. He reached down and lifted Ironhand up across his saddle, turned again and galloped into the city with the Nightbeasts at his heels.

Breakmaster saw the standard fall and, leaping off his pony, had rescued it just before the gates were slammed shut and piled high with tree beams.

King Holbian cantered up through the city, shouting for a healer. Only at the doors of Candlebane Hall did he draw rein and, after quietly thanking Beacon Light for her great courage, he dismounted and gathered Ironhand in his arms. He strode to the Candlebane Hall doors and pushed against them, but they did not move. He pushed again, stepped back a pace and, raising his armoured boot, he smashed the locks. The rush of wind from the bursting doors snuffed all the candles in the outer hall, releasing huge shadows that leapt up the walls into the smoky rafters.

'Chancellors!' shouted the King, advancing through the candles into the innermost circle.

The Chancellors were huddled around the throne, whispering together, Proudpurse cowering in the seat of the throne. King Holbian stood at the edge of the inner circle, the candle light reflecting from his bloodstained, battered armour. He saw before him the remnants of the cloak of jewels, shredded and scattered across the polished floor. He heard the Chancellors' whispers and looked down at the quiet face of the Candleman on his arm. He turned back to his Chancellors.

'Out! Out!' he whispered, violently, advancing towards his throne. 'You who dared to scheme and plot to steal this kingdom, take it now, if you dare! Stand before the people now and lead them, or forever creep in the shadows.'

Proudpurse jumped up out of the King's way and fled, followed by all the other Chancellors towards the Candlebane doors.

'Stop!' commanded the King, 'I have not dismissed you yet.'

Gently he laid the Candleman in the seat of the throne. Proudpurse would have heeded nothing, not even the King's command, but a figure stood between the doors, barring the way.

'Chancellors! Your King calls you,' Nevian said quietly, advancing into the Candle Hall.

'Nevian!' cried the King, 'Come quickly, my Candleman is gravely wounded.'

Nevian spoke briefly to a figure standing outside in the darkness and beckoned him to come forwards.

Errant strode into the Candle Hall and took the sword Nevian had offered him. 'Chancellors,' he laughed, sweeping the blade before their faces, 'let us return into the inner circle and await the King's counsel.'

'He is dying, Nevian, save him,' pleaded the King. 'He was the first man in the city I could trust. My brave standard-bearer, Ironhand.'

Nevian hurried to the high throne and took the Candleman's limp hand into his own, already the fingers were growing cold, the ends stiffening at his touch.

'He is beyond my skills, Lord. I cannot tread amongst the dead and bring them back.'

King Holbian knelt, putting his arm around Ironhand's shoulders and drew his head up to his own chest. 'Candleman,' he whispered, a tear forming in the corner of his eye, 'Oh, Candleman, Elundium will be a darker place without your sweet voice to sing it to sleep.'

Ironhand's eyelids fluttered open slowly, his lips moved in the slightest whisper, 'Who, Lord, calls the Candleman to see him to bed?' He smiled as he looked up at the King. A faraway look clouded his eyes and made him blind to those around him. He sighed, and slumped in the King's arms.

Holbian felt a hand on his shoulder and looking up through his tears saw the kind face of Nevian. 'Send for the Buryman,' he whispered.

'He will not travel in the Buryman's cart,' replied Holbian, carefully crossing Ironhand's arms and putting his own sword into the dead hands.

'Proudpurse and Overlord, they will carry him on a bier made from spear shafts used in battle. He shall have my battle cloak draped across it and I shall be mounted on Beacon Light following in honour of my dear and loyal friend. Each of the Chancellors will walk in homage to the Candleman, carrying lamps to light the way for him, who kept the light all his life.'

'And I shall carry the standard!' cried Breakmaster, falling on to his knees beside the body of his friend, weeping unashamedly in the soft candlelight.

The procession wound its way slowly down through the city. The news of Ironhand's death had travelled quickly through the city and all the city dwellers that had climbed to the top of the walls to light the King's retreat thronged the Buryman's route, standing in silence as the Candleman was carried out. Ironhand's widow walked at his side, her hand upon his, tears of grief running down her face. King Holbian laid the last square of turf on the mound over his grave and stepped back.

He looked at the sad faces filling every space in the Buryman's yard and realized just how many friends the simple Candleman had.

Nevian pressed the King quietly to hurry back to the Candlehall, Errant and Breakmaster followed in the King's footsteps.

'You are besieged, my Lord, the Nightbeasts have ringed the city. Listen to them pounding on the gates.'

Nevian paced Candlebane Hall, the bright colours of the rainbow cloak reflecting everywhere in the candlelight. Holbian turned his head towards the broken candle doors and listened. Ironhand's death had overshadowed the retreat into the city, but now he heard them and shuddered, remembering their foul nightmare shapes upon the Greenway. Roaring screams rose up from beyond the granite walls and at regular intervals a dull boom seemed to shake the city, trembling up through the foundations to Candlebane Hall, making the slender candle stems shake, spilling hot wax on to the polished floor. King Holbian spun round towards Nevian.

'What nature of beasts are these that can travel and fight in the daylight and shake the very bones of the Granite City?'

'Lord,' cried Errant, 'They wear a strange layer of armour over their eyes. Tombel slew a beast near Woodsedge, he examined the eyes and said it was the skin from a wolf's eye, stripped and stretched flat. It renders them near blind, without focus, but they can travel in the daylight and as you saw had nearly pulled Dawnrise down before you rescued me.'

King Holbian laughed bitterly, 'And I thought old age had robbed nothing of my fighting skills. Now I find that blind beasts chased me back into the city, killing my Candleman for good measure.'

Again the hollow booming noise shook the Granite City.

'What strange magic have they brought with them?' cried Breakmaster, drawing his sword.

'Whole trees,' replied Nevian, unrolling a map of Elundium on the Candlehall floor.

'Whole trees?' echoed the King.

'Yes, my lord. They are battering against the walls and the gates of the city with them. Twenty Nightbeasts hold each side of the tree trunks.'

'How long will it be before they break through?' wondered the King aloud.

'That, lord, depends on how great a stonemaster the last Mason King was when he built this city. But we must talk of attack and bold counter-moves, not defence and sieges. Too long you have hidden here sulking while the Nightbeasts have grown in power. Now is the time for action.'

King Holbian looked about him at the emptiness of Candlebane Hall, remembering how, in his youth, his captains and Marcher Marshals would have crowded around him, eager for his battle plans. He laughed at the emptiness and turned sharply on Nevian.

'What would you have me do? Send out my two Captains to be slaughtered before the very gates of the city? I have no great army to fight with, six ranks of Marchers, two strikes of Archers and twenty Gallopers. Even if I spread them around the city in defence each man would be out of sight of the next. I cannot waste them in proud moves, blind to sense and reason.'

'You cannot afford to sit here either, for the army that faces your gates is but a shadow of Krulshard's forces. The battle to save Elundium from the darkness will not be fought beneath these granite walls but far away in a place you know and dread!'

Holbian turned desperately to Errant. 'What of the Marchers you had ridden out to gather. How many had you found?'

'Sire, two thousand Marchers, sixteen strikes of Archers and ten squadrons of Gallopers had assembled at Woodsedge in a great camp. The lights from their cooking fires spread far beneath the eves of the black forest. The Nightbeasts divided, giving the Wayhouse a wide berth, but Tombel took the Marchers against them and slaughtered thousands before their

273

army had passed by. He dispatched me to tell you that in two daylights he will march on the Granite City.'

'There, help is on the way, Nevian,' the King laughed, turning back to the Master of Magic.

'No, Lord,' replied Nevian sternly, 'in two daylights all the light of Elundium could totter and fall into darkness. If the Warriors gathered at Woodsedge journey here to the Granite City turn them, Lord, send them with all haste to Underfall!'

'How, Lord?' asked the King, lifting his arms in despair.

Errant knelt, offering up the hilt of Nevian's sword. 'Lord, with first morning, as the sun heralds a new daylight, I will break the siege and ride without pausing for breath to Woodsedge and all the other Wayhouses on the Greenways' edge. Ten thousand Marchers shall gather on the Causeway Fields and Gallopers as numerous as summer corn will ride along the Causeway road.'

'Bold moves,' whispered Nevian, smiling at the King.

Holbian lifted Errant to his feet saying, 'We will win you a little Greenway, Captain. We shall ride with you as far as we dare, blunting our swords on Nightbeasts' armour and splintering our spears on their foul helms.'

'Lord,' Grey Goose cried, hammering on the broken candle doors. 'The Nightbeasts are scaling the walls. We drive them back but they climb faster than we can nock arrows on to the bows.'

'Every man, woman and child must come here to Candlebane Hall. Empty it of candles and take them to line the walls with light. Open the armoury and give every man who can fight a sword or spear.'

Candlebane Hall was quickly stripped of candles and the city dwellers, high or low born, together carried the candles to the highest ramparts and let them shine out against the darkness. Nevian watched the King, keeping his hand on the King post candle when all the others had been taken.

'You have grown brave, Lord, with the passing of the suns.'

274

King Holbian gently took the King post candle from Nevian and passed it to Breakmaster, telling him to take it down to the outer walls. Now Candlebane Hall stood bare and completely dark.

'I have tried,' the King replied, walking quickly through the doors, and breathing a sigh of relief to see the stars shining in the dark sky, 'I still have much to overcome before I dare enter the City of Night.'

Nevian smiled in the darkness and whispered, 'As I foretold long ago you have become a great King. Come let us go down to the walls and defend the city.'

First light had almost come. Dawnrise fidgeted while the blacksmith burned on a new set of shoes and nailed them securely to his hooves. Breakmaster scoured the armoury and found what legends had said the great Warhorses once used to wear, a battle coat of ancient steelsilver, so finely woven that it weighed no more than a feather and had the touch of watered silk, yet was tough enough to shatter a blade. He laid it across the horse's back and it fitted perfectly, showing the emblem of the owl in blue and gold threads. King Holbian had drawn the Gallopers into two columns in the shadows of the gates. Archers crouched between the horses. Marchers had interlocked their spears with the blades pointing outwards and waited in a long winding column that stretched back up into the city. The tree beams blocking the gates were quietly levered away, leaving a clear path for the King to gallop out on to the Greenway.

Errant led Dawnrise out of the blacksmith's forge, mounted him and rode down into the shadows of the gate.

'Errant,' the King whispered, riding Beacon Light up beside Dawnrise, 'take my standard and deliver it to Marcher Tombel, tell him to lead the Warriors with all speed to Underfall. Tell him to set the standard upon the Causeway Fields against our darkest fears and . . .' the King paused, taking a letter out from beneath his battle cloak, 'deliver this

275

letter to Thunderstone, for there will be no more messengers after you have gone.'

As Errant tucked the letter into his pouch the King gripped his arm. 'I shall miss you, Errant, brave heart, and my thoughts are ever with you, long after you have ridden out of sight. We shall ride with you as far as this column reaches, stopping only when the last Marcher is between the gates.'

The gates rattled and the locks clicked, light glowed above the horizon, the Nightbeasts battering the walls or scaling the heights retreated in the face of new daylight, covering their eyes with the wolf skin shields. Rumbling back across the cobbles the gate swung open.

'Kingspeed, messenger,' shouted the King, spurring Beacon Light forwards on to the Greenway.

'Kingspeed,' shouted every voice in the Granite City as the Gallopers and Marchers thundered out, ploughing through the shadows towards the clear line of the horizon bathed in early sunlight.

# *Nighthorses*

Morning was breaking through night's shadows, dawn was pushing the grey hours into retreat. The doors groaned and creaked, waiting for the sunrise. Watchkeepers patrolled the upper galleries, wrapped in their warmest cloaks. Only the Nighthorses stood awake, fidgeting in their stalls, stamping sparks off their shoes, tossing their heads in the torch light.

Thane had slept badly, troubled by a persistent dream that drove him from his bed of straw before the grey hours had touched the darkness. He dreamed of the ancient tumbled down Wayhouse and the door of thorns, tiny flowers opened and he smelt their heady scent, but far away upon the edge of sound a horse was running fast, pushed by fear. Tossing and turning he awoke soaked in a cold sweat, cramped fingers gripping the summer scarf. Each time he slept the hoofbeats grew louder until he saw clearly who it was the Nightbeasts chased and he leapt down on to the cold cobbled stable floor, hastily pulling on his clothes, whispering to Mulcade and Rockspray, 'Somewhere near this place fear drives a Kingsman on the roads. None will follow us, risking death on the strength of my dream. I must go alone. Will you come with me?'

The owls hooted softly, flying to perch beside the Nighthorses' stalls, pulling at their bridle chains with their sharp beaks. 'Will you fly ahead and search the roads lest I take the wrong path?' In his haste to saddle Esteron Thane missed the owls' wisdom as they tugged at the chains rattling the catches in their beaks. 'Quickly,' he whispered, 'the grey hours are upon us.' Frustrated and angry at Thane's blindness the owls rose on silent wings above the roofs of Underfall. 'We must go alone,' he whispered to Esteron, tightening the girths, 'None will follow my dream,' but Esteron would not leave the stables no matter how hard Thane tugged at the reins. 'Esteron!' he hissed in the torch light, near to tears, 'a Kingsman rides alone out there. I know my dream is a vision. It is the truth!' Dropping the reins he turned to face Esteron, a hand on his sword, 'I will go alone if I must!'

Esteron looked long into Thane's eyes and held him still, calming his troubled mind, before moving to the nearest stall, pulling gently at the chain that held the Nighthorse.

'The Nighthorses!' Now he understood why the owls had been pecking at the horses' chains and he ran from stall to stall releasing the brass catches.

'Thunderstone may flay my hide, but we shall not be alone upon the road. Come, the doors will soon open and we can take the road that the owls choose.'

Doubt crossed and recrossed Thane's mind many times as they waited for a touch of sunlight to spring the doors. An eerie ghostliness surrounded him, sitting among the riderless horses. They stood statue-still in two neat lines, not a hoof scraped the cobbles, not a bridle jingled in the half light. If his dream was just night's fantasy men would laugh and call him a fool, the Keeper would probably beat him raw but he held on to his courage tighter than the reins in his hands and waited for the sunrise.

With a deep rumble the doors swung back, scraping across the cobbles. Before them lay dew-wet empty fields. 'Which way, Esteron? We must not choose the wrong path.' There was an anxious note in Thane's whisper, 'It's getting late. Where are the owls? They would know which way.'

Esteron stood undecided between the doors, Mulcade flew to them low and fast, hooting and shrieking. Thane had heard that call before when great danger had pressed all around them on the road to Underfall.

'It is not a dream! Run, Esteron! Mantern's Forest is the road, that's the direction! Run, Esteron!' And then his voice was lost amidst the thunder of hooves, the banner of the sun blazed from Thane's arm as either side of him the Nighthorses fanned out, filling the Greenway still wreathed in morning mist. Mulcade alighted on Thane's shoulder, looking ahead with unblinking eyes. The men at World's End turned in troubled sleep as thundering hoofbeats blended with their dreams. Watchkeepers saw the horses galloping out and rang the warning bells, but it was too late, Esteron was upon the causeway, running fast towards Mantern's Forest and the Deepling Gorge.

# Underfall

King Holbian had won four leagues of Greenway in that mad dash out of the Granite City and Errant, looking back as Dawnrise galloped clear of the Nightbeasts, briefly watched the long column of Gallopers turn and magically shrink back into the city, protected by the glittering spear blades of the Marchers.

By evening time, with the sun near setting he had met Tombel in the vanguard of the Marchers running hard towards the Granite City. Tombel had argued fiercely against turning towards Underfall and Errant had to break the leather binding cords on the standard of the owl to convince him that it was the King's command to turn away. He had rested Dawnrise at Woodsedge just long enough for him to find his second wind and then, re-girthing, he had mounted for the road again. Elionbel had stopped him on the Greenway's edge and pressed into his hands a finely hammered silver fingerbowl asking him to give it to Thanehand when he reached World's End and to tell him that she raised her cup each daylight towards his safe return.

Dawnrise had taken him tirelessly from Wayhouse to Wayhouse, calling out the bearers of the tattoo mark, telling them that the King had great need of them upon the Causeway Fields, beneath the walls of Underfall. 'Hurry! Hurry!' he had shouted to them, remounting and galloping onwards. Now Stumble Hill lay many leagues behind.

'We will come!' Kyot had shouted above the armourers' racket as they hammered out new arrowheads.

Night was still master of the forest road and Errant saw nothing of the grey hours or the breaking dawn above the

285

canopy of trees. Only on the summit above the Deepling Gorge did he see morning and shafts of early sunlight on the wooden bridge.

Suddenly all around him Nightbeasts roared, black shadows swarmed on to the road.

'Gallop, Dawnrise!' he shouted, cutting the spurs into his horse's flanks. The steelsilver battle coat shone and glittered as Dawnrise leapt forwards, using the last of his strength to break through the Nightbeasts. Spear blades, cruel, hooked scythes and black double edged nightmare swords shattered against his coat, Errant struck out with the sword Nevian had given him and it sheared easily through the Nightbeast armour. Left and right he plunged the blade, drawing closer to the bridge with every stride. The wood beyond lay empty, bathed in early morning light.

Above the sound of Dawnrise's hoofbeats Errant heard the thunder of other iron-shod hooves and cried aloud with joy as the Greenway before him filled with horses and each one wore the crest of Underfall upon its battle coat. But his cry died away – the saddles were empty. Only the horse that led them had a rider in the saddle and he had a banner of light flowing from his arm and a Battle Owl on his shoulder.

Dawnrise faltered, crashing to his knees twenty paces from the bridge. Errant rose from the crumpling horse, his sword gripped tight in his hand against the circling Nighthorses, crying in a voice full of fear, 'None shall touch him while I live!'

'And none shall, save the healer of World's End!' answered Thane's voice as he dismounted and offered Errant the hilt of his sword.

'You have won the Greenway, messenger. You are safe from the Nightbeasts now!'

Errant looked suspiciously at the young man who stood before him. 'Much has changed since I left Underfall. Then the Nighthorses went into battle with a warrior in each saddle. What magic do you weave to counsel them? Who are you?'

Thane smiled, re-sheathing his sword and without a word of command the circle of horses stopped, turning as one to face outward, against the forest shadows. Thane knelt and loosened Dawnrise's girths and pulled the saddle clear.

'I am but one who serves amongst the many at Underfall. Thanehand is my name. I am the Candleman's son. I came through the breaking dawn to the sound of your fleeing hoofbeats. The Nighthorses were about me as the new sun rose and filled the road at their own wishes!'

Mulcade, having taken Thane's helm as he dismounted, stooped back to him carrying the helm upturned and filled with water.

'Mulcade is a bird of war, and fears not the dark. He found you beyond hope and showed me the road.'

Thane took the helm and began bathing the horse's wounds.

'Thanehand?' Errant whispered, reaching for the silver fingerbowl fixed on to his belt. Thane looked up, smiling. Errant offered him the bowl and he took it, puzzled.

'It is a gift from Elionbel from Woodsedge. She thinks of you each daylight, and . . .'

Errant's face clouded as he thought back further, to a funeral procession mournfully descending into the Buryman's yards. 'Was your father the King's Candleman in Candlebane Hall?' he asked quietly, but he could tell at once from the look in Thane's eyes that Ironhand was his father. Reaching out he took Thane's hand into his own. 'He ran at the King's stirrup, Thane, tirelessly carrying the standard. He was so brave, so . . .'

Thane looked away, blinking back his tears, and, lifting his hand to wipe his face the fingerbowl caught the sunlight as he moved and he quickly fixed it to his belt.

'To love is to risk everything,' he whispered, looking down at Dawnrise, struggling to rise to his feet. Quickly Thane looked back to the messenger's face. 'You have risked everything to ride to World's End. What has happened in the Granite City?

Why was my father, the humble Candleman, at the King's side?'

'The city is besieged by a terrible Nightbeast army. I ride to warn Thunderstone.'

'Then ride!' shouted Thane, leaping to his feet. 'Take any of the Nighthorses. The road is yours to World's End and tell the Keeper I shall return with your horse when he is strong enough to stand and finish the journey.'

Errant quickly chose a horse, mounted and turned in the saddle to look down at Dawnrise. 'We shall meet again at World's End, great horse, and there I shall put a battle coat of pure silver on your back.'

Turning to Thane he cried as the horse took to the Greenway, 'The King called out your name as we parted and hopes each daylight that you grow stronger!'

Thane sat in silence for a long time, bathing Dawnrise's wounds and thinking of his father. Tears kept welling up and unashamedly he wept.

'Thunderstone will marshal all the warriors to march on the city,' he whispered to Mulcade, perched on his shoulder, and then he wept again, thinking of his mother in that dark house beneath the city walls, frail and all alone. 'I cannot leave her alone,' he cried, leaping to his feet and tightening Esteron's girths. 'The King needs me!'

A voice beyond the circle of Nighthorses made him spin round, dagger drawn. 'Haste can be a bad council, Thane, and saves little in the fullness of time!'

Thane looked out of the circle and saw the old man in the rainbow cloak. He looked tired and dusty, worn out by a long journey.

'Nevian?' he asked, stepping forwards.

The Master of Magic laughed, casting back his cloak and entered the circle of horses motioning to Thane to re-sheath his dagger.

'The messenger carries grave news, but your running back

to the Granite City will only darken it a little more. Your place is here, leading the warriors of Underfall! Thunderstone needs you.'

'But Lord, surely Thunderstone will march to rescue the King before the Nightbeasts tear the Granite City down. I could be half a daylight ahead, searching out the way.'

Nevian smiled, placing an aged hand on Thane's sleeve. 'Patience, Thane, the battle for the Granite City will be won or lost here, at World's End, on a wide plateau near the stars. You must find that place and be before the black gate when the new sun rises and the battle begins.'

'But I cannot leave Dawnrise!' Thane cried, 'And where do I start looking for this plateau?'

Nevian pointed beyond the Nighthorses to the dark eaves of Mantern's Forest. 'You are not alone, Thane, nor is the road difficult to follow, for many will have gone before you marking the way. Look to the bonds I broke many suns ago.' Nevian shook the rainbow cloak and it became as leaf shadows on the forest edge that disappeared as a cloud covered the sun.

'Nevian, wait!' Thane called, running across the bridge. 'Nevian!' Movement in between the trees made him stop.

'Esteron,' he cried, retreating back into the circle, 'something moves beyond the forest eaves.'

Esteron raised his head, searched the undergrowth and then called out in a strong voice. Echoes came back from the distant hills, roaring across the tree tops, growing louder and louder until Thane realized that the sounds that he thought were echoes were in fact answers.

'The Warhorses!' he whispered, putting a hand on Mulcade's talons where they dug into his shoulder. In wonder beyond his understanding he watched the road about them fill with more beauty that he had ever dreamed could exist. The Warhorses' soft coats shone like silk in the sunlight. Their manes seemed spun on the finest looms, some so long and flowing that they touched the ground. Sheets of muscle rippled in graceful movements as they quietly walked around the Nighthorses, moving in the direction of World's End. By late afternoon Rockspray returned, he had searched for the fleeing rider along the ancient road through Notley Marsh but all that he had seen had been a fire-scorched dismal road, burned back to the boundary stones. He flew over the ring of ash and saw the refuse of Thane's great battle and marvelled at his courage for Mulcade, his brother owl, would not speak of it.

'Rockspray,' Thane whispered, as the owl flew to his shoulder, 'Will you fly for me to the Tower of Stumble Hill and warn Kyotorm that the Nightbeasts are gathering to attack. Will you bring him back to me at Underfall? Will you?'

Rockspray spread his wings, hooted softly and rose above the Deepling Bridge, flying fast towards Stumble Hill.

# Black Tunnels

Beneath Mantern's Mountain, night had spread in confusion and all sense of direction had been lost through Krulshards' greed to swallow everything into the darkness. Whips rose and fell to drive the tunnel slaves to dig, and new tunnels often ran blindly parallel to old forgotten ones with only a wafer thin wall of solid rock between them.

Many leagues below the ground, deep dust settled in the maze of empty roads and icy draughts of pure mountain air found the way to the deepest levels, bringing on a hint of summer and the smells of another world within the light. Willow rammed his aching shoulder hard against the sledge, gritty dust ground between his teeth and stung his eyes. 'Pull, Star!' he cried as the lash cut across his back, 'Pull!' But she could go no further, her old legs buckled, and stumbling she fell tangled in the traces. Tired eyes flinched as the enraged Nightbeast raised the lash, but it never finished its stroke. Willow pulled the hidden blade and, two-handed, plunged it high above his head into the monster's back. And a great strength in the steel sheared right through the hideous strips of armoured skin, cutting into the beast's flesh. The sledge slipped sideways, toppling over, a roaring neigh and flashing hooves filled the tunnel. Willow hit the tunnel side with such force that the wall collapsed, broken flakes of rock half buried him. He saw the Nightbeast crushed beneath the Warhorse's feet, saw Star trapped in the tangled traces, then blackness closed upon him.

Dust settled in the broken tunnel. The spilled ore and the collapsed tunnel wall stopped the enraged Nightbeasts from reaching Willow, but they tore at the mound of rubble, tossing great slabs of rock behind them. A wet tongue and soft lips pushed Willow's head from side to side and brought him back to consciousness as he lay in the Warhorse's shadow. The great head gently pushed him awake. 'Hurry!' a voice shouted in his head, 'The light awaits. Hurry, Willow.' He scrambled to his feet and turned towards the gaping hole where the tunnel wall had been, took a hesitant step and stopped. He turned back to the ruined sledge, where Evening Star lay trapped in the traces, struggling to rise; he knelt and took her head upon his lap, looking into her eyes. 'The Elder said to follow my heart and let it choose the path I take. I cannot leave you here to die alone.'

Reaching over he pulled the splintered blade out of the Nightbeast's back and made ready to defend his life beside the one he loved. The Warhorse fretted and pressed more urgent thoughts into Willow's head. 'Cut her loose, you fool, you were not meant to go alone. Use the blade upon the traces. Hurry!'

With swift slashing strokes Willow freed Evening Star who scrambled to her feet. They rushed for the black entrance as the last remaining blocks of rubble were being wrenched apart. Great Nightbeast claws appeared between the shifting rocks. 'Hurry, hurry! I will keep the entrance safe for a little while. Always keep the icy wind upon your face.' The voice in Willow's head fell silent as Equestrius turned to face the screaming mass of Nightbeasts swarming through the widening gaps between the wall of broken stones. Alone he stood, proud and unafraid, all Nature's beauty in that dark and crowded space against the glittering scythes the Nightbeasts carried. Rearing, kicking, biting and crushing he won what time he could. No slave had ever escaped to see the light of day or give away the secret of the City of Night. All the roads were filled with raging Beasts and the tunnellers burrowed deep into the dust in fear of their lives. But in a high, secret chamber, unknown to either Willow or the last of the Granite Kings, an ancient prisoner hung, spreadeagled by the chains that bound his blackened wrists, tortured and tormented he swung slowly in the chilling draughts.

Equestrius brought him news of the great battle far below the ground and of the sledgeboy's escape and his heart went out to the child fleeing for his life deep in the bowels of the mountain.

For Willow and Star, dark, empty, silent tunnels branched off in all directions, full of whispers but empty of fear, as the Nightshapes turned away, drawing together into solid blackness, for although they feared and hated what the Night-beasts were doing they could not help Willow and Star escape. Deep dust banked up the walls in drifts and in some narrow places almost blocked the way completely except for little gaps beneath the jagged roof, blown clear by icy winds. This gave a hint of the path they were to follow.

'Always keep the wind on your face,' the voice had echoed in his head. 'Come on, Star, paw and scrape old friend.' Willow caressed her and marvelled at how loud his voice sounded now he had no Nightbeast at his back ready to wield the whips. A life of whispers was at an end, Willow and Evening Star were free within the mountain's heart and would not go lightly back to slavery. Together they dug and scraped at the drifts of dust and squeezed through the narrow roads. Rumbling noises far behind made them dig faster, but the fragile network of tunnels held together with the settling dust had been disturbed by their retreat and rock slides had already blocked off their escape. There was no going back, the way was closed.

# The Warhorses

Underfall had armed for war. From the first clatter of the warning bells the galleries creaked and groaned beneath a rush of armoured boots. Spearmen filled the dykes, men shouted and cursed as they dressed the remaining horses for battle. Shadowspur threatened Thane's life for taking the Nighthorses. Riders already mounted spurred their mounts hard, cursing the undergrooms that ran beneath their feet burdened with the gear of war. 'Clear our path! Let none stand in our way!' but their voices were lost in the clamour.

Thunderstone stood in the main courtyard wielding the flat of his sword to drive men faster and none came near its reach as he roared out the orders. 'More swords on the Causeway. More quivers on the galleries. We would all be dead if life hung on your idleness.' But his anger and haste gave no indication of the turmoil and despair echoing in his head. 'Old fool, who snatches sleep while others stand the watches of the night. A child sees more and moves before the rumours of a war become shouts. What is more stupid than an old man, weary beyond his years, who hears nothing but his own snores; fool, fool!' The voices shouted at him and he swung his sword, catching a lad between the shoulder blades, sending him sprawling across the cobbles, scattering new arrows. The blow gave him no satisfaction, it only served to increase his shame. 'Thane must have been sorely pressed to ride out alone, taking only the owls and the Nighthorses. Why, child? Can you answer me that?' He spoke more to himself than to the boy lying before him; he reached down and pulled him to his feet. The lad tried to make a run for cover but the Keeper held on to him, looking into his frightened eyes, 'Did you hear any sounds in the night, child, or feel anything to trouble your sleep?'

'No, Master,' whispered the boy, fearing the Keeper's rage, 'I dreamed of galloping horses filling the Causeway; the sun shone on their battle coats.'

'Whose horses were they?' asked Thunderstone, sharply.

'Why, Master, they had our crest upon them. A golden owl on a blue background. There was fire in their eyes and they tossed their heads with pride.'

The lad had a faraway look in his eyes, fear gone, and for a moment the Keeper heard the roar of hoofbeats from his own dream. He smiled, and whispering as he released his grip on the lad, 'He will be safe amongst the Nighthorses for they were gathered from all the wild places. No matter what shadows fall across his path. Hurry, lad, new arrows may be bloody and blunt before this day sees an end.'

Thunderstone now gathered his captains to stand with him between the doors. He raised the blade of his sword towards the wild landscape beyond. In his other hand he held a crystal glass full to the brim with a clear liquid. Placing the glass upon the ground, he spoke to those assembled.

'Rumours and whispers will become the shouts of battle, that much I know. It is in the wind and it is in the ground we stand upon. Watch the glass.'

Great Warriors bent their heads, not knowing that magic lay trapped within the glass. None wished to seem the fool and wide-eyed fear held them to the spot.

'Watch and wait!' ordered the Keeper. The noise of men and horses preparing for war seemed to fade into the background, the liquid trembled and became still, trembled and was still again. None the wiser, the Warriors cast glances at each other, looking for the courage to ask what riddle lay in the glass. 'There is the whisper of war,' Thunderstone said, picking up the glass and casting its contents across the cobbles at their feet.

'Where, Master?' ventured Tiethorm, stepping back lest the liquid touch his boots. 'What power moved the liquid?'

300

'The rumours of war, you fool, did you not feel the tremors during the night? Whatever shook the very bones of this place must have driven Thane on to the Causeway, taking the Nighthorses with him. I thought the dotage of age robbed only me of wakefulness, I did not realize it also robbed every man about me, except young Thane.'

Thunderstone looked past those assembled, speaking almost to himself. 'Something with great power moves the ground beneath our feet. Something like a mighty wind. It is all around us; we can feel it yet we cannot touch or hold it.' Turning his mind back to those gathered about him he spoke with all the authority of the Keeper of World's End. 'I counsel you to be ready!' Then he turned to stride towards the galleries but a cry from his bowmen on the walls made him turn again, running back to the doors.

'Look, Master! The Warhorses!' came a cry from the dykes, until the shouts of the men were lost beneath the pounding hooves. The dust of their passage hung as a dense fog over World's End. The ground shook, the doors rocked to and fro upon their hinges, plates rattled on forgotten tables, drinking vessels crashed to the ground and a fierce wind blew the candle flames dancing madly on their wicks.

'Nature's army moves towards Mantern's Mountain!' shouted Thunderstone, but none heard him as the close-pressed Warhorses galloped past. 'If nothing but the shadows of death live why are they going in that direction?'

But his thoughts were broken by the sight of a rider emerging from amongst the Warhorses, hard-galloping he came, past the Marchers in the dykes who raised their spears and swords to cheer him on, straight through the mighty doors. Sparks showered from the horse's hooves as he skidded to a halt before the master of World's End.

'Errant!' Thunderstone cried, embracing him, overjoyed to see him alive and safe.

Holding Errant at arm's length Thunderstone frowned to

301

see him so ragged and exhausted. Drawing him close again he asked in a quiet voice. 'What black news do you carry that has hard ridden you into a shadow? Where is your horse, Dawnrise? He was the best and the bravest that we have ever saddled.'

'Lord, the Granite City is under siege. The road is full of Nightbeasts and is closed. I bring you this letter from the King . . .'

'Warriors!' Thunderstone shouted, turning abruptly away from Errant. 'We must rescue the King.'

'Lord, Lord,' shouted Errant above the rush of armoured feet and the clatter of hooves. 'The King sent me here to warn you that the battle for the light of Elundium will be fought here. Nevian foretold this in Candlebane Hall!'

Thunderstone held up his hands and the warriors fell silent and stood back, listening. Turning back, the Keeper took the pouch, his eyes softening.

'Forgive me my impatience, Errant,' he whispered, taking out the letter and tearing it open with the battle dagger. A single jewel fell into his hand, it flashed in the sunlight filling the courtyard with brilliant white light. Thunderstone closed his hand over the jewel and read the King's letter. It was brief and battle written, smudged and hastily sealed before the ink had had the time to dry. It told how the Nightbeasts had encircled the city with their black terror and of Nevian's predictions of the great battle to come at World's End, and how Errant would raise the bearers of the tattoo mark as he carried the letter across Elundium. The jewel, it said, was the last one from the cloak of jewels and Thunderstone, if possible, was to set it in the Great Lamp of Underfall to reflect and shine in the darkness to come.

'Keep the light burning, dear friend, for as long as you can. The pledges are at an end. If the bearers of the tattoo mark arrive too late then everlasting darkness will follow!'

Thunderstone sighed, putting the jewel in an inner pocket.

Grimly he spoke to the Warriors crowding around him. Lifting his arm with the tattoo mark of the owl in blue and gold he said, 'This light will burn as long as I live. It will shine in the darkness of despair for it knows nothing of defeat!'

Taking Errant by the arm he led him aside and asked, 'You were riding Nightbeam, the Nighthorse, where did you come by him?'

'Thanehand and the Nighthorses rescued me from Nightbeasts near the Deepling Bridge. Thane is staying with Dawnrise until he has recovered enough to finish the journey. He urged me to finish on my own.'

Thunderstone smiled, 'That young man grows more like his grandfather with each new daylight, but what of the Warhorses? Did you see many in Mantern's Forest?'

'Lord, the road was full of them, but they parted giving me the crown of the road. The dust from their passage robbed my sight of their beauty. There were many Border Runners amongst them and flocks of birds flew overhead. Do you think they are forming for battle?'

'If I knew the answer I would be a wise man, and well prepared for whatever is about to happen. But you, Errant, must eat and drink and rest after such a hard road. We shall talk again before the sun touches the horizon.'

Thunderstone wrapped his cloak about his shoulders to hide a troubled heart and walked amongst his men checking that every bow was taut, every strap and keeper was in place, lifting mens' hearts wherever he passed, for they saw not old age or defeat but Thunderstone the Keeper of World's End.

Nature's army had thinned, the leading ranks had vanished beneath the pine forests on Mantern's lower slopes, only the late-comers strode across the Causeway Fields, weary from long journeys. Dusty and sweat-covered they stretched their necks as if to finish a great race. Thunderstone withdrew his Marchers and Gallopers into the fastness of Underfall, filling the courtyards to overflowing. Swordsmen and bowmen crowded on the galleries. Not a man or a horse could move, so tightly were the Warriors of Underfall pressed, waiting to hear their Master speak. But he stood between the doors, watching Mantern's Peak that now seemed to fill the sky. The letter from his King was in his hand.

At last he turned, tired and as if at the end of some great inner debate, but he spoke with the power that Nevian had seen long ago, hidden deep within the youth, knowing that he would grow to hold World's End. Even as doubt lay all about him, true to his pledges, he spoke with pride.

'Men! You that I thought less than worthy have grown in strength and purpose and have become mighty Warriors. Horses that I deemed shadows of the truth have stood beside their brothers of legends and shown that they have the heart to match them! Ruin has taken much that we cannot see, pledges and oaths are at an end. The shackles and chains that bound you and pulled you to this place are now broken for ever. You are free to return to wherever fate drove you from.'

Not a man moved, nor a horse tossed his head; all stood in silence, for many had served a lifetime at Underfall and knew nothing of the way home or whether any still survived from old memories.

Tiethorm stepped forward, pushing his way through the host until he stood before Thunderstone. He knelt, offering his bow of oiled ash and asked the Keeper in a loud, clear voice, 'What of you, Master? Now that the oaths are broken, what will you do?'

'I have given you back your freedom. My pledge was made long ago and will hold until I die, for I am the Keeper of Underfall. I will keep it secure alone, if fate drives me to it.'

'Master, Lord of Hope,' called Tiethorm, 'In childhood I slept safely in my mother's bed, secure in the knowledge that the men of legends kept us safe. Now I know you as a man I will stand with you and in freedom bend my bow to hold World's End until the last arrow is fired.'

304

The sun, dropping towards evening, shone blood red through the great doors, seeming to set men's armour on fire. Horses neighed, men lifted their swords and shouted, 'World's End! World's End!' and Thunderstone heard in their shouts the voices of a mighty army. Tears of pride ran down his cheeks and he knew that night's shadows would hold no fear for the men of Underfall.

Pledges and oaths were cast aside and every man, old or young, knelt before Thunderstone, and in freedom chose to stay at World's End. As the last undergroom bowed his head and made the first choice he had ever had, hoofbeats rang on the Causeway.

'Rise, lad, and stand in no man's shadow, be proud of your choice.'

As Thunderstone helped the lad from his knees he recognized the youth as the one he had questioned about his dream. 'Fear not the flat of my sword, child, blade for blade we will face the shadows together.' Turning his head, he cried aloud Thane's name, for he saw him less than half a league from the doors, surrounded by the Nighthorses, their coats ablaze with evening light. 'Thane!' he cried, as the warriors fell silent, eager to hear what news he had of the road.

The Nighthorses halted before the doors, tossing their heads in the direction of Mantern's Mountain. Low murmurs passed amongst the company as Thane led Dawnrise to stand before Thunderstone. None among them had ever seen a steelsilver battle coat and they marvelled at the way it shimmered, catching the light, as the horse moved forwards, but their gasps of delight faded away as they saw the blood-caked spur marks on his flanks and the terrible Nightbeast wound across his neck and shoulders where the steelsilver coat could not reach.

Errant shouldered his way through the press of warriors and knelt before Dawnrise and wept, drawing his dagger to take his own life such was his despair at seeing how hard he had ridden

305

his own horse, but Thunderstone took the dagger saying in a quiet voice, 'He ran as his forefathers did into the legends of the world. Take not his victory, nor waste the joy of reunion. Give him your hand, for this is his moment of great honour!'

Dawnrise moved forwards, sniffed Errant's hand, brushed his muzzle on his face and whinnied softly.

'All honour to Dawnrise!' the warriors shouted. Swords crashed on shields, spear butts clashed against the cobbles and Errant led his horse into the stables and the gentle hands of the healer of World's End.

Thane stood between the doors, a frown creasing his forehead, looking towards Mantern's Mountain. Thunderstone broke into his thoughts.

'What troubles you, lad? You have seen much that others have missed.'

Thane strove for words. 'I had a dream last night. I saw the Errant Rider, I feared to wake you but the dream was a vision.'

'Yes, lad, I know that now but something else plagues your mind, speak plainly, we are on the edge of something, a great battle? Ruin?'

Thane summoned up his courage and spoke so that all those gathered could hear him. 'Beside the Deepling Bridge Nevian came to me, and counselled me to find a high plateau somewhere near the stars. He said I must find a black gate before the new sun rises.'

Thane turned his eyes back into the crowded courtyards, but none laughed as he had feared. The silence was so complete that he thought he could hear the grass bending in the wind. All eyes were fixed on him.

'I must find that place. Nevian has commanded me. Where do I look?'

Thunderstone laughed, placing a hand on Thane's arm as he went to mount Esteron. 'Wait. The impatience of youth makes an old man weary and his bones grate to chase your haste. Wait!' he paused, tugging at his horse tail hilt, speaking slowly from his memories of long ago. 'Only one man knew of such a place, and he spoke of an entrance high above the tree line. He knew nothing of its purpose or who had set it there, only that it was full of shadows, a place of fear and terrible dread. Somewhere high above the heather meadows, near the stars!'

'Who was that man?' Thane asked, jumping lightly into Esteron's saddle, 'that I may ask him the way.'

Thunderstone smiled, sadly, 'It was your grandfather, Thane. He is beyond our asking, but he told me of that dreadful place. It is there, somewhere, near Mantern's Peak.'

Thane turned in the saddle and looked at the darkening mountain.

'I am against it, Thane, just as I was against your grandfather travelling that black road, and I fear for your life beyond the Causeway Fields, alone and amongst so many shadows.'

'He will not be alone, Master,' called out a voice from the courtyard. 'You readied us for battle so we shall stand wherever the shadows gather and fight beneath the banner of the sun to march and ride wherever Nightbeasts threaten.'

Thunderstone raised his hand for silence, looking from the lengthening shadows of the mountain across the Causeway Fields and then back at the warriors filling the courtyards before he spoke.

'It is settled then, my warriors. Your going brings old legends back to life, for you travel a clear path in the Warhorses' hoofprints. Follow them to glory and heaped up honours before Mantern's Gate!'

Amidst the rush of men and horses leaping down on to the Causeway Thunderstone held on to Esteron's bridle.

'The words of Nevian are coming true, Thane. I was going to send every man and horse I could spare back to the Granite City. He said the battle would be here. I would have disobeyed him after all these years of loyal service, but you have made it otherwise. Men follow you, Thane. Guard them well beneath

307

your banner, for they know little of the terrors that await them beyond the Causeway Fields. They love you, Thane, use that love well and come safely back, my greatest Captain.'

He took Thane's hand, gripping it hard, 'Keep safe, child, on the Mountain of Darkness.'

'Lord, as my Master commands so I shall be amongst the Warriors of World's End.'

'Bonds and oaths are broken. I command only myself, the men that follow you do so in free choice. Love draws them to you. The choice of where you follow fate is yours.'

'Lord, my choice lies with all beings that yearn for freedom to see a new sun rise, to hear birdsong on the Greenway's edge and ride into morning fearing nothing the sun has yet to touch.'

'Then go with my blessing, Thane, ride hard and stir up such a wind that none can stand before you!'

Esteron reared, breaking free from Thunderstone's hand. Far away in the evening gloom he heard the Warhorse call and fretted for the road.

'Where is Rockspray?' the Keeper called, as Esteron sprang to the Causeway, taking the bridle and striding into the fading light.

'I bid him fly to Stumble Hill to warn Kyot of . . .'

Esteron galloped hard across the causeway fields, taking Thane past the running Marchers and other galloping horsemen, and his shouted reply was lost in the thunder of hooves and the great gust of wind he stirred up.

Thunderstone stood alone between the doors.

'You will not fight alone. True friends will gather before the gate of night, I know it.'

The doors began to close, Thunderstone turned, his shadow stretching long upon the cobbles. He was now almost alone within the fortress of World's End, his footsteps echoed in the emptiness. For the first time in a long life he missed the stable noises, the bustle of activity around him. Only one horse stood pulling at the hay in his manger, only one Warrior sat in the bracken on the stable floor, honing the blade of his sword.

'Errant,' Thunderstone asked quietly, 'tell me how things looked upon the Greenways. Tell me if you can what is there left to keep the light burning in this great fortress for?' Errant looked up, his eyes wet with tears, opened and closed his mouth, but there were no words.

Haste drove the spur, fear was put aside and just as Thunderstone had counselled, the way was clear to follow. Although uphill men and mounts strode with bounding strides, none looked back until they had reached the heather meadows, and then drawing breath, saw far below, the lamp of World's End shining out in the darkness of the valleys. Far away upon the ridge above the Deepling Gorge, Thane thought he saw starlight glittering on mens' helms. 'It must be a trick of the light,' he whispered to Mulcade, 'Kyot must still be far away. We stand alone.'

Somewhere above, against the shadows of tall pines, a high-pitched cry broke the evening quiet, despair and courage blended in the call for help. Esteron flattened his ears, curled his lips back, snatched at the bit and leapt forward. The voice, in desperate notes, cried out his father's name.

Willow dug and dug until his fingers bled. Star pawed and scraped and together they forced a passage through the drifts of dust. All around them the Nightshapes whispered faint mumblings of the light, faint whispers of another world beyond the night where water splashed into sunlit pools. They dug and dug until exhaustion forced them to stop and they fell asleep side by side, hands and hooves pushed into the next barrier of dust.

Cold and stiff they awoke and started digging again. 'We must keep going forwards, Star,' Willow muttered between clenched teeth. 'Even if the dust wears our skin away, leaving raw flesh, we must reach the light.'

Star snorted and dug her hooves deeper, sweat trickled down her forehead and across her shoulders. With each new drift they broke through, the air smelt a little sweeter and gradually they reached the higher levels and the tunnels widened into long dark empty roads, busy with the movement of night.

'My grandelders must have made these tunnels,' whispered Willow, now walking beside Star, a hand stretched out to feel the wall. 'Equestrius said we must keep the tunnel draught in our faces but there seem so many draughts.'

Suddenly the wall Willow had his hand against vanished, two more hesitant paces forward and they were standing in a huge cavern beneath a high rough domed roof.

'Hush, listen, Star. There is something in this cavern!' Willow whispered, turning his head from left to right, straining his shell-shaped ears for every sound. 'There! Do you hear it?' he hissed, as the dry, creaking, scraping sound echoed faintly above his head. Moving closer to Star he looked up and saw a dark shape high-pinned to the roof, held by strong chains. Slowly it turned, the iron links grinding together in the cold draught.

Star whinnied and a dark shape with wings outspread left the hanging figure and stooped down to hover just above their heads.

'Silverwing,' snorted Star in greeting to the owl, and the owl screeched quietly, perching for a moment on her withers before flying back to the figure in the roof.

'What was that?' called out Willow, drawing his blade.

Star snorted, 'It is Silverwing, the Battle Owl. He guards a great Lord that Krulshards captured long ago and left pinned to the ceiling to die.'

'What is a Lord?' asked Willow, creeping forwards and staring up at the slowly rotating figure.

The dark shape laughed as it turned, a dry crackling sound; and then it spoke. 'You may well ask, "What is a Lord?", but more important what and who are you?'

Willow hesitated, looking from the dangling figure to the owl perched nearby and then to Evening Star at his side.

'I am Willow Leaf, the sledge boy, and this is Evening Star. We are escaping to the light.'

The ancient figure bent his head, a smile crossing the wasted face, 'And I, Willow, am Thoronhand, the last Errant Rider to the Granite Kings. Equestrius has told me of your escape and my heart yearns for you to see the daylight. Hurry now, boy, you must not tarry here too long for Nightbeasts travel through this chamber on their way up to the black gate.'

'Lord Thoronhand,' Willow asked, climbing on to Star's back and reaching up towards the Galloper's ragged boots, 'Is there any way I can cut you down?'

Thoron laughed, 'These chains are thicker than a child's wrist and will need strong tools to break them, but I thank you, Willow, for wanting to help and I will ask that you do for me one task, perhaps more important than winning my freedom. On the lower slopes of this mountain there lies a place called Underfall; when you reach the light go there and warn the Keeper that Krulshards, the Master of Darkness, lives, and that he has bred new terrors here in the darkness and soon he will sweep with them across all Elundium. Will you do that for me, Willow?'

'Yes, Lord,' cried Willow, overbalancing as he reached up and touched Thoron's boots, sending the old man spinning as he fell to the floor. Silverwing hooted in alarm.

'Quickly,' urged Thoron, 'Nightbeasts are near. Go straight ahead and then take the third tunnel after the bend. I think that way leads out on to the mountainside. Hurry!'

Willow scrambled to his feet and ran towards the low entrance directly opposite on the far side of the cavern. He could hear the dry rattle of the Nightbeasts' armour and smell their foul stench.

'Come on, Star,' he hissed, leading the way. Evening Star followed as quickly as she could, bumping her bulky sides against the walls as the tunnel narrowed.

Willow's sharp ears picked up different sounds ahead, noises he had never heard before, some so loud that they thundered in his head. Dropping flat on to his stomach he crawled forward, the dagger wedged between his teeth.

311

Rounding a tight bend a brilliant white light burned his eyes. If it had been pure sunlight it would have destroyed his sight forever but morning had not yet lifted about Mantern's towering shoulders and what he had glimpsed was only the beginnings of a beautiful day. Spellbound he hugged the dirty floor, shaking his head until his hair fell in a tangled fringe over his eyes and he looked again through slitted eyelids. It was more wonderful than any of the elders' stories, pure light flooded through a metal grille about two hundred paces further up the tunnel. The grille had sharp spikes at the bottom that touched the ground and barred the way. A heavy movement near the grill caught Willow's attention. He froze where he lay, holding his breath, a racing heart made the blood pound in his ears. He had not noticed the niches carved near the tunnel entrance, skilfully fashioned to hide the Watchers, for in the niches sat two giant Nightbeasts. Willow knew that he must retreat without attracting their attention. Behind him he heard the dull pad of Star's hooves and her laboured breath rasped loudly as she climbed the winding tunnel. The Nightbeasts turned their heads from left to right and their hooded eyes searched blindly in the light.

Willow edged backwards round the tunnel bend, willing the old horse with all his mind to stand stock still. His bare foot touched something hard, he jumped and rolled over, the dagger gripped with both hands ready to strike upwards. Evening Star's soft muzzle touched his forehead and a gentle voice filled his mind, 'I heard you, Willow, we can talk together without any sound just as Equestrius the great Warhorse spoke to you telling you to cut the traces that bound me to the sledge. I have read your thoughts since the elder's death and know the pain you took from the lashes meant for my back. Come, little one, we must find another path to freedom.'

Willow guided Star backwards to the place where the tunnels branched in many directions; slowly step by step they retreated, hardly daring to breathe in case the watchers heard them. But sharp-eyed owls had seen Willow through the grille and brought the dawn birds to sing in a deafening chorus on the mountainside and their music drowned out even the greatest tunnel noise.

'Which tunnel now?' whispered Willow. 'They all look used, and they all smell of freedom. Nightbeasts' footprints tread in every direction.' Star's ears twitched and the whites of her eyes showed in the dark. Quite near she heard the rattle of Nightbeasts' armour and the tramp of feet.

'We must follow this tunnel and put as much distance as we can between us and the watchers,' whispered Star.

Without any further sound Willow moved forward; he had caught that glimpse of light earlier and it still burned within his head. The Elder in all his stories had missed the power, the sparkling beauty of the light. But, sighing, Willow remembered that neither the Elder, nor any other tunneller beyond the count of time, had seen the sunlight. He was the only tunnel slave to have looked beyond the darkness and no matter how many times he blinked or shut his eyes the image remained.

The tunnel forked, both paths looked identical, which to choose? Willow wet a dirty finger and held it up, the finger felt colder against the left hand opening. 'The draught is stronger that way,' whispered Willow. 'If only Equestrius was with us, he would know the way.'

Star whinnied and rubbed her tired head against his arm. Her need to reach the light became more urgent with each step she took, for the unborn foal she carried was growing impatient, yet she dare not tell Willow, he would make her rest and time was their enemy.

'Light,' hissed Willow, gripping the dagger in both hands. 'Look,'

The old horse pushed past him, snorting and whinnying, 'Hold my tail and cover your eyes, we have found the secret way.'

Willow stumbled blindly forward, oblivious to the sighs of lament from the Nightshapes for they knew they would change

313

if the boy escaped. Strange smells and noises filled his head until it felt as though it would burst, but a gentle voice kept him steady, 'A few more steps, child, and the sun will burn fiercely on your skin, grass and heather will lie beneath your feet. Tread carefully, the side of the mountain will be steep and strewn with rocks.'

'Can I look?' whispered Willow.

'No, the sun is at its most powerful. Wait for evening or the shade of the pine forest below.'

'Pine forests?' questioned Willow, bubbling with excitement, 'I must look.'

'No!' commanded Evening Star. 'You must wait.'

'What's that?' asked Willow, grimly, for he heard noises all about him that had not been there a few moments earlier, flapping noises near his head, rustlings in the heather.

'Is it the Nightbeasts?' Evening Star was snorting greetings to those that passed on either side of her, or flew just above her head.

'Hush, Willow,' she whinnied, passing clear thoughts into his head, 'We are passing among the Warhorses.'

'Warhorses!' cried Willow, 'I must look. Are they as beautiful as Equestrius? How many are there?' Willow would have gone on talking all day in his excitement, and was about to open his eyes when Star cut him short.

'No!' You are not to look. I will answer all your questions – all that I have the answers for – as we walk down the mountain.'

'But,' interrupted Willow, 'Birds are flying near my face. I can feel the draught from their wings. Are all the animals gathering to set us free?'

'One thing at a time,' replied the old mare, she could feel the beginnings of labour and with tired eyes sought a place to lie down.

'First, before I answer your questions I must tell you my secret. Equestrius said you had to escape in ignorance, he said I was only to tell you if we reached the light.'

'What?' exclaimed Willow. 'What could be more important than freedom itself?'

'I carry Equestrius' son and he must be born beneath the sky in freedom.'

Willow thought back to that first time he had seen Esroh near the place Evening Star was shackled and remembered how the Warhorse had commanded him to keep secret his visit to the sledge horses. Star interrupted his thoughts. 'Soon the birth will start but first we must move as far down the mountain as possible, away from the Nightbeasts' mine. Now the answers to your questions. All the Warhorses are beautiful, but Esroh is their Lord and perhaps the greatest and most powerful. The birds, the dogs, and the Warhorses are gathering here on Mantern's Mountain for another purpose, but they will help us, if the need arises.'

'Why do they gather then?' interrupted Willow.

'To free the old man, Thoronhand, the one we found hanging in chains in the high chamber. You see, amongst the wild and the free he is held in high esteem, the owls bring him food and drink, and rumour has travelled throughout the land of how Equestrius found him and Nature's army gathers to rescue him.'

'He must have been a great Lord among men,' whispered Willow.

'Yes, he was,' Star replied. 'Why I remember hearing rumours of him when I served the King as a relay horse before the Nightbeasts stole me.'

Star had led Willow down into the shadows of the tall pine trees. 'You can open your eyes now, but only for a few moments.'

He opened his eyes and gasped. Towering pine trees rose all around him, their resin scent filled his nose and a thick carpet of pine needles pricked at the soles of his feet.

'It's beautiful, beautiful!' he murmured, looking everywhere at once. 'It's more wonderful than any of the Elders' stories and . . .' then he saw all the animals moving around where they stood and his sore eyes filled with tears. Wild Warhorses stopped and rubbed their heads against his arms. Mighty Border Runners sniffed and licked his hands and face and the owls hovered and stooped down low between the trees. Willow's eyes were burning, even in the shadowy forest light and he closed them. Whispering to the old mare as he held tightly to her mane. 'All of it is so beautiful. Far better than I ever imagined it would be.'

'Hold on tight, little one, and I will take you down to Underfall. Soon night will come and it will not hurt to open your eyes.'

'What is Underfall?' he asked.

'Underfall is the strongest fastness in all Elundium. I lived there once, Willow, and served the King before the Night-beasts stole me. But we must hurry, my labour is beginning and I must find a place to lie down,' snorted the mare.

Willow had many questions he wanted to ask about fort-resses, men and the world all about him, but Evening Star began looking for a place to lie down. Willow saw that they had reached the forest edge. Before him stretched heather meadows, dark, wooded valleys and a single point of light shone far below in the inky blackness. Day had come to an end, it did not hurt to open his eyes any more, the first evening stars were climbing into the sky.

'Star!' he cried, pointing up. 'Look at the stars, they . . .' Snapping twigs and branches behind them made Willow spin round, Star snorted and neighed.

'Nightbeasts! Run! Willow, run to Underfall, I can go no further.'

'No!' shouted Willow, 'I will not leave you, I will not.' Snatching up a stout branch that lay at his feet Willow drew the dagger and cut a strip of leather from the broken harness that still hung from Star's shoulders. 'I will make a spear, just like the ones in my dream, and I will defend you.'

316

Binding the blade as tightly as he could, Willow looked down the mountainside. 'It is too far to Underfall, they will kill you and the foal. As Equestrius saved my life in the broken tunnel so shall I save yours.' Evening Star lifted her tired head, snorting through the labour pains, 'You have all the world to run in. Go! The men of Underfall must be told of Krulshards and the Nightbeasts' mine; make for the light below, run, run!'

But Willow knew he owed not only his life to Equestrius but freedom itself, and his heart told him it would be an empty world without Evening Star at his side.

'I cannot leave you, I love you,' he whispered. Evening Star laid her head on the ground and a glaze of labour filmed over her eyes. As the pain swept through her body she whispered to Willow, 'Call Equestrius's name, sing it to the stars.' Dark shapes moved between the trees. 'They are coming,' said Willow, gripping the spear shaft tightly, a quick glance at Evening Star was all he had time for as the Nightbeasts advanced, crushing and burning the heather beneath their hideous feet. That brief glance showed him the miracle of life, the tiny foal was almost born and on his hooves, reflecting in the star light, were the Warhorse rings of steel.

Willow screwed up his courage and his voice rose clearer and stronger with each word towards the stars, borne up on the evening breeze, it echoed within the very gates of the City of Night. 'Equestrius, your courage holds my blade, even as you protected me and made me strong so shall I stand between the Nightbeasts and your new born son!' Willow plunged the home-made spear and many times avenged the Elder's death, but with mighty thrusts the towering monsters pushed him backwards until he stood with his legs straddling Evening Star and her new born foal and he looked up without fear into their faces as they snarled and drooled, raising their spears to make the killing thrust.

'Equestrius! Equestrius!' Willow shouted as the stars were blotted out above his head, 'Equestrius!'

The ground shook and trembled beneath his feet and a roaring noise filled his ears, louder even than the screams of the Nightbeasts.

# The Tattoo Comes to Life

'Gallop, Esteron, Gallop!' Thane shouted and the heather beneath his pounding hooves gave off a clear night scent that reminded him of his pillow far away at home in the City of Granite. Before them Nightbeasts filled the meadows, closing in upon a tiny figure straddling an old horse that lay on her side. Beside her, first life flickered in a new born foal. As Esteron broke upon them, Border Runners leapt from the shadows of the pine trees, owls stooped from a star-filled sky and the Warhorses swept through the Nightbeast ranks, kicking and crushing all before them. Victory was quick, silence held the field and starlight sparkled on Thane's summer scarf as it fluttered in the night breezes.

Willow stood quite still, gripping the home-made spear in his hands, looking from the Warhorses and dogs to the rider, advancing through the heaped bodies of the Nightbeasts. Star struggled to her feet, her foal nickered and sought a teat for comfort.

The Riders of World's End sat uneasily in their saddles for they feared the power of the Warhorses and the great dogs that stood among them, but they feared a darker magic in the child who held the spear for none of them had ever seen such large round eyes or the shell-shaped ears before, and they knew not what he was, or what power he held, to summon the Warhorses, owls and dogs.

Thane bent low over the pommel of the saddle and gazed in wonder at Willow and the new-born foal, a miniature likeness of Esteron. 'Well met, little Warrior! Are there many more of your kind upon this dismal mountainside?'

Willow started to answer, lifting his bloody arm to point up beyond the trees but he uttered only a cry, pointing his arm in the other direction, for beating the night air beneath a massive wing span flew a mighty owl, a sword gripped in his shiny talons. Slowly he passed over them, blotting out the stars, calling to Mulcade and all the other owls that had helped to rescue Willow, 'Mantern's Gate! Mantern's Gate!'

Thane knew nothing of Eagle Owl's words or the urgency in the message, but he recognized his grandfather's sword.

Journey's end was almost in sight. Eagle Owl had seen much that troubled his heart as he flew across Elundium following the great Greenway towards World's End. Ruin, chaos and burning townships spread beneath his wing tips. Nightbeasts plundered as they moved with the shadows of death, closing in a great circle around the Granite City. Only long after passing over Stumble Hill had he seen the swift moving column of ancient marchers heading towards Underfall and recognized Tombel with his great fighting sword resting across his shoulder.

'Run!' he hooted, 'time wears all to ruin. Run!' but the brambles and undergrowth slowed them down. Tombel heard the owl's cry and lifted the marching sword high above his head where it flashed in the sunlight.

With aching wings, Eagle Owl flew across Meremire Forest, rising on evening currents towards Mantern's Mountain. Black and shadowy land slipped by beneath the great sword that he carried in his talons. Above the Deepling Gorge, starlight reflected on the helms and polished bows of a strike of archers running towards Underfall. Before them, riding a fiery little horse, a young warrior held the Great Bow of Orm in his hand, and at his heels ran two great Border Runners.

Eagle Owl hooted, urging them on, for time was their enemy even by night, they must run or come too late and find ruin as a welcome. For an instant, Rockspray rose to fly beside a great Captain Owl of days gone by and shrieked and hooted all the news of events at World's End, before stooping back to Kyot's shoulder.

Eagle Owl dare not rest or ease his grip upon the sword. Where Nightbeasts trod beneath the trees, danger flew against him, black crows attacked, flying up from wild woods that crowded against the Greenway's edge. Magpies snapped and screeched at his wing tips but none dared to touch the blade or risk his beak, for though he was old beyond counting, he was the Lord of Owls.

World's End, wreathed in shadows, showed up below. Underfall still looked secure, and upon its highest galleries one lamp shone, pure white in the blackest night. Beside the lamp, an ancient warrior trimmed the wick but even as he laboured to keep the lamp steady, his eyes were drawn towards the mountain slopes.

Eagle Owl stooped to earth, for he knew he must rest or drop the sword, and he alighted beside the great lamp, making Thunderstone leap backwards grabbing at his horse-tail sword, but surprise turned to curiosity as he recognized who perched near the lamp. 'Even you, great bird of war, have returned from the inaccessible bleakness of your mountain home. What calls you to this grim place? What is the burden you carry in these razor-sharp talons of yours? Rest, weary bird, for whatever precious touchstone lies beside you, it is safe within this fastness while the lamp burns.'

The owl let Thunderstone advance near enough to touch the hilt of Thoron's sword, for he saw before him the Keeper of World's End, full grown in power and purpose from the ragged youth of long ago when battle had darkened the Causeway road and he hooted softly before flying to perch on the old man's shoulders.

'Thoron's sword! You carry a great burden, brave owl, for few could lift such a blade, but,' he mused quietly, 'few had your strength in battle all those years ago. Why have you brought such a trophy here? Thoron has long passed into the shadows and greatly we miss him.' Thunderstone thought for a moment as he looked at the sword. 'Is it for his grandson Thane?'

Eagle Owl turned his ancient head, looking from the sword towards the black, towering shape of Mantern's Mountain and in quiet hoots told Thunderstone of his perilous journey into the Granite City, stooping low between the nightmare shapes that assaulted and swarmed the walls to collect the blade from where it hung in the armoury. 'Kingspeed' the King had called from the lower battlements where he fought among the Night-beasts, lifting his sword to glint in the sunlight. Eagle Owl tilted his head on one side and shrieked. 'Mantern's Gate, Silverwing, my brother, keeps a lonely vigil in the mountain's heart. He sent word that Thoron lives and will need the sword!'

Thunderstone lifted a hand and caressed the owl's chest feathers. His eyes searched the mountainside and he whispered, 'If only I could understand what you say or know the counsel of your words, for Thane has gone, following in his grandfather's prints towards the great gate somewhere near Mantern's Peak.'

Eagle Owl hooted, tightening his talons on the old warrior's shoulder before taking up the sword and flying into the shadows of Mantern's Mountain.


'The tattoo of the owl has come to life!' shouted Thane. 'Warriors of Underfall, follow the owl!' Thane reached down and lifted Willow quickly from where he stood, placing him on the pommel of the saddle but the boy struggled to get down. 'What of Evening Star?' he cried, 'I cannot leave her here alone.'

Thane laughed, and pointed, 'She is not alone. She has better guardians than us. Look!'

Willow turned his head and stopped struggling for he saw that a great company of Warhorses stood in a circle around the old mare and her foal.

Thane urged Esteron towards the dark pine forest that stretched across the mountain's side; Willow shouted to Star as Esteron broke into a canter, 'I will come back!' Thane leaned forwards, shouting against the wind, 'Who are you? Tell me, as we ride, all about your people and where they live.'

# The Causeway Field

Thunderstone stood, once more alone, and wept in the memory of his old friend. Around him he heard the roar of forgotten battles and saw Equion rise up to break the shadows, bringing the glory of morning to a boy without hope. Far away he heard a cry and thought for an instant that he saw starlight flash on cold steel high above Mantern's shoulders where the heather meadows began. Hooves rang on the causeway, shouts from somewhere down below brought him back to the gallery, memories forgotten.

'Who hammers on my door?' he shouted, throwing a flaming torch into the darkness. As he threw the torch, Rockspray flew to his shoulder and a strong youthful voice rose out of the darkness. 'Kyotorm, son of Archerorm, with a great strike of Archers. We follow Rockspray, we come to Thane's call.'

Thunderstone laughed, calling out in a clear voice full of hope, 'He rides to the gate near Mantern's Peak; with him are all the guardians of World's End; still I think they will number as little as one stalk of grass in a wild meadow full of weeds and thistles.'

'Which way?' shouted Kyot. 'Our quivers are full of new arrows and rest heavily on our backs.'

'Follow the hoofprints, for the Warhorses went before them. Will you take meat to eat upon the road?'

'No, Lord, we run with tight belts towards the dawn; nothing must burden us lest we arrive too late.'

As Kyot turned Sprint towards the mountain's shadowy blackness, he called in parting, 'Tomorrow we will eat your table bare. The top, the legs, even the chair you sit upon, for we have run without rest from Stumble Hill and still journey's end is not in sight.'

The darkness swallowed up the Archers, only starlight reflected on the polished wood of their bows as they ran towards the mountain slopes.

'This is no night for sleeping,' muttered Thunderstone as he paced the galleries; treading leagues beneath his feet before night passed into the grey hours, remembering all that had passed in a long life. Looking out into the beginnings of dawn, he thought his old eyes were playing tricks, for marching on to the Causeway through swirling mist advanced a great army. At first he thought the Nightbeasts had come to claim back what they had once ruled, and bring final ruin to Elundium, but as the host came closer he saw proudly held banners that brought new blood racing through his veins, for they showed the emblem of an owl in gold on a blue background. Old and faded, some as threadbare as the warriors that carried them, they filled the road. The troop of marching feet shook the walls and echoed across the Causeway Fields.

'Thunderstone! Keeper of World's End!' called Tombel, raising his marching sword to strike the door. 'Old friends have gathered at your door.'

As the hilt of Tombel's marching sword hit the door, a shaft of new sunlight touched his shoulder, casting the sword's shadow across the war-scarred wood. The locks clicked and rattled, the doors swung open, grinding across the cobbles. Thunderstone stood before them, sword drawn, casting an early sun's shadow far back into the courtyard, tears glinted in the corners of his eyes and one escaped to run down his age-wrinkled face, as he stepped forwards shedding the cares that time had heaped on his shoulders, he knew at last that he was not alone or forgotten at World's End.

Tombel looked into the courtyard, a frown creasing his forehead. 'Are you all alone in this place? The King has sent us racing across all Elundium, abandoning the Granite City to find you are safe and well and the Causeway Fields empty. We came in haste, wearing old bones brittle on a wild road. Yesterdaylight we saw a great Eagle Owl carrying Thoron's sword and took it for a sign, and marched all night without rest . . .'

'Tombel, Tombel!' Thunderstone cried, 'you may yet arrive too late. Thane led all my warriors towards the gate on Mantern's Mountain. Nevian foretold him that there the battle would be fought as the new sun rose.'

'Then we have come too late,' grieved Tombel, looking towards the sunrise. 'We have marched hard and worn our boots to ruin to stare defeat full in the face.'

A sunbeam touched the horse tail where it hung at Thunderstone's side.

'If only the Warhorses or the Border Runners were there with him, for they might buy us time!' thought Tombel out loud, looking at the horse's tail.

'They are!' cried the Keeper. 'Nature has been gathering here all winter. Thane followed in their hoofprints even as the sun was setting.'

'Then we must run as we did in our youth!' shouted Tombel. 'Better late upon the field than not at all!'

A movement on the causeway road caught his eye, a flash of sunlight on polished steel, figures hurrying towards Underfall, surrounded by an army of cats.

'Who in all Elundium can this be?' muttered Thunderstone, drawing his sword, but a loud piercing voice turned his grimness to laughter and his blade was put back into its scabbard.

'Duclos, we're here,' shouted Morolda, trying to keep the cats from hunting in the dykes. 'Leave those birds in peace,' she threatened waving a heavily ringed fist.

Thunderstone walked down on to the causeway to meet old friends. Far away memories of youth filled his mind and tears flowed down his cheeks to see how age had treated the greatest Fencing Master in all Elundium.

'Duclos! Morolda!' he cried, throwing his arms around their shoulders, 'What draws you to this grim place?'

Duclos smiled, looking over the Keeper's shoulder towards the sheer granite walls of Underfall and spoke only one word. 'Thane!'

'He cannot hear you,' explained Morolda, smiling sadly. 'He still lives in a world of total silence.'

'I know,' said Thunderstone. 'Thane told me.'

'Then he lives? My little knight is safe and he finished his journey without coming to any harm?'

'Yes,' hesitated Thunderstone, stepping back and looking towards Mantern's Mountain.

'Where is he?' demanded Morolda. 'Duclos has been plagued by dreams that Thane needs his help. Where is he?'

Thunderstone pointed towards the mountain, his words catching at the back of his throat as he told Morolda all that had happened during the last two days.

'Duclos!' Morolda shouted, turning him towards the mountain. 'He has gone up there!'

'Up where?' asked Duclos, a puzzled expression crossing his face. 'Up where?'

'No, you silly old fool, watch and pay attention.' With careful finger talk Morolda explained to Duclos all that Thunderstone had told her.

'Then by the cats' tails I must climb the mountain,' Duclos spoke more to himself than to Morolda or to Thunderstone but he took the Keeper's hand, smiling at him over his spectacles, and spoke with his out-of-key intonation. 'Throughout a life-time of toil you have kept us safe, even the cats thank you!'

'Duclos!' Thunderstone called, but it was no use, the Fencing Master had turned away, striding across the causeway fields, the army of cats at his heels. Morolda wept and whispered, 'He must follow his dream and match Thane blade for blade wherever the shadows move.'

332

# The Mouth of Night

Esteron took the bit and with each stride passed through the great army of animals moving up the mountainside. All around him he heard whispers of his father's name, for Equestrius had summoned him to be at Mantern's Gate before the dawn birds sang. Without rest he ran. Chill, clinging mists swirled and twisted around his fetlocks as he galloped into the grey hours, for dawn was in the sky, heralding a new morning's beauty and he dare not be late upon the field of battle.

As they galloped, Thane listened to Willow's story, and marvelled at how his people had survived beneath the mountain, but his heart beat faster when the lad told him of the old man hanging in chains and he pressed him for every scrap of news, no matter how insignificant.

Willow told him all he could remember of their brief meeting, even the warning about Krulshards still being alive in the City of Night. After that Thane fell silent, gritting his teeth, for he dare not think or hope to see his grandfather alive while Krulshards had him a prisoner in the city. He shut his heart against it and pressed Esteron hard towards the dawn.

The ground beneath Esteron's hooves was flattening out, morning took the sky; all about them dawn birds burst into song, night mists dissolved leaving dew sparkling in the heather as a new sun rose. 'Mantern's Gate!' shouted Thane, drawing his sword. The steep mountainside had at last levelled into a wide, heather-covered plateau. At the far side, a black entrance in the sheer rock face boiled with threatening Nightbeasts.

Rumblings far below the ground shook tiny drops of dew off the stalks of heather. 'Mantern's Gate!' Thane shouted again, halting Esteron. Looking to his left and right, he saw the

Warhorses filling the plateau right to the edge, rank upon rank of them, spreading in a great crescent, at their feet crouched the Border Runners, snarling and growling. Flocks of owls eclipsed the early morning sun, casting fast-moving shadows across Mantern's Gate. The Warriors of Underfall arrived, breathless and hot from their long climb up the mountain and filled the ground behind Esteron, seeing for the first time what they had pledged themselves to. Defeat and fear cast them down and they cried out, 'Too many! A world full of shadows, there are thousands of them!' But Thane lifted high his sword to flash in the sunlight and spoke in a clear voice.

'You came with the power of morning to break the shadows, look how they hesitate at the flash of light upon my sword! None will judge you less than men if you cannot face the Nightbeasts, you are free to choose.' Then he remembered Thunderstone's words, 'Guard well those that stand beneath your banner, for they know little of the real fear of darkness.' Twisting in his saddle he looked down into their frightened eyes and spoke softly, 'Spearmen and swordsmen, let each of you that chooses to face the shadows with me, set himself amongst the Warhorses; let their great courage keep you safe.' Without looking towards the black gate, the Warriors spread out amongst the Warhorses and each man found just enough space had been left for him to fill.

'What of us?' shouted Tiethorm. Thane turned his head and saw the bowmen of World's End standing huddled together, their eyes fixed upon the ground.

'Tiethorm!' Thane said proudly, 'you are a great Archer whose skill with the feathered shafts of death can split a single blade of grass. Keep your hand steady on the bow string, form the bowmen into a strike, move with the Border Runners, sweeping wherever they go, for the battle of the Causeway Field formed a great bond between you and they will keep you safe.'

'But we are still far outnumbered,' muttered Tiethorm, looking across the plateau, for he saw crowding amongst the

Nightshapes an army of Nightbeasts unknown to the men of Elundium, and fear of their great numbers filled his heart. 'If only we had the Great Bow of Orm,' he whispered, 'or an army of Marchers.'

Thane laughed, digging his heels into Esteron's sides, shouting, 'We have a greater gift, we have the sunlight! Come! Let us have this battle won!' Esteron surged forwards and morning breezes tugged at the summer scarf tied to Thane's arm, casting the glory of a new sun towards the black shapes spreading across the plateau.

'Wait!' shouted Willow. 'Wait! Listen!'

'What is it?' asked Thane, pulling Esteron to a halt.

'Hush! A horse is galloping within the mountain. It is getting closer with each hoofbeat.'

Esteron turned his head towards the rock face on their left, ears pricked. Thane tightened his grip on his sword and all the dogs started barking wildly, the horses were neighing and the owls were screeching. 'Equestrius! Equestrius!' shouted Willow, jumping down from Thane's saddle to the ground.

With the sound of thunder echoing in narrow valleys a great black Warhorse burst through a hidden entrance in the rock face, crossing into the sunlight. He called out the Warhorse challenge. A grey horse, muzzle whitened with age, broke through the Warhorse crescent and galloped towards Equestrius. Thane recognized her as Amarch, his Grandfather's horse, and called out her name. Amarch stopped beside Thane snorting and whinnying a greeting, turned, and neighed fiercely at the black gate.

'You have all come to free grandfather!' Thane exclaimed, sweeping his eyes across the thousands of Warhorses, Border Runners and owls assembled on the plateau. Amarch turned her head and for a moment held his eyes with her soft gentle eyes. Equestrius cantered to where Willow stood and knelt beside him, offering him a place on his back. The great crescent of Warhorses neighed, pawed the ground and knelt for the Warriors of Underfall to mount them.

'Mount them, and be proud!' shouted Thane, for the Warhorses have not consented to be ridden since the bondbreaking. Warriors – ride to your glory!'

Esteron and Amarch, side by side, moved to the centre of the crescent to face the Nightbeast army that had swarmed out of the black gate and now engulfed half the plateau. The Warhorses began to move forwards, gradually gathering speed.

'Look to the sunlight and the sharp edges of your swords!' Thane shouted above the thunder of hooves. Standing in the stirrups he turned to marshal the Marchers, urging them to keep in close formation behind the wall of spear blades the spearmen had lowered against the advancing Nightbeasts.

'Sygnis!' he cried, reining Esteron back out of the crescent, 'Bring the Gallopers forward to the left of the crescent towards that rough high ground beneath the rock wall. We must win the black gate, before the Master of Night sees defeat. Thoron lives and he will kill him if the battle turns against him to our advantage.'

Sygnis hurriedly organized the Gallopers into a flying column, fanning out into the shape of a spear. Thane wheeled Esteron back towards the black gate and saw Amarch, half a league ahead, plunging among the Nightbeasts. A part of that vision in the Learning Hall flooded into his mind as he saw her rear up, a cruel spear shaft embedded in her side.

'Amarch! Amarch!' he cried, spurring Esteron forwards, but she was beyond his reach. Fast shadows crossed the sun as stoop after stoop of Battle Owls dropped upon the Nightbeasts, tearing at their eyes. Border Runners in savage packs leapt up, biting at the Nightbeasts' faces and necks. Sometimes as many as ten huge dogs attacked together, toppling a beast before tearing it apart.

Sygnis quickly won the high ground but the Nightbeasts swept all around the Gallopers and drove them back against the sheer rock face. Thane urged Esteron towards them, slashing with his sword in despair, but he could not break through to them. Then the Marchers arrived and crashed against the Nightbeasts. He rode amongst them, rallying their hearts, lifting the banner of light above the dark shadows, yet as morning moved to noon and the sun reached its full power the Nightbeasts sneered, mocking his standard, stretching out claw-like hands to tear it down.

Pace by pace the Nightbeasts had driven a wedge of darkness between the crescent of Warhorses and the Warriors of Underfall. Now they were hopelessly divided. Thane looked up towards the black gate and saw a terrible figure wrapped in black malice. Beside him stood one-eyed Kerzolde and all about them, spears interlocked, moved the shadow circle.

'Thane!' a voice cried out behind him. Thane spun round and laughed with joy, for there, ascending on to the plateau he saw Sprint, lathered white with sweat. Kyot sat upon his back, the Bow of Orm in his hands, an arrow on the string, and behind them a mighty strike of Archers, loaded down with new forged arrows.

'Kyot, oh Kyot!' he cried, 'Amarch is injured near the black gate. Thoron is a prisoner beneath this foul mountain and the Nightbeasts have divided us. The Gallopers are against the cliff face and the Marchers and Archers are exhausted and near defeat.'

Kyot laughed, 'Let us fight side by side, brother, and win the high ground first. Draw your warriors in behind the Archers and watch the Nightbeasts fall as thick as new mown corn when the bows of Stumble Hill begin to sing.'

Thane reined Esteron in next to Sprint and length by length the horses forced a passage on to the high ground. Behind them the Archers swept easily through the Nightbeasts. Kyot turned Sprint towards the black gate and his laugh fell away to nothing as he saw Krulshards and the solid mass of Nightbeasts that spread before him.

'Who is that foul nightmare?' he cried.

'Krulshards!' Thane shouted, 'The Master of Darkness!'

'Then only death awaits in that black hole, Thane,' Kyot answered. 'It is madness to fight against such power.'

Thane grabbed Kyot's arm. 'Every Nightbeast spawned is his creation. Every dark fear and black shadow that makes you jump at night was fashioned by his hand. It is he I ride against, alone if need drives me to it!'

Thane spurred Esteron angrily towards the Gates of Night, spreading his banner to catch the sunlight. Kyot cried out for him to wait, taking his feet out of Sprint's stirrups he quickly dismounted.

'Go, dear friend. I cannot risk your life against such terror. Run to my father's house, you will be safe there.'

But Sprint snorted, arching his proud neck and bent his foreleg, kneeling he offered Kyot the empty saddle and Kyot gently stroked Sprint's neck, whispering as he remounted. 'You have more courage than the great Warhorses.'

Turning to the strike of Archers he shouted, 'To the Gates of Night!'

'The Gates of Night!' chanted the Warriors, gripping their spear shafts for the surge forwards.

Kyot searched in his quiver and selected a slightly different arrow. It was longer and had a polished tip of glass that shone in the sunlight. Fitting it on to the string he stretched the bow until it cried out to be released.

'Which one, Thane?' he cried out, aiming at the shadow circle.

'Krulshards!' Thane shouted, driving his sword through the nearest Nightbeast.

Kyot released his fingers and the arrow flew high, spinning above the battlefield, screeching over the Nightbeast army towards Krulshards. But he heard the arrow and spun round, throwing an arm up to protect his face. The arrow, true-aimed, sunk into the black malice near his shoulder, tearing through the rotten flesh until it hit bone. He staggered backwards, gripping the arrow shaft and snapped it in two. The Nightbeast

340

army hesitated, trembling in doubt, looking from its black master to the Warriors and the Warhorses.

'Charge!' shouted Kyot, laughing and nocking another arrow on to the string.

'Wait!' shouted Thane, rising in the stirrups and turning his head, looking from the black gate to the plateau's edge. 'Something is happening, Kyot, something that we cannot see. Look at the Nightbeasts.'

Kyot lowered his bow and watched that moment of doubt that had grown amongst the army of terror. Just as a breath of wind moves across the grasslands so the Nightbeasts hesitated, swaying backwards and forwards. Faintly came the sound of singing and the tramping of marching feet.

'What is happening?' hissed Kyot, the Nightbeasts were now milling in disorder, trampling on each other to retreat.

Thane laughed, pointing with his sword towards the Gates of Night.

'Look Kyot, Willow and the black Warhorse have won the gates. They lead an army of tunnellers out into the light.'

Kyot pulled at Thane's arm, turning his attention to the plateau's edge. 'Look at the standard.'

Thane shielded his eyes against the setting sun and saw Tombel striding on to the plateau.

'Tombel!' he cried out in joy. 'The Nightbeast army is retreating!'

'Then we are not too late upon the field. Forward, Marchers, forward!' shouted the greatest Marcher Captain in all Elundium.

Down through Mantern's Gate, issuing out of the darkness, cantered Equestrius, the tunnellers streamed after him, shielding their eyes against the soft evening light, singing of its beauty as they fought amongst the Nightbeasts.

Thane drew alongside Tombel, urgently pointing to where the Warhorses' crests plunged among the Nightbeasts.

'Amarch is wounded, Lord, I saw her take a Nightbeast

341

spear. She is somewhere near the black gate. Thoron lives! He is a prisoner below the ground.'

'Then we must secure the field without delay and rescue both of them! Come, Thane, lead us into battle!'

# Winning the Light

Equestrius had not galloped into battle, but had turned aside taking Willow back into the mountain's heart. A strong voice echoed in Willow's head as the secret ways swallowed them up. 'It is time to set your people free. We shall raise a great army and win Mantern's Gate from within the mountain before this day is over.'

'Free my people!' Willow queried, bursting with excitement, 'But how?'

'Quiet, Willow, quiet. Lean along my neck – in places this tunnel roof is low. Now listen. Your escape shook more than the bones of this evil mountain. Even before the dawn birds sang to hide your presence from the Nightbeasts' rest by the grille, even then your people were making ready.'

'Ready for what?' interrupted Willow, hanging tightly on to Equestrius's mane.

'Hush, child,' snapped Equestrius, 'Listen! Legends amongst your elders whispered that one day a boy would rise up and win the light. It would be a signal.'

'Signal for what?' whispered Willow, a little bewildered.

Equestrius sighed and nickered softly in the dark. 'The Elder saw it in your eyes just before his death. Your escape was the sign for the tunnellers to revolt. At this moment, in the lower chambers, they are fighting with the Nightbeasts. We shall gather them together and lead them to Mantern's Gate and the lost sunlight.'

'Equestrius,' the lad whispered, 'was that ragged old man who hung in chains a great Lord of men? And has all this happened because the animals gathered to free him?'

'Yes and no, Willow,' the great Warhorse answered. 'If you

345

pull a thread in your sleeve it moves all the threads it touches. Thus fate often pulls us all whether we wish it or not.'

'But,' said Willow, completely mystified, 'in all the Elders' stories Lords were always wearing fine clothes and looked well cared for.'

Equestrius snorted and would have laughed if he could, adding as they burst upon the Nightbeasts, 'The owls cared for him, when he was beneath the mountain, and would not take kindly to what you said. Remember, we are not always what we seem! Now raise your spear and fight.'

'Touch not the Nightshapes,' Willow cried as he led his people, 'For they are the true shapes of the night and wished us no harm. Hunt only the Nightbeasts, look into every dark hole or crack, even sift the dust through your hands to find them and destroy their evil beginnings.'

Throughout a bitter afternoon of fighting in the dark, the tunnel-slaves swept up level by level through the City of Night, driving the Nightbeasts towards the light. Picks rose and fell, sharpened spades sliced into armoured hides, and with each step the light grew stronger and the chanting voices of Willow's people made the mountain tremble.

Thane spurred Esteron towards the Gates of Night. The Riders and Marchers of Underfall cheered, lowered their spears and followed him. Kyot swept his strike of Archers to left and right and none could stand against them. Tombel marshalled his army to follow and the Nightbeasts fell as thick as summer corn beneath their feet.

'Keep the shadow circle from entering the Gates of Night!' Tombel cried to Thane while diverting a column of his Marchers along the edge of the plateau to stop any of the Nightbeasts escaping. But they did not get away, two glittering swords in Duclos' hands guarded the only other path down the mountainside and he laughed and danced, singing while the pile of dead grew around him.

Krulshards looked to the Gates of Night and saw Equestrius

cantering down on to the plateau. Before him, riding at a gallop, came Thane on Esteron with the standard of the sun flowing in the evening sunlight; and far above, beyond the sight of men, an owl hovered carrying a long galloping sword.

Krulshards spun the shadow circle faster and faster until the Nightbeasts' out-turned spear blades were humming with the speed.

'Kill! Kill!' he screamed. 'Destroy all the light and bring darkness to Elundium. Trample all to ruin! Kill! Kill! Kill!'

The circle began to spin faster, cutting through the press of leading Warriors, shredding armoured arms and legs, forcing the Marchers to flee in terror. Duclos saw the flash of sunlight on the blood-wet spinning blades and quietly crossed the battle field to stand in Krulshards' path.

'Shout all you like,' he laughed into the black Nightbeast's face, 'but you cannot harm me this time!'

'Kill! Kill!' hissed Krulshards, pushing the circle against Duclos but the swordsman sang and laughed, deaf to the threats, turning both his blades against the spinning circle, cutting into it, forcing the sharp edges of his swords inwards. Nightbeasts in the circle screamed as the swords bit into them, shattering spear shafts, iron caps and claws, and the circle fell apart. Krulshards towered, threateningly, over Duclos. Kerzolde lowered his spear to stab at the swordsman.

'The shadow! Step on his shadow!' Willow cried, darting past the swordsman.

Krulshards spun round, retreating from Willow towards the black gate. Kerzolde flung his spear and as he turned to follow his master he knocked Willow to the ground, breaking his homemade spear shaft beneath his clawed feet.

Thane spurred Esteron forwards, reached down and snatched Willow up.

Amarch saw Krulshards fleeing towards her from where she lay, mortally wounded, less than half a length from the Gates of Night. Struggling to her knees she called the Warhorse challenge and lunged at him. Krulshards felt her teeth catch upon his robe, tearing at its black shadowy folds, stopping him and pulling him backwards. Unsheathing his dagger he plunged it through her heart, ripped his robe free and jumped into the darkness.

'Who will follow me now?' he laughed. 'Is there a King among you brave enough to risk the darkness of the City of Night?'

Thane galloped to the gates and reined Esteron to a halt. He dismounted lightly and set Willow on the ground before he ran to the black entrance. He took a cautious step inside and blackness closed about him.

'Follow if you dare!' echoed Krulshards' voice, growing fainter as he fled into the high chambers.

'Thanehand!' Kerzolde hissed, leaping out of the blackness, catching his broken claw in the fine chain that held Elion's fingerbowl on to Thane's belt. 'I have waited too long for this moment. Die!' he screamed, swinging an iron mace, putting all his hatred behind the blow.

Thane jumped backwards, breaking the silver chain and stumbling towards the gates. He saw the iron mace and flung his sword against it, shattering the blade into a thousand pieces. He fell on to his knees and ducked beneath Kerzolde's second swing, rolling over he scrambled out into the light. Kyot and Willow pulled him clear of the black entrance. 'I will follow you!' Thane cried, rising empty-handed to his feet and turning back towards the black gate.

But he hesitated, shielding his eyes against the setting sun, watching the shadow of a mighty owl as it passed over the battlefield towards him.

'Eagle Owl!' he whispered, uncertainly, screwing up his eyes and looking at the sword that flashed, blood-red, in the owl's talons, catching all the glory of the dying sunlight.

Eagle Owl spread his flight feathers against the first chill up-draughts of the evening air and wheeled slowly over the black gate, searching with sharp eyes for journey's end and

Thoron's outstretched hand. Beating his wings in the thin mountain air he hovered and saw far below the cloak and helm he sought. He shrieked, stooping fast to deliver the sword but as he descended to the black gate he saw a stranger in Thoron's clothes and fanned his wings, slowing the stoop, keeping the hilt of the sword a finger's length from the hand that stretched up towards him.

'Who dares touch this sword!' he shrieked, staring with hard cold eyes at Thane, churning the air beneath his wings, rising up away beyond his reach.

A low murmur of fear ran through the warriors' ranks, spreading across the battlefield, making them hesitate. Bad omens were on their lips and whispers of defeat grew as the owl rose, spurning Thane's outstretched hand.

'Eagle Owl,' Thane cried out in despair, recognizing his grandfather's sword.

'I am Thanehand, Thoronhand's grandson, and I have great need of the blade you carry, for Grandfather is still a prisoner in the City of Night. Lend me the sword so that I can rescue him. Please help me!'

Eagle Owl hovered, turning his gaze from Thane across the upturned faces of the warriors, seeing the doubt in their eyes. Looking back to Thane he searched the young man's battle-blackened face and softly called his name, breaking the eerie battle silence that had spread across the high plateau.

'I know you, Thanehand,' he called softly.

Thane laughed, stretching his hand up towards the great bird of war, closing his fingers around the hilt of the sword.

'I will follow your nightmares!' he shouted above the sudden roar of warrior voices, 'with a new sword in my hand. For I am Thanehand, the Candleman's son, and I fear nothing in the dark!'

# Stone Angels
## Mike Jeffries

*Abaddon, the Angel of Perfection.*
*The Angel of Evil. The Angel of the Pit.*

In ancient times it was a pagan alter, washed by the blood of human sacrifice. Then it lay hidden for centuries, its perfect whiteness darkened by age, until it was possessed by a spirit. Spirit and stone fused together, taking on a shape - the shape of an angel.

The Bishop of Norwich was awed. This twelve-foot carved angel must surely be a miracle – its perfection was mesmerising. And terrifying. He had it installed with full pomp and ceremony, in his new cathedral. Then the disappearances started.

An angel? Oh yes - but not for the forces of good. Abaddon - Angel of the Pit - has entered his effigy. Now, hundreds of deaths later, he lies in the heart of Norwich Cathedral, his power building day by terrible day.

'*Stone Angels* is Mike Jefferies as a storyteller in the best tradition'

ROBERT HOLDSTOCK author of *Mythago Wood*

ISBN 0-586-21527-1

# Children of the Flame
## Mike Jeffries

*Magic, witchcraft and an ancient curse:*
*a powerful and exciting new novel from*
*a classic storyteller!*

"I can weave the power of fire and water around your babies:
they will become children of the flame."

Entwined in the coils of a curse that reaches back through
the centuries, Joel - a student, and Amy, a gallery worker -
must seek to discover the truth behind the mystery that
has brought the two of them together. Born thousands of
miles apart they both sense a powerful link to each other
and to other lives. And both are haunted by the apparition
of two shadowy figures and a huge, three-headed hound.

In the mists of time, the secret lies hidden, to be glimpsed
for a moment each time they die and are reborn; but time
is running out and the puzzle must be solved before the
wraiths claim their souls.

'Gorgeous imagination'                                    *Interzone*

ISBN  0-586-21749-5

# The Broken God
## David Zindell

'SF as it ought to be: challenging, imaginative, thought-provoking and well-written. Zindell has placed himself at the forefront of literary SF'          *Times Literary Supplement*

Book One of David Zindell's new epic trilogy is set in Neverness, legendary city of Light, where inner space and outer space meet . . . where the God program is up and running.

Into its maze of colour-coded streets of ice a wild boy stumbles, starving, frostbitten and grieving, a spear in his hand: Danlo the Wild, a messenger from the deep past of man. Brought up far from Neverness by the Alaloi people, neanderthal cave-dwellers, Danlo alone of his tribe has survived a plague – because he is not, as he had thought, a misshapen neanderthal, but human, with immunity engineered into his genes. He learns that the disease was created by the sinister Architects of the Universal Cybernetic Church. The Architects possess a cure which can save other Alaloi tribes. But the Architects have migrated to the region of space known as the Vild, and there they are killing stars.

All of civilization has converged on Neverness through the manifold of space travel. Beyond science, beyond decadence, sects and disciplines multiply there. Danlo, his mind shaped by primitive man, brings to Neverness a single long-lost memory that will challenge them all.

ISBN 0 586 21189 6